CHANGING ROLES

New York Times Bestselling Author
Melanie Moreland

CHANGING ROLES by Melanie Moreland
Copyright © 2020 Moreland Books Inc.
Registration # 1166363
Ebook ISBN # 978-1-988610-30-6
Print book ISBN # 978-1-988610-31-3

Edited by Lisa Hollett—Silently Correcting Your Grammar
Cover Design by Karen Hulseman - Moreland Books Inc.

DEDICATION

*This book is for all those
who love and care for others.*

It is a gift that is never acknowledged enough.

*Regardless of your title or profession,
we all deserve to be loved simply
for being our self.*

Thank you for reading.

1

LIAM

Familiar scenery sped by, blurred and fast under the streetlights. I relaxed against the plush leather of the limo, grateful to be heading home. I rested my head back, trying to stay calm as thoughts of the rushed escape filtered through my mind. Desperate to get home, I ditched security and everything keeping me in New York and headed for the airport. When the looks of recognition had begun, my anxiety had ramped up, but I concentrated on my goal and got to the gate and on the plane. I had purchased two seats, so I was alone, and no one bothered me. Once we landed, I sprinted through the airport, head down, my breathing returning to normal once the driver pulled away from the terminal and I hadn't been recognized. It had been a big risk, but I had done it.

We pulled up to the gates, and my sigh was long and appreciative. I had made it.

Light spilled out through the windows, shining brightly against the deep black of the night. I glanced at my watch, frowning. It was three o'clock in the morning; why was she still awake? I grabbed the bag beside me, wished Dean a good night and waved the driver away

—I was famous, but my arms worked. I was still capable of carrying my own luggage.

I entered the house, grinning right away at the sound that greeted me. Journey was blaring out of the speakers, which meant only one thing. If eighties music was playing, Shelby was ironing.

I followed the music to the kitchen and stood in the doorway, smiling at the sight before me. Sure enough, Shelby was in front of the ironing board, her head moving to the music, her socked feet tapping away as she sang in her delightfully awful off-key voice with Steve Perry while she pressed my shirts. My clothes were hanging everywhere—dress shirts, trousers, even my T-shirts, which I told her all the time didn't need ironing, were done and folded neatly on the table beside her. I had, in fact, told her to use a service to do all this, but she refused, saying it was part of her job.

I cleared my throat loudly, and she snapped up her head. She beamed widely in greeting as she grabbed the remote and turned down the music.

"You're gonna go deaf listening to this bloody shit so loud," I teased.

"Already am. At my age, hearing is the first thing to go. And it's not shit. It's classic."

I rolled my eyes at her; you would think she was twenty years my senior, not five. I stepped forward and kissed her cheek. "Hey, Shelby."

"Hi, Liam. You're home early."

"And you're still awake." I knew she had problems sleeping when I wasn't home. She often stayed up late doing mundane chores to pass the time. Her words confirmed my suspicions.

"Couldn't sleep."

I frowned. "All right there?"

She nodded. "Yeah, I'm good. Why are you home? Everett never called to say you were coming early."

I grabbed a bottle of water from the refrigerator. I took a long swallow before answering. "Right. Ah, he may not know."

She set down the iron, narrowing her eyes. "What did you do now?" She groaned.

I shook my head. "Nothing! They were idiots, Shelby. The woman interviewing me had no bloody clue. She droned on and on about some crap relating to the economy. I'm an actor, for God's sake. Not a market manager."

Shelby laughed. "But you play one on the big screen."

I laughed with her. "Hence the acting thing. Seriously, she kept asking me to talk in different accents, like I was some sort of puppet. And touching me." I shuddered. "I got tired of dodging her and her stupid questions and walked out."

"How did you get home?"

"I booked a flight, called for a limo, and presto! Here I am."

She stepped forward, concerned. "Was everything okay? Were you all right?"

Her worry touched me. "Yeah. The airline had security walk with me. A crowd got close in the airport, but he pulled me into some hidden hallway, and I stayed calm."

"Okay, good." Shelby sighed then settled her hand on her hip. "That's the third interview you've walked out of this month, Liam."

"I'm aware."

She rolled her eyes. "Temperamental British actor."

"Piss off."

Shelby chuckled as I sat down and inhaled deeply, moaning at the delicious aroma that surrounded me.

"Shelby?"

"Hmm?"

"Why do I smell turkey?"

Her voice was filled with mirth. "Because you were due back tomorrow, and I knew what you'd want when you came home."

"Brilliant girl you are. Is it ready?"

"Yep."

"I want one."

"Now?"

3

"Yeah. In fact, two. I didn't eat on the plane."

"Milk?"

"Yeah. And a shot of whiskey for after. It's been a day."

"Okay. Go sit on the sofa, and I'll get it ready."

I wandered into the den and sat, enjoying the comfort of the deep, plush cushions. I pulled off my tie, undoing the top button of my shirt, and drawing in a deep breath as I listened to Shelby moving around the kitchen, making me sandwiches.

Her sandwiches. Bloody hell, I loved her sandwiches.

The music changed, and I held back a snicker as one of Survivor's over-the-top ballads came on and Shelby started singing along with it. "The Search Is Over" it was called. She loved all this shit.

Then I did chuckle. She listened to them so often, I now knew the names of this crap as well.

But if that music was playing, it meant she was here, in my house.

And listening to her in my kitchen, I knew I loved having her around.

My head fell back against the cushion as I remembered how she came to be a part of my life.

2

LIAM

SIX MONTHS AGO

I walked through the doorway and stopped short. "Marie, what the bloody hell are you doing?"

She stood, looking guilty. "Nothing. Just...laundry."

I snorted. "You don't do laundry. You send it all out to be done. You told me it wasn't part of your job." I was quite grateful about that. I didn't want her touching the clothes I wore.

"I made an exception."

I spied the camera in her hands, and I widened my eyes.

"Why the hell are you taking a picture of my shorts?" My gaze flew to the computer sitting beside her on the desk and the website open on the screen. "Bloody hell! Are you selling my stuff on the internet?" I gaped at her, pulling my hands through my hair. "Are you daft?"

Her guilt vanished immediately. "You have plenty. I needed some extra cash."

"I have plenty? *Extra cash*? Jesus Christ! I pay you a bloody fortune to do literally nothing! And those... Those are my underwear —they're personal!" I roared.

"Fine. I'll put them back."

"Bloody right, you will." I shuddered, knowing I would never wear them again. I needed to buy all new ones now. I drew in a deep breath, finding the courage I needed. "You're fired."

"What?" she screeched at me.

I straightened my shoulders. This was my house. My stuff she was selling. Her employment with me was going to end soon anyway, but I didn't want to wait anymore. "I said, you're fired. Pack your stuff, and leave anything of mine behind. You're not selling any more of my things. Get out—*now*."

"You bastard!"

"Me? You're the one selling my stuff—that's stealing. You're lucky I don't press charges."

Suddenly, the laptop, which had been sitting on the desk beside my shorts, came flying toward me. I yelped and ducked, watching as it struck the wall behind me, shattering into pieces when it hit the floor. "Blimey, you bitch! That was my laptop!" I yelled.

The camera followed suit, as well as anything else she could get her hands on. Bobbing and weaving, I ran for the bathroom, locking myself in. Objects hit the door behind me as the whacko I had just fired screamed obscenities at me. Apparently, she didn't like being sacked. I heard her storm out of the den, and I breathed a sigh of relief before scrambling for my phone in a hurry when I heard the sounds of breaking glass and more yelling coming from down the hall.

Holy shit, she was going to destroy my house. She might be angry enough to break down the bathroom door. I hadn't thought this through very well.

I dialed my manager, Everett, who answered impatiently. "What, Liam? This isn't a good time."

"*Fuck*, Everett, neither is this. Marie has gone barmy and is destroying my house. I need you here!"

"Why?"

"*Why?*" I echoed. "Because I think she may kill me!"

"No, you idiot, why has she gone barmy?"

"I, ah...sacked her."

"Crap, Liam, you dipshit. You did what? We agreed I'd handle that while you were away! Five more days—you only had to last five more days. What the hell happened that you couldn't wait five more days?"

"She nicked my shorts!" I screamed into the phone. "My boxers, Everett! She was selling them on the internet! I couldn't let that slide. I sacked her, and now she's breaking everything in the place!"

"You never fire someone alone, Liam. *You*, especially, should never fire anyone. No doubt you cocked it up. What did you say?"

"Um, you're fired? Oh, and get out. I think that was about it."

"Yep. You cocked it up."

"Bugger that—get over here before she burns the place down!"

"On my way already. Where are you?"

"Locked in the bathroom."

He snorted. "Of course you are."

"Oh God. *Shit*."

I looked around in disbelief. How could one woman, especially one fairly small woman, do so much damage in such a short time? Everett had arrived, subdued her, called the cops, and let me know it was safe to come out of my hiding spot. I had opened the bathroom door and exited with as much pride as I could muster, considering I had been hiding from someone half my size. In my defense, I had a movie that started filming soon and I couldn't have my face mucked up, and the cow had good aim.

We stood in what was left of my kitchen. Dishes, glasses, and cutlery were smashed and thrown everywhere. A couple of cupboard doors had been torn off their hinges, and even the glass on the table was cracked. I hated that table anyway. I walked into the den and stood in shock. It looked like a tornado had blown through. The biggest insult—my Oscar that was planted in the middle of my beloved flat screen, which was still sparking and smoking. My

7

collection of movies and music had been tossed everywhere, the sofa knocked over with a few cushions torn. My desk was destroyed as well.

"She didn't take it very well," I mumbled.

Everett snorted. "You could say that."

"Maybe I should have offered her a payoff?"

"It's called a severance package here, Liam. Maybe you should have walked away and called me to tell me what was going on, and I could have handled this the way we agreed. Professionally."

I sighed. "That was another option, I suppose. Certainly not as exciting as this one."

"Good thing you've been thinking about redecorating."

My lips twitched. "Yeah, good thing."

His phone rang and he grabbed it, turning away. I walked over to the TV and stared at the Oscar protruding from the center of it, uncertain if I should try to pull it out. I looked around, unsure where the bloody electric was for it and gave up. I heard Everett's worried voice speaking low into the phone.

"It's okay, Shelby. We'll figure it out. Get on the flight I booked for you, and come to me. I'll take care of you. Promise."

I looked at him curiously. I knew Shelby was his older sister who lived in Sacramento with her husband, Malcolm. Everett wasn't fond of Malcolm and had no qualms expressing his feelings, but I had never met either of them. Why was his sister coming here? I caught his eye and raised my eyebrow in a silent question, and he shook his head at me

His voice lowered further. "Don't cry, Shelby. It's gonna be fine. I'll look after you. Don't worry about that stuff. Your flight gets you here at six, and I'll be waiting. We'll figure it out together. The car should be there for you any minute. It is? Okay, good. I'll see you soon. Love you."

He hung up with a sigh and cleared his throat of emotion.

"Problem?"

He nodded, his usual jovial face serious. "Big-time. Between the two of you, it's been quite a day."

"Your sister is coming for a visit?"

"Something like that."

I knew not to push. He'd tell me when he was ready. "Okay." I looked around. "Bugger. I hope Marie didn't get to my bedroom." I shuddered, thinking of what she might have done in there.

He clapped his hand on my shoulder. "Let's go look."

I poured myself a good shot of whiskey. Thank God the bitch hadn't made it to the living room and the bar. The den, kitchen, and dining room were disasters, although a crew had come in and cleaned the mess away. Things still had to be replaced and fixed. She hadn't made it to my bedroom either by the time Everett had arrived.

He had left last night to go pick up his sister, and I hadn't heard from him again that evening, but he had texted a short time ago to say he was coming over. A few minutes later, he let himself in and helped himself to a glass of whiskey before sitting down heavily across from me.

"Marie's been charged with destruction of private property, and I got a restraining order against her. You said you wanted it kept quiet. She agreed to leave the city and keep her mouth shut if we don't add theft or any other charges."

I nodded. "Yeah, it's fine. I don't want the publicity. I just want her gone. I certainly don't want my stuff back that she touched." I grimaced into my glass. "She was bloody mental."

Everett lifted his eyebrows. "She asked if you'd give her a reference."

I gaped. "Not bloody likely, mate. What the hell was Jack thinking when he hired her?"

"I don't think Jack was thinking with the head on his shoulders, which is why he got his own ass fired. They were sleeping together, you know."

I paused with the glass partway to my mouth. "Well, that explains a lot."

Everett nodded. "You should have let me handle it sooner, Liam."

I shrugged. "She kept the place clean, and at least there was food in the house. I didn't think it was that big a deal. I didn't know she had a business on the side, selling my stuff."

He sat back and smirked at me. "Admit it. She scared you."

I snorted contemptuously. "No, she didn't."

"You had a deadbolt installed on your bedroom door."

I was sure I had seen her in my room one night when I woke up, although she had denied it, insisting I must have been dreaming. I'd had the lock installed immediately.

"She didn't... Okay, fuck, she bloody well did. I'm glad she's gone. I should have listened to you and got rid of her months ago."

"Yeah, you should have, but it's done. I think we're rid of all the dead weight your last management team had you saddled with before me. Now, we'll find you a new housekeeper."

"I can look after myself."

He snorted. "Right."

I glared at him, but he was probably correct. I was rather hopeless when it came to the house or keeping myself on track. And the last time I had tried to fire someone, they had sold their story to the tabloids, and it wasn't pretty. After that, I agreed to let Everett handle staffing issues.

"I'm interviewing the next housekeeper," I informed him.

Everett snorted. "Like you'd know what to ask them?"

I glared at him. "I'd ask if they can make cupcakes. What kind of housekeeper can't bake?" That had always pissed me off about Marie. My own mum was brilliant in the kitchen and I liked that sort of stuff. I missed it, living here in LA.

"They need to be able to do more than bake, Liam. They need to be organized, trustworthy, run your house, and help keep you organized. We need someone with some experience."

"I want to like them this time."

He studied me for a minute. "I think I know someone who'd be perfect."

"Who?"

"You don't know her."

"You do?"

He nodded and stood, walking to the window. He looked outside for a minute, not saying anything. "My sister, Shelby, is in a bit of a jam."

"Oh?"

"Her fucking, no-good husband dumped her. And took all their savings and disappeared."

"What a wanker."

"Yeah." He sighed. "She lost her job a month ago—the company she worked for did some downsizing, and they let a bunch of the executives and PAs go. Now the asshole pulls this shit." He shook his head. "I never liked him."

"I know. I think you referred to him as 'the jackass' most of the time."

Everett nodded. "Shelby is strong and independent, and I only found out all this when she finally called me. He took everything of value and left her with nothing. He surprised her with a spa day, and when she got home, everything was gone. The apartment cleared out, their bank accounts drained. It was the last straw. She's been struggling, trying to figure this out on her own, but it was simply too much for her. The bastard ran up all their credit cards, was behind on the rent, and then disappeared."

"Good thing she called you."

"I know it took a lot for her to make that call. But I'm glad she did. With her husband gone and no job, I thought a new start would help her. She looked after me growing up. Now it's my turn to repay the favor."

I nodded in sympathy. "Crap, Everett—that's awful. What a stupid arse he must be. Good thing she has you for a brother." Understanding dawned. "You want me to hire her?"

He sat back down in the chair. "She's a hard worker, Liam, and a hell of a great person. She's dealt with being a PA for years, so she would know how to keep you organized. She needs a place to live and a job. You need a housekeeper and someone here while you're away filming, to look after the place."

I hesitated.

"She'd be a damn sight better than Marie. And she isn't remotely scary."

That was a plus.

"At least meet her." He encouraged. "I'm asking as a favor. If you don't get on, no pressure."

Everett rarely asked me for anything. Usually it was me asking the favors.

"Can she cook?"

"Like a dream. Always has."

"My favorite thing is turkey sandwiches. I love turkey. And cupcakes. I love those, too."

"I know that, Liam. I introduced you to both of those things. What does that have to do with Shelby?"

"I want to meet her, and I want her to make me a turkey sandwich and some cupcakes."

Everett shook his head. "Some interview."

I thought it was a bloody brilliant idea.

"If I like her and her cupcakes are good, the job is hers."

"Thank you, Liam. I'll let her know."

"Anything else I should know about her?"

He grinned. "Just don't call her Beaker."

I met Shelby two days later. She wasn't what I expected. Aside from the dark hair and blue eyes, she and Everett were polar opposites. He was tall, broad-shouldered, spoke loudly, and exuded confidence.

Shelby was short, tiny, her voice soft and pleasant, and she seemed quite shy. Her blue eyes were sad, filled with confusion and lingering hurt, but she smiled and shook my hand when Everett introduced us. I was surprised to find her last name the same as Everett's, but she explained she had never taken her ex's surname.

"Thank God for that," Everett muttered as he left us alone.

As we talked, I realized she was intelligent and kind. There was an aura of gentleness around her that drew me to her easily. I knew I would be able to trust her as much as I trusted her brother. I had already decided to offer her the job before she opened the basket she had brought with her and presented me with a feast.

A turkey sandwich. Unlike the deli-type offerings Marie would put in front of me, there was no processed fake meat—it was made with real turkey. The sandwich was so big, I could barely get my hands around it. There was even stuffing in it, just the way I liked it. She also handed me a carton of milk, and once I finished exclaiming over the sandwich, offered me a container of the best cupcakes I had ever tasted.

I grinned at her, my mouth full.

"Can I ask you a question?"

"This is an interview," she retorted dryly.

"Will you bake me these cupcakes again?"

"Yes."

"Will you make me turkey sandwiches every week? More, if I want?"

"Yes."

"Can you make biscuits?"

She furrowed her brow. "Like savory biscuits?"

"No, you know, cookies. Chocolate chip ones. Or peanut butter. Yeah, peanut butter ones. Can you make those?"

She laughed. "Yes, I can."

"Do you do laundry?"

"Yes."

"Can you buy me some new shorts?"

"Shorts?" she questioned.

"Underpants," I clarified. "Marie—she was pawing at my stuff. I don't know which ones she touched, so I threw them all out."

She arched her eyebrow. "So, right now—"

"I'm commando. Yes."

Her amusement was loud and rich. I grinned just hearing it as I stuffed another cupcake in my gob. They were amazing.

"Yes, I can get you new underwear."

"Shorts."

"You're in America, Britboy. You wear shorts on the beach. We call them underwear."

I grinned at her. I liked her—a lot.

She eyed me speculatively. "After Everett told me what happened, I was looking around the web, and I saw a few other posts. She wasn't only selling your underwear, just so you know."

I looked down at my T-shirt and grimaced. "Bloody hell. I thought the dresser drawer seemed empty." I pulled at the material. "I wonder what was wrong with this one?"

"It's a bit thin. I'm sure she went for the best."

"You mean she probably touched it?"

Shelby's smile was gleeful. "Oh, I'm sure she did. Many times."

"I feel dirty. Maybe you could also throw them out and get me new ones."

"Bleach works well too." She grinned mischievously. "Gets rid of Marie cooties."

I chuckled. "I'll leave it to your discretion."

"I think I can handle that."

I nodded as I shoved in another cupcake. I was subtle about it, and I was sure she hadn't noticed. I was also sure there was something else I should ask.

"Do you know how to clean a house?" I asked as cupcake crumbs blew out of my mouth. I looked at my lap. Maybe not as subtle as I thought.

Now she rolled her eyes. "Yes."

"Then it's all covered." I sat back in triumph.

Who said this would be hard?

I'd asked all the pertinent questions. Stupid Everett—what a git. "You're hired."

She smiled, even though it didn't quite reach her eyes. "You're easy."

"Tell that to your brother. He thinks I'm a pain in the arse." I winked at her. "I think, Shelby, this is the start of a beautiful friendship."

"I hope so, Mr. Wright."

"Liam."

She smiled. "Liam."

3

LIAM

PRESENT DAY

A plate appeared before me, two large sandwiches stacked on it, along with some pickles. Shelby always added some pickles, and now I was addicted to them with my sandwiches. Beside it, Shelby placed a large glass of milk and a plate of cupcakes, as well as the bottle of whiskey and another glass. Everything I needed. I grinned at the meal, already anticipating how good it would be.

"I'm going to bed now. Leave the dishes on the counter. Don't stay up all night, and don't drink too much whiskey. You know you can't handle it."

Smiling, I reached for a sandwich. She could sleep now, because I was back in the house. I was glad I had come home early. I didn't like to think of her not sleeping. "I'll eat and have the whiskey to relax. Then I'll go to bed. Ta, Beaker."

Shelby cuffed the back of my head. "Don't call me that, Oscar." Then she grinned and dropped a kiss on my head. "Night, Liam."

"Night, Shelby."

I took a huge bite of my sandwich, as she left the room to go to her suite on the top floor.

Yeah, it was good to be home.

I shuffled into the kitchen, one hand buried in my hair, the other one clutched against my stomach. I shouldn't have knocked back so much whiskey last night after Shelby went to bed.

I felt rather wonky.

I needed to find Shelby. She'd do something and make me feel better. She always knew how to make me feel better.

Instead, I found her brother sitting at my table, drinking coffee and chuckling over something on his laptop. I stifled a groan. I couldn't handle Everett at the moment.

Silently, I slid my feet back, trying to exit the room before he spotted me, but to no avail.

"Nice try, Liam. Get your sorry ass in here."

I let the groan escape this time and moved over to the table, sitting down heavily. "Where's Shelby?" I mumbled, my voice thick and scratchy.

"My sister is out doing errands. She left you something on the counter."

Anxiously, I walked over and sighed in relief at the Alka-Seltzer and Tylenol waiting for me. I mixed the tablets with water, downed them, then swallowed the painkillers. I poured a cup of coffee and returned to the table.

"Why are you here?"

Everett guffawed—a bit too loudly for my liking. "Did you not think I'd know what happened yesterday, Liam?"

I laid my head on the table. "How?" I knew Shelby wouldn't rat me out. She hid all sorts of shit I pulled from her brother.

"The magazine called, you idiot. And the studio let me know you went AWOL." He lifted his eyebrow. "Without notice or security. Not a wise move, given your history."

"Right." Of course those bastards would tattle to Everett.

"I handled it."

At his grunt, I cracked open an eye. "She was a bloody idiot, Ev.

17

The whole thing was dodgy. We were at sixes and sevens right from the start. Really, I had no choice. My integrity was at stake."

He glared at me, and I grinned. I loved confusing him with my "English-speak," as he called it, so at times, I laid it on thick. He was never totally sure what I was saying. He snorted and took a deep drink of his coffee.

"Sure, Liam. I'll be sure to tell the studio, who set up these interviews, that piece of information." He fixed me with a stern glance. "They already called. You have to make this up. That's three of their interviews you walked out on."

I nodded in defeat. "How?"

"A charity benefit. You will attend. You will be charming. And you will stay for the *whole* thing and sign autographs until your hand drops off." He glared at me. "And you won't complain once."

Instantly, my stomach clenched with nerves. "Did you call Carly? Is she available?"

Everett nodded. "Yes. And Mark. I'll be there as well."

I let out a deep breath. "Okay."

Everett went back to typing, and I leaned my head back, the medicine Shelby left for me beginning to work.

She always knew what I needed. So did Everett. I was lucky to have them.

Unlike my old management team, Everett kept things simple. He ran my career and provided me with his presence as added security most of the time, along with Mark. Nobody got near me with those two men flanking me. He used Cassidy Hawkins for PR work, though he handled most of it himself. Lily Simons was my stylist, something Ev and Cassidy had insisted on when they came on board. Apparently, my choice of torn T-shirts and jeans wasn't the best look most of the time. Ev had been my manager now for about eighteen months, and I couldn't be happier. My old manager had put so many people on the payroll, it was ridiculous, and we had argued over it constantly. He'd felt the more people I had around me, the higher my profile. The only thing I found higher was the cost. And my blood pressure. I didn't like all the people running errands, hanging around the house, and doing stupid things for me. Or more often than not, as I discovered, for my ex-manager.

When I decided to make a change, it was Everett Carter I turned to. We had gotten to be friends, and I liked him. I liked his style of no bullshit and simplicity. Everett stepped in, cleaned house, and made my life easier—better. He discussed everything with me and made sure I knew what was happening at all times. Anything he didn't think I should be bothered with, he handled, and I trusted him enough to know it was for the best. Hiring him had been the best professional decision I had ever made.

Until I hired Shelby.

She was way more than a housekeeper to me, though. Yes, she kept the house in order. But more importantly, she kept me in order. Living under the same roof for the past six months, we'd become close, and I would consider her my best friend. She was certainly my confidant and without a doubt, knew me better than anyone else—even her brother. She knew my moods, my likes and dislikes, and she catered to them. She also never hesitated to put me in my place when needed. Her gentle teasing and laughter often drew me out of a bad mood, and her no-nonsense approach to the life I led was refreshing. It was her opinion I listened to regarding scripts, her thoughts and counsel I sought when making a decision. And it was her comfort I needed when having a difficult time. With my family still back in England, she and Everett had become my adopted family here, and I would be lost without either of them.

I heard the sound of the door opening from the garage, and I smiled. Shelby was home. I knew if I asked, she'd make me something to eat. I needed something greasy and filling to help chase off the last of the whiskey hangover.

I didn't move from the chair or open my eyes when she came into the room, yet I knew exactly where she was at any given second.

"Well, look who is in the land of the living."

Everett snorted. "I'm not sure you'd call him alive yet."

I sighed as I felt Shelby's hand run gently through my hair. "Oscar, Oscar, Oscar...why do you insist on drinking? You know you can't handle liquor well."

I frowned at her and peered through one eye. "I'm *British*, Shelby. We are known for how well we handle our drink. Legendary."

She snickered, her fingers tenderly massaging my aching head. "Liam, the British are also known for their suave, smooth leading men. But let's face it, you really don't live up to either category, do you?"

I huffed in annoyance. She was right. No matter how much effort the studio and Lily put into my appearance, I would never be a legendary leading man. I was far too immature. And I was a cheap drunk.

"Put a sock in it, woman. I'm in no mood for your crap."

"How many whiskeys did you have?"

I flicked my hand dismissively. "A bunch."

Shelby moved away and I heard her open the cabinet. I watched from under my eyelashes as she held up the bottle, which wasn't missing much of the golden liquid inside. "Two, maybe three, Liam? Light ones at that, no doubt. Hardly enough to put most Brits in this shape the next day. Tsk, tsk. You are letting your people down."

"Piss off. I was shattered from being on the job all day—days, in fact—so it hit me hard. And, I'm a bloody good actor."

She chuckled as she started unloading her bags. "I never said you weren't good, Oscar. I said you weren't smooth. Or suave."

"What are you on about? Why don't you call my leading ladies and get their opinion on that?"

"Good idea. Shall I start with Carly? Or maybe Gillian?"

Everett guffawed beside me, and I gave up. Both those women, even though we were friends, knew I was a wanker. Great to work with, but not dependable.

"Fine. Sod off, both of you. Maybe I'm not smooth, and maybe I can't handle my liquor. But I'm cuter than you, Ev." I pointed at

Shelby. "And I'm way taller than you." Then I sniffed haughtily. "And the birds dig my accent."

Shelby hummed. "I'll give you that, Britboy."

"Shelby, I'm hungry."

"What do you want to eat?"

I sighed with want. "I'd give you fifty grand if you had a double-double In-N-Out burger over there. A hundred grand if there was a chocolate shake and fries to go with it."

"Is that a fact?"

"'Tis."

"Pay up."

The thump of a bag in front of me had me opening my eyes, and I grinned widely. She knew me well.

"Brilliant."

I tore into the bag, shoving fries in my gob as I jammed the straw into the milkshake, desperate for a taste of the cold, creamy liquid.

Shelby handed Everett his lunch and sat across from me with her own burger.

"Ta." I winked at her. "You're smashing, love."

Her eyes were warm and filled with mirth. "There you go with the accent again, Oscar."

"Piece of cake." I grinned. "Gotcha right where I want you."

She shook her head. "That you do, Liam. That you do."

4

SHELBY

Liam relaxed on the sofa in the den, his eyes closed. From across the room, Everett and I were going over Liam's calendar at the desk. His upcoming shooting schedule, interviews, travel arrangements, photo shoots—the never-ending train that was the life of Liam Wright.

I grinned as I took in Liam's relaxed posture. The sunlight streamed in the window, highlighting his white-blond hair and the scruff on his chin. He was tall—his legs draped over the small sofa in the den as he slumbered. In repose, he looked younger than his twenty-eight years, his skin smooth, his expression peaceful. One hand rested on the floor, his long fingers curled into a loose fist while the other was draped across his strong chest. His broad shoulders and muscular build looked good on the screen. He wore a suit like a second skin—elegant, graceful, and masculine all at the same time. His smile was blinding, and when you added in his extraordinary green eyes that seemed to glow in his face plus his killer looks, the screen loved him. He was sought after by studios, well known around town as a flirt and a playboy, yet respected and liked. He was never an asshole and had a reputation for bringing his A game to every set and treating those around him, be they a makeup artist or a co-star, with the same attitude. He always had a friendly word for everyone and was never anything but professional.

At home, he was the same way. Cheerful and friendly. Sweet. He reminded me of a puppy—wanting to please, happy to make someone smile. He thought of himself as a wanker, but the truth was he was simply Liam. Carefree and content to be looked after. There was no malice in him, only a boyish charm that covered his hidden insecurities.

Everett and I knew the truth behind his good-natured ways. The fear Liam lived and dealt with as best he could. Everett worked hard to make his career, and all it entailed, as easy for Liam as possible. I did the same for him at home. He was catered to on sets, led as to which way to go when out in public, and he relied on his team to look after him.

Our Peter Pan—the boy who refused to grow up. He'd gotten his nickname early on in his career, when he'd flippantly replied to a reporter's query about being cast in roles of characters far younger than his years.

"Are you worried about being typecast and only able to play younger men? Never growing up?"

Liam had shrugged and laughed. "Worked well for Peter Pan."

The name stuck, and he hated it, although at times it suited him. He had no idea how to run a house, handle his finances, take care of himself—or anyone else.

That was why he had us.

And somehow, needing to be needed by the slumbering boy-man on the sofa satisfied something within me. Liam and I were best friends, and I adored him. I liked caring for him, and I loved his downtime when it was only us. Those were the best times.

Despite how I had come to be in his life, I was glad I was part of it.

I startled as I realized Everett had asked me a question, and I had to ask him to repeat it. I tore my gaze away from Liam and concentrated on the task at hand. He was far too distracting—and I had a lot of work to do.

LIAM

Slowly waking, I listened to Shelby and Everett talking and planning. I was grateful I wasn't the one who had to figure the schedule, although Ev always gave me last say. I rarely disagreed since I knew he had things under control and had my best interests at heart.

Still, he always kept me in the loop, and Shelby always kept me in line. I did what they told me to do.

It worked well for all of us.

I grinned at the sounds of Shelby's amusement at something Everett said. She always brought a smile to my face, right from the day she became part of my life.

"Are you sure you'll be okay here alone, Shelby?"

She nodded. "I'll be fine, Liam. I'll be busy here, I think, while you're gone."

I chuckled. I had seen her lists. She would be busy. I wanted the entire house changed—everything that reminded me of Marie to be gone.

"I don't expect you to redo the whole house in three weeks."

"I can get a lot done."

She had been a breath of fresh air the past few days. Always smiling and upbeat despite what she had been through—she was amazing.

"Everett gave you access to a household account, right?" I waggled my finger at her. "Don't bleed me dry, woman."

"I'll clear it all with you first, Liam."

"I trust you. Do what you think is best."

She frowned at me. "Liam, this is your home. You should be picking the furniture and dishes."

"Um, not a good idea. I know nothing about that sort of thing. I'd cock it all up."

"I'll help you," she insisted. "But the final decisions are yours."

I grimaced, running a hand through my hair. "Shelby..."

"I'll make it easy on you, Oscar. Go be brilliant and leave this to me."

Leaning forward, I kissed her cheek softly. She was affectionate with Everett and treated me the same way. I found returning her warmth incredibly easy. "Ta, Beaker. Take care."

"Don't call me that!"

I raised my hand and waved.

I chuckled all the way to the car. Everett's pet name for her was perfect. When she became upset or worried, she made the strangest little bleating noise in the back of her throat—reminiscent of Beaker the lab assistant on the Muppets. It suited her.

She hated the name. The first time I had heard her make that sound, I thought she was choking, and I had tried to perform the Heimlich maneuver on her. She had elbowed me in the chest, sending me sprawling on the floor. Once I figured out what had happened, I laughed so hard she left the room in a huff. I apologized, although I fully understood the reason for Everett's pet name. She told me never to call her by that name and I agreed.

I lied.

I loved it and used it as often as I could just to piss her off and make her glare at me. She was quite cute when she glared.

She started calling me Oscar because of the statue I had shown her, lamenting over the damage it caused to my TV after Marie threw it. Shelby assured me she would find a way to have the Oscar repaired and promised to replace the TV.

"I'm not sure the Academy would be too happy to know you were more upset over the TV than the statue, Liam." She winked. "I'll keep that between us—" she paused then grinned "—Oscar."

I laughed, enjoying her teasing and liking her nickname.

But I pretended my nickname was homage to my acting skills and Shelby let me.

She was serious when she said I had the final say in things. Her emails were endless. And perfect. She narrowed down the choices to two for everything and sent me links or pictures, and I simply chose the one I liked best and replied. I did beg her to have mercy when she sent drapery choices and questions about dishes and cooking pots. I didn't give a flying fuck about any of that—as long as there was food on the plate, I didn't care what color the crockery was. Or the color of the new sheets she was purchasing for me as long as they were on my bed and Marie hadn't touched them. I told her to send me the big stuff, and I would let her choose the accessories to complete the rooms.

I was quite proud of knowing that word and decorating phrase. Shelby seemed impressed as well.

I sent the makeup artist and her husband to dinner to thank her for supplying me with them. I was grateful the email had come while Cindy was doing my makeup and she had been amused at my moan of despair when I read it. I had her type the reply to make sure it was correct. I told myself it was like someone prompting my lines off-camera.

I loved Shelby's emails for other reasons. I got to know her through her words, and I was amazed how quickly she seemed to know exactly what I would like when it came to my home. Deep, comfortable furniture would replace the ugly, hard-leather black sofas Marie had chosen. Dark wood and warm colors on the walls removed the glass-topped tables and white walls Marie had informed me were chic. In retrospect, Marie had scared me so badly, I just let her do what she wanted so she would leave me alone. It probably wasn't the best scenario, having her in my house.

When I walked into my house three weeks later, I hardly recognized the place. I loved every single change Shelby had made—especially the larger flat screen, which was now housed in a built-in wall unit, my repaired and shiny Oscar proudly displayed on one of the shelves.

I also reveled in my freshly replaced underwear and T-shirts. My dressers were full and organized.

Somehow, knowing Shelby had her hands all over them didn't bother me the way knowing that Marie had touched them had.

It was different.

Marie was scary. Psycho-shower-scene scary.

Shelby, as Everett had put it, wasn't even remotely scary. She was amazing, and I already worshiped her.

And in the six months she'd been with me, that hadn't changed at all. It had only grown.

Shelby made that funny noise, and I opened my eyes, looking at her across the room. She was staring at her tablet, her eyes narrowed and her lips moving wordlessly as she read the screen. Immediately, I shut my eyes, knowing exactly what was causing that reaction. I struggled to keep a straight face as I heard her chair push back, and her feet hit the floor in fast angry steps. My eyes flew open when her tiny but strong finger poked me in the chest.

"What the hell is this, Liam?"

I acted confused. "What is what, Beaker?"

I knew she was upset when she ignored the use of her nickname.

"This," she hissed, holding up her iPad.

"I don't know what I'm looking at."

"There is a deposit in my account for $100,000. What the hell?"

I shrugged nonchalantly. "I paid my debt."

"Are you mental? You don't owe me a hundred grand!"

I sighed patiently. "Obviously, I no longer owe you. I paid it."

"You never owed it, you stupid British moron!"

Behind her, Everett began to guffaw. He relaxed in his chair, his arm draped casually over the back as he sipped his coffee and watched us.

I subtly flipped him the bird.

Shelby slapped my hand. "Behave."

Dammit. She caught me every time.

"I told you I'd give you a hundred grand if you had what I wanted. You did. I paid up. Simple."

"You say shit like that all the time. I don't take you seriously."

I pursed my lips, teasingly. "Wait, I owe you more?" I dug into my pocket. "I'll call the bank."

"You don't owe me anything! Cancel the transfer."

"Can't. It's already in there."

"Reverse it."

"Nope. A promise is a promise."

She hovered over me, trying hard to be menacing. "I promise I am going to hurt you if you don't take this back."

"She will," Everett sang. "I'll help her."

"Sod off, you git. Stay out of this. It's between Shelby and me. And the discussion is over."

"Take it back," she demanded.

I reclined back on the sofa. "Nope."

Shelby turned and marched out of the room. I grinned widely. I'd been looking for a reason to give her a bonus, and this was perfect. I loved how she looked when pissed off—her cheeks bright with color and her eyes lit with fire as she glared at me. She was cracking.

A few moments later, she strode back in, slapping a piece of paper onto my chest before walking back to the desk. I looked down and picked up the folded slip, chuckling when I saw the check made out to me for the full amount—plus a dollar.

Without a word, I stood and went over to her, smiling innocently as I bent low and kissed her cheek.

"Ta, Shelby. But no."

And I fed the check into the shredder.

I snickered all the way to the door.

"This isn't over, Oscar."

I grinned at her. "I've already won, Beaker. Give up."

"Never."

A certified check appeared the next day. I deposited it and retransferred the money.

One hundred thousand dollars in neat, bundled twenties showed up on my bed a few days later. Ev and I dropped it off back at the bank on the way to an interview, with instructions it was to go back into Shelby's account.

Daily, a check would be sitting on my desk. I always waited until Shelby was going by to drop it in the shredder, chuckling the entire time, enjoying her muffled shrieks of annoyance. I offered to order her some new checks since it appeared she'd run out soon.

She flipped me off and kept walking.

And then she stopped. I was sitting at my desk in the late afternoon reading over the script for my upcoming movie and realized no check had appeared. No bundles of cash and no gnashing of teeth.

Had I won?

Suspiciously, I went into the kitchen. She was busy making pasta sauce, and my mouth started to water. I loved her pasta. I pulled myself up on the counter and watched her in silence. In the background, she had rock music playing. That usually meant she was thinking. Which was never a good thing for me—she was way smarter than I was. I cleared my throat. "All right, Shelby?"

She glanced at me. "Pasta for dinner, okay?"

"Sounds good. Is there garlic bread?"

She laughed. "Of course."

I glanced around surreptitiously. "Dessert?"

"Oh. I forgot that out in the car. Could you get it?"

I frowned. Shelby *bought* dessert? I grumbled to myself as I went to fetch it for her. Shelby didn't buy baked goods. Shelby *made* me baked goods. I liked Shelby's baking. *Why would she buy anything?*

I stopped short in the doorway of the garage and started to howl in amusement. The passenger side of my convertible was filled with coins, which overflowed onto the driver's side. The garage light glinted off the shiny silver of the quarters, nickels, and dimes I could see filling the small seating area of my Jaguar. A pile of coin rollers was on the floor beside the car. I had no idea how long it had taken her to fill it or how much money there was in coins, but it was brilliant.

She was brilliant.

Shelby reached around and slapped a certified draft against my chest. "I'm not helping you empty it either. Take it back, Liam. Or next time, it's all pennies." She walked away, looking over her shoulder. "And I won't only use some of the money—I'll fill your pool and hot tub with them."

I kept laughing as I looked at the $90,000 draft. She'd filled my car with $10,000 worth of coins. I wondered briefly if she could get her hands on a hundred grand worth of pennies and what they would look like filling the pool. And while I really didn't want to find out...I was enjoying this too much to stop.

I looked down at the paper in my hand. I could deposit it and let her win.

Or...I could hold on to the draft and drive her crazy. Having it in limbo would drive her nuts.

This was *so* on.

I arrived home the next day, a package tucked under my arm. I smiled at Shelby as I walked through the kitchen, stopping at her "odds and ends drawer," as she called it. I dug around and got the hammer and a picture hook, then walked down the hall.

"What are you doing?" she called after me.

Grinning, I ignored her and walked into the den. I gazed around the walls and decided I liked the one across from my desk the best.

Awkwardly, I tapped the hook into the wall, cursing when I hit my thumb while trying to avoid doing exactly that.

"Bugger."

"Not good wielding a hammer, Oscar?" Shelby's voice behind me was amused and curious at the same time.

"Piss off, Beaker. I'm busy."

"I see. Redecorating?"

I huffed. "Adding to the ambiance."

She snorted.

I glared at her. "Have something on your mind?"

"How's your car?"

I flashed my megawatt smile at her. As usual, it had no effect, and she continued to gaze at me impassively.

"It's great. I drove it to a high school that was doing car washes. They emptied it out and washed it. Their school is getting a new set of bleachers, thanks to you. Well done."

Her eyes widened.

Turning, I unwrapped my package, holding it up to admire it before I turned around and hung it on the wall.

"Perfect."

The $90,000 draft was enclosed in glass and framed.

Behind me, Shelby's mouth opened, and her Beaker noise escaped.

"You can't leave that *there*."

"I can."

"It's a waste."

I shrugged and sat at my desk. "Then take it back."

"No. It's extravagant, Liam! It's not needed!"

"I disagree." I pointed to the frame. "And it's staying there until I convince you otherwise."

She glared at me and then turned on her heel and walked out of the room. "Enjoy your expensive art, Liam!" She stopped at the doorway. "You haven't won."

"I beg to differ."

"Oh, you'll be begging, all right."

I snorted in amusement as she walked away. The flash in her eye and the heightened color on her cheeks were all I needed.

This wasn't over.

I looked forward to what she had up her sleeve next. Whatever it was, I would enjoy it. She made my life brighter and brought joy to my days.

And I adored her.

5

LIAM

A few days later, I poked at my dinner in front of me. When Shelby had fired up the grill, I was sure she was cooking steak. I loved steak.

This looked suspiciously like chicken. Only kinda flat. And there was a large pile of salad on my plate. I preferred fries.

"Problem, Liam?"

"No. I just thought we were having steak, not chicken."

Shelby's voice was amused. "It's not chicken. It's swordfish."

I took a bite of the dense flesh. "Kinda tastes like chicken."

"Trust me, it's not."

"Okay." I chewed a few mouthfuls, actually enjoying the flavor, when a thought hit me and I paused, my fork partway to my mouth.

"What now?"

"Why are we having fish? That's twice this week," I asked suspiciously.

"I thought it would be a nice change."

"I like steak."

"So you've mentioned," Shelby said calmly, continuing to eat her dinner.

"So, why are we having fish again?"

Shelby sighed.

"It's healthy."

I groaned. Shelby always made sure I ate healthily. She let me have my turkey sandwiches and the occasional In-N-Out burger, but she was constantly piling my plate with steamed vegetables and salad. She had me eating yogurt and drinking fruit smoothies. How much healthier could I get? She even monitored the baked goods I ate, only dishing them out on occasion.

I didn't want to *be* any healthier.

"Are you watching your weight, Shelby?" I asked teasingly then froze when her head shot up, and I remembered all too late that a man should never ever bring up the weight issue with a woman. "Because you shouldn't be. You're perfect," I mumbled quickly. "Just perfect. Just like you are."

"Actually, I'm watching yours, Liam."

My head snapped up. "Bloody...*what?*"

"You start filming in a month."

"And?"

"You've, um, gained a little weight."

"Haven't."

"Yes, you have. I know that during your downtime you've been eating badly and sitting more with all the lunch meetings. I thought I would help get you back on track."

I narrowed my eyes at her. "Is this about the money, Shelby?" We were at a standstill over it—the draft still hung on my wall, and I knew she hated it. "Are you punishing me by starving me?"

"*Starving* you? Dramatic much?" She paused and snorted. "Oh wait..."

I crossed my arms and glared at her.

"No, Liam. This is about you being in shape for your next role. There're a lot of action scenes in it, and I know you want to be ready."

I stood, yanking my shirt over my head. "I'm not fat, Shelby!" I yelled, poking my side. "I'm lanky. You can count my ribs. I don't need to eat fish and salad." I glared at her, trying to ignore the fact that my voice sounded like a twelve-year-old girl screeching at the moment.

She regarded me coolly. "Pull your shirt down, Liam. I'm eating dinner."

I huffed and did what she told me to do. Then sat, frowning.

"Your, ah, *bottom rib* is a little more prominent than usual when you sit," she stated.

"Piss off," I muttered, pushing away my plate.

"Eat your dinner."

"Is there dessert?"

"Yes."

Grudgingly, I picked up my fork, because really, the fish was good. I had yet to taste anything Shelby made that wasn't delicious. And, even after Shelby telling me I was fat, I still loved having dinner with her. It was one of my favorite parts of having her live here. Sharing our day. Smiling. Joking. Being scolded. It was a huge change from when Marie was here. I used to eat in the den alone. Eating with her would not have been pleasant.

Internally, I sighed. Shelby was right, as usual. I didn't want to admit my pants were slightly snug. And I certainly didn't want to tell her it wasn't because of the lunch meetings. Usually, I was so nervous that I barely ate at those things. It was more to do with the long naps I was taking daily—the last shoot had been hard and taxing, and I had been anxious for it to wrap up so I could come home. I found myself missing home more and more these days while I was away, although I wasn't sure why.

Since coming home, I loathed going out, only doing so when I had to. Instead, I opted for lazy days by the pool, naps, and watching movies with Shelby when I could convince her to stop doing whatever she was doing and spend time with me. Shelby had been extra sweet, encouraging me to "rest and regroup," as she called it, and catering to me even more than usual. I loved the attention from her. And if I was being completely honest, my pants *were* snugger than normal because I had found the stash of baked goods in the freezer in the laundry room. I'd been shoving them in my face every time I went into the room.

Which was now daily—several times a day in fact. They were almost gone.

I knew she'd find out. I only hoped she would discover it after I left to do some location filming. She'd get over being angry by the time I got home.

But I damned well wasn't going to admit it to her right now. Bloody hell—the cheek of being told I was chubby in my own home.

Right.

I tried desperately to stop the corner of my mouth from turning up. Only Shelby would calmly inform me of that fact while we were eating dinner.

We finished off our meal in silence. Shelby stood and collected our plates, and a few minutes later placed dessert in front of me.

I looked at it then back at her. "What is this?"

She sighed. "Honestly, Liam. I thought you were a smart man. You attended *Oxford*, for heaven's sake."

I leaned forward conspiratorially, wanting to make her laugh. "Actually, Shelby, I only attended a *concert* at Oxford. My PR people just left that small part out."

She gaped at me. "But they said you left before you graduated when you got bit by the acting bug."

I nodded, grinning. "I had an audition the next day, so I was only there for the concert. Technically, I *was* at Oxford—I did leave—so theoretically, I never graduated Oxford, and I started acting. It's just a slightly different spin on it."

Her eyes were wide as she looked at me. "Well, that explains a lot."

I started to chuckle, thrilled when she joined me. She was amazing, even when she was putting me in my place. "Now, what is this so-called dessert?"

"Fruit parfait."

I picked it up and studied it. "Looks like fruit and granola with something I'm certain *isn't* ice cream."

"Yogurt."

"Health food disguised as dessert? Hardly fair to tease a man like that, Shelby. Not on, really."

She picked up her spoon. "I planned on giving you some cupcakes, Liam, but they seem to have disappeared." Her eyebrow arched. "So have all the cookies. Anything you want to share?"

I shoved a spoonful of the healthy crap in my gob. I couldn't possibly be expected to talk with my mouth full, could I? I dared to glance at her under my eyelashes.

She mouthed one word at me while patting her flat stomach knowingly.

Busted.

I looked down, fighting a grin.

So worth it.

"Seriously, Lily, a tuxedo?" I complained.

The charity event had arrived, and Lily had shown up, a whirl of movement as she talked and flourished, cajoled and organized.

"It's black tie, Liam. This is a huge night. You need to be perfect. It's your favorite designer—cut just for you." She frowned. "You also need a haircut." She threw up her hands. "Why didn't you get a haircut?"

"Um, I forgot?"

"You forgot? It was on your to-do list!"

I looked over at Shelby beseechingly. Usually, she could save me from the wrath of Lily. I had forgotten but I didn't think it was that big a deal. It was a little long, but it was fine. Wasn't it?

Shelby smiled at Lily and handed her a cup of coffee. "It's fine,

Lily. I'll give Liam a quick trim. Then he can go shave and get ready. He'll look great."

"He'd better," she muttered.

Shelby chuckled and left the room, returning with scissors and a spray bottle of water. She pulled a chair away from the table and patted the seat.

Obediently, I sat and let Shelby drape a towel around my shoulders. She had trimmed my hair before, so I knew it would be fine. Lily huffed but calmed down. I shut my eyes and enjoyed the feeling of Shelby's fingers running through my hair as she snipped. She hummed as she worked, and I grinned.

"*A-ha?*" I mumbled at her. "Really?"

"Good, Liam. You're learning." She stepped to the front. "I need to be closer."

I opened my legs, and Shelby stood between them, working on the front. She was so close I could smell the light perfume of her skin as she worked away. I drew in a deep breath, letting the scent fill me, finding the unique calm that Shelby personified with it. "Don't leave a big bald spot," I teased.

She tapped my chin. "Don't tempt me."

I squeezed her hips affectionately, and somehow, my hands stayed there. No doubt to help keep her steady.

They felt strangely right there.

Everett walked in and sat. I heard him speak quietly to Lily before he addressed me. "Okay, Liam. Slight change of plans."

Shelby stopped cutting, and I opened my eyes to look at him. I didn't like his tone of voice. "What's up?"

"Carly is ill. She had to cancel."

My throat went dry. "Gillian?" I managed to get out.

"Out of town. You're stag tonight, Liam."

My stomach rolled, and the panic set in. Hard. I gripped Shelby's hips, my throat closed, and my breathing became labored.

Alone. I'd have to walk the red carpet alone.

Screaming. All the women would be screaming. Yelling my

name, crying. Grabbing at me. The memory of the night I was pulled into the crowd and mauled flashed through my head. The hands touching me everywhere and voices screaming in my ears still made me shudder. I knew I'd have security around me tonight, but I couldn't stop the panic.

I was aware of the sound of metal hitting the floor. Tender, warm hands gripped my face, and a soothing voice was in my ear, pleading and assuring me.

"It's okay, Liam. I'm right here. Right here. You're safe. Open your eyes and look at me."

Struggling, I wrenched my eyes open and stared into the clear blue eyes of Shelby. Eyes filled with warmth and compassion. Nonjudgmental, only caring.

Safe.

Home.

Shelby.

With a groan, I wrapped my arms around her, pulling her close and letting my head fall into her stomach. Her hands moved through my hair in comfort. I felt her body turn slightly.

"Everett," she hissed. "You jackass! You had to say it like that? You know he doesn't handle this well."

There was the sound of a chair moving, and then I felt Everett standing beside me. "Sorry, Liam," he apologized. "I didn't mean for it to come out that way."

I didn't lift my head, feeling embarrassed at the overreaction but unable to control it. It was my weakness. One, with a great deal of help, I kept hidden from the world. Large, screaming crowds around me. When I had first started out and became an overnight success, it was harrowing. At one event, there hadn't been proper security, and I had been pulled into a frenzied crowd. By the time they got me out, I was scratched, bruised, my clothes were shredded, tufts of my hair were missing, and I was left with an overwhelming fear of masses of people. The only way I had managed since then was with a friend to walk beside me and hold my hand, Everett and Mark, my security guy, behind me, and a Xanax before leaving the house. Although I had other women who attended events with me, Carly and Gillian were my two favorite go-to friends. It was great exposure for them, and beyond helpful to me. Since I had worked with each of them, they knew of my panic attacks but kept the information well-hidden. The same way I respected and kept their personal relationship with each other a secret.

To the world, I was a carefree bachelor who dated casually and often. Carly and Gillian were both frequent "dates," although all of us denied being anything other than what we really were—friends. The press did what they wanted with it, and none of us cared.

Only a few people knew the real truth.

But neither of them was available tonight. My panicked eyes met Shelby's calm ones.

"We'll figure this out, Liam." She glanced at Everett. "Surely there is someone else you can ask?"

He shook his head. "The gala is in three hours. I tried."

She looked over at Lily. "Lily?"

"I can't. It's my partner's birthday. I have fifty people who'll be waiting at a restaurant tonight. I can't cancel." Lily stood. "But...maybe?"

We all looked at her.

"What about you, Shelby? You could go with him."

"What?" Shelby's voice was horrified. "Me? Are you crazy?"

Lily shook her head. "No, it's perfect. You know Liam. You can keep him relaxed. You know Ev and Mark. You could go."

Shelby gaped at her. "Even if I agreed, I can't. I have nothing to wear. I don't own a fancy dress!"

Lily clapped her hands. "Well, today is your lucky day. I have a dress and shoes in the car that would be perfect for you." She blushed and added hopefully, "I designed the dress. If you wore it, it might get my name out there."

I tightened my hands on Shelby. This could work.

"Please," I asked quietly. "If you were there, I could do this, Shelby. Please."

She glanced at Everett.

"I'll be right there," he encouraged her. "You don't have to talk to reporters or anything. We'll get you down the red carpet as quickly as possible. But Liam has to go. He can't back out now, no matter what is going on."

She bit her lip, and I knew how much she hated being put in this position. She shied away from anything to do with the Hollywood lifestyle and the mass hysteria that seemed to surround me when I was in public. I knew the thought of being on that carpet tonight was almost as daunting to her as it was to me. But I needed her. I knew if *she* was beside me, I could walk the red carpet, ignore the screams, and be calm. She always calmed me.

"Please," I asked again. "I need you."

For a moment, our eyes locked. Bright blue met pleading green. Her gaze slowly softened with understanding, and I sighed in relief when she agreed. I dropped my head back to her stomach; it suddenly felt too heavy to hold up anymore.

With her, I could do this.

"On one condition."

I looked up. "You can have anything, Shelby. Name it and it's yours."

Whatever she wanted, I'd buy her.

A smile played on her lips, and then she grinned widely. "You're sure about that? Anything?"

I nodded, confused, but smiled back at her as relief coursed through me, making me almost giddy. She never asked for anything.

What could she possibly want?

She bent, brushing her lips across my forehead. She cupped my cheeks as she regarded me seriously. "The draft comes out of the frame and into your account tomorrow, Liam. And it's done."

Bloody hell.

I sat back and admitted defeat grudgingly.

She'd done it.
Game, set, and match.
She'd won.
I laughed as she winked at me.
Brilliant girl.

6

LIAM

I paced the front hall anxiously.

What was taking so long?

I had showered, shaved, and dressed in thirty minutes. Shelby and Lily had been up there for well over an hour. A couple of times, while I was getting ready, I heard muffled shrieks from the third floor, and once, I was sure I heard Shelby cursing at Lily.

She rarely cursed unless she was pissed at me, which was often. I enjoyed listening to her cuss me out, and I knew she wasn't enjoying the primping Lily had assured her she would love.

Shelby didn't primp.

It was one of the things I found endearing and refreshing about her.

She was simply Shelby. I had never seen her in a dress. Her everyday outfits consisted of either black yoga pants or jeans and a long shirt. When she had cleaned out my closet, she had snagged a few of the dress shirts I didn't want and often wore those, the arms rolled up and the tails tied around her hips as she worked around the house.

I never told her I preferred it when she wore my shirts. For some reason, it made my chest warm to see her in them, though.

Her hair was always in a bun or a ponytail. No makeup. The only item I'd ever seen her use was lip gloss.

She was naturally pretty; it was effortless. She was just Shelby.

So what was taking so bloody long?

I dragged my hand through my now-shorter hair and glanced over at Everett, who was busy typing away on his phone. Mark had arrived and was outside having a smoke as he waited patiently. Neither of them seemed concerned over the time it was taking. I glanced at my watch for the hundredth time.

"Relax, Liam. Plenty of time," Everett advised.

"What are they doing up there?"

He looked up and shrugged. "God knows."

"Go find out."

He shook his head. "Your house, Liam. You go."

"No. I don't go onto Shelby's floor. That's her space."

I had only ever been up three times. I had insisted she make over the rooms to suit her, and she had shown me the end result. The second time, I had been desperate. My head ached and I felt like shit and I needed Shelby to fix it for me, so I had bravely gone up to her room and woke her at four a.m., asking for her help. She had taken me back downstairs, soothed my head, got me medication and something to drink before she sat with me until I fell asleep. When I woke later that morning, she was still curled in the chair beside the bed, having watched over me all night. Because that was what Shelby did. She cared for those she loved, and as she often told me, she loved me like a brother. I loved her right back—she was my best friend, and I couldn't imagine my life without her. She took care of me. I was lucky to have her. When she got sick from looking after me and hadn't come downstairs for the day, I went back to her room after making her some dinner. I learned two valuable lessons. Never wake a sick Shelby. And never offer baked beans on toast to someone who was ill. I barely made it out of the room without joining her in the bathroom while she was retching after I shoved the tray under her nose, trying to be helpful.

Never happening again.

The sound of her nervous voice calling for Everett broke through my thoughts as he climbed toward the landing. I followed behind him but waited at the bottom, anxious. A few minutes later he appeared, chuckling.

"What?"

"I'll let you decide. My sister is looking rather"—he grinned and winked— "smashing, I think you'd say." He turned his head. "Come on, Beaker! Show yourself!"

"Don't call me that!"

I gaped at the vision that appeared at the top of the stairs, one hand on her hip as she glared at Everett.

I blinked as I took her in.

Where was my fresh-faced, pink-cheeked Shelby?

A woman stood there who resembled her, but who was so beyond beautiful and sexy, my throat hurt trying to stop the wolf whistle that wanted to escape.

Bloody hell. She was beyond smashing.

She was *exquisite*.

Her dress was long and red, her bare shoulders glittering under the lights from the crystals that rested over them, her skin gleaming. Her waist was cinched tight with the same glittering beads.

And her hair.

Long, dark tresses rippled freely over her shoulders, swaying as she walked down the stairs, one hand clutching the railing as her other one bunched and unbunched the deep-red fabric of her dress nervously. Whatever Lily had done with her makeup made her blue eyes seem huge in her face, and her lips were entirely kissable with the red stain on them.

I blinked.

What was I thinking?

Kissable?

45

Shelby?

Everett's sharp elbow into my side made me exhale hard. "Liam," he hissed. "Quit eye-fucking my sister."

I glared at him, keeping my reply low so I couldn't be overheard. "I am not eye-fucking—" I stopped, shaking my head.

Holy crap. I was.

What was I doing? It was Shelby. Dressed up or not, it was still my best friend, Shelby. I didn't eye-fuck my best friend.

But he was right. I was doing exactly that. She was stunning.

I frowned at him, refusing to admit it. He was much bigger than I was and could hurt me easily. Manager or not. "Am not."

I stepped forward, reaching for Shelby's hand as she drew closer. Gently, I pulled it away from her dress.

"Shelby," I breathed out. "Thank you."

She looked shy as Lily grinned beside me, almost giddy with glee. "Isn't she perfect?"

I squeezed Shelby's hand in reassurance. "She is."

"You look amazing, Liam."

I disagreed. Beside her, I was plain. She was the amazing one tonight.

Lily suddenly clucked and lifted Shelby's hand, taking something off her wrist. "Sorry, Shelby. The bracelet doesn't work. The gold doesn't go with the silver crystals. I don't have anything silver with me."

Shelby shrugged. "It's fine, Lily. I'm not much for jewelry anyway."

Lily sighed. "I wanted one show-off piece." She held up the gold cuff. "This simply won't work, though."

Inspiration struck, and I held up my finger. "Wait!" I hurried to the den, returning in a few minutes with a small case. I opened it for Lily. "Will this work?"

She clapped her hands. "Liam, it's perfect! Where did you get it?"

I grinned as I lifted the shining antique bracelet from the case. "It was my nan's. My grandmother's," I added in case they weren't familiar with the term Nan.

Shelby gasped when I took her hand and snapped the bracelet on her wrist; the tiny diamonds glittered under the lights, matching her shoulders in their brilliance. I loved how it looked on her. Like it was meant to be there.

Her eyes were wide as she looked between it and me. "Liam, I can't—"

"You can. And you are. Lily is right. It's perfect for you. Your outfit, I meant."

"I'll guard it with my life," she said, running her fingers over the intricate designs in the metal.

"One more thing," Lily chirped as she tucked a deep-red square into my tuxedo jacket pocket. "Now you look like you belong together."

For some reason, I agreed with her statement. I looked over at Shelby again, unable to take my eyes off her. The heels Lily had Shelby in made her taller, but she still fit perfectly under my arm as I tucked her into my side. "Ready?"

She swallowed nervously. "Ready."

I kissed the top of her head, inhaling her calming scent deeply. "Thank you for doing this. I'll be right beside you, Shelby."

"I think that's my line, Liam. I'm here for you, remember?"

I tightened my hold on her. "Quiet, Shelby. We'll look after each other, okay?"

Her smile could melt icebergs. Big ones.

"Okay."

I had to look away before Everett saw me.

I was eye-fucking her again.

Bugger.

The crowds were huge. Security lined the red carpet, holding them

47

back. I looked out the tinted window at the crowd and shuddered, fighting the panic, knowing I had to signal Everett when I was ready and to open the door.

The screams were loud.

It was the screaming that hit me the hardest all the time. There were times I wanted to weep with the noise level constantly pounding at my ears. I hated this part of my life.

Shelby tugged on my hand, distracting me.

She nodded reassuringly at me and silently glanced to where our hands were entwined. I looked down and sighed, releasing some tension. Our hands were so tightly clasped, I couldn't tell where her hand ended and mine began. It made me feel better.

"Everett and Mark are here. I'm with you, Liam," she murmured soothingly.

I didn't care if I sounded like a child. I needed to hear her say it. "You won't let go?"

"I promise. I won't let go."

I kissed her hand. "Let's do this."

The screaming increased vociferously when I stepped out of the car. Everett helped Shelby out first, and she turned, holding her hand out for me as I stepped into the line of vision. I hesitated before grabbing her hand and dragging her to my side. Her hand wasn't enough. I needed to feel her as close to me as possible. I wrapped my arm around her waist, holding her tightly as we made our way down the carpet, refusing to release my hold on her even when I stopped to speak to a few reporters. Everett and Mark trailed close, making sure I didn't stop long, and we made it to the door in record time. I managed to avoid the big question of who the beautiful brunette was I was holding to my side, and Shelby avoided the camera by turning her head, allowing her hair to hide most of her face. Everett told me what to say, but I was still overwhelmed by her and I forgot. I simply winked, saying I wasn't ready to share that yet. I thought I was brilliant. Everett smacked my head when we got in the door, and I growled at him. The git messed with the hair. You never messed with the hair. Took me forever to make it look like I didn't give a fuck about it. Luckily, Shelby smoothed it back in place before she smacked him for me. I liked that.

"You okay?" she asked anxiously, her bewitching eyes scanning my face.

I blinked again.

Bewitching eyes?

What the hell was wrong with me?

I wondered if I had accidentally doubled up on my Xanax. My head was certainly not reacting properly. Especially toward Shelby.

But the red carpet had been easy. With Shelby tucked into my side, I had been calm and not once had I felt the usual panic.

It had to be Shelby.

Or the Xanax.

I looked down at her.

No. It was her. It was definitely her. I beamed at her and brushed a kiss on her forehead, ignoring the flashes I could see from outside.

"Thanks to you, yes. I'm good."

She beamed at me, those lovely eyes glinting with relief.

Crap.

There went a few more icebergs.

"Is this almost over?" I mumbled to Everett. It had been a long night. We'd done dinner, the speeches, the auction, and all the bloody press and fan stuff I had been told to do. And true to her promise, Shelby was beside me the whole time, a constant balm for my frazzled nerves. She made it almost fun. Her droll comments as we walked around the room kept me distracted, and I was grateful Carly had canceled. She was nowhere near as entertaining as Shelby. Or as lovely.

He chuckled dryly. "This wouldn't have happened if you hadn't been so, ah, difficult the last few weeks, Liam. The studio..." His voice trailed off.

"The studio can kiss my arse," I muttered.

"Oscar," Shelby admonished.

I resisted the urge to roll my eyes at her. Instead, I deflected. "Did I tell you how beautiful you are tonight?"

Now, she rolled her eyes at me. "Nice one. But the diversion didn't work. Behave."

I laughed. She'd made me happy all night with her smiles and teasing. Not an iceberg in sight.

"Liam."

I looked up and grinned, the first genuine one of the night for someone other than Shelby. I stood and extended my hand. "Douglas! You're back!"

He smiled in return, shaking my hand. "Finally. What a shoot."

"You've been gone for almost five months." I indicated the empty chair beside Shelby. "Join us."

He sat, introducing himself after he greeted Everett.

I laughed, slightly embarrassed. "Sorry, Shelby. I've told you about him, but you haven't met Douglas. You hadn't been with me long when he left on an extended shoot. This is my cousin, Douglas Wright. He's a producer. We grew up together in England."

Douglas chuckled. "And he does mean that literally. After my parents died, I lived with Liam and his family. I was twelve, and this little bugger was five and refused to leave me alone." He grinned. "But we were good mates and got on really well. As he grew up, we became friends. I actually missed him when I came here to make my fortune, and I have to admit I was glad when he came over as well. He's like a brother." He smirked. "A younger, not so good-looking brother."

I grinned at his explanation. Shelby had heard many stories of our younger years back in England. He had been a great role model, and as he stated, eventually a real friend.

"Hello, Douglas."

He shook her hand. "Hello—it's a pleasure." He winked at me teasingly. "Your prettiest girl yet, Liam."

Shelby rolled her eyes. "I'm not one of his girls. I'm his housekeeper."

Douglas's eyes widened.

"Shelby is my friend, and Everett's sister. She did me a huge favor and attended with me this evening." I was quick to step in and explain. I didn't want Shelby to be thought of as my housekeeper. Of all the things she was to me, that was the least important.

"So, she's not your housekeeper?" he asked confused.

"She is, but she's my friend first," I insisted.

"Sister second," Everett piped in.

"And housekeeper third. Got it." Douglas nodded, reclining in his chair and winking at Shelby. "A triple threat."

Shelby dipped her head, her cheeks coloring slightly. I slipped my hand into hers. It felt better there.

Douglas picked up his drink. "Now tell me what you've been up to while I was slaving away in Europe."

———

Everett took pity on me and had the car pull around back, allowing Shelby and me to slip into it with little fuss. The front of the building was still mobbed, and I didn't want to face that again. I was calm, but I didn't want to push it. He and Mark took the other car, so it was only Shelby and me in the back seat.

I let my head fall back onto the headrest in relief. Peace. I lifted Shelby's hand and kissed it gratefully. "Ta, Beaker."

She fiddled with the cuff on her wrist, then held it out to me. "You need this back."

I took it, slipping it into my pocket. She had been tense about it all night, her eyes drifting to her wrist, making sure it was there all evening. "Relax. I told you it's insured. And I knew it was safe."

"It's safer now," she insisted. "It's your responsibility."

"I think it was fine on your wrist," I responded, letting my eyes drift shut.

She sighed. "I see why you hate these things, but it was worth it."

I cracked my eye open. "Yeah?" I grinned. "You liked seeing me all dressed up and hot-looking? Working the room and oozing British charm?"

She snorted. "No."

I sat up straight. "Bloody hell, Shelby. You don't think I'm hot?"

She patted my leg. "Like an inferno, Liam."

I sniffed. "Better." I rested my head back into the cool leather. "Did you have a good time?"

"I enjoyed spending the evening with you, but otherwise, not really."

"Why then was it worth it?"

She sighed and relaxed into the seat beside me. "I got the draft problem solved. Worth the sore feet and listening to the inane screams."

Then she giggled. An unusual, endearing sound she rarely made. "Seriously, Oscar. All those women need to get a life. You're not all that and a bag of chips you know. If they only knew the suave outside was covering up a git, things would change."

I tried not to laugh. But it was a lost cause. I started to guffaw. Loudly.

I wasn't all that and a bag of chips.

To Shelby, I was simply Liam. A slightly goofy, apparently leaning-toward-pudgy, strange-sounding Brit who had an abiding affection for baked goods and turkey sandwiches. And her.

She knew me. The real me.

And she still loved me.

I was good with that.

"Thanks for the reality check, Shelby."

She groaned as she unstrapped her shiny sandals. "Anytime, Oscar. God, my feet hurt."

Grinning, I lifted her feet into my lap, clucking at the pinched look to her toes. She loved it when I rubbed her feet while we were watching movies, and from the look of them right now, they needed my talented fingers. "You should have told Lily no to the shoes." I shook my head as I started rubbing the sore-looking flesh.

She sighed contently. "These were the compromise. You should have seen the death traps she wanted me to wear."

"Tell her lower heels next time."

"Next time?"

I nodded hopefully. "You were brilliant tonight. I haven't been that calm at an event—ever. I was hoping you'd be willing to accompany me again."

"Add me to your roster, you mean?"

I huffed out a long breath. "My number one spot, Shelby. You made tonight so much easier for me. You have no idea what a difference having you with me made."

She bit her lip. "What about the press? The questions? I'm your housekeeper, Liam."

"You're way more than that. We're friends. We'll talk to Ev and figure it out. I don't care about that stuff. I just want you beside me."

"Do I get a foot rub after the hell is over?"

"Yes."

"I'll think about it."

I smirked as I worked on her feet.

"I'll think about it" was Shelby's code for yes.

She couldn't say no to me any more than I could say it to her.

And I was good with that.

7

LIAM

I stumbled down the stairs the next morning, yawning, and glanced at the clock in the hall. Not morning, really. It was almost noon. Shelby had let me sleep late.

I grimaced as I heard the sound of voices and merriment coming from the kitchen. That wasn't Everett's deep tone I could hear, but it was familiar. I entered the kitchen, surprised to find Douglas sitting at the table, talking to Shelby, who was busy at the counter. She looked up and gave me a sweet smile.

I smiled back, taking her in. Gone were the glamorous gown and makeup. She was back in her yoga pants, had on one of my too-large shirts, and her hair swept up into a ponytail again.

Yet, somehow, she'd never looked as lovely to me as she did right at that moment.

"Hey, Oscar."

I shuffled over, grabbing the cup of coffee she was holding out for me, and kissed her cheek.

"Hey, Shelby." I took a deep sip and turned toward to the table. "Douglas."

"Sleep well, Liam?" he asked, amused, looking at his watch. "Rather a late start to the day."

I scowled at him. "I was up earlier for a long run. I was reading scripts in my room," I informed him haughtily. "I didn't know you were here to see me, or I would have come down sooner."

Beside me, Shelby chuckled under her breath. As she handed me a plate with a bagel on it, she leaned up on her toes, and I tilted my head to the side to better hear what she had to say. I liked her warm breath floating over my neck as she spoke.

"Being chased by a giant peanut butter cookie in your dream is *not* going for a long run. I did come to get you, but you were snoring so loudly, I let you sleep."

I glared at her. I never should have told her about that dream. She'd held it over my head ever since and never let me eat a dozen peanut butter chocolate chip cookies before retiring for the night again.

And even more important, I didn't snore.

"Shut it, woman."

She bit her lip to stop from grinning, and I couldn't help myself. I kissed her cheek again. "You'll pay for that later." I dropped my voice further, putting my lips to her ear and flexing my fingers against her ribs where I knew she was ticklish. "My wee lass."

She giggled. She loved the fact that I sometimes imitated my Scottish mum, and I loved the fact that when I did, it made her smile. Occasionally, she teased me about my "muddled" accent—a mixed-up jumble of Scottish and English rolled into my own unique sound I liked to use to make her laugh. And when she did, I would have to tickle her as I prattled on, laying the sound on even thicker, making her laugh even harder. It was one of our things we did. Like foot rubs and movie nights.

I turned back to Douglas, noticing the strange look he was giving us. I ignored it and sat, taking a huge bite of my bagel. Luckily, Shelby had loaded it with cream cheese so I could overlook the fact that it was one of the types filled with fiber and seeds. I had no idea why she thought I needed to eat bird food. It was almost as bad as the salads she forced on me, but at least there was cream cheese.

"What's up?" I asked, licking the cheese off my fingers. "I didn't know you were coming over." Shelby shoved a napkin into my hand, muttering something about being raised in a barn. I grinned at her.

"Ta, Beaker."

She patted my shoulder. "I have things to do, so I'll leave the two of you alone."

Douglas stood. "Thanks for the coffee, Shelby. I'll see you soon."

Shelby blushed and looked at me, uncertainty reflected in her glance. I realized she appeared uncomfortable, and I sat straighter. Why was she uncomfortable? I looked at Douglas. Had he done or said something to her? I wouldn't stand for that sort of crap. This was her home, too, and she shouldn't be subjected to bullshit here. Well, except from me.

I turned to him as she left. "What were you talking to Shelby about that made her nervous?"

He frowned at me as he sat back down. "I wasn't aware she was nervous."

"She was," I insisted. "She had that 'V' between her eyes. She only gets that when she's nervous."

He took a sip from his coffee. "You know her awfully well for a housekeeper."

"She's not just my housekeeper. She's way more than that."

"How much more?"

"She's my friend. *My best friend.*"

"That's all?"

"All? Isn't that enough?"

"So, if she is your *friend*, then it won't bother you at all that I came here today to ask her out."

"Out? Ask her out where?"

He sighed. "On a date, Liam."

"With whom?"

"Me, you git!"

I gaped at him. "I don't bloody think so."

"Why?"

"Shelby doesn't *date*."

He snorted. "She said yes."

What?

I spat out the first words that came to my mind. "She's married."

"Separated. She told me the basics of her situation," he assured me.

The fact that her jerk of a husband had left her penniless and floundering? That the company Everett had hired still hadn't located him, and now she was filing for desertion?

She told him all that?

Well, bloody hell. I had no response to that. I shoved some of the bird-food bagel into my mouth and chewed. I wasn't sure how I felt about this. I had never thought about Shelby dating someone. Especially someone I knew and was related to. I stared at Douglas as he nonchalantly sipped his coffee, gazing at me calmly.

"When?"

"Saturday night."

I shook my head. "Saturday night is movie night for Shelby and me. We order in Chinese—it's her turn to pick the movies—she won't miss that."

His eyebrows rose. "Again, she said yes, Liam. I'm sure you'll survive a movie night without your, ah, *friend.*"

"She is my friend," I growled. "My best friend."

He snorted in derision. "You might need to figure that out, Liam. In the meantime, I am taking your *friend* to dinner. Tomorrow night. I'm not asking your permission, but I have enough respect for you to tell you my plans."

"She's not like the women you usually date, Douglas. She's special," I informed him. "Don't hurt her. Family or not, you'll answer to me."

He shrugged. "I already figured that out. I have no plans to hurt her, Liam. It's just dinner."

I tore off another hunk of bagel, fighting the strange feeling filling my chest and, for some reason, wishing it were him I was tearing a hunk out of instead.

Bugger.

I didn't like this one damn bit.

I just didn't know why.

After Douglas left, I found Shelby upstairs in my room, making my bed. Walking over, I grabbed a corner of the sheet and awkwardly tried to help. I watched her efficiently tuck and straighten and I copied her, but my side looked like I had only now rolled out of it instead of the smooth, inviting surface of hers. She smirked and nudged me out of the way as she worked her magic on the half I had been working on. "Seriously, Liam. It's not rocket science. Even someone who only *attended* a concert at Oxford should be able to do this task."

"I think that's enough of your cheek today."

She looked over her shoulder. "What are you gonna do about it?"

I grinned. "This."

Lunging forward, I grabbed her around the waist, fake-tackling her onto the bed. I tickled her sides, avoiding her elbows and flailing arms as she twisted and shrieked for me to stop. Finally, I hovered over her. "Do you take that back, woman?"

"Yes!" She giggled as my fingers kept up their torture.

"Who is the best British actor you know?"

"You!"

"The best-looking one?"

"You!"

"The funniest? Most charming?"

"Um, you!"

"The smartest?"

Her lips twitched. "Y-you?" She got out through another titter.

I relented briefly, but I wasn't done. Her shirt had come loose, and I slipped my hand inside, ghosting her skin teasingly.

God, it was silky.

"Are you telling me or asking me, Shelby? Because I'm pretty sure I might not be able to stop my fingers in one more second." I gently caressed her skin while I grinned at her. "They do love tickling you."

Another one of her funny squeals came from her throat before she capitulated.

"You are!"

"I am...?" I trailed off, my fingers touching and teasing her. "I am what?"

"The smartest Brit I know!" she shouted. "Stop! Uncle!"

"Clever girl." I chuckled, and without a thought, lowered my head and touched my lips to hers.

Shelby gasped, her lips parting and her sweet breath filling my mouth. We were so close that her light scent surrounded me, filling my head, overtaking everything. I shut my eyes and pressed harder, feeling her softness underneath my hard body. I was overcome by the sudden desire to meld myself completely into her. My mouth, my tongue, my entire body wanted to be fused into her. Buried inside her.

My eyes flew open.

What the hell was I doing?

I lurched backward, almost stumbling in my haste to pull myself away. I ran my hand through my hair, grimacing over what I had almost done. Trying to cover my embarrassment, I shook my head and pulled Shelby off my bed. "Now look what you did. My side was perfect, and you messed it all up." I halfheartedly tugged on the sheets, trying to restore some of our usual easiness with each other.

Shelby stepped in front of me, pushing me out of the way. "I'll do that." Her voice was low and strained.

I backed away, the awkwardness filling the room. Desperate for something to say, I blurted out the first thing that came to mind. "So, blowing off movie night with me for a hot date with Douglas tomorrow?"

She froze briefly, then continued to smooth and tuck. "He asked me to dinner. I didn't think you'd mind."

"Why would I mind? You don't need my permission."

She straightened and turned, her eyes suddenly flashing. "I wasn't asking your permission, Liam."

Bollocks. *Why was everyone saying that today?*

"He's older than you are, you know."

"He is only thirty-five. Two years. He's hardly cradle snatching." Bending over, Shelby grabbed the discarded sheets off the floor. "You always said he treated you as an equal growing up despite your age difference."

He had, and I knew I was being an arse—yet I couldn't seem to help myself.

"You're not the type he usually goes out with."

From the glare she cast me, I knew that might not have been the best thing to say, but I was suddenly annoyed over the whole going-on-a-date-with-Douglas thing.

"And what is his type?"

I shrugged. "Young, sexy, good-looking actresses."

Shelby's eyes widened with shock and hurt, and I knew I had just stepped over the line. Before I could say anything, she smiled grimly and moved past me. "Well, maybe he is merely looking for a new housekeeper, Liam. We all know the Wrights handle job interviews differently from most."

"Shelby," I growled. I hadn't meant it that way.

"It's fine, Liam. Don't worry about it. I get it—believe me."

I huffed and threw my arms up in frustration. "It's...It's just you won't be here for dinner. What am I gonna do?"

She rolled her eyes. "I'll have dinner ready for you. I'll make sure my job is completely done for the day before I leave. Excuse me." She slipped past me and shut the door behind her. I could hear her hurrying down the hall. I sat on the edge of my bed, pulling at my hair in frustration. I had meant I would miss her, not that I wanted her to cook for me.

Fuck. How had that gone so wrong, so quickly?

One minute, we were us, and the next minute, I was being rude and snarky. I had totally cocked that up.

All because she was going out for supper with someone and leaving me alone.

She didn't deserve that from me. And Douglas didn't deserve what I said about him either. He didn't date a lot, and he certainly didn't go after young starlets the way I made it sound to Shelby. In fact, the women he dated, those whom I had met, always seemed pleasant. He was a good guy, and I knew he would treat Shelby well.

Somehow, though, I didn't want him dating Shelby.

I sighed. I would have to give her some time to cool down and then apologize.

She'd forgive me.

She always did. She knew I was a stupid git sometimes.

I glanced at the closed door, thinking about the look of hurt that had been on her face.

Hating the fact that I had put it there.

I definitely needed to apologize.

Only, I wasn't sure where to begin.

I walked into the kitchen apprehensively. I wasn't sure it was the best idea to approach Shelby in a room where she had access to knives, but I'd been hiding in the den long enough, and she had been in the room for a long time, so I gave up waiting.

I could dodge and weave fast if she moved toward the knife rack.

I was like a ninja.

She was sitting at her kitchen desk, tapping away on her laptop. Music was playing quietly through her speakers—country music— which meant she was feeling off-kilter. She always listened to country music when she was feeling reflective. There was a cup of coffee beside her, the steam drifting from the top of the mug.

Bollocks. She could pitch that at me as well.

Except she wouldn't. I knew she loved my face, and she wouldn't risk burning it.

Right?

I swallowed nervously and cleared my throat. She glanced at me, her eyes cool as she stared over the rim of her hot-as-hell librarian glasses.

Wait.

Hot-as-hell?

When did I decide that?

When did she get those glasses?

Without a word, I thrust the bouquet of flowers at her I had hidden behind my back. I'd slipped out while she was busy and taken care of two errands. Both were for her, and I managed to accomplish them without drawing any attention to myself.

"I'm an arse, Beaker. You know this."

She took the flowers silently, bending to smell their fragrance.

Somehow, I knew they wouldn't smell as good as she had when she'd been pressed against me earlier.

Internally, I kicked myself.

Why the bloody, bleeding hell was I thinking like that?

I cleared my throat again. "I didn't mean to upset you, Shelby. Honest."

Her voice was quiet, but at least she spoke. "I know."

"Douglas is a great guy. I didn't mean to imply otherwise. I'm sorry I said that." I paused, waiting for her to look at me before I continued. "You'll have a great time. He's the lucky one that you agreed to go out with him. What I said about the women he dates—" I drew in a deep breath "—you outshine them all, Shelby. Without even trying."

She flashed me an incredulous look.

"You are beyond beautiful, Shelby. Douglas is a lucky man," I stated firmly.

Her eyes flew to mine, and she glowered.

I yanked on my hair.

Now what had I said?

Why was she angry?

Before I could say anything else stupid, I pulled out the other gift for her.

For a second, she looked puzzled as she stared at the empty frame. Then she beamed in understanding.

"You did? You finally cashed the damn check?"

I exhaled a heavy breath. "All done and safe in the bank."

Inside my head, I added, *for now*. But I kept my face neutral.

I was good at that. It was the actor in me.

Standing, she flung her arms around me and kissed my cheek warmly. "Thank you."

She moved away and began looking for a vase.

My cheek felt nice where she had kissed it.

She looked over her shoulder. "Wanna move movie night to this evening? I'll even let you choose since I was the one to change things."

I sighed in relief. "Least you could bloody do, woman. After all, you're leaving me alone on a Saturday night to go out on the town with my more charming cousin. There better be jujubes. I think you need to make popcorn, too."

"With butter, Oscar?"

I shook my head mockingly at her. "As if it can be eaten any other way?"

She grinned at me in agreement, her eyes twinkling.

"As if."

And we were okay.

We were Beaker and Oscar again.

But I really hoped she would keep wearing those glasses.

I turned off the TV and glanced over at Shelby, who was lying propped up with cushions. Her feet, as usual, were in my lap, and I had been rubbing them while we watched the movie.

"Maybe we'll watch the second one tomorrow?" I grinned at her as she rolled her eyes.

"You cheated."

"Did not."

"I said you could pick *a* movie, Liam."

Leaning over, I picked up the box. "I chose the *Lord of the Rings* saga, Shelby. One box—one choice. We have to watch them all." I shrugged. "It's like an unwritten rule—we can't only watch one."

"I'm picking out a saga then, next time."

"Sure."

"My choice." She pointed out. "Maybe *Outlander*. That Jamie Fraser does something for me."

I groaned at her dig even as I bit back a grin. The girl had a thing for men in kilts. The truth was that I didn't care. As long as she was beside me, I'd watch some redheaded Scotsman prance around acting tough. I could run circles around him any day. Besides, I could always pretend to be absorbed and sleep while she watched it. She'd never know.

"You can't nap either. You snore. I'd know, and I'll start it over from the beginning."

Double bugger.

"I don't snore," I growled at her.

She snorted. "Um, yeah, you do."

I rolled my head to the side and grimaced at her. "Fine. Your choice next. I call dibs on the Indiana Jones one next week."

Shelby quirked her eyebrows suggestively at me. "I'm good with that—he's hot."

I chuckled at her.

Then she frowned. "But next Saturday is the hospital event, Liam."

Crap, I had forgotten. "Right." I squeezed her leg, feeling nervous as I asked, "Will you go with me, Shelby?"

She regarded me quietly for a moment. "If you really want me to."

I sighed in relief. "I do. You made it so much better."

"Okay."

"Great. I'll talk to Lily. Make sure she has a dress for you as well."

"I—"

I held up my hand. "No arguments. That's what Lily does. Tuxes, suits, and dresses. She's a walking closet."

Shelby giggled, and I smiled at the sound. I loved hearing her giggle.

"You want me to do that?"

"No, I will." I wanted to talk to Lily. I wanted to make sure she dressed Shelby in red again.

"Ask her for small heels this time."

I picked up one of her feet, digging my thumb into the arch and grinning when she moaned in appreciation. "I'll ask. And I'll rub them if she refuses. Deal?"

She sighed. "You do give good foot rubs. Deal."

"Brilliant. You tired?"

Shelby shook her head.

"Watch the second one tonight?" I winked at her. "One movie closer to your Scotsman."

"Sure."

"Can I have more popcorn?"

"Yes."

"Ta, Beaker."

8

LIAM

It was well after three o'clock in the morning by the time the second movie was over. Shelby was half asleep as she stumbled up the steps ahead of me, and finally, fearing she would fall over her own feet on the stairs and take me out with her, I scooped her into my arms and broke my own rule.

I entered her room.

Luckily, it was quick work to pull back the covers and tuck her in to bed. I bent over to click off the light, pausing as I studied her face. Her hair was dark against the white of her sheets, her skin pale and glowing in the dim light. Unbidden, I traced her smooth skin with my finger, grazing over the eyelashes that rested against the swell of her cheek. They fluttered and opened, her ocean-colored eyes gazing at me sleepily. She then smiled saucily as she whispered, "Finally got me into bed, Liam?"

I nuzzled her forehead. "Finally. I knew you couldn't resist me forever."

She yawned and curled into a ball like a small kitten. "Good job. Night, Oscar."

I passed my hand gently over her head. "Night, Beaker."

I left quickly, wondering why it was bothering me so much to do so.

I must be overtired.

My head would be clearer in the morning.

It was past noon when I stumbled out of bed and into the shower. Regardless of being up late, I knew Shelby would have risen far earlier and already been productive. I loved sleeping in, and when I was working, it wasn't a luxury I had—my calls were often early ones, so when I was home, I indulged a lot—and Shelby let me.

I got dressed, feeling decidedly off. My stomach ached and I felt tense, but I was unsure why. I felt a strange sense of foreboding I couldn't shake.

I was probably hungry.

I'd find Shelby, she'd make me something to eat, and I'd feel better. I had no idea what time her date was, but I was sure she had enough time to do that for me.

Funny, simply thinking about her date made my stomachache intensify.

Maybe I was coming down with something.

I paused at the entrance to the kitchen. Shelby was sitting at the table, staring absently into space. Behind her, playing quietly from her computer was Air Supply.

Shit. She only played Air Supply when she was feeling sad and melancholy.

Why was she sad? I racked my brain. *Had I done something again? Did Douglas cancel?*

She glanced up, and seeing me, she smiled, although her eyes remained sad. "Well, look who woke up. I thought maybe today was one of your write-offs."

I strolled in, shaking my head. "No, just a late start. What time did you get up?"

She shrugged, walking over to the coffeemaker. "About eight."

I took the coffee she offered, winking at her.

"Lazy wench."

Sipping the hot beverage, I sat while trying to find a way of asking her if she was okay. Or figure out a way of taking the sadness from her eyes.

"I heard from Lily. I texted her last night. She'll come over this week with some dresses for you to choose from for Saturday. She says it's a big night—she's pulling out all the stops."

If anything, her eyes got sadder. "Sounds like fun."

"I told her to keep the heels low. She said she couldn't make that promise."

Shelby shrugged and I took another sip of my coffee, stalling for time.

What was wrong? Didn't women like to try on dresses?

"You, um, still out for the night?"

"Yes."

Shouldn't she look happier? Was she nervous? I tried to think of what I felt like when I went out on a date.

Shit. First, I had to remember when the last date I'd gone on had been. A few months? More? I couldn't remember.

Maybe she was worried about being alone with Douglas. Or thinking about what she should wear. Women stressed over stuff like that.

A thought hit me, and without thinking it through, I spoke up. "Shelby?"

"Hmm?"

"Wanna go shopping?"

She looked at me, confused. "What?"

"I could take you."

"For what?"

"A dress, you know, for tonight. For your date."

She stared at me. When she spoke, her voice was nowhere near as enthusiastic as I thought it would be.

"You want to take me shopping. For a dress. To wear on my date."

I nodded. "You said you didn't have any dresses, so I'll buy one for you. Would that make you feel better?"

"Make me feel better?"

"You seem off. I thought a new dress would cheer you up. I'll buy it for you," I repeated.

"Why would you want to do that, Liam?"

Bollocks. I didn't like the tone she was using.

"I thought, ah, maybe you needed one?" I offered. "You know the other night, you said you didn't have any..." My voice trailed off as I took in her expression. Now she was looking pissed off. This wasn't going well, and I regretted my idea.

"I meant long gowns. They aren't something I keep on hand, being a housekeeper and all. I do, however, have a few outfits I am sure will be acceptable to wear in public with your cousin. I'll be sure not to embarrass him by wearing my everyday clothes."

I tried to make her smile. "Yeah, my shirts might not make the best date attire."

Her voice was deceptively low. "Is that what you're worried about, Liam? That I'll leave the house looking bad and embarrass you or your cousin? Maybe you think I'm not suitable to go out on date with Douglas?"

What?

I started to shake my head when Shelby stood quickly, her chair making a loud noise on the floor. She crossed her arms over her chest, and I could see she was beyond pissed. I had somehow insulted her again and now she was angry.

I liked Shelby pissed off and spitting at me like an angry kitten. She was adorable.

I hated angry Shelby; it was a side of her I rarely saw. She was downright scary. And it made my stomach ache more.

I stood. "I'm sorry. I didn't mean to upset you. I just thought you'd like a new dress. I thought I'd buy it for you. Save you some cash."

Her face got even angrier.

I should not have said that.

Jesus, what was wrong with me?

Her voice was measured. "*If* I wanted a new dress, Liam, I could buy it for myself. I don't need you to buy it for me. I certainly don't need you offering to dress me for my *date*. I don't need anyone to buy me anything. I can look after myself."

I held up my hands. "I know you can. Look, I was an arse, again. I didn't mean it."

"You said it. I think you meant it."

I shook my head. "I wasn't thinking. You looked sad, and I wanted to cheer you up."

"By buying me a dress to wear for someone *else*."

"Ah, yes," I said, although I had a feeling I shouldn't be agreeing to that statement.

She regarded me coolly.

"I'm taking the rest of the day off. I have things to do. Alone."

So, no dress shopping, then. At least not with me.

"Sure."

She swept by me without another word.

I sat, staring at the table, Air Supply lamenting some sad song in the background. I resisted the urge to pitch my mug at the computer to shut it off.

That would only make Shelby angrier.

Bloody hell. That went well. Maybe offering to buy a woman a dress to wear—to go on a date with another man—was against the rules.

Dammit. I needed to get my hands on that rule book and save myself a lot of grief.

Now the ache in my stomach was a huge, tight knot, and the only person who could make it feel better was so angry I couldn't ask her to help me.

Somehow when I woke up, I'd known this day was going to be crap.

I was right.

I decided the best, most mature course of action was avoidance.

At all costs. Give Shelby a chance to cool down.

I heard her moving around upstairs, so I ran to my room, grabbed my gym bag, and left the house.

I wasn't sure my trainer got over the shock I'd voluntarily appeared for one of his torture sessions. He was especially cruel and relentless today, reminding me why I avoided going to the gym. By the end of his session, I was a shaking, sweat-soaked mess. I hit the shower, groaning as the hot water poured off my shoulders and down my aching back and legs.

I should have snuck off to a movie.

I felt better when I left the gym, and even better once I stuffed an In-N-Out burger down my throat, hiding my face under a baseball hat and sunglasses as I went to the drive-through. I was good and didn't get any fries, but I couldn't resist the milk shake. Then I stalled for more time and stopped by my favorite music shop. It was small and off the beaten track, so I knew I was safe. They were a throwback and still stocked actual music and movies, and I killed some time browsing through CDs and DVDs for a while. I bought a bunch of new selections, some of which I knew Shelby would enjoy. We liked the classics and ones you couldn't find on Netflix, so I liked to keep them on hand. We'd watch them when she'd forgiven me.

Because she would forgive me. She had to.

Another thought occurred to me, which put a damper on my burgeoning hopes.

What if she and Douglas hit it off so well that she spends all her free time with him instead of me? I mean, how could he resist her?

"Hey, Liam, you okay, man?"

I looked up at the voice interrupting my thoughts. Ron was staring at me, concerned, and I realized I was standing there, rubbing my chest at the strange ache that had formed in it. I shook my head to clear it. "Yeah, I'm good."

I took my purchases to the counter and paid for them, then bravely headed for home.

After dropping my gym bag in the laundry room, I walked into the kitchen, the room strangely quiet without Shelby's music and presence filling it. I went to the den and unloaded the movies and music, then sat at my desk. I could hear Shelby upstairs, the occasional sound letting me know she was still home. I glanced at my watch, seeing it was almost six, which I thought was the time she said she was leaving. I remained seated, unsure what to do.

Should I go find her and apologize?

Should I stay here and let her leave, so she didn't go out upset?

Would she let me apologize?

Should I know *why* I was apologizing?

I heard Shelby's footsteps on the stairs and glanced around, panicked. I didn't want her coming in and finding me mooning about. I grabbed the script I'd been looking at the day before and slouched down in my chair like I was absorbed in the words in front of me. A few minutes later, I heard her voice. "Liam."

I glanced up, hoping to appear casual. "Hey, Shelby."

"I'm off in a few minutes. Your dinner is in the kitchen." She hesitated, then smiled softly. "And, Liam?"

"Yeah?"

"It's usually easier to read the script when it isn't upside down."

I looked at the script in confusion. "Huh. I thought it was just badly written."

She chuckled, but the sound was sad. "Have a good night." Turning, she walked away.

I sat stock-still, staring after her retreating form for a moment.

She was angry with me, and still she made me dinner. She came and wished me a good evening. She even teased me. She wasn't ready to say it, but I was forgiven.

I couldn't let her go without saying something.

I shot out of my chair, calling her name. She stopped in the hall and turned to look at me as I raced toward her. My breath caught in my throat as I got a look at her. She was in a deep-purple-colored blouse and a black skirt that was all jagged and sexy, swirling around her ankles. Her hair was up, pieces of it hanging in curls over her shoulders, and she looked, well, amazing.

Bloody amazing.

I skidded to a stop in front of her.

"I'm sorry."

She held up her hand. "It's fine, Liam. I'm sorry as well. I overreacted. I know you were just trying to be nice."

"You look amazing. Beautiful. Douglas is a lucky man."

She blushed, and it took all I had not to lift my hand and run the tips of my fingers over her cheek to feel the heat beneath her skin. I swallowed hard. "Thanks for dinner."

She nodded and turned away again.

Suddenly, I couldn't bear the thought of her walking away. "Nice shoes," I called out.

She winked over her shoulder. "Nice and flat. I don't think Douglas would be willing to rub my feet so soon in our relationship."

My heart stuttered at those words. I didn't want him touching her feet. Or any other part of her.

"Wait. Is Douglas picking you up?"

She paused at the door. "No, I'm meeting him."

I stepped forward, frowning. "Not much of a date. He should pick you up."

She wrapped a silky shawl around her shoulders. "It was what I wanted."

"I'm here if you need me."

"I know. Goodnight, Liam."

It was hard to get the word out. "Goodnight."

I stared at the door long after she had left.

But she didn't come back.

73

An hour later and after downing a rather large glass of whiskey, I felt the stirrings of hunger. I had eaten a light lunch after all. A single burger and a shake. I slapped my forehead. I forgot to tell Shelby that —she'd be proud. Picking up my phone, I texted her.

Liam: Hey—I forgot to tell you something.

Shelby: ?

Liam: I went to In-N-Out. Only had one burger and a shake. Proud?

I waited patiently for her reply. No doubt I had blown her away with my restraint.

Shelby: I'll alert the media. Go away.

I chuckled. She was impressed. I was sure she was just being polite.

I made my way to the kitchen and opened the fridge door, pulling out the plate Shelby had left me. I grinned when I saw my favorite turkey sandwiches waiting for me. I took the plate and another whiskey into the den and sat at my desk, downing the whiskey first. I ate half a sandwich and paused. Something was missing. I looked at the plate, realizing there were no pickles. Shelby always gave me pickles with my sandwich. I loved pickles. I went back to the kitchen and opened all the cupboards, searching. No pickles.

Dammit.

I returned to the den and picked up the other half, chewing away thoughtfully, wondering where Shelby would keep the pickles.

Without thinking if it was a good idea, I shot off a quick text.

Liam: I think you forgot something.

Her reply was fast.

Shelby: I think you should forget my number for the next few hours.

My eyebrows shot up. That was rather rude. I only had a question. I glanced at my sandwich. I needed to find those pickles, and I had no idea which cupboard she kept them in. I had looked in all of them.

Oh well, only one way to find out. Since I wasn't allowed to text, I called.

She answered before the second ring, her voice concerned. "Liam?"

"Hey."

"What's wrong?"

"I can't find the pickles."

"What?"

"The pickles," I explained. "You always give me pickles with my sandwich."

"I don't understand."

She didn't understand? I knew I was well on my way to getting drunk, but how much had she had to drink?

"I want pickles, Shelby," I stated slowly. "You always give me pickles with my sandwiches."

There was a brief silence. "Liam, are you ill?"

I pulled the phone away from my ear and stared at it. She *must* be drunk.

What kind of question was that? Obviously if I were ill, I wouldn't be asking for pickles, would I?

I brought the phone back to my ear. "No."

"Is the house on fire?"

Bloody hell. If the house were on fire would I be calmly asking for pickles?

She *was* drunk. An hour into her date, Douglas had her bladdered. That wanker.

"No."

"Unless one of those two things occur, don't call me again." Her voice lowered to almost a hiss. "I'm on a date, for God's sake."

Then she hung up on me, leaving me blinking into the dead phone.

Huh. Another rule, it would seem. No calls about pickles.

Except now, I was worried; if she was drinking, she shouldn't be driving. I texted her again. It wasn't about pickles, so it had to be acceptable.

Liam: I'll pick you up if you're too drunk to drive.

Then I looked at my empty glass and realized I probably couldn't drive. I sent another message.

Liam: Or send a car for you.

Her reply was swift.

Shelby: I think you're the drunk one. I am turning my phone off now. DATE, Liam. I am NOT drunk—I am on a DATE!

Dammit, how did she know I was drunk?

I sulked a bit as I picked up my sandwich. I was just trying to help. And the sandwich wasn't the same without pickles. I grabbed my phone again and called Everett.

He answered, sounding impatient. "What, Liam?"

"Hey."

"What do you need?"

"Do you have any idea where Shelby would keep the pickles?"

"What? How the hell would I know that?"

"She's your sister."

"We don't often discuss pickles, Liam."

I could hear noise in the background, the clink of china and the sound of music. "Where are you?"

"I'm out."

"Out where?"

His voice lowered. "I'm on a date. Which you are interrupting."

Bloody hell. Was everyone out on a date tonight but me?

"Are you out with Shelby and Douglas? Are you doubling?"

"What? Shelby is out on a date? With Douglas?" His voice was shocked.

Bollocks. He didn't know. Shelby hadn't told him, and now I had ratted her out.

"Never mind," I mumbled. "I'll eat the sandwich without pickles. Have a good night."

"Don't hang up, Liam."

I did.

Then I turned off the phone.

Shelby was gonna be pissed with me. Again.

I ate my sandwiches, without pickles, and carried my plate back to the kitchen. I grabbed the bottle of whiskey to save myself the trip back. I had a feeling it was gonna be one of those nights.

For some reason, I walked around the house, pausing in the different rooms, looking around, not sure what I was searching for but unable to settle. I even ended up outside Shelby's bedroom door. I flicked on the light, looking around her room, but not entering. Its warm colors and light furniture suited her well. I knew she was comfortable there, and I wanted her to be. I wanted her to feel at home. I stood looking for a while, feeling closer to her somehow, before shutting off the light and turning away. Finally, I ended up back in the den and at the desk. I sat down heavily and stared at the wall, not understanding the strange feelings or the restless, uneasy twinges I kept having.

My gaze landed on the large framed picture across from my desk, and I smiled as I looked at it. I had drawn it when I was a kid, and my mum had kept it, bringing it with her the last time she came for a visit. That had been the first time she'd met Shelby, and, not surprisingly, had loved her. The two of them got on so well I was almost jealous. Mum had given me the picture, which I had scoffed at, wondering why she had brought it. But Shelby had pounced on it, declaring it the sweetest thing she'd ever seen. She'd had it framed and hung it in here, saying it was something I had to keep.

I remembered drawing it for Mum. I also remembered my dad's hand covering mine to help me write out the words I wanted to outline and color in. It was an expression she said all the time, her Scottish accent rolling the *r* out almost lyrically.

I glanced up at the picture again.

"Home is where the heart is."

She'd cried when I proudly gave it to her.

She'd cried again, years later, when she saw how Shelby had turned it into a lasting memento and hung it somewhere I would see it every day.

I had to admit, my throat had been thick watching Mum's reaction and thinking how amazing Shelby was to have done that for me.

I took another deep draw of whiskey, enjoying the burn in my throat as I frowned.

Shelby.

She did so many thoughtful things. She took care of me. She was my friend.

My best friend.

I looked around the comfortable room. She had made this house into a home for me. She made my life easier. Better. I couldn't imagine my world without her. Simply the thought of it made my chest hurt the way it did earlier in the music store.

She was special.

My eyes were drawn to the picture again.

Home...heart...

I sat up, suddenly knowing why the thought of her out on a date with Douglas was so upsetting. Why the thought of her dating anyone made me crazy.

I knew now why I hadn't been on a date since she had come into my life. Why I loved being with her all the time. There was a reason I couldn't imagine my life without her. Why everything I did revolved around her, and why her opinion and thoughts meant more than anyone else's. The reason I knew her moods by the music she played. Because I *knew* her—all of her. Her footsteps and the cadence of her voice. She was the reason I missed home so much while I was away. It wasn't this place I was longing for—it was *her*. They were one and the same: My heart—My home.

My Beaker.

My best friend.

It hit me like a ton of bricks.

I was in love with Shelby. Completely and totally in love with her.

I sat back, stunned, the empty glass leaving my fingers and hitting the rug with a dull thud.

Holy shit.

She was gonna kill me.

9

SHELBY

I glowered at my reflection in the mirror. Why was I so pale? Slipping on my purple blouse, I hesitated, unsure whether to put my hair up or leave it down. Deciding it would be better up, I swept it into a chignon, leaving some of the ends loose and swirling around my shoulders. I stood back, gazing again. Something was missing. Then it dawned on me.

I wasn't smiling.

I wasn't excited.

I was nervous and edgy.

And not the good kind of nerves either. I was going on a date with Douglas Wright—handsome, well-known Hollywood director and producer. Women everywhere would love to be in my shoes. Yet, all I felt was this strange sensation I was making a mistake going out with him. He had shocked me so much by asking, I had said yes before I even realized what I was agreeing to do.

Slipping my feet into a pair of simple flats, I grinned, knowing Lily would roll her eyes and hate them. But they were comfortable, and it wasn't like I was dressing for the camera. I doubted I would even be spotted with Douglas. Not like when I was out with Liam the other night.

Liam.

I sat on the edge of my bed, thinking about earlier. Ever since I had agreed to go out with Douglas, things had been off between us. He was acting strange, even for Liam, and I was reacting to him by being defensive. I had every right to go on a date, just like Liam. We were both adults and could date whomever we wanted to. Oddly enough, though, the entire time I had worked for him, he never had been on a real date. His evenings, unless it was business-related, were always spent here, at home, with me. I hadn't even realized that until this moment.

I sighed. Maybe this was a mistake. I wasn't ready to date anyone yet. After the disaster that was my marriage, I wasn't sure I'd ever be ready to date again.

Marrying Malcolm had been a mistake. Looking back, I knew I married him for all the wrong reasons. My friends were all getting married and settling down. Everett had moved to LA, and I was lonely. I met Malcolm and I thought he needed me. Only he didn't. I thought I loved him. I was wrong. What I thought was love was simply the need to no longer be alone, and the only real thing he needed from me was my steady source of income and access to all my finances.

Since my parents died, leaving us with nothing, I was careful with money, saving as much as possible. I worked hard, often two or three jobs at a time, and helped put Everett through college. He worked as well and went to school; I was insistent he get his degree. When I landed a good paying job as a PA, things got easier, but we always lived a simple life. When Everett saw an opportunity in LA, he asked me to move with him, but I liked my job and stayed where I was in Sacramento. We remained close and he visited often, even after I was married. He never liked Malcolm, and, in retrospect, I should have listened to him.

In the three years we were married, Malcolm drifted from job to job, months often slipping by before he found the next one. It was always someone else's fault he lost his job, never his. As time went by, everything changed. Nothing was good enough. Our apartment wasn't large enough; our car wasn't as stylish as he wanted. I wasn't as sexy or fun as he thought I should be. Once, at a marriage-rebuilding weekend we'd attended at my insistence, one exercise had been to describe your perfect, ideal partner. Listening to the other couples, I was amazed how often they described their spouse without even realizing it, and then watched as dawning realization hit them. I'd hoped the same would happen for us. But when Malcolm spoke up, he described his ideal as tall, blond, buxom, and a tiger in bed. I sat there beside him, dark-haired and petite, knowing he certainly didn't think I was a tiger in bed since he complained about that a lot, too. I was nowhere close to his ideal, and I was beyond embarrassed. When Roni, his blond assistant from his last job, disappeared at the same time he left me, I realized how stupid and blind I had been.

We argued constantly over finances, especially the money I had saved in the bank. But having experienced the panicky feeling of nothing before, I refused to touch the money. When I lost my job, I was given a severance package, for which I was grateful, hoping it would tide us over until I found another job and I wouldn't have to touch the money I had saved.

A short time later, Malcolm disappeared with Roni, the contents of our bank account, and thanks to his hacking skills, all the savings money I had in my name as well, leaving me nothing. I also found, to my ultimate horror, he had secretly racked up thousands of dollars of debt, had neglected to pay the rent on the apartment, and I was about to lose my home on top of everything else.

In desperation, I put my pride aside and phoned Everett. He stepped in, paid off the debts looming over my head, and hired a lawyer to make sure I was protected against any further debts or problems. He also launched an investigation to find Malcolm, which to this point had turned up nothing; it was as if he had disappeared. We had begun the proceedings to dissolve the marriage in his absence, but as with everything in the legal world, it was taking time. I looked forward to the day it was behind me, knowing it couldn't happen fast enough for my liking.

The most important thing Everett had done was to bring me to LA—and to Liam.

Liam.

I felt terrible about getting angry with him earlier. He was trying to be nice; I knew he was. He didn't understand why I was feeling so sad.

I didn't know how to tell him when I didn't understand it either.

But lately, how I felt about Liam had changed.

I'd adored him from the moment I met him. Everett had talked about him so often, I felt I already knew him, even though we had never met. And then when I did meet him, the vision I had in my head didn't do him justice—in looks or personality. Liam's *interview* —for lack of a better word—had been the most bizarre experience of my life. But there was something about him, warm, sweet, and so open and honest that drew me to him. I liked being needed, and Liam needed me. Malcolm never needed me and hated it when I would "fuss" over him. He said I threatened his masculinity, which always confused me. Everett had loved, and still did love it, when I fussed over him. He said it made him feel important.

And Liam...Liam reveled in it. He soaked it up like a sponge. It didn't matter if it was his favorite sandwich, a new shirt I bought him, or how much he liked to lounge on the sofa while I stroked his head and he told me about his day; Liam needed me. He was appreciative of everything I did. In his own way, he looked after me as well and was protective of me. He was a good friend.

Except...yesterday, when he was tickling me and had kissed me. It made me feel things I shouldn't feel for a friend. I wanted him to kiss me again. Harder. Longer. Deeper.

Today when he offered to buy me a dress to wear on my date, I wanted to yell at him and tell him I wanted him to buy a dress I could wear for him. I wanted him to look at me and like what he saw. I wanted to sit across the table from him and spend the evening *with him.*

But I couldn't.

I was his housekeeper. His friend. He trusted me. I couldn't ruin that with some romanticized version of our relationship.

I wasn't girlfriend material.

I was still married, but unwanted and discarded since I had outlived my usefulness. I was also older than Liam. Five years might not seem like much to some people, but in the world he lived in, it was huge. Everything in the industry he worked in was based on looks and profile. A career could be broken with bad choices. He was a Hollywood leading man who could have his pick of women. Young, beautiful women more suited to him than I was or ever could be. I was his employee. Everett's sister.

All of those were lines he would never cross, even if he were interested.

Which he wasn't.

I straightened my shoulders. I had no idea what was wrong with me, but I needed to stop these silly thoughts.

Liam was my friend.

I had a date to go on with his cousin.

I was going to enjoy myself.

Even if it killed me.

LIAM

The more I drank, the clearer it all became.

I loved Shelby.

I loved her for the ways she looked after me, how she made everything, even the smallest of details, so much better. Her caring nature was prevalent, and I basked in it. She entered my life with no fanfare, improved every aspect, and without realizing it, also firmly entrenched herself in my heart.

I loved how she never let me forget who I *really* was. Not the mythical image that had been created about me. To her, I was Liam, friend to Everett, son of Simon and Elizabeth. Someone Shelby liked simply as a person. Someone I wanted to be—for her.

Just Liam.

Her snarky way of putting me in my place and keeping me grounded was exactly what I needed in my life. What I wanted. Her teasing was perfect for me, and I loved how she responded to mine. I loved hearing her laughter in the home I now realized I thought of as ours, not mine.

She was what I needed—and wanted. Always.

I wanted her beside me on the sofa at night, her feet in my lap.

I wanted her hands stroking my head at the end of a long day, while I complained about what happened on set, as her fingers worked their soothing magic to relax me.

I wanted her across the table, telling me to stop eating so many cookies as she shoved some god-awful bird food at me, which I would eat because she made it for me.

I flashed to the memory of tucking her in last night, the image filling my head.

I wanted her in my bed, her hair spread out on my pillow as I loved her. I wanted to fall asleep beside her and wake with her the next day. I wanted her on my arm every time I had to make an appearance, knowing her presence would keep me calm.

I was so fucked.

I peered at the whiskey bottle, trying to remember how full it had been when I started. As Shelby liked to remind me, unless it was beer, I wasn't much of a drinker. Two or three, and I was usually quite inebriated; it just hit me. I frowned as I looked at the mostly empty bottle. I was sure I'd had more than three. Or four.

I looked around. I wasn't even sure where my glass was anymore. I had been drinking right from the bottle, which wasn't a good thing.

I sighed. I couldn't feel my legs. That was definitely not a good sign.

I sat back in my chair, folding my arms across the bottle resting on my chest.

I knew what I wanted.

Now I needed to figure out how to make Shelby want the same things.

How to make her want me.

My eyes slowly drifted shut, the darkness welcome and quiet.

Maybe a ten-minute nap. That would clear my head.

Then I could figure it all out. When she got home, I'd know what to do and how to handle the whole situation.

I sighed, the sound sad in the room.

"Shelby."

SHELBY

I tried not to grin at the phone screen after reading Liam's text about his lunch. I could feel Liam's boasting, and I knew he was proud of himself for his restraint over his idea of a limited lunch. So proud he couldn't wait to tell me once he remembered. Quickly, I typed a reply and put down my phone.

"Sorry." I smiled at Douglas, who was watching me closely. "Liam wanted to remind me of something he needed doing tomorrow."

"Do you ever get time off?" he asked dryly.

The need to defend Liam was strong and came fast. "I have as much time off as I want. Liam is a generous employer." I didn't tell him I had never taken a "day off" the entire time I worked for Liam. Mostly because it didn't feel like work—it felt like I was home. "I didn't work at all this afternoon. I was busy getting ready for tonight."

He eyed me with appreciation. "Worth the effort. You're beautiful, Shelby."

"Um, thank you." Unsure of what to do next, I grabbed my menu. "Everything looks good," I mused, keeping my eyes on the menu. Liam had called me "lovely" earlier, and it had made me blush. Although I appreciated Douglas telling me how nice I looked, it didn't seem to matter as much as what Liam thought. Strangely enough, when Douglas greeted me with a kiss on my cheek, I had the same feeling as when Everett kissed me, an abiding fondness. Nothing else.

Lately, every time Liam kissed my cheek or grazed my forehead with his lips, I felt like I was being scorched with a hot branding iron. One with the initials LW stamped on it.

I shook my head, closed my eyes for a moment, and sighed. I needed to stop this train of thought. I was being ridiculous.

———

An hour later, I shoved my phone into my purse. "I'm sorry, Douglas. I thought it was an emergency."

"Did he really call you to ask where the pickles were?"

I nodded, my eyes unconsciously going back to my purse.

Hadn't I left them on the shelf beside his supper?

I was sure I had. I didn't want to put them on the plate in case they made the sandwiches soggy. I knew how much he loved pickles with his sandwiches. Did he not look in the refrigerator?

"Shelby?"

My eyes snapped to Douglas's, embarrassment warming my face.

"Did you want to call him back and tell him where they are?"

"No."

My phone buzzed with a text, which I ignored.

"You better look at that," he stated with a sarcastic edge to his voice. "After pickle-gate, the mayonnaise may have disappeared as well."

"Liam doesn't like mayo on his sandwiches. He likes Miracle Whip."

Douglas's eyebrows rose, and I flushed even more. I grabbed my phone and read his text about driving me home. Huffing in frustration, I typed a reply and, finally using my brain, turned off the phone.

"Now, where were we before we were so rudely interrupted?" I questioned with a bright smile.

A short while later, Douglas laid down his fork, wiped his mouth, and took a long sip of his wine. His eyes were kind as he gazed at me. "It's okay, Shelby. You don't have to try so hard."

"I'm sorry?"

He shook his head. "My inane cousin, in his own unique way, has managed to be with us all evening." He grimaced. "Do you know you've talked about him in every conversation we've had tonight?"

"I—"

"Even without his calls and texts, he was here. I think we both know why." He paused. "'You care about him. A lot."

"Of course I do. He's a good friend."

"You both use that phrase so easily."

"It's true."

"Is that all he is to you?"

"Yes," I said, but I couldn't meet his eyes.

"Shelby," he prompted gently. I looked up, and he smiled at me. "It's okay. It really is."

"I don't think I'm ready to date yet," I admitted. "I'm sorry, Douglas."

He chuckled. "I think there is more to it than that. But until you're ready to admit it, we'll leave it there." Reaching across the table, he clasped my hand. "Now, how about we finish dinner and have a nice evening as friends."

"Friends?"

"Yes. I like you, Shelby. You're smart and funny, and frankly, I think you're perfect for someone—I'm not the, ah, *right* Wright, though. But I would love to have you as my friend."

The *right* Wright? Did he think Liam was the *right* Wright? He couldn't mean that. It was a crazy thought. Liam was my boss. We were friends. Close ones—yes. But still, only friends.

I took a deep breath and relaxed. "I'd like that, Douglas. Very much."

"Excellent."

I picked up my glass of wine and took a welcome sip. He was a lovely man, but he was right. He wasn't for me. Handsome, kind, intelligent, and artistic—he loved the visual aspect of the world around him. His enthusiasm for it reminded me of my friend Caroline's same feelings and reactions on the vast subject.

I smiled at him over my glass, the first genuine one of the evening.

"Douglas, I have a friend who's coming to visit. She's a photographer. The two of you have so much in common."

He grinned as he winked at me. "Is she pretty?"

"Gorgeous."

"Do tell."

I walked into the house, confused as to why lights were blazing all over the place. Even upstairs. I teased Liam all the time about his thrifty ways, and he hated lights left on in empty rooms. It was as if he had a sixth sense about them and constantly followed me around, flicking them off, grumbling about wasting money.

Why on earth was there a light on in every room? Had there been an emergency of some sort?

Everything looked fine and in place as I went from room to room, turning off lights. In the kitchen, I tried not to laugh. Liam had indeed looked everywhere for pickles except the most logical, it seemed. Cupboard doors were open, items scattered on the countertops, a half-eaten bag of crisps, as he called them, left discarded as if he'd become distracted by something else.

Finally, I went to the den, expecting to find Liam dozing on the sofa.

He was asleep—or more aptly, passed out—at his desk, his head resting on his chest, his snores filling the room. I stood at the door, watching him. He was cradling something in his arms, and I edged closer to see what it was. Spying the bottle of whiskey, I wondered how much he'd drunk and why he was holding the bottle that way. Bending over, I picked up the glass lying on the rug and set it on the desk. I stood beside him, stroking his hair, grinning as he roused slowly, bending his head into my touch. His voice was thick but so happy-sounding when he realized I was back home with him. I had no idea where else he'd thought I would go, but it was nice to know it pleased him.

I was horrified to see how empty the bottle was. I had never known Liam to drink that much. It took all my strength to hoist him from the chair. I was barely able to keep him upright on the stairs; he kept mumbling about home and his heart, slouching into my side, burying his face in my neck and nuzzling me with his lips. Despite the fact that he was drunk and mostly out of it, I still felt the small shockwaves every time his mouth met my skin. Each time I admonished him, he would snigger and apologize, only to do it again a few seconds later. The sound of his inebriated giggle made me want to laugh, it was so...adorable.

He landed like a felled tree on his bed, still mumbling and trying to act sober. I could tell he thought he was being sexy, but his leer looked more like he maybe had gas, rather than could be considered amorous when he teased me, his words slurred and rather broken. Much to my amusement, any filter he did have, which was never much, was gone, and he spoke all of his thoughts out loud.

He struggled to get undressed, and I helped him pull off his pants, grateful he hadn't gone commando again. I tried not to laugh watching him attempt to yank his shirt over his head and failing miserably, finally giving up.

When he commanded that I come back so he could sniff me and show me he was the king of *his* jungle, I actually laughed out loud.

He looked so crestfallen; I bent down, kissed his cheek, and told him he would regret all this in the morning. "Good thing I love you," I teased him.

"I love you, Shelby," he mumbled, his eyes already closing.

"I know," I whispered. "I love you too," I added so softly, I knew he didn't hear me.

"No." His voice drifted off. "I...really...love—"

And he was out.

I tucked the covers around him and grabbed a bottle of water out of the small refrigerator in his bathroom, placing it on his nightstand in case he woke and needed it. I added some painkillers as well. He was going to need them. I'd make him one of my hangover brews for the morning—or more likely, the afternoon, given the shape he was in.

I stood looking at him, watching him sleep. He had already flung his arm over his face, stuck one bare leg out of the covers, and I knew he would start moving soon. Every morning when I made the bed, I was sure he'd fought dragons in his sleep from the state it was in.

His words ran through my head. *"I love you, Shelby. I...really...love—"*

I ran my fingers through his hair.

He didn't mean it.

But a small part of me wished he did.

Because I'd realized earlier that I very well might be falling in love with him.

10

LIAM

Bugger. Who turned on the floodlights?

I slammed my eyes shut and buried my head into my pillow. Bloody hell, that hurt. When had Shelby changed my plump pillow for a concrete slab?

Cautiously, I lifted my head, groaning as I looked around.

I was in agony. Every part of me hurt.

My gaze fell to my nightstand and I sighed in relief. Sitting there was a bottle of water, Tylenol, and a thermal mug of what I hoped contained Shelby's special hangover remedy.

Tasted like ass, but it worked.

She rarely broke it out, as I hadn't been drunk that often since she'd been with me, but I needed it now. I wasn't sure I'd ever had a hangover this bad before today.

Bravely, I drank the evil concoction, took the pills, and gulped down the water before stumbling into the shower. I let the hot water pour over me, working its magic on loosening my stiff muscles, easing the aches, and removing the stale liquor smell. I felt the painkillers and Shelby's magic elixir doing their job, and when I stepped out of the shower, I felt marginally better.

I decided to forego shaving, though.

My hands weren't exactly steady, and I didn't want to bleed to death.

I walked into the kitchen, expecting to find Shelby and hear all about what a wanker I had been last night, only to be greeted by an empty room.

No music playing indicating her mood, no computer on, no Shelby.

My already-upset stomach tightened further. I didn't remember much, but I had a fairly clear recollection of what happened when she came home. It had drifted through my head on rewind my entire shower.

I woke at my desk to tender fingers trailing along the back of my neck, the sweetest voice in the world whispering my name. "Liam?"

I smiled at the sound of her voice. She was here.

"Shelby. You came home. That's good."

My voice sounded rather...slurry. I wasn't sure why.

"Of course I came home."

"Our home," I mumbled. "Here. With me."

She hummed as she tugged on my arm. "Yes, Liam. Now, you need to move."

I moaned, trying to lift my head. Crap, it hurt. Finally, I got it off my chest, only to have it hit the back of my chair with a dull thud. "Bugger." The bottle I'd been holding slipped from my grasp and fell to the floor.

Shelby's voice turned from soft to horrified. "Liam! How much have you had to drink?"

I gingerly lifted an eyelid and met her frantic glare. I let the eye shut quickly.

It was safer that way. No eye contact.

I attempted nonchalance as I tried to remember. I believed it might have been a lot. The pounding in my head wasn't helping my ability to recollect anything.

"*Um. Sorry.*" *I cleared my throat. Bloody hell, my voice sounded gritty like sandpaper. I tried again.* "*What did you say?*"

"*Why are you so drunk?*"

Drunk?

I was hardly drunk. I was simply...tipsy.

I heaved out of the chair, ready to defend my honor. Except the floor moved, and I stumbled forward, the only thing preventing me from being introduced face first to said floor, was the fact that Shelby's arms shot out, stopping me and letting me lean into her.

Right. Maybe I was drunk.

But pressed against her felt nice. Really nice. I rested my face in the crook of her neck and inhaled deeply. She smelled good. She always did. I couldn't control myself as I nuzzled her fragrant skin a little.

God, it was so smooth.

"*Liam,*" *she admonished as she pushed me to stand.*

I looked at her sheepishly. "*My bad.*"

Shelby shook her head. "*Let's get you to bed.*"

I grinned sloppily at her. "*I've been waiting for you to say that.*"

She groaned. "*Always the comedian.*"

I frowned.

I wasn't kidding.

It was a long walk up the stairs, leaning heavily on Shelby. I kept finding her skin with my mouth, and she kept chiding me for doing so.

It wasn't my fault, really. My lips had their own agenda. I had to follow where they went.

Shelby, it seemed, didn't agree.

I exhaled as my head hit the pillow, it's coolness a welcome sensation. Still, I was unsure as to why the room was moving so much.

"*Because you're drunk, Liam.*"

I wasn't aware I had said that out loud.

"*You did.*"

Or that.

I felt my sneakers being pulled off, followed by my socks. My legs were suddenly cold as my pants disappeared.

"Tsk, tsk, tiger. In such a hurry for me?" I waggled my eyebrows at her, giving her one of my sexiest leers. At least I thought I did. I wasn't sure how much control I had right now over the muscles in my face. Or my body, to be honest.

Shelby shook her head. "You are going to regret all this tomorrow, Liam."

The only thing I was going to regret was her leaving my room. I wanted to sniff her again. Then I'd show her who the king of the jungle was. My jungle.

Why was she giggling?

The blankets were pulled up, and I felt Shelby's warm lips on my cheek. "Good thing I love you, Liam. Good night."

My hand clasped the back of her head. "I love you, Shelby. I really do."

"I know."

I fought the darkness descending around me, reaching out for her. "No, Shelby...I...really...love..."

Then the darkness won.

I blinked with the memories.

God, had I upset her so much she left?

No—Shelby wouldn't do that.

Would she?

Another thought had me pulling on my hair.

Had she had such a great time with Douglas that she was out with him again? My stomach lurched at the thought.

I bent over at the knees, taking in deep gulps of air as one clear memory hit me.

I loved her.

She was mine.

I didn't want her out with Douglas. I wanted her here with me. I wanted her to love me back.

As I struggled to take in more air, my gaze landed on a folded piece of paper of the counter beside the coffeemaker. I made my way over and picked up the note.

Gone to run some errands. Fresh coffee in pot. Your breakfast is on the table.

Should fix you right up. Your favorite, I think. ~S

I let out a deep gust of air. It was okay. She was out running errands, but she'd be back.

I poured a coffee and went over to the table, eyeing the covered plate suspiciously. Sometimes on Sundays, Shelby made me a fry-up. I loved those, and she only let me have them occasionally. Otherwise, it was the bird-food bagel or some other healthier version of breakfast —like those fruit smoothie thingies. I wasn't sure I could face a cold plate of bacon and eggs right now. I sat, hesitated, then lifted the lid. For a moment, I stared at the plate, and then, much to my aching head's protests, began to chuckle.

Pickles. Nothing but a large pile of pickles was on the plate.

I picked one up and started munching, the tartness surprisingly tasty this morning.

Only Shelby.

My brilliant girl.

I frowned. She *was* mine. But I needed to do something to ensure that. I finished the pickle, drank my coffee, and grabbed my car keys.

To say Douglas was surprised to see me at his door would be an understatement. "Liam."

"Hey. Got a minute?"

He waved me in. "Sure. I was just having coffee and a bagel. Interested?"

"Sure."

A short while later, we were sitting, silently eating. Inside I had to admit, although I would never tell her, Shelby's bird-food bagels were far tastier than Douglas's plain ones. She was also much more generous with the cream cheese.

Breaking the silence, Douglas spoke up, his voice slightly amused. "Are you going to tell me why you're here, Liam? I highly doubt it's for my breakfast-making skills."

I cleared my throat and looked at him. He gazed back with his usual calm demeanor as he sipped his coffee. "I–I don't want you seeing Shelby anymore."

He tilted his head as he set down his mug. His face showed no surprise at my words, but his voice was firm. "I think that decision is up to her."

I drew in a deep breath. "I'm asking you, Douglas, brother to brother. Leave her alone."

He smirked. "Throwing out the brother connection? We're only cousins, you know."

I growled at him. "You know what I mean. And if that's what it takes to get you to back off, yes."

He sat back. "Why?"

"She's special."

He nodded. "She is. She is lovely, funny, and I enjoy her company. Why would I deny myself that?"

"Because I'm asking."

"Not good enough. You said she was your houseke—ah, *friend*—why should it matter to you who she dates?"

"No. She's more," I insisted.

"I need more than that to agree to your, ah, request."

I tightened my hands into fists on my leg. "Because. She–she means something to me."

He took another sip of coffee, regarding me calmly. "What exactly does she mean to you, Liam?"

It burst out of me before I could stop myself. "I love her, Douglas! That's what she means to me!"

His eyebrows shot up, and he pursed his lips. "So definitely more than merely your housekeeper. Can I ask what brought this on?"

I glared at him. "She made me a sandwich."

"Wow. That must've been some sandwich. Maybe I should ask her to make me one."

"*No!* She only makes them for me," I spat at him.

Raising one eyebrow in typical Douglas fashion, he waited for me to keep speaking.

"She was mad at me, and still, she made me my favorite sandwich. She takes care of me. She cares for me. And I care for her. It just took me a while to figure it out. I know you think she is great, but I need you to back off."

"Hmm, not sure. I like sandwiches. And Shelby."

I was getting angry, which wasn't helping my headache. I clenched my hands on my legs, resisting the urge to punch him in his handsome face. I had a feeling that wouldn't end well for me. "Piss off. You can't date her again."

"Well, like I said, the lady may have something to say about that."

I shook my head, glaring at him. "No, she won't. She's mine. She just doesn't know it yet."

Surprisingly, he chuckled, reclining in his chair. "Relax, Liam. I was joking."

"I don't feel like joking right now, you arse."

His expression became serious. "Talk to me."

I stood, pacing, and spilled it. All of it. I told him the whole story of how she came into my life, how close we were, and my sudden epiphany last night. He listened without interruptions, waiting until I sat back across from him.

"How do you think *Shelby* feels?"

I shrugged. "She cares for me. I know that for certain. She's skittish about relationships, though, and especially wary of my lifestyle." I snorted. "And the *vast* difference in our ages."

"Yeah. Five years. Huge, that. It's only a number. Does she know your mum is four years older than your dad?"

I leaned forward. "No. I don't think I ever told her that. It never seemed important to them."

"You should tell her. It might help." He sighed. "There are a lot of successful relationships, even in Hollywood, where the woman is older. It depends on your perspective. They don't allow it to be a big deal."

"You're right. And I want the chance to explore it with her, if she's willing. I'm asking you to step back. Please."

"No need to ask. I wasn't going to see her again, privately."

"What? I thought you liked her! You just said—"

He held up his hand, silencing me. "I do like her. And she likes me. I think we're going to be great friends, Liam. At least, I hope we are." He paused as he got up and poured us both more coffee. "It was obvious last night. Shelby may have been out with me in body, but her mind was elsewhere." He gave me a pointed stare. "It was with you. I've never known a *housekeeper* to be so worried about their *employer* being alone before." He snickered. "Not that it is what we are really talking about here."

"I don't understand."

"Tell me, did you see her before she left last night?"

"Yes."

"She looked lovely. Did you tell her that?"

"Yes."

"What did she do?"

I thought about her reaction. "She blushed. She always does when I pay her a compliment."

Douglas smiled ruefully. "I thought as much. I told her she was beautiful. She said thank you. No blush."

"So?"

"My opinion didn't mean as much as yours did, Liam. What I thought wasn't as important as what you thought." He took a sip of coffee, thinking. "She tried—I could see how hard she was trying to enjoy herself." He shook his head. "She shouldn't have to try so hard. And I shouldn't have to worry about being a distant second to my idiot cousin. The only time I saw her really smile was when you texted her."

I chuckled. "She was rather pissed off about my interruptions, though."

Douglas laughed. "Yes and no. She acted annoyed, but I could see how hard she fought against calling you back and telling you where the damn pickles were."

"Not my best moment."

"She cares about you. More than she realizes or is willing to admit, I think. No matter what we talked about, somehow your name kept coming up. You were like a ghost the entire evening."

"Um. Sorry?"

"Don't be. Once we cleared the air, we had a great, friendly evening. But in the end, there was no spark for either of us," he acknowledged. "I rather suspected it when I watched the two of you together the other day. You were so...*natural* with each other. So in tune with each other. As if you completed the other one." He grinned. "And completely clueless about what the other was feeling."

"You saw all that?"

"Yep."

"Yet you asked her out." I narrowed my eyes at him. "Did you do that to push me?"

He shrugged. "Maybe. I was attracted to her, though. I have to be honest. Can't blame a man for trying. She is rather spectacular. But there was no spark."

"You didn't kiss her?" I asked suspiciously. *How could he resist?*

"I didn't even try. Neither of us wanted to. We both recognized what path we should take. Friends." He informed me. "We hugged and agreed we'd see each other at some point—probably when you were involved. She tells me she has a friend coming to visit she wants to introduce me to. So, I think we've established our baseline."

I sighed in relief. One hurdle done.

He glared at me. "But you should be telling her how you feel, Liam. Not me."

"I know. I will. I just wanted to come here and talk."

"Stake your claim, you mean."

I grinned sheepishly. "Maybe."

"Consider it done. Not that you had to convince me. I'd say your claim is safe. But you need to tell her—and soon."

He was right.

But first I had to talk to Everett.

Everett didn't seem happy to see me. Once I followed him into the kitchen and saw Cassidy, my PR advisor, sitting there, wearing what had to be one of his T-shirts, I understood why.

Bloody hell, when had this started?

Everett sighed and sat, pulling Cassidy onto his lap. "About four months ago, Liam."

Bollocks. When had I started mumbling all my thoughts out loud?

"Sorry," I muttered. "I didn't know."

Everett grinned. "We keep it under wraps, Liam. And you're easy to fool. Now, what is so important you have to show up at my door this early on a Sunday? From the sound of your inebriated mutterings last night, I expected you to still be asleep."

"I, ah, had some important errands."

"Out buying pickles, were you?" He started to laugh, and Cassidy joined him. I had to grin at his goading. His next statement wiped the grin off my face. "My sister isn't happy with you right now, by the way. I told her you ratted her out."

Bugger.

Cassidy chuckled. "He's teasing, Liam. She's fine. She knows you were rather out of it."

I sighed in relief. I really didn't need her mad at me today. Especially today.

"Liam?" Everett prompted. "Why are you here? No offense, but I have other things I'd rather be doing than waiting for you to speak, if you know what I mean." He grinned as he tightened his arm around Cassidy.

Oh God. That was too much to handle with my brain already on overdrive.

TMI.

I cleared my throat. Might as well get straight to the point. Maybe with Cassidy on his lap, I could have a head start if he decided not to take this well.

"I'm in love with your sister."

His expression didn't change. Cassidy didn't look surprised either. But she got up and dropped a kiss on his cheek, leaving the room with a small smile at me. Everett's eyes followed her. Then he turned his attention back to me.

"And?" he asked, reclining back in his chair a bit.

I frowned at him. "*Shelby*. I'm in love with Shelby."

"I'm aware of my sister's name, Liam. I'm glad you finally realized it. It certainly took you long enough."

I gaped at him. "You knew?"

He snorted. "Liam, you're the tightest son of a bitch I've ever met. My sister brings you a damn burger and shake, and you drop a hundred grand in her account? And fight with her to make her keep it? You only did that because of your feelings for her. She's the only person who brings out that crazy generosity in you. And the way you are together? How close you are with each other? A blind man on a fast horse could see it."

"I'm not that tight," I muttered even as I mused over his words, ignoring his teasing. Just because I didn't drop large sums of cash around every day or hire tons of extra people I didn't think I needed, didn't mean I was cheap. I was simply thrifty.

But with Shelby, I *was* different. Every time I heard her talk about or look at something she liked, I always made sure to buy it, and I always acted surprised when I found out it was an item she wanted. I was good at that—the acting surprised thing. I had an Oscar that said so.

Shelby rarely ever made it simple for me, though. She never said "*Hey, I want that,*" since that would be too easy for me. But I watched and listened. She had a way of tilting her head and looking thoughtful when she was interested in something, and her eyes lit up. I enjoyed her reaction of delight when even the simplest item would appear. Some odd kitchen implement I had no idea how to use. A new set of bakeware she'd stared at glossy-eyed on the TV. She'd been almost giddy last week over a new touch screen computer I put in the kitchen. I told her I wanted it—all of it. She never questioned why they were all used by her and not me.

"Um, Liam?"

I shook my head, bringing my focus back. "Sorry."

"I knew. I've known for a while. How did she take it when you told her?"

"Um, I haven't yet. I wanted to talk to you first." Feeling serious, I bent forward. "She means a lot to me, Everett. You both do. I needed to make sure this was okay with you. Man to man. Friend to friend." I paused. "I know I'm an idiot, Everett, and I have no experience with relationships. I've never had one that lasted any length of time. But I care about her. Deeply. I want to look after her. I want her as part of my life. She makes me a better person. I want to be a better person for her."

He met my earnest gaze. "You are a bit of a fuckup, Liam. But you're right. Shelby is good for you." He rubbed a hand over his face. "And you're good for her. Ever since our parents died, she's tried to be everything for me. Sister and parent. Always responsible." He smiled. "You make her happy. You bring out her silly side, and she needs that," he admitted. "She brings out your more serious side, which you need. She lights up like a Christmas tree when you're around, and you do the same thing. You were made for each other."

"So, you're okay with this?"

He shrugged. "She's a grown woman, Liam. I can't stop her. I can't stop you either." He scrubbed his face. "Her ex did a number on her. Destroyed her confidence and self-worth. Shook her badly. Don't hurt her." He drummed his fingers on the tabletop. "No business relationship will stop me from coming after you if you do."

I gave him a nervous nod and a tight smile. Everett, my manager and friend, was gone. Shelby's family— her brother—was sitting in front of me.

"I don't want to hurt her, Ev. I love her. I really do."

"She might fight you on this, regardless of her feelings."

"I know. She has a hang-up over the age thing."

"And your lifestyle, Liam. She's very private. When this gets out, there will be a lot of press. Some hard stuff for you both to deal with. Her marital status. The age thing. The fact that she works for you. That she is my sister. The rags will use anything and everything. Twist it all. We'll have to talk this all through." He paused. "If, that is, she agrees to take on your sorry ass."

"I'll protect her. So will you."

"With everything in me."

"I know."

"Good luck, Liam. You may need it. Be patient with her. She'll be guarded, that I know."

"I have your blessing?"

He laughed. "Listen to you." His face became serious. "Treat her well. Or else."

"I will."

I didn't want to know what Everett's *or else* entailed.

It would be painful, of that much, I was sure.

Very painful.

11

LIAM

I walked into the kitchen, unsure what I would find. I listened briefly, but the music seemed to be one of Shelby's regular playlists, not a sad or angry one.

Thank God. No Guns N' Roses. I'd have to run if that were playing.

Shelby was at the counter, her head down, working away. I leaned against the door and watched her in contemplative silence. Her hair was up, her shirt long and too big, meaning it was one of mine, and she had on those damn sexy glasses again. She was biting her lip in concentration as she worked on whatever project she had going on at the moment.

All around her were plates and bowls, and she was rolling something in what looked like a placemat. I pushed off the doorframe and sauntered over, trying to be casual, while my heart was beating furiously against my rib cage.

"Hey, Beaker."

She looked up, the most beautiful smile in the world lighting her face, and I had to return it in full. She was bloody amazing. And she looked good in my, *our*, kitchen.

"There you are. I was surprised when I came home to see your car gone." She snickered. "I'm rather shocked you're even awake. Where were you?"

"Errands."

"On a Sunday?"

I bit back a grin as I held up a small bag. "Yeah."

"What's that?"

I pulled out the item and held it up for her. She chuckled, her eyes lighting up with mirth. "We have lots of pickles, Liam. You looked right past them."

"I looked in every cupboard."

"You're not in England, Britboy. I keep them in the refrigerator. The jar was right beside your sandwiches."

Bugger. Never thought to look there.

She shook her head. "Sometimes you miss what is right in front of you. It's scary."

She had no idea how right she was with that statement.

"Well, you can add this to the pantry, then."

She nodded, her hands still busy. "Will do."

I edged forward, wanting to be closer to her. "What are you doing?" I asked, looking at all the things she had in front of her.

"I took a class this morning. I learned to make sushi. I'm making you some now. I got all the ingredients for your favorites."

God. I *loved* sushi.

I loved this woman.

I watched her begin to assemble another roll and inspect it. "I haven't got the technique quite right yet. But I'm getting better."

I stood behind her, watching. It looked fine to me. Without thinking, I settled my hands on her hips and my chin on her shoulder as I observed her. I felt a shiver flow down her spine as I bent closer, and I smiled. She liked me close. "It looks good. Really good."

"You can find out in a few minutes."

Her voice sounded husky. It made me want to run my lips over the exposed skin of her neck. Maybe after lunch, she'd let me. I frowned and pressed closer. "Shelby, you don't like sushi. You hate it, in fact."

"I'm making it for you."

I shut my eyes as I rested my forehead against the back of her head. Her soft hair tickled my nose. "You went to learn how to do this for me? Even though you hate the stuff?"

She lifted her shoulders in a shrug, and her skin grew warm with her blush. "You were surrounded last time you tried to go for lunch at that sushi bar you like, and you haven't had it since then. I know how much you like sushi, and I thought maybe you missed eating it. So, yeah. I learned for you."

A rush of tenderness filled me.

Always for me. Something I didn't even realize I wanted or needed, she did, and quietly took care of it.

I didn't think.

I didn't consider my actions.

I spun her around, and covered her lips with mine.

Pressing, hard, needy.

Oh God—finally.

Shelby.

For one brief, fabulous moment, I had Shelby in my arms and her mouth underneath mine. Warm, yielding, and bloody perfect.

Then she shoved me away, her eyes wide with confusion. "What are you doing?"

I stepped back, tugging on my hair. "Kissing you."

She grimaced and moved forward, sniffing me warily. "Are you drunk again?"

"No!"

I put my hands on her shoulders, shaking her slightly. "I love you, Shelby. I'm in love with you."

"Because I'm making you sushi?"

"No! Because–because I am!"

She shook off my hold. "No, you're not, Liam."

"I'm not?"

"No." She smiled sadly at me. "You're just reacting to my going out on a date last night. It's like separation anxiety for a child."

Separation...what? A child?

What the hell was she on about?

She should be kissing me back, not talking. And dammit, I didn't want her to look so sad.

"No," I stated with firm conviction. "Pretty bloody sure I'm in love with you."

"Well, let me know when you're *totally bloody sure,* and we'll talk again." She turned around, starting to make more sushi.

I gaped at her.

Let her know? I was going to let her know, all right. I was going to shag her until she was bloody dead certain.

I grabbed her and spun her back around to face me. I pressed her tightly against my chest and crashed my lips to hers again.

Damn, she was soft. Warm. Sweet. So bloody sweet.

And pushing me away again. Dammit.

She glared at me then shoved past me to the sink, tossing her glasses onto the counter. I smirked, knowing I had probably smudged the lenses when I was pressed against her. She pumped several shots of soap into her hands before scrubbing at them vigorously.

Right. No doubt she wanted to wash the raw fish off her hands before we got too carried away. Since I did want those little hands all over me, it would be best if they were clean and not smelling of seafood. Maybe I should have waited until she was finished making lunch.

I glanced down. My shirt was going to have to be washed since it already had fish on it where she had been clutching it. Shrugging, I pulled it off and threw it over my shoulder. Might as well get rid of it now.

She finished and grabbed a towel as I waited patiently. When she turned, I held out my hand, smiling at her, hoping she could see how much I wanted this, wanted her, right now. Fish or no fish.

Her eyes widened as she looked at me, and I waggled my eyebrows at her rakishly.

She stomped over and stood in front of me. Then she said the last thing I expected. "Go put on a shirt, Liam."

"Sorry. Did you want to take it off? Maybe you can do that next time."

She threw her hands up in the air. "No. There's not going to be a next time. There isn't going to be a *this* time. Stop it right now, Liam. You're not in love with me. You just panicked."

"Panicked? You think I panicked? Over what?"

"You were afraid I would leave you. Don't worry. I won't be seeing Douglas again."

"I know."

"*You know?* How do you know?"

"I went to see him this morning."

"Why?"

"To tell him to stay away from you."

When she crossed her arms over her chest, and that "V" appeared on her forehead, I should have shut up. But I didn't.

"I told him I was in love with you, and he thinks you love me as well. He said we were too close for that not to be the case. He agreed to back off."

Her foot started tapping. I ignored another crucial hint.

"I see. Anyone else have any wisdom to impart to you?"

I nodded with a wide grin on my face. "Everett told me I make you silly. He said we were good together and I make you happy. I got his blessing this morning as well."

"Let me get this straight. You have some sort of drunken epiphany about being in love with me, and the first thing you do is go tell your cousin and my brother?"

For the first time, I felt a small ripple of uncertainty. When she said it like that, it didn't sound very good.

"I, ah, figured out I loved you *before* I got drunk, Shelby. I got drunk because I *realized* I loved you."

Wait.

Dammit. That didn't sound as good as it did in my head.

I rushed ahead.

"You weren't here this morning. I had to go see Douglas and stake my claim."

Her eyebrows shot up.

Shit.

That sounded even worse. What the hell was wrong with me?

Her voice was deceptively quiet. "And Everett?"

"I wanted to make sure he wasn't gonna hurt me for fucking around with his sister."

Oh, bloody hell.

Maybe I was still drunk.

Shelby laughed, but she didn't really sound amused. The sound frightened me a little, and I backed up.

"Well, don't worry about that, Liam. Not only did you waste your time 'staking your claim,' there isn't a chance in hell you're going to be 'fucking around' with me."

I grimaced. "No?"

She inched toward me. Close enough I could smell her light fragrance. Feel the heat of her breath on my skin.

"Not unless hell freezes over."

She stepped back.

"Enjoy your sushi."

I was sure she muttered "wanker" on her way out of the room. There might have been a "fucking" in front of it as well. But I couldn't be sure. Sounded about right, though. My own stupid word-vomit was echoing in my ears. Maybe I needed to write my own rule book—one that contained nothing but do-not-do's.

I sat on the chair heavily. As my first time declaring my love, I'd say that wasn't how it should have gone.

As Everett would say, I cocked it up.

Badly.

By midweek, I was certain I was going to explode.

To anyone who saw or interacted with me, everything seemed normal. I attended various meetings, talked and planned with Everett. When he arrived on Monday morning, I only looked at him with a subtle shake of my head, and he knew. He didn't say a word to either of us an acted as if nothing was wrong. He muttered one word to me before he left that night—patience. And bloody hell, I was trying.

I studied my upcoming script daily, and even went to the gym voluntarily. Everything seemed normal.

But it wasn't. *Shelby* wasn't normal.

When she reappeared on Sunday afternoon, Beaker was gone, and she was, for the first time ever, my housekeeper.

A bloody perfect, *distant* housekeeper.

She cooked for me, even ate with me, filling the silence with horrendous idle chatter. She talked about redecorating the space over the garage that Marie used to have, constantly showing me samples I had no interest in. But I pointed and nodded obediently at the options she obviously wanted me to choose anyway, hoping she would stop and become Shelby again. She was like a person possessed by her swatches, clutching them like a talisman against me. I missed the comfortable silences we used to share.

I missed her.

Tuesday night, I made up a false meeting and escaped to the safety of Douglas's place; he called me a wanker, but otherwise let me hide for a while.

I didn't like distant, housekeeper Shelby.

There was absolutely no touching. No affectionate hugs or sweet teasing.

My schedule was printed and left by my plate every morning.

My coffee was still hot and fresh, but no longer accompanied by a pair of warm lips brushing my cheek as Shelby handed me the mug.

No foot rubs on the sofa for her while we watched movies. No head rubs for me while I talked about some funny thing that happened during the day. No teasing and putting me in my place. In fact, no movies.

She worked endlessly. Morning until night. She scrubbed and cleaned. Organized and fixed. Baked and cooked. Filled the freezer. Ironed everything I owned.

The whole time with no music playing.

That freaked me out the most.

Shelby *always* had music playing.

The house was utterly...empty. I was empty.

I walked into the kitchen on Thursday afternoon to find both Lily and Everett at the table. They looked solemn. "What's up? Fashion day not going well?" I asked lightly, trying to fight the sudden tightening of my stomach.

Lily smiled, but it looked forced. "I think we've picked a dress."

"Good."

"If it's, ah, still needed."

Bloody what?

Everett cleared his throat. "Gillian is available this weekend, Liam, if you would rather she..." His voice trailed off as I gaped at him.

"Is Shelby not coming with me?" Just the thought made me cringe. She kept me calm—I needed her.

"She wondered if maybe you would prefer someone else."

Enough of this crap. I was done. "Where is Shelby?"

"She went to get something upstairs."

"Stay here. Both of you."

SHELBY

I heard Liam's pounding footsteps heading my way, and I braced myself for what was coming. I wiped at my face, feeling exhausted.

Ever since his unexpected declaration the other day, my life had been in turmoil.

Once he uttered the words, I couldn't get away from him fast enough.

I had stormed up the stairs to my room, pacing the floor. My lips still tingled from the feeling of Liam's moving with mine. My chest ached with how much I wanted to feel them again. To feel him pressed against me. My mind was racing with his declarations. I was shocked by his words. Only, he couldn't possibly mean them.

There was no way he could be in love with me.

He could have anyone. Why would he want me?

No. He was worried about me dating again and deserting him. It had to be that simple. He was only reacting, not feeling.

I slipped to the floor, resting my head against the side of my bed, my body suddenly tired.

Liam needed to be looked after. That was what I did. The thought of me maybe not doing that was what started this change in him. He had been acting strangely since the morning Douglas asked me out. Liam didn't want to lose me—as his housekeeper.

Despite what he said about the "wisdom" imparted to him by Douglas and Everett, he couldn't be in love with me.

My head fell back as I thought about it.

What him loving me would be like.

How open and affectionate he would be. How much he would make me laugh. How it would feel to have him kiss me—really kiss me. Make love to me.

Until, of course, he grew tired of it, of me. Because he would; I had nothing exciting to offer him. He lived in a world of glamorous people;

he traveled, dined in exclusive restaurants, and attended elite functions. All of which were captured on film and posted for everyone to see. Why would he want his housekeeper to be a part of that?

When and if he changed his mind, I would lose everything. There was no way I could stay once he came to his senses. The house I had come to think of as my home. The quiet, happy life I had made here.

Liam.

I would lose Liam.

I swiped away the hot, angry tears that dripped down my face.

I couldn't risk it.

As much as it killed me, I had to keep things the way they were —platonic.

I could still be his friend, but I needed to set boundaries and act properly. Once he understood I wasn't going anywhere, he would go back to being Liam and forget his drunken epiphany.

I would rather break my own heart and still be a small part of his world than to risk him walking away from me and losing everything that meant so much.

I would rather watch him fall in love with someone else and be happy than risk me making him unhappy and regretting his ill-thought-out decision.

My head fell into my hands as I sobbed.

I had to do this. I had to be strong.

Because I couldn't lose him.

I allowed myself the time to cry it out. Then I washed my face and went back to the reason I was here.

The role I could play safely.

I needed to step back and be exactly what he hired me to be: his housekeeper.

I knew my decision came with a cost. Liam wanted me to be his wingman at the events he had to go to. Play his girlfriend, hold his hand, and cover for the horrendous panic he experienced in public. I had promised, and now I was reneging. I simply wasn't strong enough to pretend—not when he was still under the delusion that he was in love with me. It wasn't fair to him, or to me. Because for me, it wasn't an illusion. I knew I loved him, but I couldn't tell him. He needed his partner to be more than I could be for him. It was best he went back to his friends to help him out. There was no danger there of real feelings bleeding into the mix and messing things up. I had been too much of a coward to tell him, so Everett and Lily were doing so.

But from the sounds of his heavy footfalls and cursed mutterings, he was coming to challenge me. I braced myself for the onslaught. I had to be strong.

For both of us.

LIAM

I met Shelby in the hallway and, without a word, grabbed her arm and dragged her into the den, shutting the door loudly behind her.

"Are you not coming with me on Saturday?"

She looked everywhere but at me. "I thought maybe you'd be more comfortable—"

I interrupted her. "I'd be most comfortable with *you*, Shelby." I drew in a deep breath. "My Shelby. Not the perfect Stepford-wife housekeeper version that's been running around the house the last few days."

I paced, running my hands through my hair in frustration. "I realize I shocked you the other day. I know I handled it badly." I stopped and stared at her. "But pretending it didn't happen isn't working. I said it. *I meant it.* I love you."

She started to shake her head, and for the first time ever, I became angry with her.

"Don't you dare stand there and tell me I don't, Shelby. I know you think I'm a git and can't possibly be mature enough to have those feelings for you, but I assure you, I do. I am *not* a child. The only separation issue I feel is the thought of losing you to another man because I waited too bloody long to tell you how I feel." By the time I finished, I was almost yelling, but I was so upset I couldn't stop it.

Her eyes filled with tears, and instantly, my anger deflated.

"That's not what I think, Liam."

I sat heavily on the sofa. "I get it. I really do. You don't feel the same way. Or, at least, you're not ready to admit you do. I should have handled this better." My head fell into my hands. "Don't take away your friendship. If nothing else, let me be your friend. I miss you so much, Beaker." I sighed. "I need you beside me Saturday. If you can't come as my date, promise me you'll come as my friend. That's all I'm asking. Please."

For a moment, there was silence, and then Shelby sat beside me. I felt her hand slip into mine, pulling it away from my cheek. "I'm sorry, Liam."

I looked at her sad face. "Because you don't love me?"

"I do love you. Just not the way you want me to."

She was lying. I knew she was—her body language screamed it.

"Why? You can't, or you won't let yourself?"

Her eyes shut, and when they opened, they were filled with pain. "I can't handle...all of it. It's all too much. I'm not the right woman for you." Her voice dropped. "I couldn't stand losing you."

"And you're certain you would?"

"It's the logical conclusion. Your life is vastly different from mine."

"You're already a part of it."

"A small part."

"No. A far larger part than you realize."

She sighed, running a shaky hand through her hair. "Liam—"

I lifted our clasped hands and kissed hers. "I'm not going to give up, Shelby. But I'll back off. For now." I sighed heavily. "Don't keep yourself away from me. Please. Don't punish my feelings that way. Don't punish me."

She gasped quietly at my words, as if realizing for the first time how much her distance hurt me.

"All right."

"So, you'll come Saturday? Hold my hand all night? Keep me calm?"

"Yes."

"Will you stop all the bloody cleaning? I can't possibly be *that* messy." I paused. "And please, not another word about curtains and paint colors. I'll go right mental."

A small smile ghosted across her lips. "Okay."

"And your music. I never thought I'd say it, but I miss your shit playing in the kitchen. It comforts me."

"All right. I'll play my shit music for you."

"Can we be Beaker and Oscar again?"

"Yes."

I heaved a sigh of relief. "Brilliant. Can we finish the *Lord of the Rings* saga tonight? I'm dying to know how it ends. I think poor little Frodo is in big trouble."

Her laughter, however subdued, was music to my ears. "Liam, we've watched it twice before. You know Frodo destroys the ring."

I huffed at her. "Way to spoil the ending. Just for that, I want extra butter on my popcorn."

"Deal."

"Okay. Now, go and finish picking your finery." I stood and walked to the safe. "Wait." I rummaged around and handed her two boxes. "I want you to wear these."

She smiled as she recognized the bracelet, and her eyes widened at the drop earrings that matched.

"Liam, they are beautiful. I can't... What if—"

I held up my hand. "You won't lose them. You're wearing them. I want to see them on you. Lily said you'd be wearing your hair up. So, please. For me."

"All right."

"Okay. Send Everett in, please?"

She nodded and left. I sat, feeling relieved and discouraged at the same time.

Had I won the battle but lost the war?

I needed her on Saturday, but I needed her in my life even more.

My eyes drifted to the open safe where all the pieces of my nan's jewelry were stored, and I pulled out the smallest box of all. Although I wanted Shelby to wear all the pieces I had inherited, there was one piece of jewelry I most wanted to see Shelby wearing. A thought I hadn't been able to get out of my mind since I knew what I was feeling for her. I flipped open the lid, watching the light glint off the antique diamond that was nestled against the dark velvet. My nan's ring. A unique, beautiful setting—elegant and perfect, just like the woman who I knew was meant to wear it.

I sighed and put the box back in the safe. Not yet. Not for a long while. But, I hoped, one day.

I only had to convince her.

12

LIAM

Things were better after our talk, but we weren't back to normal yet. Shelby was still wary, and I tried as hard as I could to be casual—to be simply Oscar, but it was difficult. It was as if now that I realized how deep my feelings went for her, everything was *more*. I wanted to be around her all the time. I wanted her smiles and laughter. I wanted her every waking moment. I struggled every day not to overwhelm her. She felt something—I knew she did. I had to let her figure it out.

Saturday, I was anxious for the event, but not the usual sort of anxious I was used to. Because of the fact that we would be out in public and Shelby knew how tense it made me, it would be the perfect excuse to be close to her. Hold her hand. Tuck her into my side without her questioning why. For the first time in a long while, I was looking forward to going out. Everett and Cassidy were meeting us at the benefit for a brief time, as they also had another event to attend. Everett, I knew, was coming to make sure I got in safely and wouldn't leave until I was comfortable. My car would be waiting to take us home whenever we were ready to leave.

Shelby was getting ready on her own today. Lily had been by

earlier to make sure everything was okay, that my tuxedo was ready and Shelby was set. She had another client tonight, and Shelby and I told her we were fine on our own. The only thing she'd done was help Shelby do her hair.

I had been ready to go for a while and was now hanging out in the hallway, waiting for Shelby. The car was here, and I called to let her know it was time to go.

"I'm coming," she replied.

My breath left my lungs as I waited for Shelby to make it down the stairs. Once again, Lily had outdone herself. The long dress floated around Shelby as she walked toward me, one shoulder bare and glowing pale against the deep-red hue of her dress.

I wanted to run my lips across that shoulder.

I watched her as she descended. Every. Single. Step.

Thank God Everett wasn't here. I was, without a doubt, seriously eye-fucking his sister.

This time, I didn't want to stop.

She was brilliant.

More than brilliant.

Shelby was elegance personified.

Until she tripped on the last step and tumbled into my arms.

I lunged forward, catching her, and we both chuckled. I nuzzled her head as I helped her to stand back up. "Arse over elbow already, Beaker? All right there?"

She patted her still-perfect hair. "I'm good."

I arched my eyebrow at her as I settled her on her feet. She was much taller than normal.

"No-go on the low heels?"

She shook her head. "No. The dress was a little long, and I needed the height, or I'd trip over the hem all night."

"The tripping has already started, I think."

"I have to get used to them. I'll be fine." She looked dubious. "I think."

I smirked at her. "Guess I'll owe you a good foot rub later then?"

"Bloody right, Oscar. These shoes are killers, in more ways than one. Hundreds of tiny straps of death. We'll be lucky if I *don't* trip over them all night. Never mind the damn dress."

I laughed at her use of my favorite expression. "The damn dress is lovely." I raised her hand and kissed the knuckles. "As are you."

I enjoyed the blush that suffused her skin. Douglas was right—every time I complimented her, she blushed. It had to mean something. I was banking on it. "I'll hold you up, Shelby."

"You better."

"We'll hold each other up—deal?"

She nodded. "Deal."

I held out my arm. "Your chariot awaits."

She hugged my arm against her. "Let's hit it."

It was the exact sort of benefit I hated. A real industry event. A roomful of actors, directors, producers, front men, and wannabes vying for attention. There were too many egos, too much money, and far too many false smiles crowded into a small area. As arranged, the driver dropped us at the back door, and Shelby and I slipped in unnoticed, while the paps were busy snapping other celebrities and bigwigs walking the red carpet. It didn't always work, but luck was with us tonight, and we entered without incident. With her beside me, I was completely calm, not even bothered by the huge crowd inside.

Dinner was long and too loud. Alcohol was flowing freely, and it seemed to me the noise level escalated as the hours dragged by. To escape the clamor, we walked a lot, looking at the auction pieces, slipping outside often to the private balcony for a quiet breath of fresh air—at least as fresh as one could get in LA.

After dinner, I took total advantage and had Shelby dance with me repeatedly. We moved together well—as if we'd been dancing together our entire lives. I enjoyed holding her close and feeling her soft skin under my hand as we swayed. It took everything I had not to nuzzle her shoulder as I held her. I couldn't, however, stop my fingers from drawing gentle circles on the small of her back. Once Everett and Cassidy departed, I monopolized Shelby completely, maybe playing up the nervous part on my end so she stayed close. I had no shame, not when it came to my Shelby.

As the evening progressed, I thought Shelby looked pale. Twice when we were dancing, she seemed to stumble, and I caught her against my chest, looking at her with a frown.

"All right there, Shelby?"

She insisted she was fine, but I was getting worried she wasn't feeling well.

Finally, I was called on to give my speech, hand out the award I'd been asked to present, and once that was over, I made my way back to the table amid the applause. I grew concerned as I drew closer and saw Shelby. She looked as if she were in pain, but still, she smiled as I sat beside her, wrapping her hands around mine. We sat through the rest of the speeches and awards, and as the band started to play, I bent close to her. "Dance?"

"Can we sit this one out?"

"Sure." I glanced around the table. I was tired of the chatter around us. "Walk?"

She hesitated, then nodded, and we stood. I scowled as I saw her use a hand to steady herself before she joined me. We began to make our way across the floor, and I made the decision maybe it was time to go home when I saw a grimace pass over her face. I let go of her hand and wrapped my arm around her waist, surprised when I felt how heavily she leaned into my side. Something was definitely wrong. Gently, I steered us toward the front of the building, intending to get her away from the noise and find out what was wrong.

Shelby grimaced again, and then I noticed how gingerly she was walking. Worried, I tightened my arm around her waist and pulled her into the nearest alcove, gently pushing her down on the small bench against the wall. Before she could protest, I kneeled and lifted up one of her feet to rest on my knee, seeing for the first time just how high the heels were on the shoes she was wearing and how badly they were damaging her feet. I was horrified when I pulled my hand away from her heel and saw blood.

I looked at her in dismay. "Shelby, you're bleeding. Your shoes are digging into your skin! Why didn't you say anything?"

"I know," she said. "They're the wrong size. But it's almost over. I can take them off soon."

"Why did you wear them if they didn't fit?"

"Lily brought a few pair for me to try on—these looked best with the dress. Otherwise it would have been too long. I must have put the wrong-sized pair in the box after I tried them on, and it was too late to call Lily by the time I realized my mistake when I was getting ready."

"You should have worn different ones." I traced my fingers over the swollen flesh, and I knew she must have blisters under all the intricate woven leather. The skin that was visible was rubbed raw. I could only imagine what the back of her heel looked like.

"I didn't have another pair that was suitable—the dress would have been ruined."

"I don't give a damn about the dress," I muttered and started to undo the buckle on the shoe.

Shelby reached forward, covering my hand. "You can't take them off! I won't get them back on!"

"I don't plan on you doing that," I growled as I pushed her hand away, and as carefully as I could, pulled the shoes off both feet, hissing when I saw the torn flesh and blood. Shelby let out a painful sound as I set her feet on the carpet. "Don't move," I instructed her.

I grabbed my cell phone and called for the car to come immediately to the far side of the front door. I was beyond done with the event, and now I had the perfect excuse; I needed to get Shelby home. I sat beside her, removed my shoes, pulled off my socks, and shoved my bare feet back into the leather. I kneeled in front of Shelby again and gently drew my socks over her injured feet, cursing at the small whimpers that escaped her tightly clenched lips. It wasn't an ideal solution, but it would at least cover her feet until we got home. I knew blisters were easily infected. Picking up the offensive shoes, I chucked them into the silver rubbish can beside her.

"Liam! Those were expensive! You can't throw them out."

"Can. And did. You aren't wearing them again."

"But Lily—"

I pressed forward, cupping the back of her head in my hand and holding her face close. "Listen to me, Shelby. I don't give a bloody fuck about the shoes, the dress, Lily, or anything else right now but *you*. Understand?"

Her eyes were wide. "Okay."

My phone buzzed, indicating the car was out front. I stood and held out my hand. "Can you walk?"

"Yes." Shelby took my hand and stood, immediately gasping when her weight rested on her feet.

"Sod it." Leaning down, I scooped her into my arms. I didn't want her in any more pain.

"You can't carry me out of here! People will see!"

I shook my head. So bloody stubborn.

"Can. And will. I don't care who sees. Now, for God's sake, Beaker, relax and stop struggling." I paused. "Keep your head low," I warned.

Shelby sighed in resignation and buried her head into my shoulder, her body resting against me, molding to mine perfectly, just the way I knew she would. Swiftly, I crossed the foyer, my own head lowered, not making eye contact with anyone. I drew in a deep breath and walked out the double doors, hurrying to the waiting car and ignoring the constant flash of cameras around us. Luckily, we were leaving early enough that they weren't prepared, and the shouting was minimal. All they saw was two people leaving—neither of our faces was recognizable.

The driver had the door open, and I slid into the back, keeping Shelby tight against me. "Go now," I instructed.

When the car moved forward, I breathed a sigh of relief, but I didn't relax my hold on Shelby. I nuzzled her fragrant hair, and she sighed against my chest. For a few moments, the car was silent. Shelby didn't move, and I didn't let her go. She felt right nestled in my arms. As if she belonged there.

Finally, she tilted her head back, and our eyes met. Hers were wide and wary as they met mine. The air around us grew heated and pulsated with emotion.

"Thank you," she breathed.

My voice was pitched low. "Why are you fighting this, Shelby? Fighting us? I know you feel this—how right this is for both of us."

She hesitated. "I'm scared."

"So am I. But I want this—I want you beside me in all things. I want to look after you the way you do for me. I'm willing to take the risk."

"I'm older than you."

I traced her soft cheek with my index finger. I threw her own words back at her. "Barely five years, Shelby—you're hardly cradle snatching. Five years is nothing. It means *nothing*."

"I'm still married. It could be a problem for you."

"Not by choice. We'll figure it out. We can figure anything out as long as it's what you want. Everett has people looking for your ex— the fucker is hiding like the cowardly, thieving wanker he is. If we don't locate him, you can get divorced without him present. It will happen."

"Your reputation..."

"Fuck that. I don't care."

"What if it doesn't work out?"

"What if it does?"

"The press and your life..."

I pulled her closer and kissed her forehead. "We'll handle it together, Shelby. If you let me, I want to be your partner—in everything. Stop throwing up roadblocks. Let me try. Give me a chance. Give us a chance." I met her eyes. "Let me in. Tell me you feel something."

Her voice was low and shaking with emotion when she answered. "I do, Liam. So much, it frightens me."

"It almost killed me to see you walk away from me to go out with Douglas," I confessed. "I don't want you to go out with anyone but me."

"I didn't want to go," she said. "I was confused, and I had all these feelings I didn't think I should have. Then when he asked, I thought I had to try to move past whatever it was, but..." She sighed. "All I could think of—all night—was you. The only place I wanted to be was with you." Her eyes were intense. "It's always you, Liam."

Our faces were close. I could feel her breath washing over me as we stared at each other. My hands tightened on her, bringing her even closer against me. "Try, then. Please," I begged.

"I work for you—I'm your housekeeper."

"Is that your last argument?"

"Um, yes?"

Her lips were almost touching mine. "Fine. You're fired," I murmured.

"Oh," she breathed.

And then I was kissing her.

But this time, she didn't push me away.

13

LIAM

Our mouths were on each other's the entire ride home. I couldn't get enough of her. Her lips were warm and pliant, her tongue like velvet, and her taste, perfect. Sweet and uniquely Shelby. I wanted to swallow the breath she shared with me and hold it in my lungs forever. I never wanted to be without the feel of her mouth moving beneath mine again. Her quiet whimpers and murmurs only made me hold her closer, kiss her deeper, and want her more.

When the car stopped, I regretfully pulled back, but I didn't let her leave my arms. I climbed out of the limo and walked into the house, cradling her. I had her tucked tight against my chest, her arms wrapped around my neck, only letting go long enough to unlock the door and disable the alarm. I carried her to my room, setting her on the vanity in the bathroom. I stood in front of her, my hands cupping her face as I kissed her again.

Our lips had been apart far too long.

"I have to look at your feet," I whispered against her mouth.

"Don't stop."

"Shelby. Let me take care of you."

She sighed in frustration, and I leered. "Addicted already?"

She giggled as I dropped a small kiss on the end of her nose. Then I eased off the socks I had covered her feet with earlier, grimacing at the blisters I saw all over her swollen flesh. Some had already ruptured and bled, while others were still forming and looked painful.

Fuck, they all looked bloody painful.

I filled the sink beside her with warm water, planning on soaking her feet and then bandaging them.

"The dress." She protested.

I groaned. I didn't care about the bloody dress. But I knew she did. "Take it off, then."

"Right here?"

"Shelby, I've seen you in a bathing suit. I think I can handle your underwear."

"Um—"

Chuckling, I shrugged out of my jacket and unbuttoned my shirt, yanking it off, leaving me in my undershirt. "You can put this on." I wrapped my arm around her. "Come on, I'll help you." Gently, I set her on the floor, my eyes following her hand as she pulled down the hidden zipper on her dress. The deep-red gown pooled at her feet, and I swallowed when I saw what was hiding underneath the satin.

Her bathing suit, I could handle.

This, I wasn't sure about.

Red. Lacy. Strapless.

A bustier.

My gaze drifted downward.

Tiny scraps of fabric tied at her hips in the same shade of red, leaving a tantalizing strip of soft flesh between the bustier and her underwear. A strip I wanted to lick.

And the underwear...tiny straps with bows that led to...

I shut my eyes as the room became far too small and far too hot. All the blood in my body was now pooled in one place.

My hard, aching cock.

Which was at that very moment trying to punch its way out of my pants to get to that red lace.

Bugger. Shit. Damn.

I gulped in air. Tried to think of anything else. Puppies. Worms. Everett in *his* underwear. Anything but the warm, red-lace-wearing woman in front of me.

Who was in pain and needed me to look after her.

Not lift her back onto the counter and fuck her until she screamed my name.

At least once.

Three or four times, preferably.

Her voice broke through my thoughts. "Liam?"

I blinked at her and handed her my shirt. I needed to rein myself in. "Put this on, Shelby, please."

With downcast eyes, she did as I asked. I realized she thought I wanted her to cover up for a different reason than I *needed* her to cover up. I cupped her cheek. "Hey."

Her hesitant gaze met mine. I covered her mouth with my lips, yanking her close. I pulled her hips against mine so she *knew* how she was affecting me. Her eyes flew open, meeting mine that were already staring at her—trying to convey a *hard* message. I smiled against her lips. "Just for now, Beaker. Or your feet won't be the only thing that's sore."

I set her back on the counter, keeping my eyes averted. She hissed in pain as I placed her feet in the warm water. I grimaced in understanding. "Sorry. Now, where can I find bandages?"

"My bathroom has a first aid kit. Left cupboard by the vanity."

"Okay, stay here."

"Where else am I gonna go?"

I hesitated. "I'm not gonna have to touch...other things to get to the kit thing, am I?"

She smirked. "Other things, Liam?"

I rubbed the back of my neck. "Um...your girl...things, Shelby?"

"No, you're quite safe." She winked. "Just make sure you open the left cupboard. Not the right."

"Right."

"No, left."

"Bloody hell, don't confuse me! I don't have a lot of blood in that particular head right now!"

Her amusement followed me down the hall.

It was music to my ears.

SHELBY

I watched him leave, unable to believe what was happening. His reaction to me. Mine to him.

The entire evening had been torture. Liam had looked devastatingly handsome as he'd waited for me at the bottom of the stairs, and he'd seemed anxious all night, refusing to let go of my hand. Every chance he got, he wanted to walk or dance with me. I didn't have the heart to tell him how sore my feet were. When I realized I had kept the wrong shoe size but had to wear them anyway, I knew I would end up with some nasty blisters, but I hadn't expected how painful it would be. My feet must have swollen as well because the leather was digging in everywhere, and I knew the heels were rubbed raw. Every step felt like my feet were on fire.

When he saw what happened, his reaction was unexpected. I had never seen that "take-charge" side of Liam. My shoes were discarded without a thought, and he covered the sore flesh with his own socks, ignoring my protests. When he lifted me into his arms, I gave up. His hold was firm, his expression fierce in its protectiveness as he instructed me to keep my head down. Once in the car, he didn't lessen his hold, and when I finally looked at him, what I saw in his eyes made my heart race.

Open adoration and pleading. There was nothing but want and love in his gaze. No one had ever looked at me that way.

Liam's quiet, honest words had broken through my fast crumbling walls.

His warm embrace promised shelter, love.

All the things I felt were issues, he dismissed. What I saw as insurmountable, he saw as things we would work through—together.

His insistence of how right we were made me understand how deeply he *did* care.

When his lips found mine, firm, warm, and possessive, I surrendered. I knew in that moment, I wanted this. I wanted him—I wanted it all. Forever.

I was home.

Liam was my home.

His arms were my safe haven.

And I never wanted to be without them or him ever again.

I was anxious for him to come back. I wanted more of his touch. His care. His kisses. I wanted him to make me laugh again. No one made me laugh the way Liam did. I loved his way of looking at the world. He wasn't jaded and bitter the way many people in Hollywood were. He was sunny and warm.

He was Liam.

I heard his hurried footsteps and met his anxious eyes as he barreled into the bathroom.

"Good. You stayed put."

"Not much choice, Oscar."

"Bloody feet aside, Beaker, can I say you looking smashing in my shirt sitting on my bathroom counter?"

I smiled at the sincere tone of his voice. He stared at me, his feelings no longer hidden. Desire, blatant and hot, poured from his expression. It warmed me all over.

"Yes."

He cleared his throat. "All right. Let's get you fixed up."

LIAM

I finished wrapping her feet and sat back. It wasn't the best job, but I had smothered them in antibiotic ointment, and they were covered. "There."

"Thank you."

I stood with my arms leaning on the counter, caging her in. "No more high heels. I don't give a bloody fuck what Lily says looks good."

"She won't be happy."

"I'll handle her."

"They'll heal. It was my fault—"

I placed my finger on her lips. "No more. You hate high heels, and I can't stand to see you in pain."

Our eyes locked, apologetic blue meeting firm green. She nodded in silent agreement. I pressed my finger against her mouth harder, and her lips parted, the warm breath flowing over my skin. I dropped my hand to her waist and pulled her forward. "Now, where were we before your feet got in the way?"

She giggled and pushed on my chest. "I should go to bed."

My lips brushed her ear. "My thoughts exactly."

She shivered. "Liam." Her voice was low and pleading. "It's too..."

"Fast?" I finished for her.

Her eyes begged me to understand. I cupped the back of her head gently. "I know, Shelby. But I don't want to let you go. Not yet." I brought her closer. "Stay with me tonight. Just sleep with me. Let me hold you."

She hesitated. "I have to brush my teeth—and I need to change." She indicated her red-covered torso. "I don't think this is the most comfortable thing to sleep in."

"No. You should definitely take that off. I could help you with that." I grinned as I watched the dull color creep over her chest, and she began to look nervous.

"I'll loan you a T-shirt." I kissed her cheek, nuzzling her skin. "I'll behave, Shelby. Stay?"

"Okay," she whispered.

"Don't move," I instructed, chuckling at her sudden shyness. "I'll get you a shirt."

She pointed to my chest. "I can wear that one."

"You don't want a fresh one?"

Her color deepened. "No. That one will smell like you."

I looked down and grinned, pulling it over my head and handing it to her with a wink.

After gathering the jacket, I went to my room where I removed what was left of the tux, hung it up, and pulled on some sleep pants, forgoing a shirt, then returned to the bathroom.

She was still on the counter, but now in my T-shirt, her hair down and makeup gone. A damp flannel sat on the counter beside her.

My Shelby was back. Effortlessly lovely.

She grinned at me as she put down a facecloth, her expression mischievous. Unable to resist, I leaned over and kissed her.

"Why is your breath minty?"

"I used your toothbrush."

I plucked the still-wet toothbrush from the holder and smirked at her. "Bit dodgy, that, Beaker."

"I wanted to brush my teeth. I couldn't move. You said so."

"I see." I arched my eyebrow at her. "Well."

Her eyes widened as she watched me add toothpaste and use the same brush, never taking my eyes off her. When I was finished, I smacked my lips and grinned at her. "Now we match."

She whimpered.

I pulled her closer.

"You want me to behave, or can I be slightly...naughty?" I nipped her ear gently, tugging on the lobe.

"Ah..."

"Just a wee bit naughty, Shelby?" Using my tongue, I swirled a wet pattern on her skin.

"Oh...*God*... Naughty, Liam. *Please*."

I gathered her off the counter and strode into my room.

"Brilliant."

She was so bloody right in my bed. Small and warm and incredibly sexy. She fit against me perfectly. Her quiet noises were addictive, and I knew I didn't want to be without them again. Her hands tugged on my hair, holding me close as my mouth worked hers. She tasted like...*more*.

I wanted more.

I wanted all of her.

My hands delved under the T-shirt she was wearing, finding warm, silky skin. I dragged her closer as I ran my fingers under the tiny straps of the sexy red thong she was still wearing.

For now.

I wanted it off.

I tugged gently, feeling the thin material start to give way. I kissed her harder. Pulled again.

This time, it broke, and I caressed the warm, bare skin of her hip, bending my hand around to cup the plump curve of her ass.

Shelby gasped into my mouth, pulling back.

"Whoops," I breathed against her lips.

"Liam... I'm... I'm not—"

I sighed and buried my face in her neck. She wasn't ready.

Of course she wasn't.

I already had her married to me and in my bed forever even though she only admitted to having feelings for me two hours ago. Of course she wasn't ready.

I pressed my lips to her cheek in apology. "I know. I got carried away."

I rolled over, taking her with me, and she curled into my side, her head on my chest. Her fingers traced lazy patterns on my skin, their gentle warmth a calming sensation. "I'm sorry," she whispered.

"No," I insisted. "I understand, Shelby. I'll wait until you're ready. I'll wait as long as you need me to." I pressed a kiss to her forehead. "Simply being able to hold you is bloody amazing."

"I just need some time to adjust."

"I know." I ran my hand through her hair, loving the feeling of the thick tresses against my palm. I had to remember that for the first time ever in our relationship, I was ahead of her. "Sleep. Just let me hold you and sleep."

I felt her lips press to my chest. I kept stroking her hair until I felt her grow heavy with sleep. Only when I knew she was resting did I let myself fall asleep.

Holding her.

Bloody perfect.

I woke alone. I threw my arm over my face, groaning.

Where was she?

She'd been warm and close all night. Every time I woke up, she was there beside me, and I would pull her closer, needing to feel her pressed against me. She made me realize I was a cuddler.

And dammit, I wanted to wake up cuddling her.

I sat up, huffing. How was she even walking?

I flung back the covers, and grabbed a shirt, making my way downstairs where I could hear movement.

She was standing at the counter, some sort of kitchen utensil in her hand. She had the cheek to smile at me as I stalked toward her.

"Did I not fire you last night?"

"Yes. But I decided I needed an exit interview, so I gave myself back my job once the interview was over. I decided I deserved a second chance. I've been a great employee."

My lips quirked at her words. "You've been exemplary, Shelby, I'll give you that. But one question?"

"Yes?"

"Did the old you inform the new you that your boss not only encourages dating him, but also insists on it?"

"Oh yes, that came up."

My smile couldn't be contained now. I wrapped my arms around her waist, pulling her against me. "Why don't you put down the damn spatula, and I'll take you upstairs so we can discuss something else that has 'come up,' Shelby?"

"Oh, for fuck's sake," Everett huffed behind me.

Bloody hell, when did he get here?

Shelby grinned at me. "We have company."

"You might have warned me."

She giggled. "You were too busy being...bossy."

I leaned down, my lips at her ear. "I'll show you bossy when we're alone." I nipped the tender skin, smiling at the feel of her shudder.

She gasped as I picked her up and set her on the counter.

"What are you doing?"

"Looking at your feet." I turned to Everett. "Did you see this mess?"

He came over, and we both grimaced at the red welts and missing skin on her toes and heels. Everett whistled. "Nice job, Beaker."

"Shut it."

"Are you in pain?" I asked.

She shook her head. "They're much better this morning. I won't be able to wear shoes with backs for a few days, but they'll be fine." She pushed at my chest. "Can I get back to breakfast, please?" She hesitated. "I'm not really fired—am I?"

Everett snorted as he grabbed the coffeepot. "Like he could do without you."

I winked at her. "What he said."

"Okay."

I lifted her off the counter. "We'll figure it out, Shelby. Promise."

She nodded. "I know."

I took the cup of coffee from her and went to sit with Everett.

How we'd work it out, I wasn't sure.

But I knew we had to.

Everett was right—I couldn't do without her.

Ever.

14

LIAM

Shelby sat beside me, and I pulled her chair closer. I felt better when she was near. Using one hand, I picked up the bagel she had given me, while I laced our fingers together with my free hand. I also liked touching her.

Everett snorted. "Okay. Listen up. Cassidy and I have both checked, but so far, you're safe. You were recognized, Liam, and they have pictures of you two, but Shelby's face is unknown from the first night, and last night—" he winked at Shelby "—your face was buried in his neck." He chuckled. "You've been dubbed 'The mysterious Lady in Red.' You're the same woman who's shown up on Liam's arm two times in a row. Not known to the press—a mystery. They're starting to ask some questions, so things are going to change." He took a sip of his coffee as he regarded us. "I'm assuming from the display I was forced to witness and the hand-holding, the two of you have pulled your heads out of your asses and decided to explore a relationship?"

I paused before taking another bite. "I don't know about Shelby, Everett, but I assure you my head has never been 'up my arse,' as you so quaintly put it. It may have taken us a bit to get here, but it wasn't as if we were hiding from our feelings."

"I said ass, Liam."

I shook my head. "You people hurt my head. Always butchering the Queen's English. Shameful."

He looked at me like I was crazy as Shelby shifted beside me. "Whatever. Are you prepared for this media circus?"

"They can take their pictures. I can't stop them, but I'm not commenting on my personal life." It had always been my one, unbreakable rule.

He narrowed his eyes at me. "It's not you I'm worried about, Liam."

I started to argue with him, but Shelby interrupted me. "What should I be prepared for?"

Everett crossed his arms over his chest as he gathered his thoughts together. I could almost see the wheels spinning in his head.

Shelby sighed. "Just spit it out, Ev. I'm not a child."

He shrugged his shoulders as if to say fine and hunched forward, his voice earnest. "You've been pretty isolated so far. But that's going to change now that you're in a relationship with Liam. Maybe not right away, but soon enough. You're a challenge now. They will find out who you are, Shelby. And not just the fact that you're my sister." He drew in a deep breath. "They'll know you work for Liam. The fact that you're older and still married will also come up. The press will have a field day with that information. They'll find out you lost your last job and somehow twist that to make you look bad. It'll run the gamut—you're after Liam for his money, or you seduced him to get ahead in this business. They'll come up with a hundred and one false scenarios."

"Because the truth is boring?"

"They aren't interested in the truth. They're interested in selling papers. I know you've only been an observer until now, but that role is gone. You're smack-dab in the middle of it. They're gonna follow you. Take pictures. Yell things at you to get a reaction. They'll want to know everything about you."

Shelby stiffened, and I squeezed her hand.

"But why do they care?" she questioned. "They don't print things when Carly or Gillian go to a function with him. Or even any of his other dates."

"There are a few stories, Shelby. Maybe not big ones, but there are mentions. Gillian and Carly are old news. But you're brand-spanking new."

Shelby's face paled.

"You're scaring her, Ev," I hissed, wrapping my arm around her and drawing her closer.

"I don't want to scare you. But I need you to be prepared." He took Shelby's hand in his. "Cassidy and I will help you, coach you. And Liam will be there for you, but it's not an easy thing, being involved with a celebrity. I need to try to make sure you understand what you're getting into."

Shelby nodded, her voice quiet when she spoke. "It wasn't easy to let him in, Ev."

He smiled at her, the smile of genuine affection and understanding only a brother could bestow. "I know."

My eyes flew between them. It was as if they forgot I was even in the room. I felt as if I should leave and let them talk, but I didn't want to. I didn't want Ev convincing Shelby she was better off without me.

"We'll protect her together, Ev," I offered quietly. "I don't want to see her hurt either. But I can't lose her." I met his gaze. "I only just found her."

Shelby's warm eyes found mine. "We found each other," she whispered.

I pulled her back and kissed her, losing myself to the taste of her mouth and the warm scent she surrounded me in. She grounded me.

God, I needed her.

Everett cleared his throat, causing Shelby to startle and move back. I glared at him.

Bloody hell, why was he still here?

I must have muttered that out loud because they both chuckled.

The intercom buzzed.

Brilliant.

More people.

Everett stood. "No doubt, that's Cassidy. And Lily is due anytime. She said something about an urgent message from you." He paused. "I assume the shoe incident?"

I dipped my chin in affirmation. Shelby huffed in frustration.

"Okay. You have the charity dinner on Tuesday, Liam. It's the last black-tie one for a while."

"Thank God."

He looked at us. "Lots of press for this one. It's huge. We need to be ready." He eyed me knowingly. "For everything."

"Right."

"And Saturday is the library benefit. It's in the late afternoon, and it's more casual."

"Great."

"Still a suit, Liam. Shelby needs a cocktail dress. Lily knows. Not jeans."

Great. Another bloody suit. I wondered briefly if I could convince Lily no tie at least.

Everett frowned at me. "You got it?"

"Yes."

"You leave next week for some preproduction work. I've got your flights and security booked. I'll look into added security for the house while you're gone."

"Okay." Simply the thought of leaving Shelby made me unhappy.

The buzzer went again, and I scowled at him. I needed some time with Shelby; I didn't like the way she was acting. She was far too quiet.

He arched his eyebrow at me as he stood. "I'll give you a minute. I'll be in the den with Cassidy and Lily."

Finally.

Shelby walked over to the counter, her hand on the coffeepot handle, but she didn't move. My heart sank. We had barely started and now Everett had her questioning if we should keep going. I got up and pulled her into my arms. "Don't, Shelby. Please. Don't question how right we are together. We're going to be bloody brilliant."

"I could become an embarrassment to you," she whispered, not looking at me.

I slipped my fingers under her chin, forcing her to meet my eyes. "Impossible. I don't care what stories they come up with. What stupid headlines they print. I know you. The real you. That's *all* that matters to me or anyone I care about. Bloody hell, my mum loves you, and she's never even *liked* any other girl I introduced her to." Seeing the look on Shelby's face, I backpedaled. "Not that there've been many of those."

Shelby rolled her eyes and frowned. "She liked me as your housekeeper. How is she going to feel about me as your, um, girlfriend?"

I grinned. Girlfriend. I liked that. A lot.

"She's been after me to make you my girlfriend since she was here last, Shelby. She's going to be thrilled. And aside from that—I don't give a toss about what the rest of the world has to say or think." I smiled sadly at her. "Maybe I'm too much for you to take on, though? Things will change, I know that. I've been lucky lately, sneaking around unnoticed, but with the movie coming out and more press, it's going to get crazy. They'll be everywhere."

Her eyes widened. "No! I want this, Liam. I want you. I'm just worried—"

I cut her off with my mouth, kissing her deeply. As long as she wanted this, we'd make it work.

Because I wanted her—desperately.

Lily looked horrified as she studied Shelby's feet. "You should have called me. I would have gotten the other shoes to you somehow. Your poor feet!"

Shelby looked down, embarrassed, and then in a vain attempt to take the attention off herself, pointed her finger at me. "He threw them out. They were perfectly fine, and he tossed them!"

Lily started to laugh, as did I. Neither of us cared if I pitched the bloody shoes in the rubbish bin. I pressed a kiss to Shelby's head. "Nice try."

I looked at Lily. "Low heels this time."

She pursed her lips. "They're not as elegant."

"Surely to God, you can find decent shoes without six-inch heels on them, Lily." I lifted up Shelby's foot. "Or ones that don't do this to a person's flesh. Heels be damned. I want her comfortable. Find some."

Lily's face was shocked, and I realized I had never before *ordered* her to do something. I started to apologize when she winked at me.

"Hot, Liam. All bossy for your woman." She sat and opened her computer. "I'll see what I can do."

Shelby stared at me as I winked at her. "I'll leave you to it, then." I strode out of the kitchen, pausing at the door. "And Lily?"

She looked up.

"I want her in red. Both events."

I walked out grinning, listening to them snicker.

God, I loved her in red.

I let myself into the quiet house. It had been a long day, filled with Everett and Cassidy and strategies about what my relationship with Shelby would entail. I had been impatient with them both, even though I knew they were right. I hated the fact that because I cared about someone, their life would be open for scrutiny. Especially Shelby. I didn't want her hurt.

143

Shelby had been busy with Lily, and when we finally got some time alone, she looked so tired, I had to reformulate my plans of some heavy snogging on the sofa. Instead, we ended up cuddling and having a nap, which was surprisingly satisfying. I did like how she felt in my arms, but when I woke up, I had to head out to another dinner meeting with Everett, which dragged on endlessly. I ran a hand through my hair in frustration. Some of these Hollywood people liked to hear themselves talk—a lot.

I was home now, and I wanted Shelby beside me. Hurrying up the stairs, I pushed open my door in anticipation, stopping at the sight of an empty bed.

Where was she?

I took the next flight of stairs two at a time. Shelby's door was ajar, and I opened it slowly, gazing silently at what I saw.

Shelby was asleep, her book fallen on her lap and her sexy glasses barely on her nose. Her head was propped on her shoulder, her long hair falling over her chest. I grinned when I saw she was wearing one of my T-shirts. The rush of tenderness I only ever felt when looking at her filled me. I moved forward quietly, pulling off her glasses and awkwardly trying to settle her into a more comfortable position. I had never looked after anyone before, but I wanted to look after Shelby.

Her eyes fluttered open. "Liam?" she mumbled sleepily.

"Hey." I pushed back her hair from her face. "Of course it's me. You were expecting someone else, Beaker? Another charming Brit? Prince Harry, maybe?"

She giggled and yawned as she curled into a ball. "No, I only like one Brit. Most charming of them all."

"Bloody right."

"Why are you in my room?"

I nuzzled her cheek. "You weren't in my bed waiting for me, so I came to find you."

She blinked. "I didn't know if you wanted that."

I moved my lips to her forehead. "I always want you there now, Shelby. But you're tired. Sleep. I only wanted to check on you."

Smiling, she moved over. "I have room."

I didn't need another invitation. I threw off my clothes, leaving only my boxers, and slipped in beside her. I wrapped my arms around her, loving how she curled against me, her head buried in my neck. She fell back to sleep fast, and I listened to her even breathing, letting the quiet rhythm lull me into the same restful state.

I nuzzled Shelby's neck. She smelled so bloody good. With her hair up and her lovely skin on display, I couldn't resist. I knew I should. Everett was right. Walking in, the flashes and yelling had been unrelenting. Although we never stopped, or even paused for an interview, the photographers and paps had all gotten our picture together. I didn't care. I knew we were being watched now as well and pictures were even being taken, but, again, I didn't care.

"Liam," Shelby warned, but her voice wasn't much of a deterrent. It sounded breathy and wanting. I smiled against her warmth. I was affecting her as well. I wanted her. After waking up together Sunday morning, the hours since had been one long, painful session of foreplay. She was gone when I woke in the mornings, and we were both so busy that when I did see her, some cuddles and a few kisses were all we shared. I hated having so many appointments and meetings that I was pulled away from her constantly throughout the day.

I was ready for more. I felt like if I didn't shag her soon, my head would explode. One of them, for sure.

Shelby was everywhere. I could hear her voice and her sweet laughter all over the house. Her scent soaked into the air and swirled around me as I tried to work. Every time I walked into the kitchen, I could feel her stare. Every time we were close, I had to touch her. Her lips called to me. Her body beckoned. I was going crazy with lust. But we were never alone. It was like our house was suddenly Grand Central Terminal for everyone in our lives. Why, I had no bloody idea. I was sure they were all doing it on purpose. Torturing me, those buggers.

And then, tonight.

She was a siren. Lily dressed her in a sleek, red, formfitting dress, once again leaving a shoulder glistening and bare. My grandmother's earrings caught the light as her head moved. The bracelet was back on her wrist. Twinkling on the red at her shoulder was a diamond brooch I had pinned on her before we left. I had marked her with my tokens of my affection. She thought they were on loan, but in my heart, they already belonged to her. Just like me.

And she *was* mine.

Everyone here knew it.

Shelby's hand pushed on my chest. I pulled back, not at all embarrassed at having my passion witnessed. I dropped one more kiss on her neck. "Tonight, Shelby. Tonight, you're *mine*. Completely."

She shivered.

I grinned.

We ate, talked, smiled, and never once was there a time I wasn't touching her. My leg was firmly pressed against hers. Whenever possible, I found her small hand with mine and stroked her skin slowly. When speaking to someone else at the table, I casually leaned back in my chair, my arm draped around the back of hers, my finger gently teasing the skin on her shoulder, causing the most delightful shudders to race through her, making me smirk. Douglas sat at our table, his eyes crinkling with amusement as he watched us. He chatted, his companion that evening his manager, Henri. I smiled when Shelby told Douglas that her friend, Caroline, who she thought would be perfect for him, was coming to visit soon. He nodded silently, no doubt playing along with her suggestions with no intent on following them through. I was pretty sure Douglas had no plans for a long-term relationship at this point.

By the time the speeches, presentations, and donations were done, so was I. I had done my duty, and my debt to the studio was paid. I needed Shelby alone—I was finished sharing. I needed her pressed against me, and this time, I didn't plan on stopping. I was locking the doors, setting the security override, shutting off the phone, and then nobody and nothing was coming between us.

After saying our goodnights, I looked through the window at the crowd below. I pulled Shelby to my side and indicated the constant flashes. There were a large number of celebrities here coming and going by this point, and the paps were out in full force. I cupped her cheek in comfort. "Maybe I should get the car to the back."

She shook her head, although her voice sounded nervous. "I'm fine. Unless it's easier for you…"

"No." I refused to allow them to dictate my life. I wasn't ashamed to be seen with Shelby. As long as she could handle it, we would face it together. It was going to happen one way or another, so it might as well be on our terms. I wrapped my arm around her waist. "Just keep walking with your head down. Ignore the flashes. Ignore the shit they yell. Do not react, no matter what they say or shout. They're doing it to get your reaction. Don't give it to them. Just hold on to me. Don't let go, and don't stop. Mark will run interference."

"Okay."

"Ready?"

She drew in a deep breath, and I tightened my hold.

"Yes."

The flashes were almost blinding. Loud voices shouting my name came from all directions. I kept my eyes focused on Mark's back, following closely. Beside me, I felt Shelby stiffen and push herself closer to my side, turning her face away from the lights. It was worse than I thought it would be, and I knew if I was finding it loud, she must be overwhelmed. They were in a frenzy to get a reaction. Strangely, I remained calm, knowing Shelby needed my guidance and strength. I knew Mark wouldn't let anyone close to us—it was simply a matter of ignoring the noise.

By the time we made it to the car, Shelby's head was buried in my neck, and she was shaking. Once safely inside, I pulled her onto my lap, holding her close.

"Sorry, Beaker," I mumbled, pressing my lips to her hair. "All right there?"

She nodded against my shoulder, and I let her rest there and gather her thoughts as we finally cleared the area and the car picked up speed. At least we weren't being followed.

"It'll get better," I assured her. "Like Everett said, this is new. Someone or something else will get their attention." I gathered her closer. "It's like a wave, Shelby. It will crest and ease off, but we have to ride it out. Don't let it scare you away, please."

She tilted her head, and she offered me a shaky smile. "It was...loud."

"It was."

"Are they always that obnoxious?"

"Unfortunately, yes. There's a group of them that will do anything for a reaction. You have to ignore them, as hard as it is sometimes. We'll keep Mark close for the time being. And I think maybe Everett and Cassidy will come with us the next couple of appearances. No one messes with your brother."

"Do you think it will die down that quickly?"

"I don't know," I replied honestly. "It depends..."

"They're going to have a field day with the fact that I'm married."

"You're not married—there is a separation on file. Your ex deserted you, and you'll be divorced as soon as we find him or move to the next step," I stated firmly. "One of those will happen soon. Everett already has a statement prepared. It's covered."

"My age..." she whispered.

"Is not an issue for me. Case closed."

She sighed. "Well then, I guess we can only hope there is some big scandal, or an actor gets caught fucking a goat to take the heat off us, right?"

I burst out laughing. "There's *always* a scandal, Beaker. But the goat might work."

She cupped my cheek. "I'm not going anywhere."

I huffed a sigh of relief. "Good."

"But I need something."

"Anything."

"I need you. Tonight. Make it all go away, but you. *Us.*"

My mouth covered hers. "Yes. *Fuck...*yes."

If I thought Shelby was sexy the other night in her red corset, the sight of her tonight in front of me, in a lacy, barely there bra, almost did me in. I wanted to fall at her feet and worship her. Thoroughly. From the nervous look on her face, as she stood in front of me, biting her lip, I decided that was exactly what needed to be done. Keeping eye contact, I slowly sank to my knees in front of her. Gently, I pulled off the low-heeled, Liam-approved shoes, running my thumbs along her instep, smirking at her low moan as I placed her bare feet on the floor. I ran my hands up her legs, tickling the backs of her knees as she giggled, her muscles bunching against my fingers. Her eyes widened as I stroked higher, finally cupping her firm ass and pulling her toward me. I kissed her stomach as I stared at her, spreading my hands wide against the skin of her back. Her chest moved rapidly while the air around us grew heated as I stood, drawing her close. My mouth hovered over hers. "Tell me you want this, Shelby, please."

"I do," she whispered. "And I'm covered. Birth control-wise. I got tested after Malcolm..." Her voice trailed off.

I nodded in understanding. "It's been months—longer—for me. I was tested, and I'm clean too."

"Then we're good."

"Yeah," I agreed. "Good. Brilliant."

I crashed my mouth to hers, our kiss desperate and needy. She pushed and tugged off my jacket as I made quick work of the pretty red scrap of lace covering her breasts. Small clicks of buttons hitting the floor and bouncing off the dresser made me smile as Shelby pulled off my dress shirt impatiently.

"Easy, tiger," I growled against her mouth, lifting her from the pool of red at her feet and carrying her to the bed. My bed. Placing her in the middle, I stood back, grinning at the sight before me.

Shelby, naked except for the wisp of lace that covered her center, her dark hair spread across the pillows. My pillows. Her chest was heaving, her nipples erect and begging for my mouth. Her cheeks were flushed and her eyes glazed as she watched me shrug out of what was left of my shirt and loosen my belt, letting my pants drop to the floor. She bit her lip when she realized I was once again commando.

"Like what you see?" I teased her.

Her eyes widened. "You're...you're *uncircumcised*. You have a hoodie, Liam."

I looked down. *Was this a problem?* I was British after all.

"Shelby?"

"I've never...um, never seen or..."

Oh. *OH*.

Grinning, I stroked myself. "Nothing to be scared of. Just a little extra skin."

She arched her eyebrow at me sexily. "You got a lot of extra...*skin*...there."

I waggled my eyebrows back at her. "I got a lot of extra everything, baby. All for you."

She whimpered.

"You want to be introduced to all my, ah, skin, Shelby?"

She arched her back, pushing out her rosy-tipped breasts. "Yes. I'd like it closer."

Groaning, I stepped away from my pants and let her see how much I wanted to be closer as well. My cock was already weeping, aching to be buried inside her. I wrapped my hand back around my knob, slowly stroking it, teasing her. "How much closer, baby?"

Shelby rose and grabbed my arm, pulling me to her as she slid off the bed. Now she was the one looking at me, eyes locked—her expression one of raging passion. "This close," she murmured, wrapping her lips around me and drawing my dick into the warm wetness of her mouth.

Jesus.

My eyes rolled back in my head at the unexpected pleasure.

Fuck.

I buried my hands in her hair as she worked me.

Tongue. Lips. Teeth.

Licking. Sucking. Nibbling.

Her hands gripped my ass as she hummed and swallowed, the sensations driving me crazy as I hissed, moaning and bucking deeper into her mouth.

She might not have any experience with "hoodies," as she called them, but *dammit*, my girl was a fast learner.

She was far too good at this, and as much as I wanted her never to stop, she had to.

Now.

"Shelby, baby, stop," I pleaded. "Please."

She pulled back, her lips wet and swollen. "Why?" she whispered, her tongue slowly curling up my shaft, teasing and swirling the engorged head she had tenderly exposed. "You didn't like that?"

"Bloody hell, it was smashing, that was," I panted.

"Why do you want me to stop, then?" she breathed out as her lips grazed the sensitive head.

I shuddered and pulled her to her feet. "I want inside you."

Her eyes darkened even further as she lay down, her arms outstretched. "I'm waiting."

I was all over her. I licked and nipped at her creamy skin as I caressed and fondled her. I tore off the last piece of clothing separating us, pulling her legs apart as I slipped my fingers into her wetness, causing her to gasp and arch closer to my touch. I teased and caressed, kissing her, drawing out her passion until she was writhing and pleading. Needing me buried in her as deeply as I wanted to be. Slipping between her legs, I gazed at her. She was so beautiful as she stared at me, desire and longing etched in her expression. Her eyes pleaded as her body shook with desire. As desperate as I was for her, I needed her to know, to understand. This wasn't just sex for me. Not this. Not her.

I trailed my finger down her cheek. "I love you, Shelby."

I covered her mouth with mine as I buried myself inside her. We both stilled for a moment, our eyes wide and open as the feeling of being joined so intimately raced through us.

Nothing could compare to this moment.

Nothing would ever be the same.

There would never be anyone else for me.

Shelby's voice was pleading. "Now, Liam...God...*please*...now..."

With a low groan, I began to move. Deeper and deeper, I slipped inside her. Our hands grasped together, our lips pressing and sharing deep, wet, open-mouthed kisses as our voices whispered and moaned while we rocked and trembled, loved and fucked.

Watching her come was spellbinding. Hearing my name in her breathy, longing voice as she locked down around me sent me over the edge. I moaned her name into the damp, fragrant skin of her neck, panting as my orgasm twisted and turned, burning me with the intensity of the feeling.

I gathered Shelby into my arms, holding her tight. I was too overcome to speak, and for moments, the room was quiet except for the sound of our deep breathing. Shelby's lips ghosted over my chest, the sensations like a butterfly alighting on my skin. I ran my hand through her dark hair, my caresses gentle and light. It was as if the intense, burning passion had faded to a warm, downy blanket of emotion that wrapped around us. I had never experienced anything like it. I never wanted to be without it again.

I nuzzled her forehead, smiling as she gazed at me. "Ta, Beaker."

She smiled the way I knew she would. She loved it when I said "ta."

She traced my lips with her finger. "Wow."

I grinned against her touch. "Bloody right, wow." I pulled in her finger, sucking it gently, swirling my tongue around the digit as I stared at her intently. Nipping the end, I released it with a kiss as she stared back at me. I grinned at the look of sudden desire that crept back into her eyes and pushed myself up, keeping my weight on my elbows as I hovered over her. My lips trailed up her neck, my tongue bathing her skin roughly. "Advantage of dating a younger man, Shelby." I nipped at her lobe playfully. "We're..." *bite* "always..." *lick* "ready..." *kiss* "for..." *nip* "the..." *nuzzle* "next..." *thrust* "round."

The way her arms draped around my neck, pulling me to her, it appeared she was as well.

Brilliant.

15

LIAM

"You should turn on your phone," Shelby murmured from her spot in my arms. "I'm sure Ev has been trying to call. It's almost two in the afternoon."

I kissed her damp shoulder, running my lips up her neck, loving the shiver that went through her whole body. "Not happening. I'll turn it back on tomorrow."

She leaned her head against my shoulder. "I'm surprised he hasn't shown up."

I smirked down at her. "He might have. I changed the passcodes on the gate and the house. He can't get in." I tilted up her chin, dropping a kiss on her tempting lips. "I'm not ready to share you again. Not yet. I want you to myself today. He and the rest of the world can bloody well wait."

She nestled back into me with a quiet sigh. "Okay."

Cupping my hands, I filled them with water, dripping it down over her shoulders, watching as it ran past her collarbone and over her breasts. Smiling, I cradled them, stroking her nipples, watching as they pebbled under my touch. I loved how responsive she was to me.

I hadn't stopped touching her since we got home. We made love twice in the night, once this morning, then I shagged her in the kitchen—totally interrupting her attempts to make us something to eat. I bent her over the counter, taking her roughly as she screamed my name. I couldn't help it—she was wearing my shirt from last night, most of the buttons missing and the ends tied loosely around her hips. And a pair of my boxers. She said it was because I tore hers off; I was certain she wore them deliberately, knowing what it would do to me. What did she expect as she stood there looking all tousled and sexy?

I had no choice.

Afterward, we sat on the floor, feeding each other the remnants of the meal she'd tried to make. Finally taking pity on her, I drew a warm bath and slipped in behind her, content simply to hold her, feeling her close.

Until she moved once too often, brushing up against my ever-hardening cock.

Although I never had much, I had lost whatever control I might have possessed over my own willy. It was as if he had a fucking mind of his own, and it was centered on Shelby completely. Her pussy was his own drug of choice, and now that he'd had a taste, he was addicted. Big-time.

I brushed her ear with my mouth, my voice a low rumble. "Shelby, I know you have to be sore. We've been going at it for hours. Either stop moving, or I won't be responsible for what happens next."

She chuckled, the sound feminine and knowing. "I think you'd be totally responsible. I think you'd be happy to claim responsibility."

I groaned as she crowded against me. "My dick wants to shag you...again."

She pressed her lips against my throat, scraping my skin lightly with her teeth. "Poor OJ."

"OJ?"

There was another nip followed by a giggle. "Oscar Junior."

I pulled her close, letting my hard dick press against her. "May I remind you, Beaker, there is nothing *junior* about my cock?"

Her breathing picked up, and she panted against my neck.

"Yes, Liam...remind me." She lifted over me, then slammed down on my aching erection, causing the water to rise and spill over the edge of the tub, hitting the floor like a small waterfall. "Remind me *hard*."

I hissed as she repeated the action. There wouldn't be any water left in the tub if we kept this up. And I was okay with that. We had lots of towels.

So, once again, I gave in. I had no choice. It was two against one.

OJ and Shelby.

What a team.

I was so fucked.

Thank God.

"Liam, are you listening?"

I tore my eyes away from Shelby and looked at Everett. He was frowning at me, and I searched my brain, trying to remember what he had been talking about. I'd finally turned on my phone and reset the security code so he could once again get through the gates. He wasn't overly happy with me when he got here and couldn't gain access to the house or when he saw the rumpled state of both his sister and me. It wasn't my fault she looked so sexy making coffee I had to snog her until he showed up. He should have arrived faster.

I nodded. "Excellent. Right. Next week."

He sighed. "You'll be gone for a week, back for a week, then you need to head to New York for a few days for another location shoot, and then you're home for the rest of the filming. I'm still working with the studio about your promotion schedule for the release of *Nighthawk*."

My gaze drifted back to Shelby. Her head was bent over her laptop as she typed away, her hair falling over her shoulder in dark waves. The late sunlight streaming in behind her caused a burnished glow around her head. I thought about how soft her hair was, how thick it felt when my hands were buried in it, kissing her, shagging her, or when her mouth was wrapped around...

"Liam!" Everett slammed his hand on the table.

I snapped my gaze back to him. "Back home. Brilliant."

He narrowed his eyes. "Stop eye-fucking my sister. We need to go over this entire schedule. Give it a break, and concentrate."

I *was* eye-fucking her again. I couldn't help it; she was far too irresistible when she was that close to me. I smirked at him. "Well, if you'd leave, I'd stop the eye-fucking and commence with the real—"

He threw up his hands. "That's my sister! Jesus! Shut up!"

I grinned. "Aye. *Your* sister. Not mine."

He groaned, dropping his head into his hands. Shelby looked over at us, a smile curving her lips. "Liam, behave. Stop freaking Everett out."

I winked at her. "It's fun."

"Oscar." Her voice held a warning tone.

"Fine," I huffed. "I'll behave. Now, where were we?"

Everett pulled out a file. "They got a lot of pictures of you two the other night. Clear ones. They're now scrambling to find out who Shelby is—that's three times in a row she's been out in public with you." He pushed the file toward me. "It's only a matter of time."

I looked through the file. They were clear—innocuous for the most part. My arm around her, walking into the building. The two of us smiling at each other as we walked. A couple of grainier ones inside. The ones of us leaving, our heads lowered, Mark in front of us as we headed to the car. The last one I paused at and studied closely. It was taken before we left the building, obviously with a zoom lens. I was talking to Shelby, my hand cupping her face as I instructed her what I needed her to do when we left. She was gazing up at me, her hand wrapped around my wrist, and the moment the camera captured was oddly intimate. I returned my gaze to Ev, who stared back at me, serious.

"We could issue a statement. Get ahead of this frenzy," he offered.

"No. I'm not commenting on my personal life. I'm actually surprised they haven't figured it out yet. Shelby comes and goes from here all the time. They must have a few photos of her on file."

He glanced toward Shelby and shrugged. "Your household staff has never been a topic of interest before. I don't think they've realized the mysterious woman in red and your housekeeper are the same person yet." He dug through some photos and held up two—one of Shelby in her gown with me, and the other a shot of her leaving the grounds taken at some point, her hair up, sunglasses on, wearing jeans and a baggy T-shirt, probably one of mine. "They hardly look like the same woman." He lifted a shoulder in apology. "Sorry, Shelby."

Shelby waved her hand. "It's fine, Ev. I hardly recognize myself once Lily gets through with me."

I took the photos, studied them, then smiled at Shelby. I held up the picture of her taken on a regular day. "I prefer you like this. You don't need all the other stuff. You're perfect when you're simply you."

Shelby blushed, and Everett rolled his eyes, shaking his head. "Cheeseball."

I flipped him the bird, and he chuckled then became serious again. "They will figure it out, and soon, and then the shit is gonna hit the fan. Cassidy has been taking calls and fielding inquiries all day. It'll only increase. They were all around when I came through the gates. They'll surround the library event. I've already instructed the organizers we'll need extra security."

I rolled my eyes. I was looking forward to that event. It had never garnered much media attention in the past, and I was hoping it would be the same this year. Everett didn't seem bothered, though.

"It's been growing and getting bigger every year since you came on board. It's more publicity for them. They're not surprised."

I hated this part of my career. The constant intrusiveness of being chased by photographers over the most mundane things. I could never figure out what was so fascinating about me buying a bag of crisps at the corner store or why a hundred photos had to be taken while I did. It was only a bloody bag of crisps—hardly newsworthy. I was grateful I would be busy filming for a while. At least on set I was insulated from all this craziness. And Everett would make sure Shelby was okay while I was gone.

I looked at Shelby, who returned my gaze calmly. I turned back to Everett. "We carry on."

He huffed as he shut the file. I grabbed the last picture before he could pull it away. I rather liked it.

"*My* sister," he muttered in warning.

"I'll keep her safe," I assured him.

Shelby smiled at us both.

Shelby ran her fingers through my hair again, and I frowned. "I don't want to go next week."

"You have to. It's your job."

"I'll miss you."

She kept playing with my hair. I loved it when she did. "I'll miss you as well," she whispered, her voice soothing. "But it's only a week, and then you're home. We've been apart longer than that before."

"I didn't know I loved you then."

Her eyes softened, and she leaned down to press her lips to mine. "You'll be fine. You're always so busy on set anyway, and I'll be here when you get back."

"What will you do while I'm gone?"

"I think Caroline is coming while you're gone, so I'll be busy with her."

"You still plan on introducing her to Douglas?"

She nodded. "They're perfect for each other."

"Aside from the fact that he lives here, and she lives in Chicago. Yeah. Bloody perfect," I snorted.

"She's a photographer, Liam. She can work anywhere. She used to come visit me in Sacramento all the time."

"Well, good to know you have it planned out for them." I stroked her cheek. "I don't know if Douglas is in the market for a relationship. Don't be too disappointed if it doesn't happen the way you hope, okay?"

She smiled. "It's fine. But I have a good feeling about them."

I grinned at her. "I have a good feeling about you."

"Oh yeah?"

I pulled her head down, kissing her inviting mouth. Her fingers threaded deeper into my hair, holding me close as we lost ourselves. She nipped my lip as I pulled back, looking rather mischievous. Her voice was husky. "Liam...I'm thirsty."

As strange as that seemed at this moment, I pushed off the sofa, heading for the kitchen. "What do you want?" I asked over my shoulder.

"OJ."

I stopped midstride and looked back.

Did she mean...?

She sat stock-still, grinning widely at me. "A great *big* shot of OJ."

I narrowed my eyes at her. "You really don't want to be testing me on that, Beaker."

She quirked her eyebrow at me, still grinning.

Quirked. Like a challenge.

"Would that be a...*hard thing* for you to manage?" She giggled.

I covered the distance back to the sofa in two strides, pausing only to swoop her into my arms and head for the stairs. "I'll show you hard."

She nuzzled my throat. "I hope so."

If I thought I adored Shelby before, the last couple of days had sealed the deal for me. Being with her, being able to touch her, kiss her anytime I wanted was amazing. I followed her around like a puppy dog at times, hating to be in another room. I only wanted to be where she was, no matter what she was doing. Even letting her get ready alone today was hard. But so worth it when she appeared at the head of the stairs.

She was cracking today.

I smiled at her as she came toward me. Her dress was still red but had some frothy black stuff on it and was shorter this time, showing off her lovely legs. Her feet had healed enough that she was wearing heels, although lower than Lily would've liked. The only jewelry on her today was the bracelet, but she still wore some token of mine on her body.

I had even cajoled Lily into letting me go without a tie since the event was less formal. It always took place outside in a massive garden, where people milled about at will. The speeches were minimal, the auction being the large draw. I always donated several things to it: signed scripts, a visit to the set of a movie I was working on; I even had dinner with a family one year. Whatever would net the most money for their cause. I got my love of books from my mother, and I did this in her honor every year. She got a kick out of that and loved knowing I helped the library and its many programs keep going. I had a soft spot for any cause that had to do with children. Most of my charitable contributions, either monetary or timewise, were donated to these types of causes.

Everett and Cassidy were going with us, as well as Mark. I was secure knowing I would be safe with them, and having Shelby beside me, I was quite calm. She was the perfect antidote to my panic attacks. It was as if needing to protect her made my own anxiety dissipate.

I crooked my arm. "You ready to do this?"

She stood on her toes, and I leaned down to meet her. Her full lips grazed mine. "I'm right here, Liam. I won't let go."

I kissed her again. "Me either."

I looked out the window of the car as we pulled up outside the building. "Bloody hell." It was a frenzy out there. Stirrings of panic began in my stomach, and I swallowed nervously.

Beside me, Shelby squeezed my hand. "Maybe...maybe I shouldn't go in. If you went without me, they'd just leave, right? No picture, no story?"

"No!" I gasped out at the same time both Everett and Cassidy said it, albeit a little less forcefully. I turned to her, gripping her hand hard. "I need you, Shelby. Please."

Everett spoke up, his voice calm. "It'll be fine. They can't move from behind the barricades. Mark will be in front, and I'm right behind you. There's no red carpet, no reason to stop. Just get out and walk. Cassidy will handle anything she feels is necessary. We'll leave out the back when it's done." He covered Shelby's hand with his. "I warned you. You need to make up your mind right now. You okay to do this?"

She straightened her shoulders. "Yes."

I huffed out a sigh of relief and winked at her, trying to remain composed. "Ta, Beaker."

She laughed, and I steeled myself.

"Let's do this."

The flashes were endless and the shouting loud. They were relentless.

Who's the arm candy, Liam?

Flavor of the week, pretty boy?

Planning on another fuck and run, Liam?

How do Carly and Gillian feel about your new toy?

How long until you dump her for someone new?

Shelby stumbled when one woman, presumably a fan, screamed out to "get your dirty mitts off my man," but I held on tight, and we made it inside as quickly as possible.

I pulled her into my arms once the door was closed, my eyes meeting Ev's over her shoulder, both of us worried about her reaction. He was right; the pressure was getting more intense every time we went out together.

"Not fucking cool," I muttered. "They're the ones that make up most of this shit about me, and then they act like it's the truth! I'm not the party boy they write about!"

Shelby drew back, shaking her head. "I can't believe they do—" she gestured wildly toward the door "—that. Just because you have a new date?" She sighed and shook her head. "I should go out there and tell them you're just a guy who can't find the laundry basket or the bloody toilet half the time. You fart and burp with the best of them. That ought to cool them off." She huffed. "And dump *me*? Huh. Maybe I'll dump you first, pretty boy." Then she grinned and started to giggle. Cassidy joined in her merriment.

Everett and I gaped at her before we joined in.

I kissed her head in silent gratitude. Instead of freaking out, she was handling it like a pro. And making me relax.

But she was paying for the toilet remark when we got home.

They hounded us the entire event. Cell phones and cameras were out everywhere we went. I knew photographers were set up all around, their zoom lenses pointed at us, following our every move. Being outdoors, there were only so many places we could hide, so we chose to ignore it all and enjoyed ourselves the best we could. I knew both Ev and Cassidy would be busy with all the media, considering the number of pictures being taken. I also knew Shelby's identity would be made public and the anonymity she presently enjoyed would be over. Our life was about to change. As if she knew what I was thinking, she kissed me softly on the cheek. "So worth it, Liam," she whispered.

I hugged her close, unsure how I got so lucky to have found her, but grateful I did.

I only hoped she felt the same way a few weeks from now.

Because this was only going to get worse. The closer I got to a movie release, the more attention I received; it was simply the way it was for me. With publicity for *Nighthawk* ramping up, I would be under more scrutiny for a while. It always died off once the hype for the movie was over, but it never ended completely. I had gotten better at evading them a good deal of the time, but there were times, like now, I couldn't avoid them. Add in a new relationship, and they would be that much more virulent.

I looked down at Shelby, who was talking to Everett, her hand clasped in mine.

I would do whatever I had to do to protect her from this side of my life, as much as I could. She was a very private person. I knew she hated this aspect, but she would accept it because of me. I wanted to make it as easy on her as I could.

She was too important to me.

I wanted to make sure she felt I was worth it.

Always.

16

LIAM

I woke up, my hand searching for the warmth of Shelby, only to find the bed cold. Bloody hell, it didn't matter how late I kept her up, she was always awake and on the go long before I was in the mornings.

Yesterday, after sneaking out through the kitchen of the hotel and into the waiting car, successfully avoiding the paps, we had gone to dinner and spent some time with Cassidy and Ev, as friends, not colleagues, at one of my favorite restaurants. It was small, far off the beaten path, and private, and I knew the owner well. He always put me in the back room so I could enjoy peace while I ate. The four of us laughed and talked, feeling relaxed. Cassidy and Everett made a good couple—him exuberant and funny, while her quieter, more serious personality kept him level. I enjoyed watching Shelby and Everett interact—the love between them plain to see. She obviously doted on her little brother, and he cherished her. They shared stories of growing up, each trying to outdo the other, making Cassidy and me chuckle several times. It turned into a great evening, and I loved spending time with Shelby, simply being us.

Sunday, we spent alone, Shelby helping me pack and get ready to leave on Tuesday. She knew I didn't want to go but kept the packing and prepping lighthearted, even promising to pack some cookies in at the last minute for me. I pouted, trying for cupcakes, but she patiently explained how smashed they would be when I arrived. I managed to refrain from telling her I would happily still eat them, no doubt even lick the container clean, since I wasn't sure how she would feel about that confession. Instead, I kissed her warmly for the cookies. Any excuse to feel her mouth underneath mine was good with me.

After the packing and organizing were done, we spent the rest of the day together and blissfully alone. We cuddled on the sofa, I chased her around the kitchen, shagging her senseless when I caught her, and generally enjoyed the day together. She made my favorite dinner, we watched Indiana Jones movies until late in the night, and I made her laugh when I pinned her on the sofa, attempting to discover her "hidden treasures" with my "mighty pickaxe." I tried not to be too insulted by her amusement.

I ran my hand down my chest, landing on my morning wood, stroking my erection slowly. It would seem a part of me *was* on the go and ready. Sadly, my dick was no longer satisfied with my own hand. It wanted Shelby. *Her* hand, her sweet pussy, or *God*...her mouth. Her talented, wicked mouth.

Or even better, all three. I was sure I would never get enough of any of them. Or how I was going to do without her over the next week —OJ was not gonna be happy with my hand as her replacement.

Jesus... I needed her. Now.

I threw back the covers, intent on finding Shelby and bringing her back to bed, then fucking her until she screamed my name. I loved hearing my quiet Shelby become loud and vocal. I loved how her pussy felt, clenching and squeezing my cock as she came around me. Grabbing my sleep pants, I jogged down the stairs, confused at hearing the sound of voices. I could hear both Everett and Cassidy talking, and I grimaced. I didn't want company this early in the morning. What the hell were they doing here? We didn't have a meeting planned until later today. I was leaving the next day, and I wanted this final morning alone with Shelby. Glancing down, I knew I couldn't walk into the kitchen right now either. I might scare someone.

Seriously, scar them for life.

Shelby knew what wonders my pants kept secret, but Everett might not like it and Cassidy might rethink what she was doing with him once she saw the heat I was packing.

As I neared the kitchen, I heard Shelby's worried voice. "Liam is *not* going to be happy. Can we hide this?"

Shit. The other day. The paps. The yelling. The pictures of Shelby and me. They had found out who she was.

Those bloody bastards had posted pictures of her. With, no doubt, some ridiculous story to go along with them. She would be terribly upset.

That killed my erection. Fast.

I burst through the door. "What the fuck have those tossers done?"

Like a unit, three bodies turned toward me, blocking Shelby's monitor.

"What?" I growled. "Are they saying shit about you, Beaker? I told you not to look at that crap! It's garbage! Meaningless!"

Everett held up his hand. "Try to remember that, Liam."

I reached for Shelby and pulled her close, wanting to offer her comfort. "It's okay, Shelby. It's all shit. Remember, we talked about this. We'll ignore it."

Her eyes were wide, and she bit her lip. But her eyes weren't upset; they were almost mischievous. Was she trying...not to laugh?

"Let me see."

I bent close, scanning the screen.

"MAID" FOR EACH OTHER
—SHE NEEDED THE JOB—
HE NEEDED THE COVER

I frowned at the headline. I didn't like this. Not one bit. My eyes widened as I read the article.

You better be sitting, ladies. Our sources have it that Liam Wright is now dating closer to home. His home. The mysterious Lady in Red, as she has been dubbed, is none other than his maid.

I glanced over at Shelby, reaching for her hand, squeezing it in comfort.

They'd figured it out fast. Bastards.

I went back to the badly written text.

Why his maid? You would think this leading man, the heartthrob of Hollywood, could have his choice of leading ladies to squire around town on his arm, rather than the person who shines his silver. Except, the information we have received tells us that is the only thing she does shine.

It seems that Peter Pan is a little too fond of those green tights.

Liam Wright, romantic leading man, is playing for the other team.

I read that twice.

Green tights? Playing for the other team? *What other team?* I looked at Shelby, scowling, but she was too busy biting her lip and not looking at me.

My eyes went back to the screen.

Rumor has it, Mr. Wright's past dates got tired of being his cover. Tired of being nothing but arm candy and left with only a kiss on the cheek at the end of the night. If they were lucky.

But who could resist these lovely ladies? Why would a man even try?

Trusted sources say, only a gay man.

I blinked. I read it again.

They just said I was gay.

I stood abruptly.

"Gay?"

I looked at the three people staring at me. "They're saying I'm...gay?"

Why did my voice sound so screechy?

Everett stepped forward. "Garbage, remember, Liam? Just bullshit."

"But I'm *not* gay, Everett." I waved my hand at the screen. "I don't play for the *other* team. I've never had another man's...*bat* in my hand! Or any bloody-where-else in my body." I drew myself up to my full height and flexed my muscles. "Seriously, why would they say that?"

Everett shrugged and Cassidy grinned. "Well, you do rock the metrosexual look at times, Liam."

Shelby smirked. "That one photo session you did—"

I gasped. "Piss off!" I started pacing. "This is low—even for them. I want this retracted and an apology issued. Call Samuels now and get him on it. Threaten to sue them if we have to."

"They don't come out—" Everett paused and chuckled at his choice of words "—and *say* you're gay, Liam... They say it's a rumor. You need to calm down. If we make a big deal of this, you'll come across as homophobic."

"I'm not homophobic, but these are lies. *Pure lies.*"

I pulled on my hair in anger. "Those fucking wankers! I love women! I've loved lots of women! Shagged them until they screamed my bloody name! And never once was it yelled in a goddamn baritone!"

Shelby turned to me, glaring. "Exactly how *many* women have you shagged *and made scream your bloody name,* Liam?"

My eyes widened as she stared, giving me the best bitch brow I had ever seen.

I swallowed heavily.

Bugger. This bad day just got a lot worse. She was right pissed about that statement.

"Um, just a figure of speech. Not many at all in the scheme of things. Really."

She narrowed her eyes, and I gave her my best innocent face. "None of them meant anything. Not like you, Shelby."

"Hmm."

"I never told anyone else I loved them. Only you."

Her face softened and I sighed. Crisis averted. That one anyway.

I threw up my hands. "The point is, none of them were men!"

Cassidy snorted. "Glad you're showing Shelby how not to overreact there, Liam."

"I'm not overreacting! I'm defending myself. I've never done any ball-handling!"

"Other than your own, you mean?" Everett guffawed.

"Get stuffed," I growled at him, starting to pace again.

"I think that's the point of this article," Cassidy stated dryly.

Stopping mid-pace, I pointed my finger at Shelby. "Ask her—she'll tell you. I shag her daily. I shagged her twice last night. In fact, I was so randy this morning, I was coming down here to find her and do it again. We probably wouldn't have made it out of the kitchen!"

Everett grimaced, his head falling into his hands. "Oh God, that's my sister you're talking about. TMI, Liam. Too much fucking TMI!"

Shelby piped up, sounding far too happy for what was

happening. "It's true, though. He, um, shagged me so hard on Saturday, I could barely get off the table."

Everett stood with a boom, the chair toppling over behind him as he spat out the coffee he'd been sipping all over me. "We *eat* at this table, for fuck's sake!"

"Bloody hell, you just spewed coffee all over me, you git." I wiped at my chest.

"Stop talking about shagging my sister!" he yelled.

Shelby giggled. "Well, according to the article, you're used to men spewing liquid at you, Liam."

I swung around, glaring at her. "You think this is funny? Not only are they saying I'm gay—even worse, they're calling *you* a bloody maid!"

I hated that her role in my life had been described that way. Even before I fell in love with her, Shelby was never just that. Maid wasn't the right word. I couldn't even begin to think of a word that encompassed all she was to me.

"You're so much more than that," I informed her. "You always have been."

She refused to be upset. "No hand service, though," she quipped.

"Shelby!" I roared. "This is *not* amusing!"

"Maybe I should issue a statement saying you fuck me so much, I can barely walk. That should help quell the rumors," Shelby mused.

I slammed my hand on the counter. "Yes! Bloody brilliant!"

"No! Stop this, both of you. No one is issuing statements about fucking," Everett snarled, frantically pointing his finger between Shelby and me.

Cassidy, who had been unusually quiet, suddenly started to snicker again as she bent over, reading the computer screen.

Ev and I looked at her. "What?" Everett asked.

"Well, further into this riveting article, it indicates that, ah, you and Liam may be closer than just manager and client. And being your supportive sister is another reason Shelby is acting as Liam's cover."

Everett stormed over to the computer, swearing as he read the screen.

"Call Samuels," he hissed. "We need to prepare a statement."

I leaned against the counter, crossing my arms over my chest. "Oh, now it's not so amusing when they think *you're* my bitch, right, Everett?"

He turned, glaring. "Trust me, Liam. If we were in a relationship, I would *not* be your bitch. You'd be mine."

"I doubt that, you overgrown pansy. You are not my type, mate."

"Well, you're not mine either, string bean. Trust me, by the time I was through with you, they'd be peeling you off the ceiling."

"Whatever, you daft moron." I sniffed. "I've got moves you've never seen before, wanker."

He stepped forward, poking me in the chest as he yelled, "You're the one who's been wanking—"

The strangest sound came from behind me, interrupting Everett, and I turned to Shelby. She was standing against the counter, tears rolling down her face as the most Beaker-like sounds escaped her lips. Cassidy was standing beside her, biting her lip, and then the two of them started shrieking with amusement.

Startled, Ev and I stepped back.

Bugger. Shelby was so upset, she was hysterical. I shouldn't have made that quip about all the shagging with other women. It probably sent her over the edge.

She gasped and tried to control herself as she pointed her finger between Everett and me. "This is the two of you 'handling' things and being calm?" Then she burst out laughing again, even harder, if it was possible. Beside her, Cassidy was cackling so hard, tears were streaming down her cheeks.

Everett and I traded glances. "I think we need to do something," I muttered, indicating the two women losing it in front of us.

"What?"

I searched my brain, trying to remember what to do for hysterical people. "Um...slap them, I think?"

Everett waved his hand. "Be my guest, Liam."

I looked at Shelby, who was still laughing so hard she actually snorted. Doing exactly what I told her to do. Ignoring the bullshit. Understanding dawned on me as I watched her reaction to the stupid article. She was right, as usual, and I was being the daft one. She was handling it properly, and I was overreacting.

I shook my head. "Not me. I'm a lover, not a fighter, Ev." I nudged him with my elbow, realizing the humor myself. "You should know that—" I winked "—*my lovah*."

He gaped at me.

And then we were laughing—all of us.

17

LIAM

Sitting around the table, all of us now composed, Cassidy spoke. "Okay, Samuels will be contacting the magazine, threatening libel and slander. And as much as you hate to comment, Liam, I'll issue a statement, confirming you are in a loving, committed relationship with a trusted member of your staff. It will also say that while you value any relationship built on love and trust, you are not now, nor have you been at any time in your life, gay."

"There's nothing wrong with being gay," I insisted. "I have gay friends..." My voice trailed off as Cassidy held up her hand.

"You're rambling again, Liam. Shut up. I have that covered."

I nodded. "Right. Excellent suggestion. Thanks."

Beside me, Shelby snickered. I pulled her close and nuzzled her head. She was calm, and it helped to calm me as well. Her way of seeing the humor of the whole situation was exactly what I needed.

Everett crossed his arms. "Well, it's out now." He grinned widely. "Or at least, Liam is."

I shot him a withering glance. Shelby giggled again as Everett chuckled and Cassidy smacked him. He looked injured, then cleared his throat and became serious. "They know you're a couple, and from

174

now on, the scrutiny is going to get worse." He turned to Shelby, his expression now one of concern. "Are you sure you're up for this crap? You're going to be followed and questioned. Your privacy is shot."

I regarded her anxiously as she gave Everett's words some thought.

"We knew this would happen," she said quietly. "I knew Liam was too well-known for our relationship to remain private. It frightens me some, I admit." Her hand squeezed mine. "But it can't last forever—surely they'll get tired of our relationship, and someone else will pique their interest. Right?"

I turned, pressing a kiss to her head. "Eventually, yes. But we don't know when. This could last a while. Scrutiny is always the worst when I have a movie coming out. And the fucking studio almost encourages it. The paps will follow you. Shout at you to get a reaction. Crowd you. They'll interrupt your day—even grocery shopping will be difficult." I looked at Everett. "Should we hire someone to be with her?"

Shelby gasped beside me. "Like a bodyguard? I think that's slightly excessive."

Everett tapped the top of the table. "Shelby, you have no idea how intrusive these people can be. What happened the other night is just a small glimpse of how they can act. Liam is right. Someone with you, who can run interference, is a good idea."

For the first time today, she looked upset. "I don't like the idea."

"I don't like the idea of you being subjected to the likes of these assholes," I snapped, suddenly angry as the humor faded and reality set in. Why couldn't she understand this? She knew how much I hated this part of my life. "They can be vicious, Shelby. It's like nothing you've ever gone through." I stood, pacing. "You are about to find out. And it's not going to be fun." I'd experienced it far too often, and now, because of me, Shelby would as well.

Until recently she had been in the shadows of my life—someone on the edge to whom they paid no attention. Now, she was front and center. A prime target. We'd discussed this already, but I had hoped we'd have a little more time before we had to deal with it. I stopped pacing and looked out of the window at the sun reflecting off the pool, the light shimmering on the surface, much like the panic that was now simmering below my skin. A shudder ran through me.

Could we handle this situation?

Could Shelby?

Arms draped around me, and Shelby's warmth pressed into my back. Turning, I wrapped myself around her, and we stood together, drawing comfort from our quiet embrace.

I said my fear out loud. "It might make you change your mind about us."

"Nothing can make me change my mind. If it makes you feel better for me to have security, I'll do it," she whispered. She tilted back her head, her eyes filled with worry.

"I have to keep you safe, Shelby. It's only for a little while. Please understand that. I have to make sure you're okay."

She huffed a sigh. "I know. I don't like it. But I do understand." She cupped my cheek. "We'll figure it all out. I'm not going anywhere, Liam."

I pressed her against me, kissing her deeply.

I needed to hear that. I needed to know she was still with me.

I buried my hands in her hair, holding her close to my face, kissing her. I needed her taste to calm and center me. I groaned as I pulled her nearer, my emotions suddenly raw and needy.

Some part of my brain registered Everett and Cassidy leaving the room.

"I can't lose you," I murmured against her mouth. "I can't even stand the *thought* of it."

"You won't," she insisted, running her hands down my back. "I'll be right here when you get back. I promise. I'll be waiting on your gay ass to come home to me."

I chuckled into her hair, knowing she was trying to lighten the mood. "Of all the angles I thought they'd go with, I never thought about that one." I grinned down at her. "I was sure they'd point out what an old lady you were. Cradle snatching and robbing me of my virtue and all."

Shelby mock-glared at me, but her tone was serious. "They probably will soon enough."

I kissed her. "And it will be as false as this one. Equally insulting and filled with lies."

She nodded. "I know, it was rather insulting. Like the only reason you'd date me is because you're gay." She huffed dramatically. "I'm not that hideous. I've got moves too, you know."

"I know that, Beaker. I've seen some of your moves. Or were you holding back on me?"

She grinned at me. "Not telling."

The way she looked at me made everything else fade away. I didn't care about reporters or false stories or anything outside this room. Only her. Only us.

I pressed my forehead against hers, my voice serious. "Thank you. For today...for keeping me calm. For everything." I sighed. "I love you, Shelby."

She tightened her arms around me. She rose up on her toes, brushing her mouth over mine. "I love you, Liam."

Three small words.

Words I desperately wanted to hear.

Ones I wasn't sure she'd ever say.

Nothing else mattered.

Because everything right, everything true, was here in my arms.

"Shelby—" Crashing my mouth to hers, I let my lips and tongue tell her how I felt about her statement.

I dropped my face into her neck, breathing her in deeply.

She loved me.

My Beaker.

Mine.

Together, we'd figure this out, because I wasn't letting her go. Ever.

I pulled her tighter, feeling my emotions beginning to overtake me. I wasn't used to this intensity. Feeling the depth of such a powerful emotion for one person. Worried about them. Not wanting to leave them.

With Shelby, though, I felt it all. And right now, it was crashing over me.

She held me close as she returned my passion. "Say it again," I pleaded against her mouth.

"I love you, Liam. So very much."

"How long?"

She smiled as she traced my bottom lip with her finger. "Since you smirked at me and told me you were sitting there, interviewing me, commando."

I looked at her in wonder. She'd even been ahead of me in this, only she kept it to herself. "All this time? You kept it to yourself? Even after I said I loved you?"

"It took me a while to admit it to myself," she confessed. "I was afraid there were too many obstacles, too many reasons for us not to be together. I was afraid I wasn't good enough for you. I didn't think I could fit into your world. As your friend, I could at least be close to you."

I shook my head. If anything, she was too good for me.

"And now?"

She sighed wearily. "I'm tired of holding the feelings in, Liam. I'm tired of trying to stay away and only be your friend." She drew in a deep breath. "Malcolm let me know, so often, I was a failure as a wife because I never made him happy. I never did anything right in his eyes. Everything that went wrong was my fault. All the time. Even his inability to keep a job."

I waited. She rarely spoke about her ex. All I knew was their marriage had ended long before he left her, and that when he did leave, he took everything they had, leaving her in a vulnerable financial position. Everett had disliked him intensely and hated how he treated Shelby.

"I swore I would never let my guard down again. I was too busy trying to fix what was wrong with me, to make him happy, I didn't see what he was doing or that Everett was right, and Malcolm was only using me, until it was too late. Once I lost my job, and the only income for us, I was no longer of any use to him, and he left." She snorted, "Taking everything of value with him."

"Not everything, Shelby."

She looked up. "What?"

"He left the most valuable thing behind—you. He was just too much of an idiot to know that."

"He never made me feel that way." Her quiet voice revealed her vulnerability.

"I'll show you that—every day, if you let me. I know it took me a while, but I want you to know how much you mean to me. Let me in and trust me. I won't let you down, I promise."

"I want that, Liam. Very much."

"Hey." I waited until her eyes met mine. "We can have both, Beaker. You *are* my best friend—the added bonus is we love each other, too. It's the best of both worlds. And you, *you*, are perfect for me. Never doubt that."

The smile I loved so much lit her face. Warm, open, and filled with love.

"You're the best of both worlds for me as well."

I tugged her closer and kissed her deeply.

There was nothing left to say.

She had said it all.

"God, I miss you," I sighed into the phone. "This week is never going to end."

Shelby sighed. "You've only been gone two days, Oscar."

"Two bloody long ones." I paused. "Don't you miss me?"

Her voice became shy. "Yeah, I do."

"Where are you sleeping, Shelby?" I asked huskily.

"In your bed. It smells like you."

I shut my eyes, groaning. I could see her there, her dark hair spilled across the pillow as she slumbered, curled up like a contented kitten. I wanted to be behind her, tucked around her soft body and feeling her warmth pressed against me. I could feel myself stirring, my cock aching at the thought of being close to her again. "I'm not letting you out of our bed for days when I get home," I growled. "I'm gonna shag you senseless."

"We don't have to stick to the bed," she whispered, teasing me. "I like the kitchen...and the sofa."

"What about the desk—and the stairs? You like those too?"

She whimpered.

My head fell back against the chair. This woman was going to be the death of me. I also knew I had to change the subject and fast. I had a wardrobe fitting in a few minutes, and at the moment, I couldn't possibly walk in there. "Behave, Beaker."

Then I cleared my throat. "Any trouble today?"

She sighed quietly. "Ryan took me to the store to pick up some things. It was fine."

"Fine?"

"He drove. I hid."

"Did they follow?"

"No."

"Really?" I was surprised. There had been a crowd outside the gate when I left and at the airport, yelling their inane questions with flashes going off so often it was like one steady bright light in my eyes. Even flanked by Everett and Mark, I felt exposed, and I worried constantly about Shelby. I made Everett promise to stay close while I was gone, before he left me at the gate. Ryan had come highly recommended by Mark, and he and Shelby had hit it off right away. The man was massive—almost as big as Mark, and he looked bloody menacing with a scowl that said, "Back the fuck off," although his demeanor in private was far more affable. He, too, assured me no one would get near Shelby while I was away, and she was under his protection. I'd been fairly sequestered since arriving in New York, but I was more concerned about Shelby. She hadn't left the house since I'd departed, and today was the first time she had gone out.

"I had Ryan drive out with his windows open so they could see I wasn't in the car. They hung around the gates."

"Wait. I thought you just said you went out?"

"I did. I was in the trunk. Ryan let me out at the side entrance. I did my shopping and hid on the way home again. I chatted at him from the split seat in the back. He told me all about his wife and how they met."

I burst out laughing. "Whose idea was that?"

"Mine."

"Oh, Beaker, you are bloody brilliant." I chuckled. "But that is rather dangerous. I don't think I like the idea of you rolling around in the trunk, unrestrained."

"You'd rather I be restrained, Liam?"

"I'd like to restrain you."

She giggled. "Hold that thought, Oscar."

"Oh, baby, I will." Then I became serious. "They'll catch on."

"I know. But I fooled them today, and I'll handle tomorrow when tomorrow comes."

She still astonished me how coolly she was handling this pressure. "You are truly amazing," I praised her. "I can't believe how well you're coping with this mess."

"You're worth it."

God, I hoped she kept thinking so.

I heard my name and I sighed. "I have to go."

"I love you."

"Ah, Shelby, you have no idea how bloody much I love hearing you say that. I love you too. I'll call you tonight."

I hung up, thinking. Ryan had driven her, and all went well, but I didn't want her in the trunk, as genius as that was today. And soon she would refuse to let him drive her if she felt she could do it on her own—I knew that for a fact. She would want to start testing the waters. Her car was older, a Honda that had seen better days—it was also the base model. No tinted windows, no air conditioning. She said she didn't need it for errands. But things had changed. I didn't want her that exposed when she left the house.

My name was called again, and I grabbed my phone, dialing Everett.

It was time to upgrade Shelby's ride.

And I had $90,000 burning a hole in my pocket to pay her back.

Perfect.

18

LIAM

I never thought the week would end, and I was thrilled when I finished ahead of schedule. I caught the first flight out so I would be home early in the day instead of late that evening. I had Everett keep the change a secret so I could surprise Shelby. With the early departure, I even slipped through the airport undetected. I hoped it would happen at LAX as well. I wanted to arrive unannounced.

God, I had missed Beaker.

She had been amazing all week. She kept her cool and her sense of humor, even when other stories surfaced about the fact that she was older and divorced, accompanied by pictures of her looking less than glamorous. I didn't care about the age difference or the photos, and I was thrilled they had gotten the second part wrong. Once they found out she wasn't yet divorced, it might get uglier. Although Everett thought the divorce would happen any day now. The lawyer he had hired was pushing it through as quickly and quietly as possible.

Cassidy issued a simple statement, and otherwise, we ignored what was being said as best we could. Ryan had proven himself a man of his word, helping Shelby get around safely the whole time I was gone. I knew the shouting and flashes bothered her, but she remained composed, which, in turn, kept me calm. I was gobsmacked at her attitude. She was brilliant.

Everett had a car waiting for Mark and me, and as usual, he chose a different style of vehicle so it wouldn't be recognized. That meant there was a chance I could get past the crowd at the gate quite easily if they didn't realize it was me in the back. As in the past, Mark would stay in the car and depart after I was safely in the house.

Entering my home, I headed straight for the kitchen, disappointed to find it empty. I saw two coffee cups on the counter and figured Shelby must be out with Ryan. I checked the garage, surprised to find her car gone. Had they taken hers? Where was his car? That seemed unusual. But I could smell turkey cooking in the oven, which meant she couldn't be far. She was getting ready for me to come home.

Grabbing my bag, I went upstairs, walking into my room and breathing in the scent of Shelby. The top of my dresser now had bottles and jars on it—Shelby's lotions and perfume, which filled the air with her fragrance. It made me long for her to get home. I tossed my bag in the closet and came out, stopping dead at the sight in front of me. Sitting in the middle of my bed, eyeballing me back, was a cat.

Well, maybe a kitten more than a cat. Striped gray, chocolate, and white, with huge paws and wide blue eyes, it blinked at me warily as we stared at each other. It had an amusing face on it—sort of a tough-guy expression with a pug nose, and a small scar along the side of its face. The baleful glare made me grin. I wasn't overly fond of cats as a rule, but this one was rather...cute.

I approached the bed slowly. Where the hell did it come from? And why was it on my bed? It stood, stretching, arching its back, and walked toward me, sitting on the edge of the bed and extending its paw, patting my hand. Unsure what it wanted, I lowered my hand and awkwardly stroked the furry head. Immediately, it began to purr, pushing against my hand and looking at me with its blue eyes, pleading.

"Um...hello, cat," I murmured. "How did you get here?" I sat beside it, shocked when it crawled up onto my shoulder, curling into my neck, purring. I sat for a few minutes, running my fingers through the fur on its back. Obviously, this was Shelby's handiwork. Maybe she was so lonesome, she thought a kitten would be a good idea. I knew she had trouble sleeping when I wasn't here, and maybe the kitten helped. Everett told me once she had been like that all her life —unable to sleep in an empty house. He had sheepishly admitted it might've had something to do with him forcing her to watch scary movies with him when they were younger. Maybe the kitten made her feel better. I would ask her when she got home.

I settled back against the headboard and let the kitten sleep. I rested my head on the wood, and I felt my eyes drift shut. I'd just sit here until Shelby got home.

A noise startled me, and I opened my eyes, meeting the sleepy blues of the kitten, who wasn't happy about being disturbed. I glanced at the clock and realized I'd been asleep for almost an hour.

The noise came from downstairs, which meant Shelby was home.

I lifted the kitten from my shoulder and got off the bed. It followed me to the edge, giving a plaintive meow as I started to walk away. Turning around, I picked it up, grinning as it settled right back onto my shoulder, promptly digging its claws into my neck and curling up tight. I guessed that was where it liked to be.

Quietly, I went downstairs and peeked in the kitchen. Shelby was clearly not only oblivious to the fact that I was home but was searching for something in the bottom cupboard. All I could see of her was her tight ass sticking out of the open cupboard door, the black yoga pants accentuating her curves. My cock hardened thinking about burying itself between those plump cheeks.

I set the kitten on the floor, ignoring the pitiful look I got from it. Grinning, I snuck up behind Shelby, grabbed her hips, and pulled her sweet ass tight to my groin as I crouched over her. "Tell me, Shelby, why is it I came home to find a strange kitty in my bed? We both know I only want one little pussy waiting for me there." I thrust forward. *"Yours."*

Shelby yelped, her head hitting the cupboard as she pushed backward, scaring the kitten, who was trying to crawl up my leg, causing me to yell as its sharp nails dug into my calf. I stumbled back, taking Shelby with me, landing on the floor with a loud "oomph" as all the air escaped my lungs. The kitten jumped in fright, meowing loudly as Shelby scrambled off me, her pointy elbows digging in. Except as she rolled and sat up gasping, it was my turn to be surprised. Instead of warm, blue-colored eyes, startled, hazel ones met my shocked green.

That was not my Shelby.

From the garage doorway, there was a loud gasp. "Liam?"

I turned my head and gaped at Shelby standing in the doorway. Pushing and scrambling, I backed away from the unidentified woman on the floor, who was staring at me, partially amused, partially horrified.

My gaze bounced between them. The kitten jumped back on my lap, crawling right to my shoulder like that was its rightful place.

Shelby's voice was dry. "I see you've met Fuzzball. And introduced yourself, as only you can, to Caroline." She waved her hand. "Are you trying to add her to the list of women who have screamed your name, Oscar?"

I shook my head violently. "Bloody hell, Beaker! I thought it was you—I missed your sexy ass, and it was beckoning to me!" I clambered to my feet. "It was all wiggling and lush—"

Her eyebrows shot up, and I realized what I had said. "I mean... Oh shit." I hung my head in defeat, groaning. "Oh bugger," I mumbled, squeezing my eyes shut.

I was so fucked. And not in a good way.

The woman sitting on the floor—Caroline apparently—began to chuckle. She glanced over at Shelby. "Charming," she stated sarcastically. "A hornball. You neglected to add *that* to your list of attributes when describing your boyfriend."

My ears perked up. Shelby had been listing my attributes? Maybe I could salvage this mess.

With a flourish, I stood and extended my hand. "Forgive me, Caroline. Allow me to introduce myself. Liam Wright at your service. May I help you up?"

With a grin, she allowed me to pull her off the floor. She was taller than Shelby, dressed in a snug T-shirt and yoga pants that showed off her curves and muscles. Short, dark hair framed her attractive face. Freckles scattered across her nose, and the golden color of her skin indicated a lot of time spent in the sun. Her hazel gaze was intelligent, and her wide mouth showed faint laugh lines beside it, hinting at her sense of humor.

A sense of humor I needed right now.

"I, ah, apologize for the arse grabbing. I thought you were Shelby." I shrugged. "I don't have many strange birds rooting around in my cupboards, waving their arse at me."

Her eyes widened again, and behind me, Shelby let out one of her Beaker noises.

"Does she wave her *arse* for you a lot?"

"Not as often as I would like, I admit."

"But you like to grab it?" Caroline questioned, her eyes dancing.

"As often as she lets me." I winked at her. "And often when she doesn't as well."

A real smile broke out on her face. "Nice to meet you, Liam." She winked right back at me. "Nice *grip* you have there. And, um, I would say from the feel of your *welcome,* you're happy to be home."

"Bloody happy."

"Sorry it was the wrong ass."

I waggled my eyebrows at her. "A pleasure anyway."

"Maybe I should leave you alone to say a proper hello to the right ass."

"That, Caroline, would be greatly appreciated. Maybe we can have coffee after?"

"I'd like that." She indicated the ball of fur sitting on my shoulder. "I realize you are rather possessive of your, um, *pussy*, but would you like me to take him while you have some time with Shelby?"

God, I loved this woman already. She was cracking.

I lifted her hand and brushed a kiss over her knuckles. "Thank you. That would be brilliant. A little private time with my other, ah, *kitten* would be appreciated."

Behind me, Shelby's Beaker noise escaped. Again.

Caroline left the kitchen, carrying the kitten who I now knew was male and Shelby had named Fuzzball. I would have to address that, but first, I had another kitty to soothe.

Turning, I looked at Shelby, giving her my best sad eyes and smile. "Oops."

She stared at me. "Can you ever do things like a normal person?"

"Um, no?"

"You grabbed my friend's ass, Liam." She waved her hand toward my crotch. "You ground your...oh *God*—"

I grinned sheepishly. "In my defense, I thought it was yours."

"So you said."

I stepped forward. "Again, in my defense, I didn't know she was here."

"She got here late last night. We went for breakfast. I wasn't expecting you."

"I finished early," I explained, slipping my arm around her waist. "I was anxious to get home to you."

"I think Caroline knows just how anxious."

"I like her."

"Yeah?"

I nodded. "She's feisty." I pressed closer. "But I like you better."
Her cheeks darkened. "Yeah?"

I chuckled as I pulled her against me, my lips at her ear. "Her ass was nice, Shelby, but nowhere near as spectacular as yours. I have no idea how I got them confused." I squeezed her rounded cheeks firmly. "I'd like to show you how anxious I really felt. How much I missed you." I squeezed again. "And this."

Her eyes, the warm, rich blue I missed so much, looked at me from under her lashes. Her arms wound around my neck. "Show me, then."

With a groan, I tightened my hold and crashed my lips to hers. I commanded her mouth instantly, delving and tasting, needing to show her exactly *how* much I had missed her. One hand stayed on her hip while I buried the other into her thick hair, tilting her head and controlling the kiss. Her low whimper was all I needed to lift her onto the counter, stepping between her legs as I reacquainted myself with the sweetness that was Shelby. Her hands tugged and pulled on the back of my hair, keeping me close, wrapping her legs around my hips as she welcomed me home. I wanted to lose myself in her taste forever.

It was only the sudden, sorrowful, and loud meow that broke through the fog clouding my brain. I wanted Shelby. I wanted to tear off her clothes and shag her right here on the counter until she was panting and screaming my name. Then I wanted to take her upstairs, make love to her in our bed, and then shag her all over again on some other surface of the house. God knew there were plenty of places I wanted to try.

But we weren't alone.

If the meow hadn't done it, the quiet, "Sorry, he escaped," did. I stepped back, my breath ragged and bent down, picking up the kitten that was clawing at my jeans, trying to climb his way to my shoulder.

Caroline stood in the doorway, uncertain if she should leave or stay. I smiled at her, tracing my thumb across Shelby's bottom lip. God, I loved to bite that lip.

"Someone likes you," Shelby said quietly.

I looked over to the kitten that was nestled happily again by my neck. He did seem to have taken to me. "Pussies do like me." I winked at her. "I mean, what's not to like? Where did he come from?"

Shelby gave me a pointed look, rolling her eyes, before explaining. "I was dropping off a donation at the shelter. He was abandoned, and he needed a home—he was down to his last day." Her eyes were pleading. "I couldn't leave him, Liam. I couldn't."

Her tender heart made my own ache. She cared so much about everything. "It's fine, Beaker. He's welcome." I tickled his chin as he purred happily. My new mate. "But we aren't calling him Fuzzball. That is all sorts of wrong. He needs a good, strong, male name."

"What's wrong with Fuzzball?"

I leaned down, my lips against her ear. "I already have one soft, fuzzy pussy in the house I like to play with. This wee guy is gonna be my mate. He needs a different name." I bit down on her lobe, pulling it with my teeth.

She shivered and swallowed; her voice was husky. "What are we calling him?"

I looked at his rugged face and big paws. He was going to be a monster when he grew. I grinned at her. "Thor."

"Thor?"

"Yeah. He looks like a tough little bugger. I like it." He licked my finger. "See, he agrees."

She rolled her eyes but agreed. "Okay, Thor it is."

I grabbed her chin and kissed her. Hard. Deep.

"Thor and I are hungry. We need you to take care of that for us."

Her eyes crinkled as she grinned saucily. "For food, right?"

I kissed her again, pressing my lips to hers firmly. "For now." Then I grinned. "I smell turkey?"

"Yes."

"I want sandwiches."

She stared at me, slowly trailing her tongue over her bottom lip.

"I want you even more," I murmured.

"Caroline," she whispered. "I can't just kick her out."

Pulling back, I winked at her. I wanted her alone—and soon. "I've got it covered."

I turned to Caroline, who was watching us with a smile. "Come in and join us, Caroline. I have to make a call, but I'll be right back."

I scratched Thor under the chin as I walked down the hall, dialing the phone.

"Hey Douglas, can I interest you in the best-tasting sandwich you've ever had?"

I grinned at his enthusiastic reply.

"Great. Come on over."

19

LIAM

Lunch was great. Douglas was as crazy for Shelby's sandwiches as I was, and in my opinion, ate far too many of them—I even had to share the pickles. I sat back, watching Caroline charm the pants off Douglas. She was funny, smart, and articulate. They had many shared interests including her photography. Turned out he knew her work and was a fan. She, in turn, admired his films.

Shelby, as usual, was right. They were perfect for each other. But I wanted them to be perfect for each other somewhere else.

They were far too comfortable sitting at my table, eating and talking. I wanted Shelby to myself, but she seemed to be enjoying their company a little too much. I needed to remind her why I invited Douglas over in the first place. I was hoping he would take Caroline out for a while, and I needed to make him think it was his idea.

Shelby was driving me mental. Every time she leaned forward, I caught a glimpse of the top of her breasts peeking out from her shirt. I wanted to touch them—with my tongue. Her voice seemed huskier today, her laughter sultrier, which made me need to feel her lips underneath mine. When she moved her head, I could smell the fragrance of her hair. I wanted to bury my face in it. Each time she shifted in her chair, I wanted to feel her moving underneath me. Or on top—I wasn't picky right now. When her hand would land on my thigh, my cock twitched a little trying to get to her. It was like a fucking heat-seeking missile and Shelby's pussy was the target. He wanted her. *I* wanted her. Soon.

I needed her to understand that.

Casually, I stood and strolled to the refrigerator, grabbed the jug from the shelf, took a glass from the cupboard, and set the orange juice in front of Shelby with a loud thump. Smiling, I poured her a glass and pushed it toward her.

Douglas looked at me. "Did I miss something?"

I shrugged. "Shelby is thirsty. I can tell. Parched, in fact. She needs some OJ. She has a severe deficiency—it's a medical thing. She needs lots of OJ."

Caroline frowned, looking concerned. "Shelby, you never said anything."

Shelby's cheeks flushed. "It's nothing. Liam is overexaggerating." She shot me a look.

"She had a glass at breakfast, Liam," Caroline assured me.

I nodded. "Good. I'm after her all the time to make sure she gets enough. It's my *job* to make sure she gets enough. I give her at least a couple of good solid shots of OJ a day. More, if she lets me." Turning my head, I winked at Shelby. "It's packed full of natural goodness."

"I think I'm fine right now," she murmured.

I shook my head. "No, you really need some. *I really need to give you some.* I want you *full* of OJ."

She giggled. Then she started to laugh. She picked up the glass and started to sip as she chortled.

Caroline and Douglas shared a look, and Douglas shrugged as if to say, "I have no idea." Then he addressed Caroline. "I understand you're here to see Shelby, but I know some great spots where you could take some wonderful photos." He looked over at Shelby. "If you don't mind me stealing her away for a few hours? I mean, you're welcome to join us, but with your following out there..."

Shelby smiled. "It would be nicer for Caroline if you took her, not to mention safer. They won't follow you."

That reminded me. "Where is Ryan? You didn't go out for breakfast on your own, did you?"

She didn't quite meet my eyes. "No. Ryan was with us."

"Did you drive?"

"No, he drove us. I sent him home after we got back. We didn't plan on going out again."

"Where is your car?" I asked, because she still didn't have her new one yet.

She and Caroline shared a quick glance. "Um, I took it in for service."

I pursed my lips. Something was up, and she wasn't telling me. Feeling my gaze, she looked up. "Later," she mouthed. Grudgingly, I let it go.

For now.

Caroline spoke up. "Are you sure you don't mind, Shelby?"

She shook her head. "No. You go and enjoy the afternoon. I'll help Liam unpack, and I have a few things to take care of." She assured him. "Will you be back for dinner?"

Caroline started to nod as Douglas spoke. "Why don't we play it by ear? We'll call you later."

I liked his idea. I hoped it was much later. I smiled benignly. "Of course. I know Shelby wants Caroline to see everything. Take your time." I pretended to yawn and stretch. "I need a nap. I'm knackered —it was a long week, and I was up early this morning. And I've got a few phone calls to make." I stood. "I'll let you get on." I extended my hand to Douglas. "Enjoy your afternoon." I kissed Caroline's cheek. "So...*lovely* to have met you, Caroline. A real pleasure. I look forward to seeing you again."

She grinned. "I doubt anything will ever compare to that

introduction, Liam. See you later." She waved, and I knew Douglas would be hearing all about this morning at some point during their time together. I also knew I'd never hear the end of it. I held up my hands.

"Jet lag and wishful thinking, Douglas. Keep those in mind." My hand brushed Shelby's shoulder as I left the room. "You know where I am if you need me."

I headed upstairs, knowing Shelby would join me as soon as we were alone. After giving Thor a head rub, I grabbed a quick shower. Coming out, I grinned at what I saw on my bed. Shelby, curled in the center of the bed, wearing only my T-shirt from earlier, Thor snuggled against her as she tickled his head. He obviously enjoyed her touch as much as I did. I could hear him purring from where I stood. Shelby had drawn the shades, the room cast in dim light, restful and soft.

Shelby glanced up, her eyes dancing as she saw me.

"Are they gone?" I smirked at her.

"Yes."

"The door locked?"

"Yes."

"Brilliant."

Shelby quirked her eyebrow. "Medical condition, Oscar? Seriously?"

I ran a towel through my hair as I walked toward the bed. "I spoke the truth."

"Do tell."

Leaning over, I picked up Thor and placed him in the basket Shelby had bought for him. He wasn't overly happy, but he didn't move. I loosened the towel at my waist, allowing it to fall to the floor. My cock was already hard; OJ knew Shelby was *right there,* and soon he would be buried deep in her warm, wet heaven. I ached for her. Shelby's eyes were wide as she watched me slowly stroke myself. "You have a raging fever that only I can cure."

She leaned back on her elbows, my T-shirt pulled taut across her breasts. I could see her nipples, hard and straining under the cotton.

"Is that so?" she teased.

I crawled on the bed, my cock pulling and surging to get closer. "Yep. You need an injection. An OJ injection." I shook my head. "I won't lie to you, Shelby. It will probably take more than one injection to cure you." I waggled my eyebrows at her. "Probably...mul-ti-ple." I said the last word slowly, running my tongue over my lips as I leered at her.

For a minute the room was dead quiet.

"Oh my God," she whispered. "Everett was right. You do make me silly."

Then she giggled.

And I pounced.

Having her under me again was perfect. She was perfect. Our mouths pressed, tongues claimed, our hands stroked and sought out curves and dips as we rocked together. I held her tight, devouring her mouth as I thrust deeply, needing her as close as possible. She whimpered and moaned as she clutched my shoulders, my name falling from her lips like a prayer while I pushed and pulled, the heat between us blistering.

I cursed and moaned as I felt my orgasm building—too soon and too strong to ignore. Desperately, I slipped my fingers between us, finding her clit, and stroking. "With me, Shelby. I need you to come with me, baby."

She cried out in her release, the sound of her passion music to my ears as I succumbed, breathing out her name. The pleasure was so intense it was almost painful as I gasped and clutched at her small form, finally collapsing on her chest, panting and mindless.

She pressed her lips to the top of my head. "I missed you."

I sighed against her neck, leisurely trailing my lips up to her mouth, kissing her with the lightest of pressure. "I missed you. So much."

I rolled slightly, tucking her against my chest, not ready to let her go yet. "How the hell did we live together for six months and not do this every fucking day?" I wondered into her hair. "I must have been blind."

"We weren't ready."

"Was it worth the wait, Shelby?" I asked, suddenly uncertain and needing her assurance.

"Yes," she answered simply.

I lifted her chin for another kiss, my hand tightening on her shoulder. She stiffened, and I heard the small gasp of pain escape her lips. "Beaker?"

"It's nothing."

I sat up, flicking on the light and straddling her, effectively pinning her to the pillows. I ghosted my fingers over her shoulder, and I frowned at the bruise I could see forming there. I met her nervous eyes. "How?"

"It was an accident."

"What kind of accident?"

She hesitated. "Did someone touch you?" I hissed through my teeth. I was going to kill whoever had put those marks on her.

"They tried."

"Start talking, Shelby. Before I lose it."

She sighed. "You were right, Liam."

"About?"

"Caroline and I went for breakfast without Ryan this morning. I thought it was early enough we'd be okay. There were only a few of them hanging around."

I already knew where this was headed. "And?"

She huffed. "They followed us. I got nervous and called Ryan. He met us at the restaurant, but it was like the few had multiplied—

there were so many of them, so fast. They were surrounding us and yelling all sorts of things. One of them got too close, and I stumbled back and fell, hitting my shoulder. Ryan got there right then and pushed the guy out of the way. He hit the car with his camera, denting it. Ryan got us into the restaurant and took care of them outside. He had my car sent to the shop and drove us home after—yelling at me the whole way." She pouted. "Everett called and yelled at me too."

"I told you—"

Her eyes beseeched me as she cupped my face. "I know you did. I was stupid, and I thought I could handle it. Please don't be angry. I have enough people angry at me."

I leaned into her touch. "I'm not angry. But you have to understand—"

"I do," she assured me. "It was a mistake. I won't do it again. I promise."

"Everett yelled at you?"

"He called me by my full name and everything. He was really mad." She sighed sadly. "He said now they'll print a story about me being drunk in the morning and falling down and my bodyguard assaulting a member of the press."

Sounded about right.

But she looked sad and worried. I hated that she'd learned this lesson, but I also knew she'd learn many more. No doubt Everett would be here at some point this afternoon, and we'd hash it all out. But for now, I wasn't going to lecture her. I wanted her to smile. "They'll probably link you and Caroline together as well." I waggled my eyebrows at her. "Maybe I'm doing both of you—together." Then I grinned at her. "And they'll see her with Douglas. No doubt, we're sharing the two of you. Keeping it in the family and all."

She covered her mouth as she giggled, her eyes lighting with mirth. Her shoulders relaxed as she realized I wasn't going to yell at her. I didn't care about her dented car or what they would print. I only cared about her being hurt. She only cared about those she loved not being angry with her.

"I understand, Shelby. I do," I assured her quietly. "I only lasted about three days the first time I had a meltdown." I ran my fingers down her soft cheek, wanting her to know I wasn't angry with her. Never with her. Only at the situation we were in. "That was how I met Everett. Did he never tell you the story?"

"No. I assumed you met at some industry function."

I shifted. "Nope. I became an actor by accident. I was visiting Douglas, and as a laugh, he let me have a walk-on role in a film he was making. I was spotted by another producer visiting the set and given my first break. It was a small role, but it led to another, and then I was hired for a leading role." I huffed a long breath. "That movie took off like wildfire—totally unexpected by everyone. I was hounded and had no experience, nothing. Douglas tried to help, but I was a bit stubborn and insisted on making my own way."

Shelby laughed quietly. "You, stubborn. I can't even imagine it."

I kissed her forehead. "Hush. So in the meantime, I had hired a manager. My first mistake of many. He was" —I snorted— "useless. To him, any press was good press—any picture of me was a good thing in his eyes, no matter how intrusive." I rolled over, tucking my arm under my head and pulling Shelby close. "I had been trapped in a hotel doing a press junket for a few days and had to get out. So, I did much like you and jumped in the car, thinking I'd be okay. I ended up in some bar across town, believing I'd lost the reporters following me. But not long after I got there, a couple of the tossers walked in and sat at a table nearby, staring at me, waiting for me to do something. They would throw out remarks to try to get me to react."

"What happened?"

"I started getting angrier, and after I had a couple of ales, decided I was gonna confront them and give them what they wanted. Maybe even throw a punch or two and show them who was in charge. I figured if they thought I was tough, they'd leave me alone." I chuckled at the memory, tracing small circles on Shelby's skin with my fingers. What an idiot I had been. "I was about to get up when this big guy beside me slapped his hand on my shoulder and told me I needed to stop thinking what I was thinking and just ignore the fuckers."

"It was Everett?"

"Yeah, it was. I growled at him, I think, and he laughed, then introduced himself, ordered us another round, and calmly explained exactly what would happen if I followed through with my plans. I had been muttering out loud, it seemed, and Everett heard enough to know what I had planned."

"What did you do?"

"He told me he had a much better plan and asked if I was up for it. Of course, I said yes because anything was better than sitting there with those wankers so close, irritating the hell out of me. He explained his car would be out back, to give him five minutes, and winked. He said to follow his lead, and then he raised his voice, telling me to get over myself, stood, and walked out the front door." I started to grin, remembering what happened next. "A few minutes later, I got up and loudly announced I needed to take a piss then pretended to stagger down the hall. I slipped out the door and into his car." I shook my head. "We were long gone before they even realized they'd been played."

Shelby was giggling with me. "And then?"

"We went to his place and got right drunk off our heads. It was the start of a great friendship. The next day, there was an article about my rude and drunken behavior in a public place." I looked down at Shelby, grinning. "I was quite thoroughly chastised by the studio. If only they knew how drunk I'd been in a much more private place, they would have been horrified."

"How did he become your manager?"

"Jack and I hadn't been getting on—at all. We argued constantly, and then one day he informed me I should stick to acting, and he would handle the rest of the stuff, since he was much more capable than me."

I sighed. "The day I was mobbed, he was there—twenty feet away, watching. He did nothing to help. He stood and watched as they tore at my clothes and hair. Groped at me. Grabbed my junk. He did nothing but make sure lots of pictures were taken." I shuddered at the memory. "He thought my panic attacks were amusing. He never cared about me. Only the dollars I added to his bank account."

"What a jerk."

"Yeah, he was. He loved to spend my money. All under the guise of 'helping' me, when really it was just helping himself and his friends. It took me a while, but the argument we had that day was it for me. I walked out, went to Everett, and made him an offer. He only had two other clients, but I liked how he treated them—with respect." I rubbed my face roughly with my hand. "He had been much more than a friend for a while. Always there to advise me or help if I needed it. He always had my back—something I knew Jack didn't anymore. Whatever was better financially was the direction Jack seemed to be taking. I knew it was only going to get worse. The more famous I became, the more we argued. Jack proved he wasn't loyal to me—only the money I made him. Everett was a true friend, and I knew I could trust him. He had proven it time and time again.

"Bloody hell, it was an awful scene when I fired Jack. Everett was there, doing most of the talking, thank God. And my lawyer was there. It got ugly. But once it was done, things got much better." Smirking, I rolled again, making Shelby gasp in surprise as I hovered over her. "Then I fired that nutjob, Marie, and got you. And my life became pretty bloody perfect."

She smiled at me, her gaze filled with love. We were close enough I could see the flecks of gold amidst the blue of her eyes. Our eyes held as the heat built back up around us.

Fuck, I wanted her again.

I drifted my fingers across her shoulder. "Does it hurt?"

"Not really. Just a little achy."

Leaning down, I brushed my lips over the bruise. "I'll kiss it—and anywhere else you're aching," I murmured, trailing my lips to her ear. "Just show me, and I'll make it *all* better."

I liked the shiver my touch caused.

She wound her arms around my neck, pulling me down to her sweet mouth.

I went willingly.

20

LIAM

My phone buzzed with an incoming text. Shifting carefully so I didn't disturb Shelby, I grabbed it off the nightstand.

Everett: Picked it up. On my way. Be there in 10. She is going to kill you, btw.

I grinned—there was that chance. Looking down into Shelby's sleeping face, I decided the chance was worth the risk. And I knew exactly how to get her on board with my plan. I snickered quietly to myself.

I was pure genius.

Pressing closer, I nuzzled the sleep-warmed skin of her cheek, ghosting my lips over her skin. "Shelby, my darling girl. Wake up."

Her eyes opened, her sleepy smile welcoming. "Hi."

"Everett is going to be here any minute. We need to get up."

She pulled the covers tighter and snuggled into my chest. I wrapped my arms around her, enjoying the feel of her being close.

"Is he coming to yell more?"

"I'll make you a deal. I won't let him yell. But you can't yell either."

"Really?"

"Promise."

"Okay."

Chuckling, I got up, grabbed some jeans and a T-shirt from the drawer, and threw them on. Bending, I grabbed Thor, placing him on my shoulder. "Get dressed and come downstairs."

"Commando, Liam?"

I winked at her. "My girl likes me that way." I paused at the door. "Come on, Beaker."

"I'm coming!" I heard her get out of bed as I walked down the hall, and then she called out, her voice suspicious. "Wait—what are you up to Oscar?"

I kept walking.

Shelby walked around the vehicle silently, stopping a couple of times to glare at me, then she would move again, opening the doors, peering inside, but not saying a word. I heard her rummaging around the front at one point, and I braced myself for her wrath.

Finally, she stopped in front of me. "You bought a new car."

"SUV—the safest one in its class. It's an Acura MDX."

Everett grinned. "It's a sweet ride. This thing is loaded."

"Why does the registration have my name on it, Liam, if it's your car?"

"SUV," I corrected.

"Fine," she huffed. "Your *SUV*."

"Ah, tax purposes."

I looked at Everett, who nodded with approval.

Good one.

I probably shouldn't have raised my hand for a fist bump while Shelby was looking.

Big mistake.

"You better not have bought me this, Liam. If you did, you can take it back...*right now.*"

I shook my head. "No refunds."

"So, you did buy this for me?" she spat out, crossing her arms over her chest. "Is my car not good enough?"

And there it was. I looked at Everett, who shrugged as if to say, "You're on your own," and faced Shelby.

"No, actually, it's not."

Her eyes narrowed and I moved closer, keeping my voice soothing. "Shelby, this SUV is safe. A nav system, completely synced with your phone, extra air bags, tinted windows, air conditioning."

She snorted. "You sound like a car salesman. Why do I need that stuff? I'm fine without it! I've done without all of it until now!"

She walked into my web so easily, I was surprised.

"Things have changed now. This—" I patted the top of the SUV "—will keep you safe. Now you can drive with the windows up and be comfortable in the heat." I jerked my head toward the front gate. "They can't take pictures of you through the tint. Pull down the visor and wear sunglasses, they won't get much of an angle from the front either. You don't even have to roll the windows down to get in the gate—there's a remote inside the cab." I added a little incentive. "Once this—us—dies down, I won't worry as much when you're out on your own." I didn't add it would be a while before that happened. Then I went in for the kill. "I would think, after what happened this morning, you'd want to make sure Ev and I don't worry as much. We hoped you'd accept this, knowing how much it would mean to both of us."

Her eyes widened, and she looked over at Ev, who stared at her, his face grave. She looked back at me, and I struggled to keep a straight face as he took a bow behind her. I kept my expression serious. "I don't ask much, Shelby, but I am asking you to do this one thing. Drive this car. For me."

She looked at the vehicle and then back at me. "It would make you feel better? Worry less?"

"Yes, it would. Please."

Her voice became suspicious. "Does this have anything to do with the money?"

Bloody hell, my girl was a smart one. "No, Shelby. This has everything to do with your safety and my peace of mind," I stated firmly. "It never even crossed my mind."

She studied my face, which I managed to keep smooth, only conveying shock at her suggestion.

"Just checking," she murmured as she looked back at the vehicle again.

My lips twitched as I dared a glance at Everett, who was smirking at me. I should have gotten another Oscar for my performance. Fooling her wasn't easy.

She sighed in defeat. "It is a lovely color," she murmured.

I pulled her against my chest, wrapping my arms securely around her. "It's called 'Performance Red Pearl.' You know how much I love you in red." I patted the hood. "And it sparkles. You love sparkles."

She looked at me, no longer annoyed, but smiling.

"Oh."

Everett groaned. "I am out of here." He chuckled. "Cheeseball is back in the house." He shook his head as he walked away. I ignored him. *Cheeseball* was working right now, and I was taking full advantage of that fact.

Lowering my head, I bit down on her sensitive lobe. "The windows are dark enough we could snog in the back seat somewhere. Just for fun."

"*Oh.*"

I kissed the shell of her ear, tracing the pale skin with the tip of my tongue. "We could get in now and try it if you like." I lowered my voice. "It would drive Everett crazy." I opened the back door. "You wanna test it out?"

She whimpered.

I had her.

Score.

The stories printed the next day were quite close to what Everett had predicted. Apparently, I was seeing Caroline as well as Shelby, which caused her to drink. One of the photographers got pushed while trying to break up the two of them, since they were about to start physically fighting over me. I glanced at Shelby, who was chuckling beside me.

"*Hot*, Beaker. Catfight." I waggled my eyebrows at her, relishing her giggles. Of course, no mention was made of the fact that they were long-standing friends, or that Caroline was staying here and they had left to go for breakfast together. I shut off the monitor, shaking my head. It would never change. Half the time, even legitimate interviews misconstrued my words, twisting them to make it seem like I said something other than what I had stated. I was tired of it, and I had to admit, it was wearing me down.

I sat, sipping my coffee. "Is Caroline still asleep? What time did she get home last night?" I had crashed early, Shelby beside me reading, and Thor purring on my head as he snuggled in.

Shelby smirked as she placed the plate of French toast in front of me. I dug into the unexpected treat, famished. "She texted me to say it was late and she'd stay at Douglas's."

I paused, my fork midway to my mouth. "That wanker. He stole my other woman!"

Shelby laughed. "You Wright men are hard to resist."

"It's the British thing. I keep telling you. Resistance is futile." I pulled her into my lap, kissing her with syrup-covered lips.

"So it appears," she agreed. "It's not like Caroline to move so quickly."

I took another bite of French toast, chewing thoughtfully and chuckling as Shelby stole a bite off my plate. "Douglas isn't usually one to act like this either," I agreed. "I guess you were right. They are perfect for each other."

Her eyes lit up, and she moved closer. "I'm sorry, I couldn't hear you. What did you say? I was *what?*"

Laughing, I kissed her—hard. She was adorable. "You were right. One hundred percent right." Then I smirked. "And I am going to have fun with them when they eventually resurface."

"Liam? If you embarrass her, she might decide to spend less time with Douglas. And more time here."

I frowned, not understanding her point. Caroline was here to see Shelby after all. "And?"

"If she's here, we won't be alone. And then I couldn't do this." With a grin, she slipped off my lap onto her knees in front of me. Her hands began a torturous circuit up my thighs, gliding under the loose legs of the board shorts I was wearing and teasing OJ. He instantly became far more interested in the fact that her mouth was *right there* than the fact that French toast was close to my mouth. I dropped my fork as Shelby tugged on the material, lifting my hips as she pulled him free of the suddenly restraining fabric.

When her mouth closed around me, wet and warm, my head fell back, thoughts of breakfast, Caroline, or anything else leaving my head, at least the one on my shoulders. The only thing in the entire world that mattered was the sexy woman kneeling in front of me with my cock in her mouth. Dammit, she was good at pleasuring me.

"*Oh fuck...*Shelby..." I groaned.

Her eyes were filled with mischief as she pulled back, teasing the head with her tongue, the pink tip gliding and licking, making my eyes roll back in my head. "You really want Caroline here all the time before you leave?"

"No," I panted, shaking my head, understanding her completely now. And in utter agreement. "Caroline should spend lots of time with Douglas. She can come back after I leave," I gasped. "Not saying a bloody word."

She winked. "Good plan."

My reward was her mouth on me again.

Both OJ and I rejoiced.

Loudly.

Later in the afternoon, I handed Douglas another beer, grinning at the expression on his face as he watched Shelby and Caroline chatting, floating around the pool. "You are a goner there, big bro."

He glanced at me, frowning. "I just met her, Liam. Hardly a goner."

"Hmph," I mused, throwing myself back into the lounger next to him, staring at Shelby. Her blue bathing suit was nowhere near small enough for my taste, but since we had guests, it was probably for the best. They might not like the reaction I would have to her more revealing suits. As it was, I had to keep OJ on a short leash and distracted. "Well then, you'll be happy to know Shelby is planning on keeping Caroline busy over the next few days. You won't have to worry about her being too...clingy or anything."

The bottle paused in midair and Douglas glanced at me. "Oh."

I hid my grin. "Problem?"

"No." He paused. "But I thought you were home the next few days. I, ah, was planning to take Caroline around, show her some great photo spots and, um, you know, let you have some time with Shelby before you left for your shoot. You know, as a favor."

"Ah. Such a selfless gesture on your part." I rolled my eyes. "You are so full of it."

He joined me in my laughter. "I am. Bloody hell, Liam, she's fabulous."

I agreed. "She's great. I like her."

His eyes were focused on her. "I like her too...a lot."

"She's feisty."

"She's smart, funny, and sexy as hell," he pronounced. "She makes me laugh. I like how she makes me feel when I'm with her. So at ease and happy."

"So, not bringing her back, then."

He shook his head. "Not if I can convince her to stay for the night. I already promised her a tour of the studio tomorrow."

"The way she's looking at you, I don't think it'll be too difficult to convince her." I pointed out. "And the way the two of them are scheming over there, I think it's being decided for you."

He grinned, taking another swig of his beer. "I'm surprisingly good with it." He swallowed. "I'll make sure to give her back after you're gone. I know she wants to spend time with Shelby."

"I think Shelby is thrilled her matchmaking worked. She doesn't mind Caroline spending time with you."

"And you are all for it," he stated dryly.

I didn't bother to hide my amusement. "Whatever makes Shelby happy."

He snorted but didn't say anything else for a few moments.

"When do you leave?"

"Sunday."

"You don't sound enthused."

I shrugged. "It's fine. I hate leaving Shelby these days, even if it's only for a short time. She's handling all of this well, but I keep thinking something is going to go wrong."

"She's strong, Liam. She loves you."

"I love her."

His voice was serious. "I know. It's good to see. She's changing you—for the better."

I had no response. He was right.

He took another sip of beer. "Aunt Liz know about this?"

"Yes. I called and told her. She was thrilled but told me it took me long enough."

"Sounds like her."

Merriment drew our gazes again, and I grinned at the sight of their two beautiful heads bent close together, giggling. I liked seeing Shelby relaxed and happy. "Will she be getting a call from you soon, Douglas?"

His eyes left Caroline and met mine. He huffed out a sigh. "Yeah, you wanker. She probably will be."

"That means a Scottish invasion. An epic one." I turned on the

Scottish accent. "Both her laddies in love? With such bonny wee lassies?" I sniggered. "Ooch, me boys! When do I get grandweans? I've been waiting to change nappies for some wee bairns for sooo long." I drew out the words. "Dad won't even come to hold her back. She'll be full-out mental with happiness."

He laughed. "She'll be daft." He fixed me with a stern look I knew he was struggling to maintain. "She's *your* mum. She stays with you."

I knew he was full of it. He adored my mum and always complained when she didn't spend enough time with him on her visits. "She'll want to spend time with Caroline as well. We'll share."

"I'll do sixty-forty. And you're the sixty."

I knew he was only bluffing. He'd try to steal her more often—he always did. "Done."

"Okay." He stood. "Let's go join the ladies." He looked back, meeting my gaze. "We'll keep an eye on Shelby, Liam. And Ryan and Everett are here." He sighed. "I'll even bring Caroline back while you're gone, so Shelby isn't alone. She'll be fine."

I drained my beer and stood beside him. "Thanks. I am worried. It's only a week, but it seems..."

He gripped my shoulder. "I know. We'll make sure she's okay."

"Good."

I needed to know that.

I kissed Shelby, a fierce, deep kiss as I pulled her against me. I didn't want to go. The past few days had flown by too fast, and now I had to leave again. She eased back, panting. "The car is waiting."

"It can wait another few minutes," I growled, capturing her mouth again.

I pressed my forehead against hers. "Don't go out without Ryan. Please, Beaker."

"I won't."

"Call Everett if you need something or you're scared."

"I will."

"Caroline—"

She cut me off. "Caroline is with Douglas, Liam. She'll be over later today. We're going to do some fun things this week, and I'll be sure Ryan is with us. Douglas is also coming at times. The rest of the time, I'll be fine—just like I always am. You'll be home by the weekend. Don't worry so much, please."

"I'm sorry, I...I don't want to go. I don't want to leave you."

She pulled me back with one last kiss. "You have to. It's your job. Go do what you do and be brilliant. I'll be right here when you get home."

"I'll call you when I get there."

"Okay."

I walked toward the car, turning partway down the steps. "Maybe from the airport, before I get on the plane."

"Whatever you need to do, Oscar," she giggled.

"Go back to bed. It's early," I instructed her firmly.

The car door was open; Mark waiting for me.

I turned around as I got in the car, for one last look at my Shelby. Leaning on the doorframe, wearing one of my T-shirts and leggings, her hair tumbling past her shoulders in total disarray from my hands, she was breathtaking to me.

She was home.

I lifted my hand and slid into the car before I ran back to her for one last kiss.

Because I knew one would never be enough. I needed more of her. More kisses, more time.

I took out my phone and texted Everett.

Liam: Clear my schedule as much as possible. No more time away from home for a while.

He replied quickly.

Everett: Okay. Will do what I can.

I sighed. I rarely demanded much, but I wanted this. More than anything.

Liam: Just take care of it, Ev.

His reply was brief.

Everett: Done.

It was what I wanted. I'd do this movie, all the publicity the studio wanted for *Nighthawk,* and then I would take some time off. Maybe take Shelby away for a holiday. The two of us on a deserted island or something—just somewhere private we could be alone and I could spoil her. I'd like to do that.

About halfway to the airport, my phone buzzed, and I looked at it, expecting to see another return text from Ev. Instead, there was a picture from Shelby with the text —**waiting for you right here** —and I had to smile. She had taken a selfie, lying in our bed, resting on my pillow with Thor beside her head, curled into her dark hair. She was smiling into the camera, her eyes half-closed and sleepy-looking. She was so damned sexy, and she had no idea.

I wrote her back.

Liam: I love you in our bed.

Her return text made my heart clench a little more.

Shelby: I love you everywhere.

God, she was brilliant.
The next week couldn't go by quick enough.

21

LIAM

I yanked my T-shirt over my head, grabbed my duffle bag off the floor, and shoved my few personal items in it. I looked around the trailer to make sure I hadn't left anything behind. Satisfied, I pulled the door open and went to find Mark. The location shoot I was involved with was done, and I was ready to go back to the hotel. I had an interview later in the afternoon and a flight home the next morning. I had a few days off, then the film I was working on would continue to shoot in LA, meaning I would be home.

I hated being away from home now. Being away from Shelby.

I clambered down the steps, surprised to see Mark headed my way, his face dark and scowling. My stomach tightened at his expression. "We need to go, Liam," he informed me quietly. "Now."

"Go where?"

"Back to LA. Everett booked a private plane. We'll go to the hotel, get your stuff, and head to the airport."

I grabbed his arm. "What happened?"

"Shelby. She's been hurt. She needs you."

Panic shot through me at his words, and my breath caught in my throat as I struggled to stay calm. "Screw the luggage," I growled. "They can send it. Let's go."

"Stay calm, Liam," Mark muttered, grabbing my arm, hustling me onto the plane. I looked behind me one last time at the crowd of photographers at the gate. They were too far away for me to hear what they were yelling, but I knew something big had happened to cause all this mayhem.

"Why aren't Everett or Cassidy answering their phones?" I snarled, throwing myself into one of the plush seats. "What the hell is going on? What happened to Shelby?"

"Fasten your seat belt. I'll tell you once we're in the air."

I was about to tell Mark to fuck the hell off and tell me now, but I held my tongue. I wasn't acting like myself due to worry about Shelby. Being an asshole to him wasn't going to help the situation. Without saying another word, I buckled myself in and leaned my head against the headrest, drawing in deep breaths and wishing we had stopped at the hotel. I could use a Xanax right now. But since I didn't have any on me, I concentrated on my breathing and tried to think about something calming.

Except, the one thing that made me calm was Shelby.

And she was hurt. How hurt, I didn't know.

My pulse picked up, and my heart started racing.

"Mark?" I gasped, struggling for breath.

"Yeah?"

I swallowed heavily, trying to get the words out. "Is...is she going to be okay?"

"Yes. I need to get you to her, Liam. In one piece. Stay. Calm."

I let out the pent-up air. "Okay."

As soon as the plane leveled off, I sat up. "Tell me. Now."

Wordlessly, Mark handed me a copy of one of the daily rags. The one I loathed the most since they were notorious for printing more lies than truth, yet their sales were unbelievable. People ate up that bullshit.

I was horrified at the headline.

Shelby Carter's Husband Breaks His Silence. "I was dumped for a richer, younger man. She used me. Now she's using him."

Fuck.

Malcolm *fucking* Johnson had reappeared.

I scanned the article, my hands gripping the paper so tight, it started to tear. The article was full of lies and accusations. His version of the story was she left him to pursue me, wanting a younger, richer man. *She* was the one who made off with the money, leaving him high and dry. She played him. She'd played me. Used her brother's connection to get to me and bided her time until I fell for her. He was ashamed to say how often he had caught her cheating with younger men in their marriage, but he had tried hard to make it work, because he loved her deeply. He called her a pathological liar and stated that she was desperately trying to hold on to her youth by being with younger men. He was shocked to discover, while he was away trying to come to grips with his pain, he was being divorced and cast aside.

I stopped reading and looked at Mark.

"This is total bullshit. We can prove all this is false. Tell me Everett has Samuels on it."

Mark nodded.

"Shelby must be shattered," I muttered. "No wonder Everett sent for me."

"That's not why."

"What?"

"This hit the media this morning—Everett and Cassidy had no warning. Shelby had an eye doctor appointment this morning. When she came out of the building, she was surrounded."

My stomach dropped.

"Ryan wasn't there?"

"He was. There were too many of them, Liam. He tried. He's injured as well."

I threw myself out of the seat, pacing the aisle and cursing. I slammed my hand on the top of one of the seats. *"Fuck!"*

I spun around. "What happened?"

"Everett said it was a mob, and they were lying in wait for them. They were rabid. Pushing and yelling, shoving copies of the article in her face. There were too many of them, and Ryan tried to get Shelby back to the car. There were repairs happening on the stairs—work being done on the handrail. Things escalated, and somehow..." He paused and took in a deep breath. "One of the reporters grabbed at her, and Ryan pushed him away. The reporter took a swing at Ryan, and it caught Shelby. She stumbled backward and began to fall over the railing. Ryan grabbed her, but the railing gave way and he went over, and they both fell to the concrete."

Shelby.

My legs gave out, and I sat heavily, staring at him.

"How bad?" My voice was hollow as I asked.

"Luckily, it was only one flight of stairs. Had it been higher, things would have been much worse. Still, Ryan took the brunt of the fall. Somehow, he twisted Shelby, so she was on top of him. Protecting her body with his. She hit her head on the railing as they went over. His body landed on a concrete border surrounding the bushes, which caused the bulk of his injuries, then he hit the pavement. Shelby's arm was broken, she's bruised, and she was unconscious when she arrived at the hospital."

"Unconscious?"

He nodded. "She's still unresponsive, Liam."

I buried my hand in my hair, and a funny choking noise came out of my throat.

"Ryan?"

"His injuries are extensive. Shattered hip, shoulder, and leg, broken ribs."

My voice became pleading. "You said she'd be okay."

"She will be, Liam. You have to believe that."

"Everett is with her?"

"Yes. He won't leave her."

"Get me to her."

He leaned forward, clapping my shoulder. "I will."

It was the longest five hours of my life. The entire time, I paced and fumed, becoming more enraged as the minutes ticked by. The flight attendant stayed as far away from me as possible after I snarled at her when she offered me a beverage. I knew Shelby would tell me off for being rude and I should apologize, but I honestly didn't care about my behavior at the moment. The only thing I cared about was trying to figure out how to get this bloody plane to fly faster and get me to Shelby. Knowing she was not only emotionally hurt, but physically injured because of those fuckers and their irresponsible actions, made me livid. It was all I could do not to tear the plane apart with my bare hands.

I read and reread the shit that passed as an article, cursing at the blatant lies within it. I knew why he'd done this: money. He must've seen pictures of Shelby and me when he'd slid out from whatever rock he'd been hiding under. Discovered he was being divorced didn't sit well, and he'd figured out a way he could cash in on our relationship. And the rag he'd sold his story to was infamous for never checking facts before printing.

I felt grim satisfaction in knowing by the time my lawyers were through with them, they wouldn't have a press left to print anything on. I planned on destroying them, and I knew Everett would be right beside me when I did it. I was going to hit them with everything I had at my disposal.

And Malcolm Johnson.

He was going to answer for what he'd done. His lies had caused this whole fucking disaster. Because of him, Shelby was lying injured in a hospital bed. I stopped my pacing and plopped into my seat, dropping my head into my hands. The thought of her—Shelby—hurt was tearing me up inside. More than once I had dry heaved in the bathroom simply thinking about her lying there, unconscious and bleeding. I couldn't stand the idea of her being in pain. I had no idea how I was going to handle it when I arrived, but I knew I had to—I had no choice.

I had to be strong for her. And for my friend Everett. I knew how he adored his sister and how deeply he revered her for the way she'd looked after him when their parents died. He had to be suffering right now as well. Tears ran down my cheeks, and I swiped them away in anger.

I couldn't do this right now. I couldn't fall apart. I inhaled a deep breath.

It was time to grow up and be the mature person they could lean on.

The way they had allowed me to lean on them for so long.

"Liam."

I looked up at Mark's quiet voice. "We land soon. There'll be a car waiting."

"Any change?" I knew he'd been using the plane's satellite phone to check in with Cassidy—I could barely think, never mind talk. Everett hadn't left Shelby's bedside. The only message I asked to pass along was to make sure Shelby had the best care available and a private room. Anything she needed, she was to have. He assured me Cassidy would take care of it all.

He shook his head. "No. Ryan is out of surgery, though. He did well."

"Good."

"Almost there. Hold on."

I shut my eyes. "Thanks."

I had no idea what was waiting for me.

We landed in a private area of the airport and taxied into a hangar. As soon as we hit the ground, I was on the phone to Samuels, who had been in contact with Cassidy. I gave him instructions on what I wanted to happen. If he was surprised at my sudden take-charge attitude, he was smart enough to keep his mouth shut. I called my parents, who sent their prayers and told me to keep them posted, then called Douglas from the car, knowing Caroline would be with him. He knew what had happened, was horrified, and wanted to do something to help. He told me as soon as I had news to contact him. He was keeping Caroline away from the hospital until he heard from me. We both knew it would be a mob scene there, and it was best for her to stay at home.

Cassidy had arranged for the car to bring me to a service entrance, so I was able to get inside the hospital without incident. The paps were all hanging outside the front and sides, waiting for me to show up later. Cassidy had issued a statement saying I was on a later flight; therefore, they weren't expecting me yet. She was waiting for me by the elevator, pale and tense. She flung her arms around me, and I held her, grateful for the sight of a friendly face. Pulling back, I scanned her anxious eyes. "Is she awake?"

"No." She paused, her voice quiet. "She's in a coma, Liam."

I tightened my hands on her arms. "Coma?"

Her eyes glimmered with tears. "That's what they are calling it now. There's no brain swelling, though, which is a good sign. The doctor can tell you more."

"I need to see her."

She nodded. "It's family only, but Everett made arrangements for that to be overlooked."

I snorted. That wouldn't stop me. Nothing was stopping me from seeing my Beaker.

"You haven't seen her?"

"Only briefly." She squeezed my shoulder. "She's really banged up. Lots of bruises and cuts. Her head is also bandaged."

My stomach lurched, and I covered my mouth, hoping I didn't heave again.

"They have her on pain meds. They promised Everett she was comfortable."

"*Now*, Cassidy. I need to see her now," I insisted.

"I'll take you to her."

She was still and silent. Even when sleeping, Shelby moved; her nose scrunched, mouth pursed, fingers twitched, toes curled, and her legs shifted constantly. And when she wasn't moving or twitching, she mumbled. Often my name, and frequently it was followed by a low sigh or giggle. Usually watching and listening to her was entertaining for me. But seeing her lying there, utterly motionless, brought tears to my eyes. She was small and fragile-looking, her head swathed in thick, white gauze, her hair almost hidden, only the ends peeking out at the back. She was deathly pale, with bruises and scrapes scattered over one side of her face. Her arms were covered in more bruises, one arm encased in heavy plaster, the other lying limp on the bed. An IV was hooked up, the needle piercing her skin, and I swallowed deeply looking at it, the tears beginning to fall down my cheeks.

Shelby *hated* needles.

Monitors beeped and made strange noises in the stillness of the room. Oxygen was steadily pumped into her. Beside her was Everett —her brother, my friend, looking more broken and lost than I had ever seen him. Always so strong, so much larger than life, he sat beside her, her small hand enclosed in his, just staring at her as if he were willing her to open her eyes and look at him. He hadn't even looked up to see me enter the room, his every sense focused on his sister. His shoulders were hunched, his body tense. I wondered how he would react to seeing me. He must be angry—this was my fault. Because she loved me, she was hurt. I brought her into this crazy life I led. I promised him I'd keep her safe, and I had failed.

"Everett," I murmured, surprised to hear how raspy my voice sounded.

His head snapped up, and our eyes met. His blue ones, so like Shelby's, were swirling with pain and grief as they met mine. Standing up, he lunged, and the next thing I knew, his huge arms were around me and we were both sharing our pain. When I felt his shoulders shaking, my own emotions peaked, and I gripped him hard. "I'm sorry, Everett. I'm so fucking sorry."

He pulled back, shaking his head. "This is not your fault, Liam. Don't even go there." He shook my shoulders. "This is on that asshole."

"I promised you—"

"And you kept your promise."

My eyes went to my girl—my silent, still girl, and I swallowed the sudden lump in my throat, struggling to get my emotions under control. My fingers twitched with the need to touch her. I had to feel her skin under my fingers and know she was still *here*. That I could still *feel* her. I had never experienced the helplessness threatening to overwhelm me.

Everett's hand was a heavy, comforting weight on my shoulder. "She needs you strong, Liam. I need you strong. We have to get her through this—and she *will* get through this—and we need to nail that bastard. To the motherfucking wall."

I exhaled. He was right. "I know. We will." I looked at him. "Can I, ah, have a moment?"

He wiped his eyes. "Yes. I'll go see Cassidy and give you a few minutes. We have a private quiet room down the hall. I'll be back."

He turned to me before he left. "Talk to her, Liam. She needs to hear your voice and know you're here."

The door shut soundlessly behind him, and I moved to the bed. Gingerly, I picked up Shelby's hand, bringing it to my lips, surprised at how warm it was. I bought it to my face, leaning into her palm. "I'm here, my darling girl. I'm sorry I couldn't get here faster." I swallowed as the tears threatened. "But I'm here now. Open your eyes, Beaker. Open them and tell me off for taking so long. Make me laugh." Turning my face, I kissed her palm, the noise of the machines beeping and whirring the only sounds in the room.

Tenderly, I traced the skin of her uninjured cheek, sighing. "Okay. Have it your way. You sleep. But I'm not leaving. Not until you open your eyes and call me Oscar." My voice cracked. "Until you tell me you love me, my fine British arse is staying right here." I bent closer. "I'll have lots of time for bank transfers and surfing the net for expensive gifts. Think about all the money I'm going to spend on you while you're napping."

She didn't move. No twitches or flexing of her fingers. No sweet smile to my attempted teasing.

Silence. Stillness. She was lost in a world where I couldn't reach her, no matter how hard I tried.

I broke.

I buried my face in her hand, the wetness of my tears running down her arm.

"Come back to me. Don't leave me, Shelby. I love you. Please don't leave me."

22

LIAM

That was the only time I broke. When Everett and Cassidy returned, I was sitting, stroking Shelby's cheek, holding her uninjured hand, and telling her about the antics of the idiot costar I had been working with, assuring her he was even more of a screw-up than me. "Hard to believe, right, Beaker?"

When I saw Cassidy and Everett watching me, I forced a smile and got to work.

"I want Samuels and Mark." I paused. "And figure out how to get Douglas and Caroline in here."

Cassidy arched an eyebrow at me, no doubt wanting to know what my plan was. I shrugged at her. She'd know soon enough.

"Now."

I turned back to Shelby.

The hours that followed were one surprise after another for them all. Including me. Early the next morning, I left a somber Caroline to sit with Shelby since I refused to leave her alone for even one minute in case she woke. I filled Caroline in before I left the room. "They just moved her. And checked her drip. She should be okay while I'm gone. But I'm only down the hall."

"We'll be fine, Liam."

"She likes it when you talk to her."

"I will," she assured me.

It took all I had to walk away. This meeting was going to be quick.

I walked into the room, looking at the faces waiting for me. Everett and Cassidy looked as tired as I felt. Douglas was pacing, anxious. Samuels was his usual business-like self, but he was tense. I started right away.

"Samuels, I want a large cash reward offered. No questions asked. I want the location of Malcolm Johnson, and once we have it, I want him arrested."

"Which charges do you want me to start with..." His voice trailed off at my angry glare.

"Figure it out!" I snapped. "He stole everything of value that belonged to Shelby, and he deserted her. He caused this entire fucked-up situation. He's lied and cheated. He needs to be held responsible for a lot of shit. Pick one. Pick them all. Just do it!" I pulled a hand through my hair. It needed a trim again. I would have to remind Shelby of that when I went back into her room. "I want him found—*now*—before the asshole gets his money and leaves town again.

"And I want a lawsuit launched against the rag. Throw everything at them. Everything. I want them out of business."

"Everything?"

"Crush them."

I took in Cassidy, Everett, and Douglas, who were all watching me. "Use your contacts. I want the names of the paps in the crowd. There were so many cameras going off, someone captured what happened. I want to know *exactly* who put their hands on Ryan and Shelby. Who the hell is responsible for sending them over those stairs."

I had already read the reports and heard the stories from eyewitnesses on the news. There was also a video a bystander had taken. The scene was chaos. Too many reporters, and only Ryan and Shelby, desperately trying to get away. Amidst the shouting and pushing was the moment when the altercation broke out. Watching Shelby get hit and fall backward, and the way Ryan dove after her, protecting her as they went over the railing, horrified me. The sheer panic on her face broke something inside me. Seeing them lying on the concrete, her unconscious and Ryan gravely hurt, was ghastly. So was the fact that the mob barely stopped, snapping pictures of them lying injured and bleeding. It was someone walking by who contacted 9-1-1—the paps were too busy getting their pictures or running away. The entire scene made me ill, and Everett had the same reaction.

"What are you planning, Liam?" Douglas asked.

"I'm taking them down. The police are looking for them, but they'll take too long. The paps won't talk to them willingly. I saw lots of familiar faces in the crowd. The lowest of the low." I barked out a laugh. "Even some legit reporters were there. Offer enough cash—one of those bastards will give up their competition, no problem. I want all the pictures and proof."

I drew in a deep breath. "And as an added incentive, whoever gives me what I want gets a one-on-one with me." I paused. "Two hours of my time. No holds barred."

Everyone stared at me as if I'd lost my mind.

"Liam, you never—" Cassidy began.

I cut her off. "When it comes to Shelby, there isn't a 'never,'" I informed her. "In fact, call a press conference. Now. Today. I'll issue the statement myself about the reward. I have a few things I want to get off my chest."

Everett frowned. "Liam—"

I held up my hand. "No. Don't say it." I scrubbed my face roughly. "If this had happened to anyone else, and a child had been hurt, we wouldn't be having this conversation. There would have been a huge outcry and an immediate investigation. But because it was the girlfriend of a celebrity—of mine—it's no big deal? The police are dragging their feet—as if it's not urgent. They act as if I should accept it. Well, I don't. I will *never* accept it. The paps hurt Shelby and did nothing to help once she and Ryan were injured. All that mattered was a goddamn photo and story." I sucked in some much-needed oxygen and pointed down the hall. "My entire fucking life is down there. She's in a coma because of them. Ryan may never walk properly again. Someone needs to be held accountable for this bloody atrocity. This is not about my privacy. This is about much more." I slammed my fist into the wall. "Fuck!"

Suddenly, I was exhausted. Leaning against the wall I'd just hit, I let my head fall to my chest. I sighed deeply and lifted my gaze, meeting Everett's eyes.

"I can't let them get away with this, Ev. You know I can't. I have to do this."

"Liam, you don't talk about your personal life," Everett said as he frowned at me.

I braced my hands against the small table in the room, ignoring the throbbing of my knuckles. "I will give and do whatever it takes to make sure those bloody fuckers get what is coming to them—especially criminal records. If giving up a few personal details will make it happen, then so be it." I shook my head. "I'll read whatever statement you prepare, Cassidy. But I want it good. Plain. Honest. You got me?"

"I'll take care of it." She jotted some notes. "I'll handle the questions after, though, all right?"

I turned back to Samuels. "Once we have the names, I want restraining orders against all of them. Personal lawsuits brought forth."

"That's always tricky, Liam."

I shrugged. "It'll send a message. Make life hard for them, at least for a while. I'm through playing and being nice. They hurt the most important person in the world to me. It's time they paid.

"Everett—cancel everything. Appearances, interviews— everything. Tell the studio I'm on hiatus. Taking a personal leave of absence. I don't care how much they bitch or what they threaten to do. Until Shelby is home and well, I'm not going anywhere."

He watched me with unguarded admiration. I knew he wasn't used to seeing me like this, but it was high time he did.

"Mark, I want extra security. Someone by the elevator. Outside Shelby's door. Twenty-four seven. No one gets near her room that shouldn't. The paps are getting restless down there, and they'll start looking for ways to get on this floor. I've already cleared it with the hospital."

He nodded. "Done."

I turned to Cassidy. "Any word on Ryan?"

"I got him the private room, as you requested. He's still coming out of it. They have him heavily sedated." She paused. "His leg, hip, and shoulder were crushed, Liam. Badly. With all the damage, he'll probably never work security again. If he can work at all."

I frowned at the news. "I'll take care of him."

From the corner, Douglas spoke up. "Let me help, Liam. You concentrate on Shelby, and I'll run point for you on this." Drawing in a deep breath, he continued, "Let me handle the press conference. I'll speak on your behalf and for Shelby and Ryan." He turned to Everett and Cassidy. "Let my staff help you. I'll tell them to give anything you need top priority so you can spend your time with her as well." He chuckled darkly. "My lawyer, Geo, is a rottweiler, and I'm sure he'd love to pitch in with the lawsuit. He loves taking down those wankers. I'll call him in to help you, Samuels."

Our eyes met across the room. He projected the same calm, cool exterior all those who knew him would recognize. But for someone like me, who knew the real person, I could see how upset he was. His hands that normally would be resting relaxed beside his legs were clasped in tight fists, while a beating pulse jumped erratically at the base of his throat. He already cared for Shelby, and he wanted to help. He was family, and his words carried a lot of weight here. He was as private as me, so for him to offer to do all this was a big gesture. From the expressions on Everett's and Cassidy's faces, I knew they thought it was a good idea. He would be far calmer than I would be, and although part of me wanted to be the one saying the words, I had to do what was best for Shelby and Ryan. Douglas's voice and leadership would be seen as a statement to many.

"Let me do this, Liam," he insisted. "I want to do this for you and for Shelby."

"Thank you, Douglas. I accept your offer."

"Good. It will happen later today."

Everett stood. "Okay. Let's go over this. Liam—go back to Shelby. I'll ask someone to come in and look at your hand."

I nodded, not caring about my hand, only about Shelby. I was already feeling anxious being away from her, even though she was only a couple of doors down and Caroline was with her. I wanted her to hear my voice and feel my presence beside her.

Selfishly, I wanted to be the first person she saw when she woke.

"I also want to check on Ryan."

"I'll check on him and let you know when he's awake," Cassidy assured me.

"Okay."

I paused at the door and glanced behind me. They were all looking at me with new expressions, ones I had never seen before. Maybe it was respect. Or relief that I had finally grown up.

I nodded at them. "Thank you."

And I went back to Shelby.

I pressed Shelby's small hand to my forehead. "Please, baby. Wake up. It's been too long. I need you."

She slept on. I ghosted my fingers over her cheek as I kissed her hand. "Beaker, I'm getting desperate. I swear I'll send Cassidy to the house to empty the freezer, and I'll eat every baked good you have stashed in there. My pants will explode, I'll get so fat. You don't want that to happen, do you?"

Nothing.

I buried my face in her palm.

I needed her to come back. I wasn't sure how much more I could take.

A hand settled on my shoulder. "Liam. Take a break."

"No."

"You've hardly left her side. Cassidy says Ryan is awake and his wife is there. He's finally coherent enough for visitors, and he wants to see you." Everett's voice was weary. "I want to sit with my sister for a bit. Go see Ryan, and then Douglas will catch you up."

I looked into his exhausted face. Neither of us had left the hospital, taking turns napping briefly. Cassidy and Douglas were both working tirelessly on my instructions. Watching Douglas address the press yesterday had been astounding. He was articulate, cool, and fierce. There was no doubt of his contempt for what had happened, and his stern and unflappable demeanor was exactly what was needed, given the situation. He represented the Wright family well. I would have been too emotional, no matter how hard I tried. I owed him a large debt of gratitude.

I was rarely out of the room, Everett stepping away only on occasion. But I made sure everyone else was being looked after. A hefty donation to the hospital made sure the quiet room was ours for the duration, and they agreed to my security people. An extra bed was wheeled in so anyone needing it could sleep. I made sure food was delivered and they all ate. I looked after the nurses and doctors on the floor with food. But I had barely moved from the spot beside Shelby, sleeping in the chair and choking down a sandwich when I was forced to. The only time I left her was for a quick update from someone or a fast bathroom break. I hated even leaving her that long. I felt better when I was beside her, holding her hand, stroking her arm, and talking to her. It was only in the deep of the night, when the entire hospital was silent and we were alone, that my fears overwhelmed me and I gave in, laying my head beside hers on the pillow, my lips close to her ear, begging for her to wake up. Otherwise, I remained steadfast in my determination to be strong.

I wasn't sure, though, if I was fooling anyone.

Malcolm Johnson was now in police custody. The owner of the cheap motel he had been staying at was only too happy to give him up for the reward offered. The charges leveled against him were long and deviously clever thanks to Samuels's and Geo's legal minds. The one thing he had that we wanted and could help him was his signature on divorce papers. I knew they would get it too, and his reward for doing so would be very little. He hadn't realized that part yet. He was done.

"More news?"

"Yeah. Douglas wants to tell you." Everett sniffed, trying to lighten the atmosphere. "You need a shower too. Lily was by again and brought you some stuff to change into."

I noticed his hair was damp and he had changed. Looking down, I realized I was in the same clothes I had arrived in, unable to bear the thought of leaving her for that long. Everett was right. I needed a shower and to go see Ryan. My gaze fell to Shelby.

"You don't want her waking to see you looking like this, Liam," he urged. "You're a wreck. She'll kick both our asses."

I chuckled, because he was right about that as well. Standing, I pressed a kiss to her cheek. "I won't be far, my darling girl. Promise."

I swore I felt the flutter of her eyelashes and I pulled back quickly, but her face remained serene and motionless. I was imagining things again. Earlier, I'd thought I felt the press of her hand in mine but had finally put it down as my imagination when I tried to get her to do it again. Her hand remained unresponsive.

I was beyond exhausted and strung out. I kissed her one more time. "Come back, Shelby. I need you, baby."

The hot water felt good pounding down my back. I let it run over me as I washed my hair, soaped, and shaved thanks to Lily's thoughtful supplies. She'd been here often, bringing items and dispensing hugs. She went daily, checking on the house and Thor, feeding him and making sure he was okay, knowing how much Shelby loved him. She sat beside Shelby, chatting about the red dress she had found she knew I would love for our next big night. She winked at me across the bed as she whispered she also knew how much I would love what she had found to go under the dress. I had smiled, grateful for her friendship and care of Shelby.

Dressed in fresh clothes, I sat with Ryan and his wife, listening to his broken apology. I held up my hand, interrupting him. "You fought for her, Ryan. You were trying to protect her. You owe me nothing. I owe you. I will forever owe you." I looked between him and his wife, Lesley, a pretty woman who looked nervous, worried, and troubled. Her husband was hurt, facing months of physiotherapy to be able to walk again. The fact was he would never be a bodyguard again—the pins and plates that now held his leg, hip, and shoulder together would never allow him the flexibility or strength he would need to do that job. I knew she was worried about him and their future. I knew what I had to do—what Shelby would want me to do.

I sat back and smiled at them. "Ryan, you have nothing to worry about. Either of you. Your hospital bills and any physiotherapy are covered. Anything else you need, as well. You will be kept on my books as an employee for as long as you want to be. No lost wages."

He shook his head, even as Lesley's eyes widened and began to fill with grateful tears.

"I can't accept your charity."

"It won't be charity, Ryan," I insisted. "I plan on you sticking close to Shelby and me. Mark needs help with scheduling things, and I need someone with your tactical background on my team. I've already had Samuels draw up the papers. It's not open for discussion. You're covered."

"I don't know what to say."

"You were injured trying to protect the woman I love. I saw the video. I know what you did—how you risked yourself for her. You showed both of us true loyalty. That deserves a reward." I stood, not wanting to be away from Shelby for too long. "Don't worry about money or the future. Just get well, Ryan. A job is waiting when you're ready."

After a tight hug from Lesley, I left the room, feeling better. Shelby would be pleased. I could hardly wait to tell her how much better Lesley looked with those few words.

I studied the pictures Douglas handed me. "We're sure?"

He nodded. "Mark confirmed it. Like you suspected, those tossers threw their so-called colleagues under the proverbial bus, and fast. Those two were definitely the ones pushing." He tapped the picture. "And he threw the punch that caught Shelby."

I grimaced, thinking about the second part of the offer I had made. I didn't care about the money. "Who gets the reward?"

Douglas smiled. "Well, you got lucky, Liam. A reporter from *Features* was on the edge of the crowd, but not part of it. He was there doing an interview in the building when they saw the crowd and went to investigate. He and his cameraman happened to be at the right angle and got these. I was able to verify his cell was one of the numbers that made a call to 9-1-1." He motioned to the stills I was looking at. "You can see who was behind Shelby and the two paps arguing with Ryan. There's no doubt. The magazine wants the money donated to a charity, but they do want the interview." He grinned. "We got a lot of offers from tons of rags and paps with pics, but these were the clearest—" he shrugged "—and they were among the first to arrive."

I felt a flash of relief. They were, at least, a reputable publication.

I pointed to the faces in the pictures, stabbing the paper hard. "I want them punished."

"The police already have copies. Charges will be laid as soon as they finish their investigation." He held up the pictures. "But these helped tremendously. Samuels and Geo have a long list of restraining orders they will try to put through. All the pictures we collected showed many people you would like to see kept away." He squeezed my shoulder. "A lot of your friends are taking up this cause, Liam. Other celebs are speaking out about the paps and their intrusiveness. Maybe with many voices, we can bring about change."

I nodded, even knowing how difficult a fight this would be. "That would be good." I huffed out a long breath of air. "I know I said it before, but you were bloody amazing yesterday, Douglas. This is all moving quickly because of the press conference."

He waved my thanks aside. "Your idea, Liam. I was only the calm voice." He studied me. "How are you holding up?"

I met his eyes, allowing my pain to show through. "I need her to be okay." I rubbed at my chest, pushing on the ache that persisted. "I can't be okay without her anymore."

"She will be. She's strong, Liam. Her body needs a chance to heal." He paused. "I spoke with Aunty Liz today. She wants to come and be here with you. I told her I thought that was a good idea." He watched me for my reaction. "She'll be here tomorrow."

I blinked. My mum would be here tomorrow. I hadn't even thought to ask. I knew Douglas was keeping her updated, but the thought of having her close was pleasing and brought me some much-needed comfort. Being a retired nurse, she could help me when Shelby came home.

Because Douglas was right. Shelby was strong.

And she would come home.

She had to.

Everett listened as I filled him in, standing on opposite sides of Shelby's bed. He shook his head when I finished telling him everything Douglas had said. "You, ah, you've been amazing, Liam. I'm proud of you."

I ducked my head at his praise. Lifting Shelby's hand, I kissed the skin. "It's all her."

He grinned. "Told you she was the right person for the job."

I kissed her fingertips again. "Bloody perfect, actually."

A gentle flex against my lips had me freezing on the spot. My eyes flew to Shelby's face. "Beaker?"

Her eyes moved, fluttering quickly, and if I hadn't been looking, I would have missed it. Everett and I shared a glance. We had both seen it.

He bent lower, his voice almost commanding. "Shelby. Open your eyes for me."

We both watched anxiously and were rewarded with another flutter. Then another. I pressed my lips against her palm. "Shelby, baby—*please*." My voice caught.

Slowly, so slowly I wasn't sure it was happening, her eyes opened. Closed. Opened. Blinked. For a brief moment, they were unfocused and bleary. She blinked again, this time frowning as her head tilted toward Everett.

Her voice was quiet and rough, like a small fragment of an echo in the room. "Ev?"

His shoulders bowed in relief as he assured her, "I'm right here, Shelby."

She stared at him for a minute, licking her dry lips. I grabbed the jug of water and ice chips they refilled constantly and pressed an ice chip into her parched mouth. "This will help," I whispered, unable to make my voice any louder with the lump currently residing in my throat. She was awake. She was talking.

Shelby's huge eyes regarded me as she sucked in the ice chip, her eyes falling shut as she sighed and smiled softly. "Good," she breathed.

I kissed her hand, wishing it were her sweet mouth. "Do you want another one, Beaker?"

Her brow furrowed as she accepted the chip, and then she looked at Everett questioningly.

"What? What do you need?" he asked gently.

Her eyes moved back to me briefly before she spoke again, this time her voice a little louder. "Who is that? Why is he holding my hand and calling me Beaker?"

My heart plummeted. I met Everett's wide gaze with panic.

She didn't know me?

I struggled to remain calm.

"That's Liam, Shelby."

"Oh." She looked at me again and then motioned for Everett to come closer. He bent down, and she whispered at him. "Is he your lover?"

He straightened up quickly, shock written all over his face. I looked around wildly.

What? Did she...

Then it happened.

The most endearing, tiny squeak of a noise.

She giggled.

I gaped at her.

She winked at me, her eyes closing again. "You're not the only one who can act, Oscar."

Her shaky hand slipped from mine, cupping my cheek, her fingers moving restlessly on my skin. Her eyes were warm when she reopened them and gazed at me, her love shining through her tired stare. And in the middle of one of the most poignant moments in my life, I started to laugh.

Joyfully.

Loudly.

My girl was back.

23

LIAM

The room was quiet. Finally, everyone was gone. The doctors and nurses had checked and rechecked Shelby's vitals and responses while Everett and I waited and paced anxiously. They were all pleased, but they warned us Shelby would need time to recuperate from her injuries, including any residual effects from her head trauma. Although she was doing amazingly well, we had to be cautious. Her body needed to recover and heal. Even though she had been unconscious, she was exhausted and needed a lot of rest. Her head was admittedly fuzzy, and a couple of times she had to stop and search for words, but the doctors were sure that would change and go away as she grew stronger.

Beyond grateful she was awake and doing better, I assured them and Everett I would make sure she had everything she required. More than anything I wanted to get her home, where she would be in familiar surroundings and I could care for her. I knew she'd respond well when she was comfortable. With my mum coming to help, I was confident Shelby would be in good hands.

Shelby insisted everyone go home and get some sleep. I encouraged it too, knowing full well I wouldn't be going anywhere.

Until Shelby went home, I wasn't leaving.

After kisses and hugs, we were, at last, alone. Shelby watched me with soft eyes as I dipped a cloth into a basin of warm water. "I'd rather have a shower," she murmured.

"Tomorrow. The doctor said tomorrow," I assured her, gently lifting the heavy plastered arm and wiping the warm cloth over the exposed skin, doing the same thing to her other arm. "You may get to go home tomorrow, and you can have a nice soak in the tub. Sound good?"

She nodded, watching me as I slowly, tenderly, wiped her clean. I smiled at the shaky sigh she emitted as I caressed her face and neck with the velvety cloth I'd had Cassidy pick up for me before she left. "If not, we'll get you a shower. But this will have to do until then, my darling girl."

"Okay," she breathed.

"What did you do to your hand?" she asked, tracing her fingers over the bruises on my knuckles.

"Ah, I sort of introduced it to the wall," I admitted sheepishly.

"Oscar," she chided gently, shaking her head, which caused a small grimace of pain to cross her face.

"Do you need some pain medication?" I asked, already reaching for the call button.

She stilled my hand. "No. It's fine. I'm fine."

Dropping the cloth, I cupped her cheek, tracing a small circle on her skin with my thumb. "I don't want you in any pain. I can't stand the thought of you in pain. You have to tell me," I pleaded. "I want to look after you. You have to tell me what you need."

"I only need you."

"Oh, Shelby." I brushed my lips against hers. "You have me."

"I'm sorry I scared you." Her voice was barely a whisper.

"You did. All of this did. They were talking about the next step and feeding tubes..." I drew in a shaky breath. "I thought...I thought I lost you."

"No," she murmured. "I'm right here, Liam." She pressed my hand closer to her warm skin. "Right here."

I was suddenly unable to speak. Gingerly, she moved closer to the edge of the bed and patted the mattress beside her. I started to shake my head, but she pulled on my hand with a breathy, "Please," and unable to resist her, I carefully stretched out beside her, cautious to avoid her bruises. Turning slightly, she buried her face in my neck, her breath tickling my skin as she shuddered. I draped my arm over her, loosely holding her, wishing I could be closer, but her cast prevented us from pressing together. The feeling of her being beside me, awake and talking—the sheer relief of it—hit me. Tears began to drip down my face, soaking into the pillow under my head. Shelby stroked the back of my head as she murmured gentle hushing noises meant to calm. Her tenderness only made the sobs worse, and I gathered her as close as I dared, letting my emotions rage until I was spent.

And then, I slept.

My eyes flew open in the dimness of the room, only to find Shelby looking at me. "Hey," she soothed. "It's okay."

I caressed her cheek. "I fell asleep. I'm supposed to be looking after you, and I fell asleep." I snorted. "What a git."

"Everett said you refused to leave me and that you barely slept."

"I couldn't leave you."

"He told me everything. He said you were so strong and handled everything. You impressed him, Liam. And that isn't easy to do with Everett."

I shrugged, feeling somewhat embarrassed. "I did it for you. You needed me. They needed me."

"Thank you for looking after me," she breathed out.

I kissed her. "I'll always look after you," I said, realizing for the first time in my life, it was true. She would always be more important than anything or anyone else. Especially myself.

She smiled in understanding. "So, with everything you've been doing, a nap beside me is okay."

"I should get up and let you sleep."

"Or you could stay, and we could sleep together."

I grimaced at the tight quarters. "You're not...uncomfortable? It's kind of a small bed. They might not like me in here with you."

"I'm good. Deb was already in and tsked. I told her I needed you here. She said she'd allow it this once."

Deb was my favorite of all of Shelby's nurses. "I'll send her some flowers."

"Good."

"Do you need anything? Are you in pain?"

"No. Deb gave me some pills. All I need is you."

I tightened my arm and brought her closer to my chest. "You have me."

"Good."

I pressed my lips to her head and stroked her hair gently until I felt her relax and sleep. Almost instantly, the twitches started, and I rejoiced at her signs of normal sleep. I was worried she would slip away again. When she breathed my name and smiled, I relaxed and allowed my eyes to drift shut again. Shelby was right—I was exhausted, and I needed to sleep so I could care for her better.

And with her beside me, I could rest.

The next time I opened my eyes, Everett was staring at me, shaking his head. "You can't stop touching my sister, can you? You had to sleep with her?"

Before I could answer, Shelby's groggy voice piped up. "Piss off, Ev. I asked him to."

I grinned widely and kissed her head that was still buried in my chest. "What she said."

He shook his head, but then started to grin at the two of us. "I spoke with the doctor. They are gonna do the CT scan, remove all the tubes and medical stuff, and if all is okay, Shelby can come home."

Carefully, I lifted off the heavy plaster Shelby was resting on my side, slipped off the bed, and smiled at her. "Good news, Beaker."

She nodded, relief evident on her face. "Especially the *stuff*."

I knew she wanted the IV and Foley gone. She wanted to try to get up and walk. She wanted a bath. She wanted to come home.

I wanted her to come home.

"Soon, baby."

"And your mum will be there?"

I grinned. "Mark is picking her up soon."

"Thor?"

"Lily has been looking after him. He'll be glad to have you home."

She looked at me beseechingly. "Can you get them to come check me out faster?"

I loved the fact that she was asking *me*, not Everett. She wanted me to take care of it—take care of her. Bending down, I kissed her. "I'll go find the doctor."

She walked. Shaky and hanging on to me for dear life, but she did it. She passed all their tests, and the CT scan was clear. They removed all the "stuff" she hated, and when they let me back in the room, they told me I could take her home.

The doctor left the room, and I wrapped my arm around her. "I'll get you home, and you can have your bath, Beaker. And sleep in your own bed."

She pressed her lips to my ear. "Your bed?"

I kissed her. "Our bed," I promised.

She drew in a shaky breath. "Will there, um... Will there be..." Her voice trailed off, but from the nervous tone and the way her hand clutched mine, I knew what she was worried about.

"We're going out another way," I assured her. "Cassidy has called a press conference for later this afternoon. It's at the front of the building." I grinned. "They'll all be gathered there, waiting. What a shame when they realize I'm not showing up. Just Cassidy. But by then, we'll have gone through the tunnel and out the back service entrance. You'll be home before they know you're even awake." I pulled her closer. "No crowds, my darling girl." I crooned in her ear. "No one will get near you."

She looked up, her eyes wide and scared. "You promise?"

I hated the fact that now she was as nervous as I was about what waited outside the door. Those fucking wankers. All of them. I wanted to hurt all of them.

But I only nodded and held her close. "I promise."

"Can I see Ryan before I go? I want to thank him."

I had told her what I'd done for him and Lesley, but of course, she would want to thank him herself. "Yes. I'll take you to him."

"Will he be okay after we go?"

"I'm leaving him security. He'll be fine."

"And then we'll go home?"

"Yes, Shelby. Home we go."

Escaping the hospital had been easier than I anticipated. After Shelby saw Ryan and Lesley, the discharge papers were signed, and we left. They allowed us to use a staff elevator that led right to the parking lot underneath the building, and flanked by Everett and Mark, we were ready in case we ran into any press, but our departure went unnoticed. I held her all the way home, strapped in and safe. The gates were clear of everyone; no doubt, any stragglers were still at the hospital waiting for the press conference.

Mum was waiting when we got home. She stood in the entranceway, a small figure, dressed in her usual cardigan and skirt, her white hair a cloud around her face. Her green eyes were bright with tears as she watched me carry in Shelby and carefully set her on her feet. Mum wrapped her in a gentle hug, swaying side to side.

"Ooch, lassie, all ye been through. Oh, let me see ye." When I heard the sound of Shelby's muffled sob, I saw my mum's arms tighten. "There, there. I'm here now."

Shelby eased back, unable to talk when their embrace broke, her eyes misty.

Watching Mum hug Everett and Mark made me smile. They both loved her and looked forward to her visits. Mark bent low for his hug, but Everett picked her up off her feet.

"Liz," he said. "So good to have you here. Maybe you can keep Liam in line for a while."

She turned to me, a smile only she could offer lighting her face. She held out her arms.

"Laddie."

Her embrace was home. Lavender, Mum, and tea. She wrapped her arms tight around me, and despite the fact that I towered over her, for a moment I was a lad again, seeking the comfort of her touch. I felt the tears gathering behind my closed eyes at the wave of comfort her embrace brought. I was grateful to Douglas for bringing her to me.

Then she stepped back and cupped my cheek. "Ooch, yer too thin. Do they not feed ye here?"

I met Shelby's tender glance, and I cleared my throat, needing to lighten the moment. "Shelby only gives me bird food, Mum." I shuddered. "And yogurt." I bit back my grin at her horrified expression. "I ordered in some roasts and such." I gazed at her imploringly, ignoring Shelby's snort and Everett's muffled "bullshit" he coughed into his hand. "I was hoping you'd cook for me."

"Ah, laddie, yer mum is here now. I'll look after all ye." She turned and clapped her hands. "Let's get this lassie up the stairs and

243

settled. Everett," she called. "You come back tomorrow. I'll have dinner, ye poor soul. All ye been through."

"I will, Liz." He grinned.

"I've done stuff," I mumbled as I lifted Shelby. "Lots of stuff. I have lists too. Lots of lists. I deserve dinner too."

Shelby looked at me, fighting a grin. "You have." She assured me. "You've been the best."

"I know," I assured her. "I've been awesome."

She agreed, "Awesome."

Everett was laughing as he bent and kissed Shelby's cheek. "I'll check on you later, and I'll see you tomorrow."

He and Mark left, and my mum indicated the stairs with an impatient sigh. "Are ye daft? What are ye waiting fer? Take her up, Liam. She needs to rest."

I didn't argue. There was no doubt who was in charge now.

Lily was waiting upstairs, and they both clucked in understanding when Shelby begged for a warm bath, insisting she didn't want to get into bed before she got the smell of the hospital off her skin. The gauze was gone from her head, leaving only the thick bandage over the stitched skin, the dark bruising visible around the area. Lily assured me she could clean Shelby's hair without hurting her, or getting the site wet, since one of my instructions said that wasn't supposed to happen for a few days. I showed her the list.

I had many lists. I had asked questions of every doctor who came into her room and even hounded the nurses for information. I had written everything down and made sure I was well prepared to care for Shelby. I had never cared for anyone before, and I wanted to make sure I did it correctly. I was grateful Mum was here, though. She was much better at all this than me. She had chuckled when I showed her all the lists. I had one for Shelby's list of medications, her bandages, what to expect, various instructions, doctor's numbers, coma recovery websites. I had them all. I was determined to be the best caregiver possible for Shelby.

Steam billowed around us as I helped Shelby off with her clothes. She was too shy to strip in front of my mum, so she was giving us some privacy and letting me help her get in the tub. Shelby was still shy in front of me at times, which I found rather endearing. She had no reason to be shy because, to me, she was the loveliest woman I'd ever seen. OJ agreed, although we knew today wasn't about getting her naked for the usual reasons. I had ordered him to stand down for the next while. I only hoped he listened. Shelby naked was usually a good day in our books.

But that thought vanished when I saw Shelby's leg, hip, and arm where she had fallen. Her damaged skin was a mottled mass of blue, purple, black, and green. Several areas were chafed, scraped, and sore-looking. I was amazed she could walk, given how painful it had to be. Caring for her became the only idea in my head. Both of them.

Gently, I touched her as I looked into her weary expression. "Are you sure you should get in the bath?"

She nodded, the movement slow so she didn't cause any pain in her head. "Your mum put on this waterproof cast cover." She motioned to her arm. "I won't get the cast wet. Lily will help with my hair. If you lift me in and out, I'll be fine. The doctor said it was all right."

"I'll be sure she's fine, love," my mum called out behind me. "She'll feel better with a soak."

Still, I hesitated. "Maybe I should check the lists one—"

"Liam Reginald Wright, pick up the wee lass, put her in the tub, and get out! When she's ready, I will call ye back. Stop hovering!"

Shelby widened her eyes, and she tried not to giggle as my mum gave me shit. I rolled my eyes at the use of my full name but did as she instructed, lifting Shelby and gingerly setting her in the tub. Her eyes shut as she sank under the water, and a small gasp escaped her lips. I froze, not letting her go. "Beaker?"

"It's okay. I'm fine. It just stung a little. Let me go, Liam."

I loosened my hold but not before I found her ear. "Never."

My mum walked in and tugged on my shoulder. "Get out, you silly prat. Go make me some tea and be useful. I'll call when we're done." She smiled at Shelby, picking up the towel I had dropped on the floor. "Let's get you clean and into bed, lass. Maybe my daft son will relax then."

I glared at Mum, and she pushed my shoulder. "Out, lad. Let me look after your girl."

With a final look, I left them to their devices and stomped down to the kitchen, grabbing Thor, who was waiting for me on the edge of the bed, and placing him on my shoulder. My little mate had missed me, and judging from the feel of him, Lily had been feeding him far too much. He wouldn't fit on my shoulder much longer.

I put the kettle on, grateful for something to do, then sat at the table, Thor purring in my ear as I stroked his head, glad to have me home. I was glad too, but I hated being pushed out of the bathroom. I was used to Shelby needing me, and I kinda liked it.

Thor jumped to my lap then to the floor, and I watched, amused, as he thumped his way over to his food bowl, squatting down and loudly munching on his kibble. From the amount in his bowl, I knew why he felt so heavy.

The kettle boiled, but I knew it was too soon to make the tea. My stomach growled, and I realized I hadn't eaten all day. I rummaged through the refrigerator and made a quick sandwich, eating it standing at the counter. It was nowhere near as good as one of Shelby's, but it would do. Figuring Mum might be hungry, I made her a plate of some cheese and crackers, thinking that would please her. By the time I was done, I heard my name being called and hurried upstairs to help Shelby out of the tub. I met Lily in the hall.

"She's all ready for you. I'll be back in a couple of days, Liam. I'll let Shelby rest tomorrow."

Grabbing her, I pulled her into a tight hug. "Ta, Lily. You've been smashing."

She giggled. "Your accent gets heavier when your mum is here. You know that, right?"

I shrugged sheepishly.

She ruffled my hair. "It's cute, and I'm sure Shelby loves it. I'll let myself out."

Grinning, I went in to help my girl out of the tub. She looked much happier than when I left a while ago. After my mum slipped out of the room, I lifted Shelby from the water and set her on her feet, wrapping a fluffy towel around her.

"I got you wet," she sighed, bunching my T-shirt in her hand.

I stepped closer, grazing my lips to her ear. "That's usually what I do to you, isn't it?" I bit down gently. "Beaker?"

She blushed, and I stepped away, chuckling as I pulled my shirt over my head. I picked up another towel and awkwardly started patting her dry the way I had seen her do so often. "I missed your blush."

"Stop it," she giggled.

"I missed that sound too." I kissed her, suddenly serious. "I don't want to be without it again."

"You won't be. I'm right here, Liam." She wrapped her hand around my neck, pulling me close, her breath wafting over my face. "Right here."

I nodded, unable to speak. I looked up to see my mum watching us with a gentle smile as she handed me one of my loose T-shirts Shelby liked to sleep in. "Bring yer lass, and let's get her settled, love. She needs her rest. And I need some tea." She rolled her eyes. "I'll get ye a fresh shirt, too."

I was quiet as I tugged the shirt over Shelby's head, pulling away the towel. I helped her into bed and tucked the blankets around her, making sure she took some pain medication.

"I'm right downstairs. I'll be up soon to check on you."

She captured my hand with hers. "I'm right here," she murmured.

Closing the distance between us, I kissed her deeply, burrowing my head in her neck, breathing her in. She smelled like Shelby again —light and floral, and like home. I kissed her, showing her without words how happy I was she was home.

"I love you," I murmured against her lips.

She lay back on the pillows, her smile one of understanding.

"I know."

Mum's eyes were warm as I handed her the cup of tea. "Ta, love."

I sat heavily beside her, suddenly exhausted.

"Maybe ye should go have a wee nap with your lassie."

"You sound like Nan."

She winked. "It's the Scot coming out, yer da would say."

I nodded as I shut my eyes. I was tired. A contented sigh escaped my mouth as I felt my mum's fingers stroking my head.

"You love her so much. 'Tis a lovely thing to see."

"Truly, I do."

"I'm glad ye finally saw it. I told ye before, it took ye long enough. Ye were blind, love."

"I wasn't that bad," I insisted.

"Oi, Liam, ye're daft. Ye've been in love with her from the start. I saw it when I was here last. Ye simply weren't ready to admit it. I thought ye'd finally come to yer senses when I saw the picture of the two of ye together and noticed her wearing Nan's bracelet. I knew she meant something special for ye to let her wear that jewelry."

I snorted. "Yeah, okay, it took me a bit longer to figure it out."

She huffed a sigh. "Well, ye always took after yer father in that department. I love that man dearly, but he is rather slow at times."

I barked out a laugh as Mum sipped her tea and nibbled on the crackers and cheese I gave her. She set the empty plate and mug on the table.

"Good cuppa, son. Ta."

I sighed as she once again ran her fingers through my hair. We sat in comfortable silence for a while. Then she spoke up.

"Yer doing a good job, Liam."

I opened one eye and peered at her. "Yeah?"

She smiled as she kept stroking, her voice approving. "I was teasing earlier, but I see it. Ye've changed, my boy."

"How?"

"Ye've grown up. 'Tis a good thing to see."

"I want to be what she needs, Mum."

"Ye are, love. Yer exactly what she needs. And her, ye. Yer good together. I thought as much last visit."

I swallowed and looked at her. "I was so scared."

Her eyes were filled with understanding. "But still, ye handled it well. Shelby told me what all ye did." Her voice softened further. "That's what we do for those we love, Liam. We put them first."

"I want to give her Nan's ring. I want to marry her."

"Ooch. That'll be grand. I'd love her for a daughter."

"She still thinks she's too old for me."

"Nonsense. I'm older than your da. It's never meant a thing. It's only a number."

"That's what I told her."

"Keep telling her until she believes ye."

I sighed and Mum grinned. "Her age is perfect fer ye. She is mature and loving. I love ya dearly, laddie, but ye are such a git. She brings out yer age in ye. Makes ye better."

I chuckled. Even my mum thought I was a wanker. But she was right—Shelby made me a better man. More responsible.

"I'll talk to her for ye. Give her me thoughts."

"Ta, Mum."

The room was silent for a moment, then I spoke.

"I want to marry her at home. In England."

"Your da and I would love that."

I grinned sheepishly. "She has to say yes first. To both things. Marrying me, and doing it in England."

Leaning forward, she kissed my cheek. "She will, love. She will."

"I hope so. I want it more than anything."

"Liam—"

"What?"

"What if she wants to leave here?"

"You mean this house?"

"No." Mum paused. "This...life. Go somewhere quieter."

There was no hesitation. "Then it's done. Whatever she needs. Here, England, somewhere else—as long as it is with her, I'm good. She matters more than anything."

Mum smiled and sighed. "Then I'm happy as well."

I left Mum napping on the sofa, Thor curled beside her. She insisted she was too comfortable to move, muttering something about sending her one of these sofas as I left the room. Upstairs, I opened the door, smiling at the sight of Shelby in my bed.

Our bed.

She was tucked in, sleeping on her uninjured side, her arm propped up on a pillow. Mum had gathered her dark hair up in a ponytail on top of her head, and she looked comfortable and peaceful. Not wanting to disturb her, I began to back out when her eyes opened, and she smiled sleepily. "Come here," she murmured.

"Do you need something?" I asked quietly, caressing her head.

"You beside me."

That, I could do.

Toeing off my sneakers, I crawled in, gently easing the pillow out from under her arm and resting the cast on my hip. "Better?"

She snuggled closer. "Much."

I nuzzled her head, breathing her in.

"Where's Liz?"

"Napping with Thor."

"Ev?"

"He'll be over tomorrow with Cassidy. They were both tired, and I told them to go get some sleep." I yawned. "We all are." I kissed her head. "And you should be resting."

She sighed. "I will now you're here."

"I'll always be here," I murmured drowsily.

"Good. Me too."

It was the best thing I could hear before I fell asleep.

"Mum, that was brilliant," I praised, pushing back from the table.

"Ta, love."

Shelby stood slowly. "I'll make tea."

I opened my mouth, then shut it quickly as she glared at me. She'd improved a lot in the few days she'd been home and was tired of me "fussing." In fact, yesterday she took great delight in shredding my printed lists while I watched in abject horror. I worked hard on those damn lists.

I decided not to tell her I had digital ones. God knew what she'd do to my phone.

Everett and Douglas both patted their stomachs in appreciation. "No one can beat your roast, Aunty Liz." Douglas grinned.

Mum smiled widely, loving the compliments and attention. She'd been in her element today with everyone around. She already adored Caroline, and I could tell she'd decided she would like to add her as a daughter, as well. Given how close Caroline and Douglas were, it didn't seem too far of a stretch. It appeared we Wright men might be slow to find the person we loved, but once we did, we wasted no time at all. After the first few days here, Caroline gave up any pretense of staying with us, all of her things ending up at Douglas's place. She had been such a good friend to Shelby and me while Shelby was in the hospital. I was thrilled for Douglas, whom I had never seen looking happier.

"Dessert anyone? Shelby and I made cupcakes."

251

I groaned, having eaten too much to have any—even Shelby's cupcakes. Luckily, everyone else agreed, so we decided to postpone it for a while.

Everett stood, holding out his hand for Cassidy to join him. "Why don't we go talk, Liam?"

I nodded stiffly. I knew what he wanted to talk about. Mum spoke up. "Ye all go in the other room and I'll tidy up. I'll join ye in a bit, and ye can give me the highlights."

Caroline stood, picking up some dishes. "I'll stay here, too."

I wrapped my arm around Shelby, and we went into the den, sitting and making ourselves comfortable.

"Okay," Everett began, looking at Shelby. "First thing. Malcolm. We met with him."

Shelby stiffened beside me. I hadn't gone with Everett—he and Samuels were worried I wouldn't be able to control my temper if I saw him in person, plus the fact that I didn't want to leave Shelby for any length of time. I couldn't stand to be away from her right now.

"I saw him yesterday with Samuels and Geo. His girlfriend dumped him a while back, and he's alone now. All your money is gone, Shelby. He's blown everything he took, and he hadn't been paid in full by the rag yet. He spent what they paid in advance. I doubt he'll see any other money since we have more than enough proof how inaccurate the story was. Add Liam's suit against the rag and they are probably looking at bankruptcy, so his gravy train is gone." He shook his head in disgust. "God, I hate that asshole."

"My divorce?"

"Will happen fast." Everett cracked his knuckles. "Trust me." For the first time, I noticed some faint marks on his hand, and I raised my eyebrows at him in a silent question. I had a feeling Everett had "helped" Malcolm reach his decision. Everett met my eyes with a quick, almost unseen nod. I was surprised at how glad I was to know one of us got to him—I wasn't usually violent, but that asshole deserved it. I'd make sure to find out all the details later, but right now, Shelby remained blissfully unaware of our silent exchange.

"I don't care about the money. There wasn't that much to begin with, I suppose. I just want to be rid of him."

"Samuels had the papers drawn up. Malcolm signed. It's a matter of rubber-stamping now. The rest of the charges, his lawyer can figure out." Everett assured her. "Good luck with his public defender. He's looking at a nice long stint in jail—years. We weren't the only ones looking for him. Good thing his greed overpowered his brain. He should never have come out of hiding so publicly."

"So, it will be over soon? I'll be...free?"

Everett reached over and took her hand. "Yes. Free to move ahead with your life with Liam. Malcolm will be rotting away in prison for a long time, which is where he should be."

Shelby breathed a small sigh of relief. I pulled her closer and kissed the top of her head.

"Good. The wanker deserves it," I muttered. "I hope his cellmate likes him. A lot."

Everett and Douglas chuckled, before Everett turned serious again.

"The paps."

I waved at Everett. "We'll discuss that later." I knew charges had been brought against the two who caused harm to Shelby and Ryan. The rest was an uphill battle. There were fewer of them hanging around outside, but I was smart enough to know they were lying low and I would never get rid of them entirely. No matter how many charges were laid, how many rags went under, there was always a new one that would open up. There would always be a demand for *that* shot—*that* scoop. Sadly, it was the nature of the business. But anytime I could slow them down, cause them grief, I was all for it.

And when they hurt those I loved—it was gloves off.

But right now, I didn't want to discuss it in front of Shelby. Talking about it made her headaches worse, and she had been having a good day. Not a single headache and she was able to talk without hesitation.

He nodded in understanding.

"*Features* has asked for their interview. They have one other request," he said slowly, exchanging glances with Cassidy.

"What?"

"They would like Shelby to join you."

The words were out of my mouth instantly. "Not bloody likely."

Shelby squeezed my knee, her voice calm. "Why, Ev?"

"They would like to hear from both of you. They want to talk to you as a couple. About being a couple. They are also willing to use the pap angle and how it affects your life."

I shook my head. "No. They get me," I snarled. "That was the deal."

But Shelby shocked me. "I'll do it."

I gaped at her. "What?"

"As long as you're there, I'll do it." Her gaze was imploring. "It affects me a lot, Liam. I think I can offer a different perspective here." She gave me a pointed look. "Plus, they were the ones who identified the paps who hurt me. I want to give something back to them."

"Shelby—"

"Please."

"Shelby is right," Douglas interjected. "She would be a good addition. You can speak together." I glared at him, then saw Everett and Cassidy nodding in agreement.

I huffed, knowing when I was outnumbered. "Fine. But not until she's stronger." I frowned at her, almost daring her to argue with me, but she nodded in agreement.

"I'll set it up and explain the ground rules," Cassidy assured me. "I'll be there to run interference if needed and so will Everett."

"Okay. Next?"

"The studio wants you back."

I knew that was coming, but still, I groaned. I wasn't ready to leave Shelby yet.

"I'm fine." She assured me. "Your mum is here. Caroline is close."

"You only have three weeks to go, Liam. David has been great working around your understandable absence, but you're needed to finish," Everett urged me. "You need to complete this movie. It's all being shot here, so you'll be home every night. Then you have a couple of weeks of promos for *Nighthawk*. After that, I've cleared your schedule for the next month. I even got them to have Megan and Seth handle the out of country promotion for *Nighthawk*. You only have to make appearances here and in New York." He grinned. "By then, Shelby will be up to going with you, if you want. You'll have a bunch of interviews and two red carpet appearances."

I felt Shelby tense beside me. This incident had left her with her own fear of crowds now. Everett noticed and hastened to assure her. "I'll be right beside you. No one is going to get to you with me there."

She relaxed. "Okay. Good."

"All right," I agreed. "I'll go back next week."

"Great."

"No more projects for a bit, right?"

"Nope. You're done for a while until you find something you want to do. I've got some scripts at the office for you to look over."

Beside me, Douglas cleared his throat and handed me a thick script he took from his messenger bag. "I've got something as well. I want you to look at this, Liam."

"What is it?"

"My next movie—something I've been working on for a couple years. I'm excited about it—so excited, in fact, that I'm putting my own money into it. I want to control this one. You'd be perfect for the lead."

"You never said anything."

"No. I've been keeping this close to my chest. I found the book in a used bookstore—not exactly a best seller—but it blew me away. I tracked down the author and bought the rights. She was amazing, and I even had her help write the screenplay. She also thought you were perfect for the part." He winked. "She looks forward to meeting you."

I frowned as I looked at the script. It was huge. "When?"

"Spring, maybe early summer. And I'm filming back home. It's going to be massive. I'm thinking about a four-month shoot, minimum. My team is scouting locales now."

"England?"

"And Scotland." He grinned. "Aunt Liz's cottage is gonna be one of the locations I use. It's perfect. It's a historical piece. Read it. It's a great script." He leaned back. "Epic, if you ask me."

I thought about the cottage we used to go to when I was younger. Right by the water, in a small village—there were a lot of great memories there for me. The cottage was over one hundred years old and had been in my mum's family the whole time. It would make a great backdrop for a historical film. Beside me, Shelby was flipping through the pages, pausing occasionally.

Four months. Four months away from here, back home where things were less intrusive—especially off the beaten path. I could even add on some extra time at the end and take Shelby to all the places I knew she wanted to see. Show off where I was born, let her see where I grew up, and meet more of my family and friends back home. Make it a vacation for us.

Shelby moved closer, her eyes gleaming with mischief as she pointed to a page in the script. "There're dukes," she murmured. "Swords."

"Liam would be playing a Scottish lord. A laird," Douglas offered with a wink.

Her smile grew wider. "A *kilt*, Liam. You'd have to wear a kilt."

Everett and Douglas chuckled at the glee in her voice.

I nudged her with my elbow. "Like that idea, do you, Beaker?"

Her cheeks colored slightly, even as she shot me a cheeky wink. "As long as you wear it...properly, Oscar."

I started to laugh, pulling her against me. "Fancy a trip across the pond then, lass?"

Her eyes were bright with excitement. "I'd love that!" She tapped the page and mouthed "kilt," at me again.

I kissed her before turning back to Douglas. "I'll read it."

SHELBY

A Month Later

Movement caught my eye, and I looked over, smiling at Liam. Lowering my book to my lap, I watched him sleep. He had one arm tucked under his head, the other lying across his bare stomach, his fingers twitching as he slumbered. He slept more peacefully these days, with me beside him—his days of dragon-slaying rare, but tonight he was more active than normal. Leaning over, I caressed the hair falling over his forehead, pushing it back and grinning when it fell right back into disarray across his face. He needed a haircut again but refused to have it done until I could do it. He was looking a little shaggy but steadfastly declined.

I gave the air cast on my arm a glare. It had felt like heaven when they cut off the heavier, plaster one and replaced it with this much lighter alternative, but I was still anxious for this one to be gone, too. I was allowed to remove it to bathe, but that was about it. I had to wear it for another week or so, then I was done.

I looked at the clock with a grimace. It was well past one o'clock, and yet I still couldn't sleep. I didn't want to admit to Liam how nervous I was about the interview in the morning. If he thought it was bothering me in any way, he would cancel. Even with him beside me and Everett not far away, the whole idea of talking to a stranger about myself, my ex-husband, and my relationship with Liam seemed bizarre. Never having been one for gossip of any kind, the idea that people were curious about me seemed odd. But I'd agreed to do it, and now I simply wanted it done. Liam was finished filming, and he still had a few days before his publicity appearances. I was flying to New York with him, and while part of me was excited to go somewhere I had never been before, the larger part of me dreaded the public part. I wasn't sure if I would ever be comfortable again in a crowd.

Liam's fingers twitched again, and I frowned. He'd been rather quiet tonight, almost nervous, tugging on his hair often, muttering to himself, and now his sleep was restless. Maybe he was also feeling anxious. Knowing how much it relaxed him, I moved closer and ran my fingers through his hair, smiling as he sighed quietly in his sleep, a small smile of contentment on his face. I loved how much my touch soothed him. How I soothed him.

My fingers slipped through his soft hair as I gazed at him, still slightly amazed I was here, beside Liam Wright. I had fallen in love with him hard and fast, struggling for months to be the one thing I thought I *could* be to him—his friend, never thinking he could possibly love me back. Surrounded by so many people who only wanted to use him and take from him, he trusted few people, and I was determined to be one of them. To those who really knew him, he had a naturally warm and open nature and a need he kept hidden from the rest of the world. His panic attacks were crippling, and when I realized my presence helped him, I fell in love with him even more. His need for me only fueled my feelings, and when he had confessed to loving me, it seemed almost too good to be true. I was scared of the what-ifs—what if it didn't work out, what if he decided I was too old for him, what if... There had been many, but he made me realize they were *my* fears only—not his, and that he did, indeed, love me. And as with everything else in his life, when Liam did something, he did it with his entire being. His love was all-encompassing, reaching out and surrounding every aspect of our life.

He had changed a great deal in the past few months, starting subtly before we finally admitted our feelings and coming into his own when I was injured. He had slowly grown into himself and found his hidden strength. When I'd been hurt, he'd blown everyone away with his take-charge attitude and the way he had cared for everyone around him, especially those who were used to caring for him. He said he grew up; I felt he simply recognized he *could*, that he'd had the strength all along but only now had finally grasped it. He hadn't stopped since then, taking over more of his own decision-making and finding a deeper focus when working. Always professional, his co-actors noticed a quieter depth to his work. The producer he just finished working with had nothing but good things to say regarding what he brought to the role, especially after returning to the set.

I looked over at the large script sitting on the nightstand. Douglas was right—Liam was perfect for the role. A strong, intense, historical character, with the backdrop of the rugged coasts of England and Scotland, the movie was aggressive in its reach. Liam was at the exact right place in his life to do justice to the character. I knew he'd be brilliant. He was thrilled at the prospect of working with Douglas as well as filming back at home. The script was covered in notes Liam scribbled as he read it repeatedly. He was so convinced of the success of the movie, he was partnering with Douglas on the making of it—neither of them wanted the influence of a studio clouding their vision. Rumors were already swirling about the Wright boys and their giant venture, due to the vast scope of this project. It was the first time since I met Liam that I had seen him this excited about a role. I was thrilled to watch him as he and Douglas sat and planned. I was going for the whole shoot; Liam refused to consider anything else, saying he wouldn't be able to be apart from me for any length of time. He had already rented a large house for us. Douglas had one nearby as well. Caroline had some commitments but would be joining us whenever she could. Liz was beyond excited "her lads" would be close for such a long period of time and had many things arranged already for all of us.

Ryan and Lesley were going to be staying at the house. Liam had exercise equipment installed, and the guesthouse was being remodeled to suit Ryan's needs. Liam would have the peace of mind knowing the house and Thor would be looked after, and Ryan had a purpose to keep going while recuperating, until Liam returned. Ryan had made huge strides already, and I knew Liam and Everett had plans for him once this project was over. Liam's generosity knew no bounds when it came to Ryan.

My gaze drifted back, and I was surprised to see Liam's green eyes watching me intently.

"All right there, Beaker?" he asked quietly.

I felt bad I had woken him.

"Should I stop?" I asked, indicating my fingers that were still pulling through his hair. "You seemed a little restless."

"No. I like it." He pulled my hand down, kissing the inside of my wrist. "I like it when you touch me." Then he frowned. "Why aren't you asleep? Are you really okay?"

"I was reading and lost track of time."

"You ready to sleep now?"

I knew I wasn't, and lying there beside him, trying not to toss and turn wouldn't work. "Soon. Will the light bother you?"

"No."

I sat back and lifted my book, adjusting my glasses. I tried to lose myself in the words, but I found myself reading the same passage over and over. My eyes drifted over to Liam, only to see him staring back at me.

"You're supposed to be sleeping."

"I like looking at you."

I tilted my head. "Are *you* okay, Liam? You seemed...distracted tonight."

He tugged on his hair again, and I grabbed his hand, pulling it free. "Stop that, Oscar. You'll be bald soon and lose all your appeal to the masses. Then what will you do? Be a judge on the X *Factor*?"

I gasped as I suddenly found myself underneath a grinning, teasing Liam. "Would I still appeal to you, Shelby?" he growled.

Giggling, I buried my hand in his thick hair. "You would. But then I couldn't do this." It was his turn to gasp as I pulled him down, our mouths fusing together. Our tongues met, sweeping and sweet as we kissed intensely. He moaned low in his chest as he pressed me deeply into the mattress, his body hard and unyielding against mine, and I reveled in his closeness. It had taken days after I came home from the hospital for him to touch me with anything but the sweetest of caresses. It was only after I almost lost it on him that he was able to make love to me without worrying he would hurt me. The last few days, he had been more like his usual self, but this was the first time I'd felt his control slide away and his passion fully unfurl as he lay on top of me, his lips demanding, his body surging against me. His cloth-covered erection was trapped between us, and in one swift movement, he lifted my leg over his arm, grinding his hardness into me. I moaned out his name as I bucked against him, wanting, *needing*, more of him.

Closer. So much closer.

So much deeper.

"Liam...*oh God*...please," I pleaded.

"Shelby...*Jesus*...baby..."

He sat up, his chest heaving. His hair was wild from my fingers. His eyes were dark and hooded, his lust clearly illustrated by the straining material of his sleep pants. "I want. *God, Shelby, I want—*"

"Tell me," I urged. I wanted the same thing. I knew I did.

He dropped my leg and bent down, his face close, his eyes earnest. "I want... I want you to marry me."

I blinked.

That wasn't exactly what I wanted right now.

"*What?*"

LIAM

She was blinking at me, her cheeks flushed, eyes bright with desire, and her hair spread out like a dark ribbon against the pillow. She was so beautiful, it made my heart ache. "*What?*" she asked, confused.

Fuck.

It was the sushi all over again. I had cocked it up.

I had wanted to ask her all evening—planned on asking her. I wanted to show up at the interview the next day with her as my fiancée—I'd even had the ring in my pocket all night. Mum was spending the evening with Douglas, so we were alone. I knew Shelby would hate a big production and would want a proposal done privately. It was the perfect time to ask her. Us—here—in the place we fell in love. But I couldn't find the right words and never seemed to find the right moment.

And judging from the look on Shelby's face right now, this wasn't the right one either.

I hung my head, cursing.

I looked up, meeting her bewildered gaze. I brushed a tender kiss to her forehead, grateful she didn't fling me off and stomp away. "Sorry, Beaker. Sometimes I feel so much when I'm with you, the words just...burst out."

I began to move away, but she tightened her hand on my arm. "So, you didn't mean it?"

"Of course I meant it. I love you, Shelby. I want to marry you. I want you by my side at every event. I want kids and laughter and your smile across the table every day. I want it all with you."

I sat back with a grimace. "I wanted to ask you all night. I was just so bloody nervous, I couldn't."

"So, you waited until we were..."

I looked down at OJ, who was still standing proud and erect, knowing Shelby's pussy was inches away, and I huffed out a groan.

"Yes. OJ thought it would be more romantic if he got involved in the asking. Because nothing says romance more than a ginormous erection bobbing in your face when asking the woman you love to marry you."

I was rewarded with a smile for my inane explanation, and I shrugged in resignation. "I cocked it up, Beaker."

Her lips quirked as if she was trying not to laugh.

"Ginormous, Liam?"

"It's a word." I indicated my hard-as-steel erection. "And accurate."

"Been saving that one for a while?"

Beyond glad she wasn't furious at me, I grinned in relief. "A bit."

Shelby sat up, her face close to mine. "Ask me again, Oscar."

Relief, happiness, and pure joy tore through me as I reached over and grabbed the small box I had stuffed under my pillow, pressing it into her hand. I cupped her sweet, loving face, tenderly stroking her cheeks with my thumbs. "Shelby, my darling girl. I want you to marry me. Be mine. Let me be your life. You're already mine." I drew in a deep breath. "Please."

She sighed, the sound low. "Yes."

I opened the box and gently slid the ring onto her finger. It was still slightly swollen from the break, but the ring was perfect for her. The same way she was perfect for me.

"It's beautiful."

"So are you."

Bright blue eyes shimmered in the dim light. "I love you."

I pressed my lips to hers. "And I, you."

We fell back onto the pillows as the kiss deepened.

"I think you have some unfinished business to attend to," she whispered as she bit down on my earlobe, arching her body up into mine. She slipped her hands into my waistband, tugging it down with impatient fingers. "With your *ginormous* OJ."

"Oh, baby, you are right. So bloody right about that."

OJ wept for joy. He loved this woman.

She wrapped a leg around me, drawing me close to her warmth.

God, *I* loved this woman.

The interview was almost done. It had been decent, and as if sensing her nervousness, Tony had mostly stuck to directing his inquiries to me first. The questions were fair, honest, and I answered them all in the same manner. I did get rather worked up over the issue of the paps and their intrusiveness in the lives of people, including myself. Shelby had to squeeze my hand more than once when we discussed the day of the "incident," as Tony referred to it.

"You seem almost confused by the public's interest in you." Tony addressed Shelby.

"I am," she admitted. "I don't even understand their fascination with Liam."

"He's a celebrity."

Shelby pursed her lips. "He's an actor. That's his job." She lifted a shoulder. "He can't really shoot a gun or fit his car into a tiny spot with some fancy brake work and the twist of a steering wheel. He doesn't slide out of bed in the morning wearing a tux and walk around the house all day in character, quoting romantic lines and being funny."

"What does he do?" Tony queried.

"What other men do. He wakes up and drives me crazy for most of the day, disrupting my schedule, wanting to be fed, asking where his glasses or keys are." She met my gaze with a wink. "Stealing cookies or cupcakes when he isn't supposed to."

I leaned close. "I steal kisses too," I murmured, brushing my mouth over hers.

Color flooded her cheeks, and she pushed me away. "The point is, he's human. Not the characters he plays—he's just Liam. Why it's fascinating when he drives to the store or goes out on a date, I don't understand. And I really don't get the fascination with following me around the grocery store, seeing what kind of peanut butter he prefers." She looked right at the camera and winked. "Jif, by the way."

Tony laughed, and I joined him. "Shelby's right. I'm an arse, and, frankly a bit of a git. It takes a lot of work to make me look smooth. According to Shelby, the suave thing is unattainable unless I'm acting."

"You two certainly seem down to earth."

Shelby lifted a shoulder. "We're just two people."

"There must be something special about him," Tony urged. "Something that made you fall in love with him."

"His heart," Shelby replied promptly. "Liam has the biggest heart I know. And although he doesn't slide out of bed wearing a tux, I love the smile he gives me when he wakes up."

"Why?" Tony asked.

Shelby looked at me for a moment. "Because it's *my* smile. He has hundreds of them, and a lot of them are what the public sees. But in private, the smile I get is the one that tells me how much I'm loved. It's the most special one of them all. And in the mornings, when he's still drowsy and not ready to face the world, he still has that sweet, wonderful smile for me." She looked at the camera with a shrug. "Maybe before you read the rags and all the lies they print, you should remember the person they're talking about is real. Not a character." She laid her hand on my arm. "He's someone's son. Part of a real, breathing family. Friend. Human first, actor second. He acts for a *living,* and he gives it his all. He doesn't deserve the lies. None of them do. They give so much of themselves to entertain. Let them have a little privacy in return."

I had no choice but to kiss her again—camera or no.

She was bloody brilliant.

When Tony addressed me, I liked being able to confirm that Shelby was divorced, and would have been sooner if the wanker hadn't been hiding and living under an assumed name while using the money he had stolen from her to do so.

"Shelby is older than you," he stated, lifting an eyebrow. "Does that concern you?"

"No."

"Hollywood is known for valuing youth above all else."

"Then it's a good thing it's not Hollywood I'm in love with," I retorted. "I didn't fall in love with her age. I fell in love with her soul. Her mind. Her tenderness." I winked. "Her turkey sandwiches and how sexy she looks in red helped, of course."

Tony chuckled. "So the future doesn't bother you?"

"It would if she weren't a part of it," I said. "My mum is older than my da. Never made a bloody bit of difference to them or to me growing up. Shelby is thirty-three. I'm twenty-eight. Next month, I'll be twenty-nine, and it's four years. Makes no difference. As my mum says, it's a number. When Shelby's fifty-five and I'm fifty, it won't even make anyone blink. It shouldn't now either."

"Good way to look at it."

I held Shelby's hand. "It's the only way to look at it. Bottom line is, if it were reversed and I were older than her, we wouldn't even be having this discussion. I'd be patted on the back for snagging a younger woman. We need to change our mind-sets."

He lifted an eyebrow. "It sounds as if Peter Pan is growing up."

I rolled my eyes. I hated that nickname, although at one time, I deserved it. "About bloody time, I think."

He asked a few more questions about our beginning, and I gave a witty rendition of how we fell in love, leaving out most of the idiotic stuff I had done over the course of our relationship.

When Tony asked about the ring on her finger, Shelby blushed, and we confirmed it was what it looked like, and we were engaged. He asked her how I proposed, and I held my breath, hoping the words "He did it while trying to fuck me with his ginormous erection" didn't leave her mouth.

She smiled softly as she answered. "In his own unique way, Tony. As only Liam could."

"Did you do anything to celebrate?"

Her lips quirked. "I had OJ," she quipped and started to chuckle.

Tony looked at me. "OJ?"

I nodded, trying not to laugh. "Nothing says love better than a big shot of OJ, Tony."

His brow furrowed. "The party-boy actor celebrates his big moments now with orange juice? That's a little, ah, different."

I had to roll my eyes. The press had decided I was a party boy and dubbed me as such. It was never accurate.

"We have OJ as often as possible," Shelby assured him. "Liam hand-squeezes it for me."

I wrapped my arm around her, chuckling. "I do."

Tony looked confused. "You take your OJ seriously."

Shelby started to laugh. "You have no idea."

I grinned as I realized something, watching her amusement as we shared our secret joke. Everett was right; I did make her silly. And I loved that fact. I made her laugh, and she made me...*better*. In everything.

He shrugged. "Well, whatever floats your boat."

Shelby laughed harder and I joined her, pulling her closer as I chortled into her hair, knowing I had found the perfect woman for me.

Tony looked at us like we were nuts.

And we were—for each other.

24

LIAM

SIX MONTHS LATER

I walked out of wardrobe, shoving material into my bag, anxious to get home. We'd done an overnight shoot, and Shelby had stayed behind. One night away became two, and the sap I had become—I missed her. I hated being away from her now at all.

Not looking where I was going, I ran right into Douglas, who shook his head as he stared at the item I was carrying.

He raised an eyebrow at me. "Again, Liam?"

I smirked at him. "What can I say? My lass loves me in a kilt."

He groaned. "Because of your girl's fetish, I now have to listen to wardrobe screaming about another missing kilt?"

"Nope. I had Abby order me my own. I even had her find the McKinnon family tartan. Nan would love it." I grinned widely. "*Shelby* will love it."

"No Wright?"

"Sadly, no, but Mum will love I found her family's tartan."

He snorted. "Yep. Aunty Liz will be stoked to know her family tartan is adding to your sex life."

I winked at him. "She'll do anything for some wee bairns," I drawled in my best Scottish accent.

"Jesus, Liam. You only married Shelby two weeks ago."

I clapped him on the shoulder. "No time like the present. Shelby isn't getting any younger—her words, not mine."

He stopped me as I went past him. "Really, Liam?"

I nodded. "Really, Douglas. Me, a dad. Can you imagine?"

He chuckled. "Heaven help that child."

I turned around. "They'll have you to steer them straight."

"Too right. Now get home to your wife."

I grinned as I looked down at the heavy band I now wore on my left hand. Given to me by Shelby.

My wife.

I wasn't sure I'd ever stop smiling when I heard those words. Sitting in the car, I thought about our time here and the day I married my Shelby.

Sitting on the warm grass at the back of the house, we looked out over the water. I nuzzled Shelby's neck. "Happy?" I asked quietly.

"Yes," she hummed. "It's lovely here. Peaceful."

By peaceful, I knew she meant private. Since we had arrived in England a couple of months ago, life had been different. Filming was going well, and for the most part, we were ignored by the locals. People let us come and go, smiling at us when we would appear in one of the pubs for dinner or drinks, offering a warm greeting, and then letting us be. We made this our base, staying at hotels when needed to shoot other scenes, but coming back here in between. We both loved it. We took full advantage of the privacy, strolling the sights, visiting with friends and family, and simply enjoying being us. Liam and Shelby. Oscar and Beaker. We avoided London and other big cities, but the couple of times we had been there, we had managed to slip in and out under the radar. But we both preferred the quiet of the small towns.

Shelby had healed well. The scar that ran just under her hairline would forever be a reminder of how close I came to losing her. Her arm was back to a hundred percent, and away from the pressures and scrutiny of LA, she blossomed. Some days, she visited the set, sitting and watching as I worked. Other days, she spent with Mum, who was a permanent fixture, it seemed, and Caroline who had arrived and decided there was so much beauty here, she could happily stay and work to be close to Douglas and Shelby. So, she did. Dad came to join us when he could, and I loved having my family around. Everett and Cassidy had both been over and were coming back in a couple of weeks. I knew Shelby missed her brother and was looking forward to his visit.

An idea that had been taking hold surfaced as I held her close. I knew this was a good time to ask her.

"Shelby," I murmured, suddenly nervous again.

She twisted in my arms. "What is it?"

"I want to get married."

She smiled at me. "I think we already established that, Oscar." Holding up her left hand, she winked. "I have proof."

"I meant now. Actually do it. Here."

Her eyes widened. "Here?"

I nodded. "My family is here. So is Caroline. Ev is coming over with Cassidy. I'm sure I could convince Lily to make a trip as well. Mum and Caroline would help, and we both want it simple. We could arrange it."

"What about the press? What if word leaked out?"

I shook my head. "I already talked about it with Mum. It won't be big since neither of us wants that." I grinned. "In fact, we won't tell anyone. We'll just invite them for dinner and surprise them all."

"Where?"

"Right here." I indicated the large piece of land we were sitting on by the water. "We can rent a marquee, have the pub cater a dinner after, and say our vows in front of the people who mean the most to us. Exactly what you said you wanted. A quiet, happy day. No fuss."

I stopped talking, letting her think it over.

"You'd be okay with something simple?"

I brushed back the hair blowing across her face. "I'd take you into town and marry you right now if you'd let me." Then I smiled. "But me mum would kick me arse if I did."

She giggled, knowing how true that was.

"How casual?"

I slid my hands over her bare calves. "Whatever you want. You can wear one of your pretty skirts if that's what you want. But if you want a fancy dress, I'm good with it. I'll even wear a tie for you." I winked at her. Since we had gotten here, casual had been the look for both of us. With the heavy costumes I wore daily, I was happy to be in jeans and T-shirts for the most part, when not filming. Shelby had taken to wearing skirts and billowy blouses, which drove me insane with lust when I saw her. She had no idea how sexy she was to me. More than once, I had to take a break filming when I saw her appear on set, watching me. My trailer had been well used as I shagged her senseless a few times, my mouth covering hers to keep it private. Although the smirks from people around the set led me to believe it wasn't the case; I chose to ignore them. I didn't want Shelby's visits to stop.

"Maybe just a suit?" she mumbled against my throat; her lips moving over my skin. "You don't need a tie," she added.

"And you?" I asked hopefully.

"The dress I saw last week—the one I thought was lovely but had no place to wear it? In the vintage shop?"

I remembered the dress, or at least remembered telling her to buy it. The color had caught my eye—the deep red standing out in the window as Shelby had gazed at it. I loved her in red, and I knew she'd look lovely in it; although I had no idea what the dress itself looked like anymore. "Buy it," I ordered her. "Marry me in it."

She tilted her head. "Yes."

I pulled her down on the blanket with me, my body covering hers. Our mouths met in a long, slow, deep kiss. Our tongues stroked softly, celebrating the moment. I pulled back panting. "You'll be my wife."

"Yes."

"Forever."

"Yes."

I hesitated as I looked at her. "Shelby—"

"What is it?"

"I want children with you."

"I want them too."

"Soon?"

"Well, I'm not getting any younger."

I kissed her hard. "Stop it." I growled. I hated when she brought up her age.

She frowned. "In this case, it's true, Liam."

"Then I guess we need to get married soon and get you pregnant— fast." I winked at her. "What a hardship that is going to be. All that shagging."

She giggled. "Indeed."

I turned serious. "You want that, Shelby? Children? With me? Soon?"

She pulled my mouth to hers. "I'll throw my pills out tonight, if you want."

"I want."

The day was perfect. Everyone was surprised and excited when they discovered our plans, arriving to find tables set out, complete with flowers and candles. I waited with the local vicar as Shelby made her way to me, taking the trip alone, the way she wanted.

"I give myself to you," she explained.

The sinking sun caught her hair as it floated around her shoulders. It glimmered off the antique hair clips I had given her to mark our day. The lace of her red dress lifted in the breeze, catching the same shimmering rays. She glowed with happiness as she took my hand and let me make the final few steps of our journey at her side— where I planned to stay for the rest of my life. The scent of the white roses she carried would always remind me of this day and her beauty.

She smiled at the tie I had added, patting it gently. It matched the garter I knew the dress hid. I planned on helping her remove it later—with my teeth.

I was talented that way.

She made it through her vows, her voice clear although quivering at times. I wasn't able to read the words I'd written. My damn allergies must have acted up, and for some reason, they were nothing but a blur on the small piece of card stock where I'd written them. I did what I did best and winged it. I promised her many things, which included my undying devotion, foot rubs, movie marathons, and all the OJ she could possibly handle.

My adlib made her laugh, although most people were mystified at my insistence that vitamin C was a daily necessity and had to be included in my marriage vows.

"Oh, Oscar," she whispered. "Only you."

I winked at her. "Only me for the rest of your life."

"I'm good with that."

I kissed her before we were pronounced husband and wife.

No one objected too strenuously.

There was lots of music and dancing after the vows. Shelby's smile was brighter than the sun when I swept her into my arms as "The Lady in Red" played, and our guests clapped and shared our joy. And of course, many wishes and hugs were given. My mum cried. Shelby cried. Even Ev got weepy. I was fine except for the allergies.

Only a few people knew what the day was for, and they all helped. Douglas arranged for one of the cameramen to film the vows and take pictures. Mum and Caroline made most of the other arrangements and no one got suspicious. We had a completely press-free day to remember. Us, our friends, and family celebrating love.

Celebrating us.

And now as the car pulled up to the house, I was anxious to see my wife. Anxious to hold her and then tease her with the kilt. We had left for Scotland a couple of days after the wedding. The first time Shelby had seen me in a kilt, her eyes had widened, and it had been *her* dragging me off somewhere private. I had snuck a kilt home with me the first weekend and had to pretend not to know how it disappeared come Monday. It had gotten rather...torn by Shelby's anxious fingers as she yanked too hard trying to discover exactly what men wore under their kilts.

She was delighted to find I was a traditionalist.

I replaced the torn one after confessing to Abby and asked her to order me one of my own. I even got a spare one in case.

But when I got into the house, it was Shelby who had a surprise for me. Leaning against the door, she leered at me as I took in her appearance, OJ hardening at the sight before him. If I thought she was sexy in a skirt, nothing prepared me for the vision awaiting me.

Shelby—in a kilt and a waistcoat. Nothing else.

Her arms and neck were bare, the silky skin glimmering in the sun, her hair tumbling down her shoulders, gleaming in the light. Her breasts were spilling out the front of the tight vest. Her kilt—way shorter than the one I wore, sexier, showing off her slender legs to perfection, her feet bare, toes wiggling in anticipation as she watched me look at her.

"Hello, my handsome laddie," she drawled in a perfect Scottish accent I'd never heard her use until now. She had obviously been practicing. "Fancy a go?"

If the hot rush of desire I felt was anything like what she experienced when she saw me in a kilt, I now understood her need to see me wearing one more often.

I wanted her.

Now.

Hard and fast.

Right against the wall she was standing beside.

Wearing her fucking kilt.

I stepped forward, shutting the door behind me, reaching up blindly to snap the lock. I didn't want any unexpected visitors.

"What you have on under yer kilt, me lass?" I crooned as I stepped closer, dropping the bag I was carrying.

"Why don't ye come closer and find out fer yourself?" she replied with a wink, her chest rising and falling rapidly.

"Aye, I intend to," I grinned. "I hope yer ready..."

She arched forward, pushing off the wall, her eyes widening as she took in the ginormous bulge I was now sporting. Reaching down, I cupped my heavy erection as I arched an eyebrow at her. "Brace yerself, lassie."

In two long steps, I had her pressed against the wall.

The buttons on the waistcoat made dull pings as they hit the floor, the material shredded from my strong hands. I didn't care. I'd buy her another one.

My pants hit the floor, her anxious fingers making short work of the buttons and zipper. My shirt had already been yanked over my head and disappeared.

In one move, I had her sexy legs wrapped around my hips. Our bare chests pressed to each other's, warm, silky skin meeting coarse, unruly hair as they joined and heaved together.

One flick of my wrist and I found out she was bare and ready for me.

I possessed her mouth with mine. Deep, plunging, hot, needy.

I stroked her heat with my fingers. Warm, wet, slick.

My groans were low and urgent.

Her whimpers were keening and wanting.

I surged forward, my cock slamming itself into her heat.

We both gasped.

Swiveling hard and fast, I pinned her to the wall with my hips, holding the nape of her neck with my hand as I consumed her mouth, never letting go of her sweet taste.

She held me tight, grasping my shoulders in desperation as I took her. She gave and gave, and I took and took.

Hard.

Pivoting. Thrusting.

Lifting her higher. Spreading her wider.

Driving deeper.

Demanding, taking even more.

Needing all she could give me.

Her entire body locked around mine as she screamed her release into my mouth. In one long, final thrust, I gave her everything I had, groaning and gasping her name.

Slowly, we sank to the floor, a mass of entwined limbs and soft, sweet kisses and caresses.

"Welcome home, Mr. Wright," she murmured against my shoulder. "I missed you."

I chuckled into her hair. "Aye—A grand welcome at that, Mrs. Wright."

The sun was dipping below the trees, the reflections bouncing off the glass in the window. Shelby curled around me, her head tucked in the crook of my neck, while she drew lazy circles through the sparse hair on my chest with her fingers. I stroked the curve of her shoulder, enjoying being beside her this way.

"Any other surprises for me, Beaker?"

"I didn't know your reaction to me wearing a kilt would be so... powerful." She lifted her head, eyes dancing as she smiled. "I might have worn one sooner."

I captured her lips with mine. "I liked it."

She giggled. "I noticed."

"Indeed."

She settled closer. "How did the shoot go?"

"Once the weather cooperated, fine. Douglas got what he wanted. He thinks about another six weeks and we'll wrap."

Shelby sighed. "Oh."

I tilted up her chin. "That was a sad sigh. Do you not want to go home?"

She shrugged. "I miss Thor and seeing Ev. But I like it here, Liam. I like the quiet and the peace."

"I do too." I sat up, dragging Shelby with me. I pulled a pile of papers I'd been hiding from the bedside table drawer and handed them to her. She read them, her brow furrowing in confusion. Then her eyes widened, and her head flew up in shock as she realized it was an offer to purchase the house we'd been using as our base in England. We'd both fallen in love with it. I'd married her there, and I wanted to give it to her.

"I didn't know the house was for sale," she gasped. "You want to buy it?"

"I asked the owner if he would consider selling it."

"You want to move here—permanently?"

"No. Not yet anyway. But we both love this place, and we could use it when we come here to visit. It's close enough we can get to Mum and Dad and easy to get to London..." My voice trailed off at the look on her face. "It was only an idea. I won't do it if you hate the thought, Beaker."

She shook her head wildly. "I don't hate it. At all." Her fingers traced the page she was holding. "You can...afford this?"

"Hey."

I waited until she looked at me. "*We*. We can afford this. What's mine is yours. Remember?"

She nodded slowly. I knew she still had a hard time comprehending my wealth. When I'd repaid Everett what he had put out to cover the debts her ex had left her saddled with, she'd had trouble accepting it, but I had finally persuaded her it was for the best. It had taken weeks to convince her to use the account I had set up for her once I "fired" her as my housekeeper. She still wanted to discuss her purchases, even though I wasn't the slightest bit concerned with any of them. I humored her though, since I knew she had to get comfortable with the concept.

Her eyes looked back at the paper she was holding in a tight grip.

Confused by her reaction, I pulled open her shaking fingers. "Shelby? Talk to me."

"I want this, Liam. I want to be able to come here. More than visit," she confessed in a quiet voice. "I want to bring up our children in a calm, peaceful place." She hesitated, biting her lip, then finished her thought. "I don't want them surrounded by the craziness of LA."

"Why are you nervous to tell me this?" I asked her, confused. She had to know I would give her anything she asked for, material or otherwise.

"You've already given up so much for me."

"Such as?"

"You spoke to the press about your private life. You've changed your lifestyle, you—"

I cut her off with a finger pressed to her mouth. A low laugh escaped my lips as I pulled her into my lap, the papers now forgotten. "Yes, you're right. I gave up a meaningless, lonely existence where I was so afraid of the crowds I had to face, I drugged myself to leave the house. I gave up rattling around in a huge house that was only a place to crash until you came in and made it a home. I filled my life with work, empty things, and meaningless drivel." I admonished her gently, "Shelby, you gave my life meaning and a sense of purpose. I gave up *nothing* but a few minutes of privacy and my immaturity. I gained *everything* with you. I grew up because of you—*for* you. You're my best friend, my lover, my wife." I spread my hand over her stomach. "You will be the mother of my children. And if you want to move here, we will. As long as you're with me, I don't care where we live," I admitted. "I was hoping to convince you to let me buy the place and use it for vacations, thinking maybe, eventually, you'd want to be here more. I'm thrilled you want it as well, my darling girl."

Tears filled her eyes. "Really?"

I tucked a loose strand of hair behind her ear. "Why don't we plan on splitting our time for a while? I'll finish up my commitments to Douglas and a few other obligations. The house here needs some renovations to make it what I know we'd need to live here permanently. We can go back and forth after the shoot is done, and we'll do whatever feels right. Mum and Dad can help oversee any work that needs doing here."

"Your career?"

I shrugged. "If the filming is done in the States, we have a house there. If I'm not working, we're here. Easy." I teased her stomach with my fingers. "You know how I feel about this, Shelby. As soon as our first child comes, I'm sticking close to home. I don't want to miss a moment of you being pregnant or miss watching them grow up. I want all the milestones, from conception onward."

She started to talk, but I silenced her with my mouth, pressing a kiss to her full lips. "My choice, Shelby. I choose us. I choose you. Every. Single. Time." I drew back, caressing her cheek, but my tone serious. "You are my world now. Please tell me you know that."

She nodded. "Sometimes, I think I'm dreaming."

I winked as I kissed her again. "There are times when I'll piss you off, and I'm sure you'll think you're having a nightmare."

Giggling, she wrinkled her nose at me. Unable to resist, I kissed the end of it, making her giggle again. I loved hearing that sound.

Her hand covered mine that was still resting on her stomach. "What if we just made a baby?" she asked.

My smile was wide. "Nothing would make me happier. We'll simply fast-track our plans."

"You're amazing," she whispered. "I'm the luckiest woman in the world."

She gasped as I laid her on the bed and hovered over her. "I'm the lucky one. You are everything to me. Everything."

I kissed her with all the adoration I was feeling.

"I love you, Beaker."

Her smile lit up the room.

And my heart.

"I love you, Oscar."

EPILOGUE

LIAM

We did make a baby that night. Or one day the next week. Shelby bought more than one kilt, and she wore them a lot. I wore mine too, so we were both in a frenzy most of the week, it seemed. Either way, by the time we arrived back in the States, Shelby was well and truly pregnant. And as usual, I was blind.

Shelby seemed a bit off and tired. I was crazy wrapping up the movie with Douglas, doing last minute-reshoots and making sure everything was complete before we left. When the words "It's a wrap," finally left Douglas's mouth, I was grateful to head home.

The house was quiet when I walked in. It seemed strange. No Shelby music, no off-key singing in the kitchen. No Mum. She had been here when I left yesterday, planning on keeping Shelby company as we did a few overnight retakes, then finished off the day.

Had she left without telling me?

I found Shelby in bed, propped against the headboard, a book open on her lap and her sexy glasses perched on her nose. I tried not to show my surprise.

It was only eight, and Shelby was in bed? She was wearing a

thick wrap, and I could see the edge of lace peeking out from a long sleeve under it so she wasn't planning any sexy times.

So, why was she in bed?

"Where's Mum?" I asked.

"She went to Douglas's. She and Caroline had plans."

I frowned. "You weren't included?"

"I wasn't feeling up to it."

Now, I was concerned. I approached the bed. "All right there, Beaker? Should I call in a doctor?" I scratched my head. "It's early to be in bed."

She smiled. "I'm tired."

I sat, reaching for her hand. "My point exactly. You're never in bed at eight."

"I've never been pregnant before."

I was about to reply, but the words dried up in my mouth. My grip on her hand tightened.

"Preg-pregnant?" I swallowed. "Are ye sure, lass?"

She laughed. "Oh dear, you're channeling your mum. She was so excited, she could barely talk."

I shook my head to clear it, then moved closer. "You're carrying my baby, Shelby?" I laid my hand on her flat stomach. "In here?"

"It tends to work best there, yes," she replied, her eyes twinkling.

For a moment, I was struck dumb.

Shelby was pregnant.

I was going to be a dad.

Talking about it, planning it, making flippant remarks about it—none of it was real. It was a thought, an image—an idea. None of it prepared me for this moment.

For the surge of joy.

The instant worry and wonder.

The insane terror of the idea that I was going to be responsible for a child.

A baby.

My baby.

I stood and let out a whoop. I danced a fast jig. I lunged forward and kissed Shelby's sweet, smiling mouth—hard. I cupped her cheeks and rambled incessantly, promising to be a good dad. I dropped to my knees, pushing away the blanket and shawl, kissing her stomach, and talking to the small being inside.

My being. Our being. The one we made with our love.

Then I gathered Shelby in my arms and held her.

My family encompassed in my grip.

I held my entire world at that very moment, and I shed my own happy tears, which mixed with Shelby's.

I was ecstatic.

I had a beautiful wife, a successful career, and a baby on the way. I had never been happier.

We had lots to celebrate that night. At least until Shelby fell asleep, her head on my shoulder as I talked and made plans. When I noticed her silence, I watched her for a while, filled with the wonder of the moment and of her.

I kissed her brow and let her sleep.

I had a feeling my child was going to wear her out for a long time to come.

To nip things in the bud, I allowed Cassidy to release a statement saying while out of the country, Shelby and I were married and were now expecting our first child—news we welcomed with a great deal of happiness. I still refused to talk about it or my private life, but I decided to get ahead of the rumors this time. Shelby was already glowing, and I knew soon enough she would start showing. She already had a small bump I liked to run my hand over and press my lips against while I chatted to the baby.

Our baby.

I drove her doctor crazy with my questions, read far too many books on the subject, and once again, made everyone laugh with my lists.

This time, I made multiple copies so when Shelby was fed up

with me checking them and fed them through the shredder, I had extra handy.

I went to every doctor's appointment, held Shelby's hair during her bouts of morning sickness, rubbed her sore shoulders, and brought her crackers to quell her queasy tummy. Quickly, I learned the three new faces of Shelby while her body raged with all the additional hormones, some of which frightened me no matter how often they appeared.

HS: Horny Shelby. My favorite one. OJ loved it, as well. We both actively encouraged that hormone.

IAS: Instantly Angry Shelby. We weren't big on this one.

ES: Emotional Shelby. Our least favorite.

Often, I could sideline ES with HS if I moved fast enough and it was the right sort of day. Frequently, IAS dissolved into ES. I was never sure. When I brought up the subject with Dr. Emily, wondering if there was some sort of indicator I could find so I knew which Shelby I would find waiting for me when I walked through the door, she actually smirked at me while Shelby glared then cried. I hugged Shelby while looking at Dr. Emily with my "*See what I mean*" expression. The doctor simply shook her head and her return look said, "*Live with it.*" So I did.

I added it all to my lists. My lists were a great comfort to me. Shelby hated my lists.

I also drove Shelby crazy with my constant worrying.

Nothing could happen to her or to the baby. I made sure she kept her stress to a minimum, I added extra security, a driver, and as often as not, went with Shelby wherever she was going, until the day she told me I was smothering her. And then sobbed because she thought she'd hurt my feelings. After that, I tried to give her a little more space, but I was never far away in case she needed me. If she had any idea how often I contacted her security when she was out, IAS would have shown up and maybe taken up permanent residence. Luckily, Ryan understood my over-the-top concern and kept me covertly informed. I gave Lesley the job as housekeeper, leaving only the part of keeping me on track to Shelby. No one could help keep me on track like my wife.

And nobody could cook like my wife.

I couldn't live without her turkey sandwiches and cupcakes.

Especially the cupcakes.

Which was the reason I was currently being scolded by IAS. Vehemently.

I had to admit when she was hissing at me in anger, almost spitting in her fury, she was highly adorable. She resembled a rather pudgy kitten, all bristled and ready to attack. Her Beaker noises were loud and passionate, one hand resting on her rounded stomach, while the other gestured wildly. I tried hard not to smile as she cussed me out. That only made IAS angrier.

She *did* tell me she was making the cupcakes for Ryan and Lesley—I admitted that to her. I didn't think they'd miss one.

Or three.

Apparently, I was wrong. Very wrong. And my plea of sympathy cravings wasn't working.

Now I had ruined the *entire* day.

I braced myself for what I knew would happen next. I hated this part more than anything. I watched anxiously as Shelby's face changed, the anger draining away as quickly as it started, and her voice trailed off. I waited, counting in my head for what would happen next.

5-4-3-2-1 and....

She was in my arms, sobbing out her apology for yelling. For being such a horrible person. I was the best husband in the world. She loved me so much. Chuckling at the complete about-face, I gathered her close and rocked her in my arms as I crooned tender words to calm her. I hated seeing her cry, but her hormones were so out of whack, it happened almost daily, and always after the angry hormones made their appearance.

I kissed her head as her sobs eased off and pulled back a bit to

gently wipe away the wetness from her cheeks. She gazed at me with sad, teary eyes.

"It's okay, Beaker." I grinned. "It was a short one this time."

Her bottom lip started to tremble again, and I did the only thing I could think of to stop a second weeping session. I used the one hormone I could count on—HS. Cupping her face, I crashed my mouth to hers, sweeping my tongue in and kissing her deeply. It took her about two seconds to catch up, and then we were on. Her hands gripped and yanked at my hair, pulling me closer. I tilted her head to get deeper into her mouth, panting and groaning at the sudden passion. It was only the sound of the throat clearing behind me that reminded me we weren't alone.

"You know," Everett's amused voice spoke up. "That's how you got into trouble in the first place."

"Actually, there was a wall involved." I smirked as I winked at Shelby, stroking her warm cheeks. "And a very sexy kilt."

"TMI, Liam!" he snapped and walked out of the room.

"You started it!" I yelled after him.

Shelby giggled, and I sighed with relief.

"Sorry," she whispered.

"So am I. I shouldn't have eaten the cupcakes. They looked too good to ignore."

"I shouldn't have yelled."

I chuckled. "Yell all you want. But I'd prefer it if you didn't cry. I hate it." I pulled her back into my arms, nuzzling her hair. "It makes my chest hurt when you cry."

"You love me too much."

I tightened my hold. "I do. It's a shame."

The buzzer went, and Shelby huffed.

"Do you want me to tell Lily to come back another time?" I asked gently as I led her to the table, trying not to eyeball the cupcakes still sitting there. One emotional outburst today was enough.

"She's here with dresses for the Oscars. I need to choose one." She grimaced. "If I can fit into anything she brings. I'll be almost six months by then, and I'm already fat! Maybe I should stay home." Her lips started to quiver, and I quickly kneeled in front of her, trying to stave off the tears.

"No. I need you with me." Douglas and I were presenting two categories, and I needed her beside me on the red carpet; I needed to be able to see her while on stage. "You'll be the most beautiful woman there," I insisted, laying my hands on her rounded bump. "You are not fat, my darling girl. You're pregnant."

She sniffed. "You're just saying that because you *made* me fat. Your OJ injection did all this."

"First off, I am proud of my injection. And secondly, I am not saying that because it's my fault. Which it's not. You are sexy, Shelby —and you're only getting sexier. I love how you look, round and curvy with our son. I can hardly wait to see you all dressed up for me."

Gently she placed her hands over mine. "Our son," she whispered.

I kissed her full mouth. "My sexy wife." Leaning down, I kissed her tummy. "My healthy son."

Lily walked in. "My beautiful dresses. You'll be stunning when I'm through with you. And you should see the shoes I found. Tiniest heel ever!"

I stood, chuckling. "I doubt you have anything with you as beautiful as she is, Lily. But you can try." I winked at Shelby. "There better be a red one in there. You know how I love her in red."

Shelby's face flushed at my words, but she smiled warmly.

"Liam," she called quietly as I walked away, knowing better than to stay and offer fashion advice. My outfit was chosen and ready, Lily sworn to secrecy. Douglas and I were both wearing dress kilts to do the presenting in homage to *The Highlands*. Shelby didn't know yet— I knew she'd love it, my only hope being she didn't attack me until we left the ceremony. I'd hate to have to walk onstage with a torn kilt.

I turned back, smiling at her.

"Take the rest of the cupcakes. I'll make more tomorrow."

Grinning, I covered the distance between us in three strides, hauling her up and kissing her breathless. Then I grabbed the plate and left quickly before she could change her mind. I'd share my score with Everett.

Well, at least two of them.

Shelby was beautiful at the Oscars. Beside me, she glowed as brightly as the jewels she wore under the lights. Her red dress left her shoulders bare and flowed like a waterfall over her rounded tummy. She took my breath away when I saw her walk down the stairs toward me, and I was beyond proud to have her on my arm. Having her close and seeing her in the audience kept me calm and focused. She always kept me centered, and my need to make sure she was okay overrode anything else. By the end of the show, she was exhausted, and I was more than happy to shake a few hands and take her home for a nice foot rub. Douglas and Caroline stayed behind for the after parties, giving him a chance to talk up *The Highlands* even more. The buzz about the movie was already high, and he wanted to make sure it stayed that way until its release in the fall.

Shelby had, indeed, loved the kilt, her hand delving under the plaid, constantly teasing my bare skin as soon as we were in the limo. The only saving grace was we had stopped to pick up Douglas and Caroline, sharing the limo, and she behaved once they joined us. I was grateful for that; my sporran was large and, if she had kept up her teasing, would have stuck out at a frightening angle, given the ginormous erection I was sporting. I pressed my lips to her ear, nipping the lobe and grinning as I promised her that we'd be alone for the return journey and both OJ and I would happily be at her mercy.

"I'll have the driver take the long way home and put up the privacy screen," I assured her. *You can sit on my lap, and I'll let you touch my sporran as much as you want."*

I loved the way her eyes lit up.

287

. . .

We stopped only once on the way out to the waiting car. The reporter who had interviewed us months earlier caught my eye, waving us over, and we stopped to chat with him. Tony was full of well-wishes on our marriage and upcoming birth, which we happily accepted. We talked briefly, and I made sure to do some shameless plugging for *The Highlands*. Just as we were turning to leave, he grinned at Shelby.

"Still an OJ fan, Shelby?" he asked. "I remember you were pretty big on it."

She grinned at him as my hand tightened on hers in shared amusement. "Absolutely. I have as much OJ as possible these days."

I nodded. "I keep her pretty full of OJ, Tony. Her cravings are endless. In fact, she'll have some in the limo."

Shelby giggled, and I chuckled as I wrapped my arm around her, nuzzling her head and ignoring the flashes happening around us. With her beside me, laughing, nothing else mattered.

He shared our amusement, not understanding the joke, which only made it funnier to Shelby. "You two are cute, even with your orange juice fetish," he acknowledged as he shook my hand. "Perfect for each other, I'd say."

Walking away, I kissed her head. "He's right," I murmured as I helped her into the car. "We are perfect for each other."

She beamed at me, her happiness radiating from her lovely eyes. "We are."

I had to kiss her again.

And I didn't stop all the way home.

Holding my newborn son in my arms was one of the most profound moments of my life. Watching Shelby work to bring him into this world was unbelievable. I was astounded at her strength. Throughout her entire pregnancy, she had been the calm one, always brave, never panicking, often laughing when I ran to my lists to check on things. But seeing her today made me realize she was truly amazing.

"One last push," Dr. Emily said.

Shelby panted heavily, her cheeks red, sweat dripping down her face. "I can't," she pleaded. "I need a rest."

I pressed the damp cloth to her head and leaned close to her ear. "One more, my darling girl. I want to meet our son, and you're the only one who can give me that." I pressed a kiss to her skin. "For me, Shelby." I gripped her hands. "With me, now."

She bore down, an inhuman cry bursting past her lips. For a moment, there was silence, then I heard the most beautiful sound in the world.

A long wail.

"He's here. You did it, Shelby." I kissed her—hundreds of tiny kisses rained all over her face and shoulders. My hand shook as Dr. Emily let me cut the cord and, finally, laid our son in my arms.

I gazed at his small face. Red and wrinkled, he was perfect. He frowned as he shoved his fist into his mouth, already seeking food. I smiled through my tears.

"That's my boy."

Gently, I laid our son on her chest. "Someone has been waiting to meet you, my lad," I whispered as I nuzzled both their cheeks, one so small and soft and the other warm and damp with joyful tears. Shelby's blue eyes shimmered with emotion as she looked at our son.

My own eyes grew damp again as I looked at them. My family. Blinking, I smiled at Shelby and our son. "Does he still look like an Adam to you?" I asked. We had both liked the name.

"Yes." She stroked his downy skin as he snuggled into her warmth. "Adam Everett Wright."

I nodded, bending low to kiss them both again.

My wife and my son.

My world.

I shifted anxiously in the meeting. I didn't want to be here. I wanted to be with Shelby and Adam at his three-month checkup, but the appointment had been moved up, and I couldn't get out of this meeting. My mum was with her, but I liked to go to all the appointments with them. The fact that Shelby had been a little under the weather the last couple of weeks made me want to be there as well. She promised to make sure the doctor would check her out while she was there. She seemed more tired than usual, even with Mum there to help look after Adam, and I was worried, even though Shelby assured me it was normal for new mothers to be tired.

Douglas kicked me under the table, and I brought my mind back to the business at hand. I enjoyed being partners with him but hated all the business stuff we had to deal with. When the meeting was finally done, we made our way to our cars, separating quickly. He knew I was anxious to get home, see how things had gone, then discuss our upcoming project with Shelby. Some of the location work would mean being away from home, and I hoped she would be up to some of the traveling with me—at least the shorter trips. Douglas and I had discussed hiring a private plane so the trips would be more comfortable for her and Adam. Both Caroline and Mum could come with us, if Mum was here for a visit. Since Adam was born, she had been a constant visitor.

Entering the house, I made a beeline for the kitchen, finding Mum with Adam. She was cooing at him as he blinked at her. I gathered him up, breathing in his baby scent—something I loved. As I nuzzled his little face with mine, the whole day faded away, and all that mattered was the tiny, warm body nestled against mine. He was already growing fast; I hated to be away from him. His blue eyes, so much like Shelby's, shone with happiness as I held him, and as usual, I felt the overwhelming rush of love for my baby boy flow through me.

"Where's Shelby?"

"She's, ah, lying down. She just fed Adam."

Her voice sounded strange.

"Is she okay? Did everything go all right at the doctor?"

She stood and took Adam from my arms. "Go see yer lassie."

Panic crept up my spine. "Mum? What's wrong?"

She narrowed her eyes at me. "*Nothing* is wrong. But go see yer wife, Liam."

My legs couldn't move. Something was wrong.

Mum cupped my face with one hand, her voice soothing. "She is fine—I swear. But she needs ye, lad. Go to her."

My feet carried me to our door, and I slipped inside. Shelby was on our bed, a box of tissues beside her. When she looked up, her eyes were red and swollen as they filled with fresh tears. I was quick to cross the room, kneeling in front of her, holding her hands, my imagination running wild with fear. "Tell me," I demanded hoarsely.

Tears trickled down her cheeks, and I reached up to wipe them away.

"Do you remember when I got ready for the Oscars, and I was worried because I was fat?"

I nodded, unsure why she was thinking about that night. "You weren't fat, you were beautiful."

"What did you say to me that night when I was lamenting about my loose, flowy dress?"

I racked my brains. "Um, I said when we went to the Oscars next time for *The Highlands,* you could wear something racier if you wanted because you wouldn't be pregnant then."

She stared at me, her lip quivering. "Wrong," she said. "I won't be able to."

I frowned, not understanding for a moment, and then realization hit me.

"No way." I gaped at her teary face, before dropping my gaze down to her stomach. "But...we were protected, and you're breastfeeding!" I sputtered. "My lists said it lessened the chance! *And* we used condoms!"

"Your lists were wrong. I'm pregnant, Liam. Again." She shook her head. "And that one night..."

Oh.

Right.

She'd been in the kitchen late one evening, making us a snack, only wearing my T-shirt. When she'd bent over to grab something, showing me her sweet ass, I had moved in; one thing led to another, and the snack was forgotten. So was the condom. We'd had just gotten the six-week clearance and neither of us was planning on it in the moment—but it happened. And now...

All I could do was stare at her.

Pregnant.

How would her body handle this?

How would Shelby handle this?

"What did the doctor say? Is this...safe? For you?"

"I'm fine. She says I'm very healthy. We may need to take some precautions, but she says I should be fine."

I hesitated, swallowing the lump I could feel growing in my throat. "Do you want this, Shelby?"

Her eyes flew to mine. "Yes!" She paused. "I'm still in shock, but Liam, you don't—" Her voice caught.

I thought about what lay ahead. Another nine months of hormones. IAS, ES, and HS—all of them would be back. Anger. Tears. Throwing up. Worry. But then at the end—another child. Our child.

I looked up at her as she watched me. Nothing else mattered. We'd make it through as long as we were together. I'd make sure she had the best care, and I would look after her. I'd take all the yelling and the tears because she'd need me to.

"Yes," I insisted gently. "I want another child." Standing, I captured her mouth with mine. "I love you."

A small sob escaped her lips, and I sat beside her, pulling her onto my lap and letting her cry as my mind raced. We were both in shock.

"We'll get some help," I assured her. "I know two babies less than a year apart will be hard." I chuckled. "Irish twins, Beaker. We're having Irish twins."

"It's entirely your fault," she sobbed. "If you weren't so damned irresistible, I wouldn't be knocked up again!"

I hummed into her hair. "I told you before, Shelby. OJ is packed full of natural goodness. And determined, it would seem. It was only one time."

She let out a giggle, and I nuzzled her hair.

"We'll be fine." Drawing back, I swept the hair away from her damp cheeks. "We said we wanted two close together—" I paused with a grin "—maybe not this close. But given your advancing years, it might be a good thing." I kissed her nose teasingly. "We can have our family done before you're totally decrepit."

She smacked my chest but grinned. She knew I was trying to make her smile. I waggled my eyebrows at her. "OJ did himself proud."

"I'm probably going to be really fat this time." She sighed. "I haven't had a chance to get back into shape yet."

I hugged her close, knowing she needed my reassurance. "I love you really fat. I think I proved that last time." It was true—I couldn't keep my hands off her. "And besides, you're in amazing shape. Perfect, in fact."

"The press will have a field day."

"The never-ending pregnancy." I groaned. "Everett is gonna kill me."

She sighed, nestling her head into my neck. "He'll be fine. He loves being an uncle. Although I'm sure he'll tease us both mercilessly. So will Douglas."

I held her, stroking my hand through her hair in soothing passes as we both lost ourselves to our thoughts.

"I want to talk to Dr. Emily."

"I already made an appointment for next week. She asked if you would be bringing your notebook."

I would be. A new one. This was a whole different ball game, and I needed lots of notes. "Maybe we need to decide on the house in England soon."

"Your mum and I talked. I thought maybe we could go over in a couple of months, check on the work, and get it ready? Go back after the baby is born?"

"I like the sound of that. We can enjoy some time with our children."

"I'd like that too."

Tilting up her chin, I smiled at her. "Thank you, my Shelby. For my son, for this rather shocking but blessed piece of news—for everything." I stroked the skin on her cheek. "I'll take good care of all of you. I promise."

"I know you will. You already do."

A cry echoed in the house and I laughed. "Meanwhile, our son wants us—well, probably you. I'll go get him."

"I'll come down. Your mum, no doubt, is bursting. She was so excited at the doctors. Another 'grandwean.'"

"She's going to be giving Douglas a hard time about this, you know. I bet she tells him to man up." I puffed out my chest. "My boys are a determined lot. He has a lot to live up to."

Shelby giggled. "I bet you're right."

I wrapped my arm around her as we walked down the stairs. "Maybe we'll have a girl this time, Beaker. I'd like that."

"Maybe," she agreed. "We have a fifty-fifty shot."

With a grin, I nuzzled her head. "If not, we can try for number three."

With a glare, she pushed me away. "I don't think so, Oscar," she muttered. "And I am cutting you off until I'm back on birth control after this baby is born." Shaking her head, she stomped away to the kitchen, leaving me laughing since I knew she didn't mean a word of it.

IAS was back.

And so it began.

Shelby's eyelids fluttered open, her eyes unfocused and confused. "Liam?" she whispered groggily.

Cupping her pale face, I pressed a gentle kiss to her forehead. "I'm right here, my darling girl."

Her voice became anxious. "Olivia?"

"She's perfect, Shelby."

Tears welled in her eyes, running down her face as a small sob escaped her mouth. "You promise?"

Pressing my forehead against hers, I reassured her. "She's fine, baby. I promise. I was holding her. She'll be back in a few minutes."

She shifted, wincing, and I stood to help her get more comfortable, moving her gently. "Easy, love, you just had surgery. You're going to be sore."

Gripping my hand, she kept crying, her voice weak. "I was so scared."

"So was I. Dr. Emily was amazing, and Olivia is fine. You'll be fine. Everything is okay," I reassured her.

"I want to see her."

"Soon, baby. I need you to rest."

"You promise," she pleaded, unable to relax.

I grabbed my phone, holding it up so she could see the pictures I had taken. "Look, I'm holding her—and there is one of Mum with her. She's fine, I promise. Rest a little more, and when you wake up, she'll be here and you can hold her."

She relaxed a little seeing the pictures. I stroked her hair softly as her eyes drifted shut. She was still under the influence of the anesthesia they had administered. I scrolled over the pictures as I sat beside my wife. Our daughter was tiny. Adam had weighed almost ten pounds when he was born, and Olivia Elizabeth Wright had barely broken the five-pound mark. But her delivery had been fraught with drama—too much blood and pain—and when Dr. Emily made the decision to do an emergency C-section and put Shelby under, I was terrified. Seeing Shelby lying unconscious again brought back many bad memories, and I'd struggled to stay calm.

But they were both fine. Shelby would recover, and my daughter, although tiny, was healthy, and I would take them both home soon. Where I knew she would be greeted happily by a loud little boy who, no doubt, was driving his nan crazy, wanting his mummy.

I wanted her home, too.

As soon as she was well again and able to travel, we would return to England and build a life there. The house was ready, and so were we. We wouldn't need the security that surrounded us here. We would both relax. Ryan and Lesley would stay on at the house in LA with Thor. They were taking over the third floor that had been Shelby's, and the rest of the house would stay our home for when we were here in the country. It didn't seem fair to drag the cat back and forth with us, and Thor had taken a great liking to Ryan, his broad shoulders the perfect place for Thor to perch on. I knew he would be well looked after.

Thanks to Mum's help, we'd found a wonderful woman who would aid Shelby with the children once we got to England. We had met Joanne last time we were there, and she had come over a short time ago to help us on this end. Adam adored her, as did Shelby, and I knew Joanne would be a great friend to her as well as a big help. She was a kind, loving person and exactly what we all needed in our life. Her soon-to-be husband was now the groundskeeper at the house, and they lived nearby in a cottage of their own—it was perfect for us all.

After finding out Shelby was pregnant again, I only accepted smaller parts since *The Highlands*. Ones that kept me close to home and my family. Douglas put off the project we had been discussing, but we were now revisiting the idea since he planned on filming in England again. It would work well for me. The part excited me enough to consider taking on a bigger role again. *The Highlands* had won huge at the Oscars including Best Picture, Best Director for Douglas, Best Actor in a Leading Role for me, among other awards.

Shelby had been so proud and excited that night, I'd been afraid she'd go into labor right on the spot. The bookshelves in the den now held three golden statues, gleaming symbols of my career, and yet their importance was diminished compared to the health and happiness of my family.

As I watched her sleep, I made a decision. This pregnancy had been too hard on her. Through it all, she remained cheerful and upbeat, but it had been a struggle, and watching her had been difficult for me. We had been blessed with two healthy children, for whom I was grateful, and they were enough. With all the research I had quietly done, I knew I didn't want Shelby back on birth control pills; the side effects were simply too frightening to me for that. I was going to tell her I was getting a vasectomy. I had spoken with my doctor about it, and he told me if I wanted, I could freeze some of my boys in case we changed our mind in the future. But I was sure after everything she had gone through, Shelby would agree. We'd both said we would like two children, and no matter how I teased her about a third, today had been too scary for me even to contemplate it. I only had to convince her to let me be the responsible one and have the procedure. I chuckled to myself. People were still getting used to the idea of me being grown up. My days of Peter Pan were long behind me—for the most part anyway.

Slowly, I caressed her hair, smiling as she sighed in her sleep. The change was because of her. She made me responsible. Her love gave me the strength to grow up and become the man I was supposed to be. I was still a git, and I would forever mess things up and say the wrong thing at the exact wrong moment, but Shelby insisted it was part of my charm. My mum insisted it was my dad's contribution to my DNA. But as long as the two most important women in my life loved me, I was okay with it. Thank God they both had large capacities to forgive my constant cock-ups.

The door opened behind me, and another important woman in my life was brought in. Eagerly I stood and accepted Olivia from the nurse. I pressed a soft kiss to her warm cheek, pushing back the pink bonnet that covered her hair. The almost white wisps glinted in the light, and I grinned. Shelby said she wanted our daughter to look like me. She may have gotten her wish.

I looked up to see Shelby was waking. "Let's go and introduce you to your mummy now, baby girl. She's been anxious to meet you."

Gently, I placed her in Shelby's waiting arms, sighing at the sight.

My girls.

A few hours later, I was smiling so wide, my face hurt. Mum and Dad were in the room, along with Douglas, who was chatting with Everett and Cassidy. On the bed, nestled together, was my family. Adam was snuggled into Shelby's side, staring away at Olivia, his blue eyes round with excitement. Caroline was in the corner, the quiet click of her shutter letting me know she was capturing this sweet moment for us. Shelby looked up, her eyes meeting mine. Peace and contentment radiated from her warm gaze, and I knew she saw the same in mine.

We were surrounded by family, friends, and so much love.

In the middle of it all—the nucleus of my entire universe.

My Shelby.

I was the luckiest bastard in the world.

I could see the years ahead of us. Birthdays, holidays, watching our kids grow. Love, laughter, tears, joy. All of it with Shelby beside me.

Before Shelby, I was just Liam—an actor.

Now, I was so much more.

A son, friend, husband, lover, and father.

All in one.

My greatest role ever.

YOU REALLY DIDN'T THINK THE STORY WAS OVER...

SEVERAL WEEKS LATER

I wiped my hands on my pants, looking around the waiting room, feeling nervous and jittery. The room seemed excessively warm to me.

I leaned over to Shelby. "Is it hot in here?" I asked, feeling the sweat trickle down the back of my neck.

"No, Liam. The room is quite cool." She studied my face. "You are a little flushed. Are you feeling okay?"

"Yeah, I'm fine," I responded, shifting in my seat. "These chairs are uncomfortable."

"Actually, they are really nice for a waiting room."

"Huh. Bloody hot, though."

"Nerves, I think," she murmured.

"I'm not nervous," I lied. "It's a simple procedure, with few, if any, side effects," I quoted. "Except OJ will be shooting blanks. Big, copious amounts of blanks. Nonthreatening, nonimpregnating blanks."

She patted my hand. "You're rambling."

I nodded. "Right."

She was correct. I always rambled when I was nervous, and

fuck, I *was* nervous. I was sure I would breeze through today, but the closer the time came, the tenser I got. The thought of all those sharp instruments doing things that close to my cock… One wrong move…

I swallowed heavily, wondering if anyone would notice if I ran from the room—aside from Shelby. Somehow, I doubted it would shock her.

I glanced around, noting we were one of only two couples in the room. There were a few guys on their own as well, but it was early, and the office wasn't busy. I bet I could be back in the car before anyone really figured it out.

"Mr. Florida?" the receptionist called out.

For a moment, the room was still, then she called out the name again. "Mr. Florida?"

Dammit.

Right.

That was me.

I stood, taking Shelby's elbow and dragging her up with me. She frowned and pulled back. "Liam, that's not—"

I shook my head. "Incognito, Shelby," I hissed and headed to the door leading into the clinic area. I hadn't been recognized yet, and I hoped it would stay that way. The damn doctor had come highly recommended, but he'd refused to allow me to come in after hours or to clear his schedule. He was a grumpy bugger.

"Other men need me as well, Mr. Wright. I'll put you in first thing in the morning, and we'll use a different name. Wear a hat. Trust me, not many paparazzi hang outside my office."

I almost refused, but then remembered how important the anatomy that he would be working on was to me. I didn't want some run-of-the-mill doctor, and I certainly didn't want to piss off this one. He would be handling my junk, and OJ was far too fond of Shelby for me to risk any malfunctions caused by an angry physician. So, here I was, answering to a fake name.

We followed the nurse to Dr. Buckley's office and sat down.

"He'll be in soon, and then I will come and take you back to the procedure area," she informed us.

I nodded as Shelby murmured her thanks. She looked at me after the nurse had left.

"*Mr. Florida?*" she asked, her eyebrows lifting in question.

"In homage to OJ," I explained with a straight face, waiting for her reaction. I didn't wait long.

She giggled, covering her mouth with her hand. "Oh, Liam, only you. Most men would go with Mr. Jones or Mr. Smith. Something forgettable. But you go with Mr. Florida." She shook her head. "Good job."

I grinned. "I thought you would like it."

She leaned forward and kissed me. "I like you."

I pulled back, wagging my finger. "None of that, Shelby. I am about to undergo delicate surgery. I can't have OJ springing into action because you got handsy. God only knows what complications that would cause."

She laughed again. "For one thing, I am not getting handsy. For another, Olivia is only five weeks old, and you're not touching me until you've been clipped. We agreed."

I winced. "Can we *not* use the word clipped?"

"Snipped?"

I shook my head.

"Neutered?"

"Bloody hell, no."

"Tied off? Fixed?"

"No."

"What, then?"

I sighed. "How about we don't even name it. Or discuss it."

She bit her lip, trying not to laugh. "It's gonna be hard not to talk about it while you're sitting around icing your junk for the next few days."

"Shelby!"

"Sorry."

I sat back, muttering, "I thought you'd be more sympathetic."

She patted my hand. "I tried, Liam. You're the one who insisted on throwing yourself a vasectomy party and calling it the 'Last of the Spermians.' Should I remind you what the cake looked like?"

"That was Everett. I asked for a simple white cake. Not a beheaded, limp dick."

"The balloons you put everywhere?"

"Douglas's idea to use the old condoms. I'll buy more until we're sure the stragglers are gone," I insisted.

Shelby sighed.

"I was trying to make light of it," I admitted. "But frankly, Beaker, I'm scared stiff."

She raised an eyebrow, and I chuckled. "No pun intended."

Shelby clasped my hand in hers. "If you're unsure, we can postpone or you can change your mind, Liam."

"No. I need to do this for you. For us. I don't want you on those bloody pills or the shots, I hate condoms, and I want to have sex with you as much as I want without worries or looking for whatever form of birth control we try."

"Would me getting pregnant again be such a terrible thing?"

I reached over and stroked her cheek. "I can't go through that again, Shelby. Seeing what you went through. Knowing if we didn't have such a skillful doctor, things could have been different. I will never risk you. Ever. This is my responsibility, and I am handling it."

She smiled. "I love you."

"Good. I hope you still love me if he slips and damages my dick in any way."

She winked. "You still have fingers. And a tongue. I think we'll manage."

I returned her smile, the silence falling between us. I studied her hand. Her rings caught the light, the wide band of diamonds setting off my nan's antique ring. I loved seeing it on her hand, and knowing she was mine. Forever.

If I survived this procedure.

The sweating started again.

"Jesus," I muttered. "Someone turned up the heat again."

Shelby rolled her eyes. "Relax, Liam. Everything is gonna be fine."

"You aren't the one having your junk rearranged."

She snorted quietly. "My vagina sympathizes."

I began to laugh. She was right and had already been through enough. I hadn't squeezed two humans out of my body in the span of a year. I was just getting a simple procedure. It was fine. I was cool, and all was good.

Then the doctor walked in, and I passed out.

I woke up to Shelby's worried expression and the doctor's impatient frown.

"Really, Mr. Wright. A little over the top, I would say."

"He's nervous." Shelby defended me.

"Not necessary. You'll be walking out of here in twenty minutes, Mr. Wright. Cock intact, unlike your dignity. You ready?"

Bloody hell, he was a right miserable bastard. And my head hurt from smacking it on the wall as I collapsed in the chair. But I wasn't going to let him know that.

I stood. "Ready." I bent and kissed Shelby. "We'll always have Scotland," I said with a wink. "Remember me in a kilt."

She laughed. "I'll be right here."

It took everything in me not to ask if she could stand beside me and hold my hand. A strange man was already going to be manhandling my balls. I needed to maintain some sort of composure. My dignity, as I had been informed, was long gone.

I really should have taken the valium they offered. I wondered if it was too late, and then Dr. Buckley turned to me. "*Now*, Mr. Wright. I don't have all day."

I guessed I had my answer.

I shivered in the procedure room. Whoever had been playing with the thermostat was at it again. It was fucking freezing. As I sat on the table, my ass was frozen, and I felt the goose bumps rising on my skin, the gown they put me in not helping against the cold. The nurse, a pretty Asian American lady named Ren, bustled around, making sure Dr. Buckley had everything he needed to kill me—I mean perform the simple, everyday procedure that would result in minimal discomfort for me.

Jesus, I wanted Shelby.

Dr. Buckley walked in, wearing a mask, gown, and gloved up. I swallowed hard.

Shit was about to get real. This was my last chance to escape. Condoms weren't so bad. I eyed the door, calculating my chances.

Except the pretty nurse proved to be exceptionally strong and pushed me down on the table.

"You lie down for snip snip," she sang.

I grasped the edge of the thin vinyl pad that passed for a mattress. I twisted the sheet, holding it tight. Dr. Buckley sat at the end of the table, talking to Ren. He arranged the draping, the cold air hitting my balls, making me shiver more. He muttered something which made Ren chuckle as she lifted her eyes to mine. I was pretty sure they were talking about my junk. I felt the need to defend myself.

"It's cold in here," I snapped. "Shrinkage, you know."

Buckley snorted, muttering something about egos, and Ren laughed. Then they fell silent in preparation.

What happened next was torture that went on for hours. Or fifteen minutes when I checked the clock. But it was horrendous.

The blade being drawn across my scrotum was slow and scary. The Betadine on my balls was like being dunked in a vat of ice, and I squealed at the cold.

Ren rolled her eyes.

The "pinch and burn" of the anesthetic was more like an

explosion of agony in my balls, the fire hot enough it should have done the job the surgeon was determined to take care of.

I groaned, grabbing the foam mattress hard in order not to launch myself off and run like hell. I could picture the headline—

"Actor Liam Wright caught streaking on Hollywood Boulevard, his ass hanging from an open johnny gown as his balls slapped and twisted in the wind. He was blubbering and screaming about saving his junk as he was hauled away to the loony bin."

Then blissful numbness set in, and I relaxed a little. But all too soon, it felt as if Dr. Buckley was trying to pull a kidney down through my nutsac.

"Did I request my inner organs get moved?" I yelped. "I'm not paying extra for that service," I informed them.

"Part of the procedure," he muttered, pulling harder. "Damn and blast, if our health care wasn't so fucked up, we could do this in a hospital with you knocked out. Damn government and their cutbacks."

"Is it easier?" I gasped, trying not to move in case he got pissier.

"For me, it is," he snarled. "Then you'd be quiet."

"God, you're a grumpy bugger," I muttered.

He glanced up. "You would be too if you stared at dicks all day."

I had to give him that one.

Finally, after years and years, it was over.

He stood, stripping off his gloves. "Stay there for a few minutes. Then Ren will help you up, and you can go."

"How long should I stay in bed to recover?"

He snorted. "That depends on you. Nothing strenuous, no sex for a while. A bag of peas or an ice pack will help the ache. I'll give you some painkillers to take if you need them. A couple of days, you'll be fine. There will be a recovery instruction sheet with your prescription." He paused in the doorway. "My wife, Mary, is a fan. Leave an autograph."

I stared at his retreating form, grateful Mary liked me. Lord only knows what he might have done if she hadn't.

Then I snorted internally at his words. A couple of days? I was pretty sure I would need at least a week to get over this.

Maybe more.

———

At home, I eased onto the sofa in the den with a groan.

"Do you need some pain meds?" Shelby asked, running her hand along my head. I sighed and leaned into her caress. It felt good.

"Yeah," I pouted. "It hurts." It wasn't as bad as I'd feared, but I didn't want to tell her that. I wanted her to spoil me. I loved it when Shelby spoiled me.

"I'll get the ice too."

"Okay. And, Shelby?"

"Yes?"

"I'm hungry. I couldn't eat before, and now I'm starving. Did you- did you cook turkey like you promised?"

Her voice was amused. "Yes."

I opened my eyes and met her gaze. "Could I have a sandwich?"

"Yes."

"Any, ah, chance you made cupcakes? I think I need a little sugar."

"Of course you do."

Everett walked in. "How are you feeling?"

Shelby left the den as I started telling him of the horrific morning I'd had. I knew he'd understand. And he did, covering his dick with a wince as I told him of the procedure.

"Jesus," he muttered. "How long you down for?"

I laid my head back. "Days and days, I think."

Shelby came in, carrying a tray. She slid it onto the table and handed me a bag of peas. "Nice try, Liam. I'll give you two. This will help."

I glanced at the label. "Organic peas?"

She smirked. "Only the best for OJ, Liam."

"Damn straight, woman."

The cold was heaven, dulling the ache my testicles felt. The painkillers took care of the rest of the discomfort. The sandwich filled the emptiness of my stomach, and the cupcakes were a welcome bonus.

After eating, I went to bed, and my mum carried in my weans. Olivia lay on my chest, a warm weight I welcomed. Adam snuggled into my side, and soon, they were both asleep.

Shelby moved around our room, tidying and humming as she went. The sound of her voice, the scent of her closeness eased me, and with a sigh, I realized it was over. I had survived the procedure. All in all, I handled it really well.

Shelby laughed softly, leaning over the bed, stroking my hair.

"Yep. Really well, Mr. Florida."

I chuckled with her, comprehending the fact that I had spoken my thoughts out loud. I was a rambling git who liked to mutter his thoughts out loud when drunk or slightly stoned. I always had been, always would be, and yet, she still loved me. I was the luckiest bastard in the world.

She cupped my cheek. "I do, Liam. I really do."

That was all I cared about.

"I love you, Shelby." I captured her hand in mine and kissed it. "I really love you."

She smiled. "I know."

I patted the bed. "Join us."

She nestled beside Adam, resting her hand on my chest. I sighed in contentment, listening as her breathing became deep and even.

I laid my head back and joined my family in sleep.

ACKNOWLEDGMENTS

As always, I have some people to thank.
The ones behind the words that encourage and support. The people
who make my books possible for so many reasons.

Beth, Trina, Melissa and Jess -
thank you for your feedback and support.

Carrie, Ayden, Jeannie, Freya -
I love you and am honored to call you friends.
You humble me.

Deb and Peggy -
thank you for your support and keen eyes.

Lisa - your humor as always makes the red strokes of your pen easier
to handle.
Thank you for your patience and the "gentle" lessons you give me.
I will learn them one day—but not today.
Okay let's face it—probably never. You are stuck with me.

Melissa - thank you for the beautiful covers and teasers.

Karen, my dear friend and PA. I am so grateful for you. For your
friendship—
For having you with me on this journey.
For the laughter, the tears, and the shared moments—
I love you.
Thank you.

To all the bloggers, readers, and
especially my promo team -
Thank you for everything you do.
Shouting your love of books—of my work—posting, sharing—your
recommendations keep my TBR list full, and the support you have
shown me is so appreciated.

To my fellow authors who have shown me such kindness, thank you.
I will follow your example and pay it forward.

My reader group, Melanie's Minions—
love you all.

And always, my Matthew.
You are my world.
My beginning and my end.
My everything.

OTHER BOOKS BY MELANIE MORELAND

Vested Interest Series

BAM - The Beginning (Prequel)

Bentley (Vested Interest #1)

Aiden (Vested Interest #2)

Maddox (Vested Interest #3)

Reid (Vested Interest #4)

Van (Vested Interest #5)

Halton (Vested Interest #6)

Sandy (Vested Interest #7)

Vested Interest Box Set (Books 1-3)

Insta-Spark Collection

It Started with a Kiss

Christmas Sugar

An Instant Connection

An Unexpected Gift

The Contract Series

The Contract (Contract #1)

The Baby Clause (Contract #2)

The Amendment (Contract #3)

Standalones

Into the Storm

Beneath the Scars

Over the Fence

My Image of You (Random House/Loveswept)

Changing Roles

ABOUT THE AUTHOR

New York Times/USA Today/Wall Street Journal, international bestselling author, Melanie Moreland, lives a happy and content life in a quiet area of Ontario with her beloved husband of thirty plus years and their rescue cat, Amber. Nothing means more to her than her friends and family, and she cherishes every moment spent with them.

While seriously addicted to coffee, and highly challenged with all things computer-related and technical, she relishes baking, cooking, and trying new recipes for people to sample. She loves to throw dinner parties, and enjoys travelling—here and abroad—but finds coming home is always the best part of any trip.

Melanie loves stories, especially paired with a good wine, and enjoys skydiving (free falling over a fleck of dust) extreme snowboarding (falling down the stairs) and piloting her own helicopter (tripping over her own feet). She's learned happily ever afters, even bumpy ones, are all in how you tell the story.

Melanie is represented by Flavia Viotti at Bookcase Literary Agency. For any questions regarding subsidiary or translation rights please contact her at flavia@bookcaseagency.com

Connect with Melanie

Connect with Melanie

Like reader groups? Lots of fun and giveaways! Check it out at Melanie Moreland's Minions

Click **HERE** to join my newsletter for up-to-date news, sales, book announcements and excerpts (no spam)

Visit me on the internet at www.melaniemoreland.com

facebook.com/authormoreland

twitter.com/morelandmelanie

instagram.com/morelandmelanie

CPSIA information can be obtained
at www.ICGtesting.com
Printed in the USA
LVHW041252210320
650787LV00005B/1460